Lord Wraxall's Fancy

Lord Wraxall's Fancy

ANNA LIEFF SAXBY

BLACK
lace

Black Lace novels are sexual fantasies.
In real life, make sure you practise safe sex.

First published in 1996 by
Black Lace
332 Ladbroke Grove
London W10 5AH

Typeset by CentraCet Limited, Cambridge
Printed and bound by Mackays of Chatham PLC

ISBN 0 352 33080 5

For CMN

Prologue

To: Mistress Prudence Fortescue
Fortescue House
In the County of Surrey, England

Mid-Yeare's Day, 1718

Honour'd sister, I hope this finds both you and my Daughter Celine well, as it leaves me. I am pleas'd to report that Government House is now ready to receive Guests. I would be oblig'd therefore if you would send Lady Celine to me on board the Challenger out of Bristol. Celine is full Eighteen and it is time to think of making a suitable Alliance for her. I have a Gallant for her in my Eye, but pray say Naught to her of this, as Nothing has yet been agreed. Tho' the Incidence of Smuggling has been much decreas'd by my firm Measures, the Depredations of Pyrates still continue troublesome. I hope by Yeare's End to have the notorious Tremaine (Ringleader of these Scoundrels) hanging from the Gibbet in Market Square. You need not fear to send my Lady Celine, however. The Challenger will be convoyed as far as the Windward Islandes by the Man o' War Intrepid.

I have, Madam, the honour to remain, Your Humble Ob't Servant

James Fortescue (Bart), Governor General for King George I of the Islande of St Cecilia in the Caribees

1

Chapter One

A warm wind blew, bringing with it the scent of frangipani and the cries of tropical birds. Southern stars burned overhead, waking an answering phosphoresence in the ocean. The merchant ship *Challenger* dipped and curtseyed, her sails as swollen and silver as the moon that hung above.

Lady Celine Fortescue clutched the cloak tight over her silken nightgown as she tiptoed past the long wicked shapes of the sleeping cannon, and up the final companionway to the deck. Her heart pounded and the pulse in her throat felt as if it would stifle her.

Every tenet of her upbringing, every principle taught to her by the maiden aunt who had raised her, screamed that what she was doing was wrong. She could turn back, even now, but Celine knew that she would not.

She was a different girl to the one who was content to stay at needlework in the dull Surrey mansion. When she had looked out of the carriage window and seen the ocean for the first time she had felt a shock in her breast. It was if something very small – as small as a seed – had broken open.

On the voyage it had grown. Rain storms had fed it: the languid airs of the tropics warmed it to maturity. It drove her on with a reckless hunger for she knew not what.

This urgency was opposed to everything she had been taught. It must be some inheritance from her mother, Lys. Something that did not show in the portrait of the haughty Creole beauty – except, perhaps, as a mocking glint in the wide dark eyes.

Celine had never known her mother: she had died young. But Celine had spent long hours staring at that portrait.

Lys had an oval face the colour of old ivory. She had been painted in oriental dress. Palm trees bowed behind her, and on her dark hair she wore a crown of flaring native lilies. Celine felt that the strangeness swelling like a bud inside her might flower tonight into just such a scarlet, hungry thing.

She hurried through the darkness, her bare feet silent on the deck. Liam was waiting for her, striding impatiently by the rail. Celine's heart faltered as she looked at him. He was so handsome; tall, with hair that held all the shadows of night and long-lashed eyes, so startlingly blue that even moonlight could not leach away all their colour.

She ran the last few paces to his arms. They slipped round her, under the cloak, and he strained her slim body to him. Celine thrilled at his touch. They had never been so close before: there had always been watching eyes. At most their hands had met, lingeringly, and once they had stolen a kiss. Now the night was their own.

'I dared not hope that you'd come,' he whispered.

'I nearly didn't,' she confessed, rubbing her head against his shoulder. 'But the moonlight called me and – oh, Liam! – we must talk! You must speak to my father when we arrive at St Cecilia!'

He bent his head and covered her face with kisses. His hands moved on the silk, sliding down the sweet curve of her back.

'I fear it will be useless,' he murmured. 'My branch of the O'Briens are nobodies – poor nobodies, for all we're descended from the ancient kings of Ireland. I'm only an officer by courtesy, because the cargo supervisor always

4

is. Perhaps, when I have made my fortune in Virginia . . .'

'My father loves me too well to see me unhappy.'

'How can you know that?' said Liam gloomily. 'He hasn't seen you since you were squalling in your cradle.'

'My mother was a great beauty, and I am held to be her speaking likeness. No, no,' she laughed, putting up a hand to still his lips, 'No compliments. This is important. She loved my father from the moment she saw him: she left family and friends to follow him, gave up the tropical heat that was life itself to her, and withered quickly in the cold of England.'

'Rest her soul, poor lady,' murmured Liam.

'When my father sees me, it must recall her to him,' said Celine. 'It will soften his heart. Remembering her love, how could he be unjust to mine?'

Liam made no answer, but his arms tightened around her. Where her high breasts pressed against him Celine could feel the rough gold braid on his waistcoat. Her nipples tautened under the thin silk of her nightgown, and she made an unconscious purring sound, deep in her throat.

His hands slid down across her hips, only a whisper away from the naked flesh. Celine moved sinuously, rubbing herself against him. She opened her mouth under his demanding kisses as a blossom opens to the bee.

Their tongues met and his hands clasped her buttocks, pulling her against her loins. The feel of his strong, hard-muscled body pressed close against her delighted Celine.

'Ah, God, I want you,' he whispered.

When his hand strayed to her breast, Celine tensed a little at the unaccustomed caress. But she loved him so much, surely it could not be wrong? And the feel of his fingers was so delicious, so exciting. As he teased her nipple she felt pleasure go sizzling straight from the hard, pink bud to the pit of her belly.

Pushing her back against the rail, Liam began to move his hand in small circles on the softness of her breast. He

5

was breathing hard, and there was an increased fierceness to the movement of his mouth on hers. He thrust against her, pressing his lower body to hers with little, rhythmic motions. There was a hardness, a long bulge in the fabric of his breeches, pushing against her with each stroke.

Something inside her quivered at the feel of it, and instinctively Celine's body began to answer his. She wanted – she did not know what, only that it was more than this.

'Yes,' she whispered. 'Oh, yes, Liam!'

He groaned and, for a moment, the increased power of his thrusts echoed her new, bewildering need. Then, with shocking suddenness, he pulled away.

He was trembling, and his eyes looked wild. He held her at arms' length, his fingers digging into her shoulders with a cruel grip.

'No,' he said, hoarsely. 'I will not take you: not like this. I know your lovely innocence. I can't abuse it so.'

'But I don't understand!' cried Celine. 'Don't you love me?'

'More than my life,' said Liam, in a smothered tone. 'More than my honour. But not more than yours. If you were my wife – but it's impossible.'

The night was sultry, but she shivered. All the warmth that his caresses had raised in her was fading away.

He saw that she was chilled and huddled the cloak around her. Placing a firm arm about her waist, he turned her to look with him over the sea until her breathing slowed and the tension left her body.

A burst of flying fish skimmed across the moon's track. Far above, the lookout scanned the distance with his spy-glass. A cloud hung there, marking where the island lay.

'Land Ho-oo-oo-o!' he cried, from the skies.

'I must go,' said Celine, unwillingly. 'We must part for a little, my love. And be so polite and proper when we meet at disembarking.'

She smiled, and turned her face up to Liam's. He

could not answer her goodbye, but pulled her close, and told it with a kiss. Her mouth opened under his for an instant, sweet as honey, and then she was gone.

Lady Celine stood on the quayside, in the relentless sun, being bustled and stared at by strangers of every shade and variety, from ebony to palest pearl.

Though it was still early in the morning, the heat was intense. The chests and shoulders of the black, half-naked stevedores shone as if they had been oiled. Market traders fanned themselves with palm leaves. Velvet-eyed wantons leaned from the windows of waterfront houses, bending low to display their breasts, and threw orchids down to attract men from the sweating throng passing beneath.

A little crowd of women had gathered at the dock, calling up to the sailors in lilting voices. They danced, swaying their hips. Celine could not keep her eyes away. She was half envious of the thin, loose dresses; half shocked by the way the clinging fabrics accentuated the nakedness beneath.

She herself had dressed in her finest to impress her father. Her rose calico gown was looped up over a petticoat of white lawn. It had falls of Valenciennes lace at the elbows, and a lace fichu round the shoulders. Pink ribbon bows decorated the front of her satin bodice.

She wore a straw hat tied with white ribbons, and the French shoes which had high red heels. Bess had laced her waist to nineteen inches, and it was hard to breathe. Her corset was damp with perspiration. She could feel droplets trickling down her back, like tiny fingers.

And still no-one came for her.

She felt very alone. Liam was busy on board with the cargo manifest. There had been no time to do more than exchange a touch and a look before he was hustled away to the hold with his lists.

Celine's trunks had been unloaded and dumped unceremoniously beside her on the quay. Bess Brown, her maid, stood guard over them, goggle-eyed, crossing

7

her fingers ostentatiously when anybody particularly black looked her way.

Celine swayed, and brushed the back of her hand across her forehead. It came away wet.

'This insufferable heat,' she said, faintly. 'Is there nowhere we could wait in the shade?'

'What's that?' said Bess.

Celine followed her gaze. At the end of the quay a long, red-roofed building stood, its double doors wide open. The dark within promised coolness. Perhaps she could find a drink of water there, and a chair to sit on.

She lifted up her skirts and began to pick her way along the dock. Bess pattered after her and laid an anxious hand on her arm.

'I think it's a warehouse, milady. You can't wait in a warehouse!'

'I'll wait in a stable if I have to,' said Celine.

'But someone might steal the luggage!'

Celine rounded on her maid. 'Go back and swelter with it, then,' she said crossly 'Go! Tell my father where I am when – when he comes. I can't stay in this inferno! I must get out of the sun before I die.'

Hurt, Bess walked back to the trunks and shooed away two sharp-faced urchins who were investigating the locks. She seated herself on the biggest box with Celine's jewel-case held jealously on her lap and set herself to endure.

Celine walked up the two shallow steps to the entrance and took a few paces within.

'Ladies on the left,' said a crickety voice from the gloom.

She turned towards the voice, peering into the dim recesses of the chamber. The room was wider than it was long, with a closed door at each end. Tucked in the deep shadows of a corner she made out a high desk facing her, and a tall stool behind the desk, where a tall man sat. He kept his head bent, scratching away with a quill pen.

Celine raised her chin. She was not used to being ignored by the lower orders.

'I wish to wait here in the cool,' she told him, in her best Fortescue manner.

The clerk raised his head. He was dry and biscuity. He looked at Celine's breasts slyly from under short sandy eyelashes.

'As you wish, madam. Ladies' gallery through the left hand door.'

'What is this place?' asked Celine.

'Dick's Bum Barracoon,' said the clerk.

'I beg your pardon?' she exclaimed in astonishment.

'Dicks Bum,' he enunciated carefully and pointed with his quill pen. On the wall behind a noticeboard read: DIIJKSBOOM & D'SILVA: 1698. ESCRAVOS – OPERARIOS – TRABLHADORES.

Celine wished she had paid more attention during her Italian lessons. At least – was it Italian? She decided to pursue the main point.

'Where can I can sit?' she enquired.

'Upstairs,' said the clerk. 'Plenty of chairs. Empty in the mornings. Ladies mostly come later in the day. To see if there's anything they fancy.'

He gave her breasts a last long stare and bent once more over his ledger.

Celine hesitated. 'And a glass of water?'

'There's lemonade,' he said without looking up. 'Or rum punch.'

The lure of comfort and a cool drink quickly outweighed Celine's suspicion that Aunt Prudence would disapprove. Heels tapping, she crossed the room and turned the handle. The door swung easily on its hinges and she entered a little lobby, blessedly cool between stone walls. A stair led upwards to a second door.

Pleasantly intrigued, she ascended the staircase and opened the door.

She found herself in a long gallery. A railing on the right overlooked a wide central space. Frivolous little gilt chairs stood about in groups. Most were unoccupied, but at the other end of the room sat two or three young matrons, richly dressed in the French style, and a severe dowager in Spanish black.

Celine curtseyed politely to them. The dowager stared and then inclined her head the least possible degree. The others drew their heads together and whispered, looking sidelong over their spread fans.

A mulatto woman in decent grey, wearing a white apron and headdress, dusted a chair close to the railing and ushered Celine into it.

As Celine sat down a burst of male laughter sounded from below. Leaning forward, she found herself looking down into a rectangular arena. A canvas awning was stretched above, blurring the fiery sunlight. Sawdust covered the floor, here and there scuffed up in little heaps.

Diagonally opposite her, steps led up to a rough wooden stage. A naked black girl stood on it, arms outspread. Diffused light woke gleams in the flesh of her pert young breasts, and on the sultry curve of her loins.

'Seventy guineas!' cried a hoarse voice.

Celine craned her neck. Directly below, a group of rakish-looking men were clustered around a table loaded with bottles. A couple wore fashionable brocades, with small-swords and diamond buckles, but most favoured riding dress. One or two were in shirt-sleeves, their fine coats discarded. They lounged at their ease, smoking long pipes.

The girl turned slowly, showing every inch of her body to the men.

'Eighty!' shouted a middle-aged man in purple velvet.

Celine stared. She raised her hand and pressed it to her mouth.

'Eighty-five!'

It was a slave-market.

The auctioneer, a grimy creature in brown fustian, turned his face up to the gallery, and the dowager raised a chalk-white finger.

'A hundred guineas!' cried the auctioneer.

10

The man in purple swore, and poured a glass of rum.

'One hundred once! One hundred twice! Sold! To Mother Midnight.'

'I'll be visiting your house soon, then, Mother!' called up a pallid fellow in green, and the dowager smiled faintly and bowed.

The slave girl folded herself back into her simple garment and was led away to the holding cells. The mulatto woman returned with a tall glass of water, flavoured with sugar cane and the juice of lemons. She placed it at Celine's elbow on the broad top of the railing and rustled away. Celine took a grateful draught and, her thirst assuaged, leaned forward to peep down into the arena: another sale was beginning.

The auctioneer raised his hands. 'And now,' he said with a knowing smile, 'Lot Nine, my lords and gentlemen! 25 years old, luscious as a peach, and famed throughout the Caribbees for her voracious appetites, the one you've all been waiting for –'

'I lose patience rapidly,' said one of the men in an icy voice.

The auctioneer blenched. 'Your pardon, my Lord Viscount,' he quavered.

The fear in his voice surprised Celine. She stared. The man who had spoken stood a little apart from the others, with one high boot planted on the seat of a chair.

Though no longer young, he was as slim and strong as a Toledo blade, and he radiated the same deadly menace. He faced away from her. Dark hair, streaked with threads of silver, hung about his shoulders and down his back. His shirt was open, deep ruffles of lace fell over his hands, and he swung a riding crop between slender fingers.

'I'm sure you aren't going to leave me waiting much longer,' the man said. His voice was quiet, but it stung like a whip.

The auctioneer bowed, and beckoned hastily. A woman, swathed in white draperies from head to foot, stepped slowly across the arena to the stage.

11

The man in purple, who had been singing a dirty ballad over his rum, perked up and groped at his periwig, pulling it askew.

'Going to bid for her, Wraxall?' he enquired jovially. 'I'll wager this one could exhaust even you. They call her the Nassau Hurricane.' He smacked his lips. 'Insatiable, I give you my word.'

The dark haired man half-turned. Despite the heat, Celine shivered at the sight of that thin, swarthy face, with its cynical mouth and deep, heavy-lidded eyes that seemed to hold the knowledge of every vice.

'It takes more than mere quantity to satisfy me,' he drawled, as he straightened up and strolled across to the platform.

The auctioneer stepped forward eagerly to disrobe the waiting woman. But the Viscount was before him. He struck like lightning, lashing the other man aside. The blow sounded loud as a pistol-shot and the auctioneer cowered back, one hand clasped to his cheek. With horror, Celine saw the quick blood bloom between his fingers.

The dark haired man tossed down his riding crop.

'Burn that. And learn to keep your hands away in future. If I think her worth the purchase I would not want to have to scrub your grease from her skin.'

He circled the woman, moving slowly, looking her up and down. Celine watched him as he prowled closer. She felt a touch of last night's strangeness. A pulse beat fast in her throat. Tight chamois riding breeches clung to his loins like a second skin, outlining the lean hips and the powerful muscles of his thighs. His fine linen shirt hung loose about him: the tanned skin of his chest was lined with pale scars, mark of the duello.

Now he was so close that he brushed the woman's veils as he moved. He did not seem to handle them, and yet the diaphanous swathes began to fall and unwind. They slipped away, layer after layer, showing first her shape and then a glimpse of tawny flesh, until the

12

woman stood exposed and naked, rising like Venus from the foamy pool of fabric at her feet.

She was honey-gold and rounded, with swelling hips and breasts like ripe fruit. Ruddy brown hair hung in a curled mane down her back, and crouched like a fox at her groin. The rakes growled their approval.

His fingertips began trailing over her skin as he continued to circle. Rose brown nipples sprang erect under his touch and the woman sighed, closing her eyes. She began to move a little, responding to his caresses.

Celine shifted restlessly on her chair as she watched. She could feel the texture of her lacy petticoats as they slid across her naked thighs above her garters. The lining of her bodice brushed against her bosom.

The woman was shuddering, her hips rocking. The Viscount stood behind her, pressed close, one hand cupping a round breast while he teased its sensitive tip to hardness.

Celine's mouth opened slightly, and she moved back and forth on the hard seat, pressing her thighs tightly together. She blushed, imagining how it would feel to be touched and played with in such a wanton style.

The legs of the woman on the stage were parted now, and the Viscount slipped his right hand between them. She writhed against him sensuously as he explored the swell of her mound under the damp, curling hair. He titillated and massaged her with slow skill. She moaned, urging him to enter her.

Celine clasped her hands and pressed them hard into her lap, feeling a thrill deep inside. She watched, avidly, as the man thrust his fingers again and again into the wet flesh between the woman's thighs.

And then he raised his head and looked Celine full in the eyes.

She froze, unable to turn away from him. The dark, knowing stare stripped her of every pretence. He saw her excitement, he understood her body's desires better than she did herself. Insolently holding her look, he slowly slipped two fingers in and out of the panting

13

woman's sex. It was as if he had Celine there, naked under his touch.

Then the woman cried out, shrill as a bird, and he broke his gaze to glance down at her, smiling thinly.

Released, Celine thrust herself quickly back from the railing, knocking over her forgotten glass. It smashed on the floor below, narrowly missing the man in purple velvet. He leapt to his feet with a startled oath and turned on her, shaking his fist. Then he grew still, staring up at her. His hand unclenched and fell to his side. His face turned deathly pale.

'Lys . . .' he whispered.

One of his companions touched his arm.

'What is it, Sir James, are you ill?'

'My wife . . .' he faltered. Then his eyes narrowed and his face flushed to scarlet. 'No, damme, it's my daughter!'

Celine started to her feet, one hand at her throat.

'Get down from there!' roared Sir James Fortescue. 'Get downstairs, you baggage, you saucy piece! Hell's fire, where's my hat!' He snatched it from a friend's hand and stormed out.

Unwillingly, Celine felt her gaze drawn back to the man standing on the podium. He was fastening his shirt and tucking it into the tight breeches. When he saw her looking he laughed, white teeth snapping. As she fled down the stairs to face her angry father she could still hear him laughing, loud and long.

Head bowed, biting her lip with mortification, Celine stood on the cobbles outside the slave-market, enduring the tempest of her father's wrath.

She was a jade, a doxy, a shameless light-skirt. She had made herself a scandal in the island before she'd been there an hour. Bess, who had rushed to defend her mistress, eyes flashing, came in for her fair share of the abuse. What kind of a servant was she, to let his daughter cross the threshold of a barracoon, a place where no lady would set foot!

14

'There were others – ' Celine began.

Sir James snorted. 'Fine ladies!' he exclaimed furiously. 'Mother Midnight and her cronies! Why, your name will be a by-word in every bawdy-house from here to Havana before the month is out!'

'Forgive me,' said Celine in a small voice.

Her father mopped his face with a large pocket handkerchief and glared at her.

'By God, but you're like your mother,' he said. 'Well, it can't be undone now. No need to cry. Best we get you home and out of the sun. Where's your baggage? Stap me, all that? We'll have to send a cart.'

As Sir James gave loud orders for the carriage to be brought round, Celine glanced quickly up and down the dock. Liam stepped forward out of the shadow of the ship.

Celine flushed, feeling as if he could read the experiences of the past hour in her face. He moved swiftly to her side. She looked up at him, remembering the things she had seen, and a flutter of excitement stirred within her.

The carriage, drawn by two horses, rumbled across the quay towards them. A footman leapt down and opened the door.

'Father,' said Celine, shyly. 'This is Mr O'Brien.'

'Honoured to make your acquaintance,' said Liam, with a respectful bow.

Sir James responded with a nod. 'Your servant, sir. Any relation to the Earl of Fermanagh?'

'I'm afraid not,' said Liam.

'I didn't think so,' replied Sir James.

'Mr O'Brien is one of the ship's officers,' said Celine. 'He was very kind to me on the voyage.'

'Was he, by God?' said Sir James, glowering. 'Friendly, I dare say? Looked after you?'

Liam drew himself up, his blue eyes sparking with anger at the older man's contemptuous tone.

'I assure you, sir . . .' he began, with chill politeness, but Sir James had already turned away and was hustling

15

Celine before him to the carriage where Bess sat waiting, ensconced in the forward seat.

'Good day to you, sir,' said Sir James, climbing in after Celine and slamming the door. He leant back on the cushions, scowling. 'Damned Irish upstart. Got his eye on your fortune, I warrant,' he muttered. 'Drive on!'

Chapter Two

*F*ort George, the island's sole town, was built on the slopes of a hill, overlooking the harbour defences. Twisting streets, bordered with palm and casuarina trees, climbed up to Government House.

Celine's bedchamber was hung with blue, and bare-bottomed cupids rioted over the coved ceiling. French windows opened onto a deep veranda; their brocade curtains blew in the night wind from the sea.

She crouched in a polished copper bathtub, while Bess sponged her with cool water. Her long dark hair was pinned up on top of her head, and flickering candlelight played across her nakedness, outlining her with gold.

Scented water spilt across her back and trickled in the downy crease of her bottom. It coursed over her breasts, making their pink tips tighten. Droplets hung like gems in the triangle of black curls at her loins. Bess hummed softly as she soaped Celine's smooth swelling buttocks and long legs.

'There, you're done,' she said at last.

From the great ballroom downstairs, Celine could hear the squeaks and trills of musicians tuning up. There was to be a dance tonight in her honour, to introduce her to island society. She glanced at the ormolu clock ticking above the fireplace, and dried herself quickly.

17

'You're sure he's coming, Bess?' asked Celine, tossing the towel aside.

The maid stood on tiptoe to drop the chemise, a wisp of rose-coloured silk, over her mistress's head.

'You've asked me that every day for a week,' she said dryly. 'Take hold of the bedpost, milady, I've got to lace your corset.'

Celine obeyed. It was no good arguing when Bess was in this mood.

'Don't tease, Bess. I just want to hear it again.'

'All the *Challenger*'s officers have been invited. And Mr O'Brien said he'd walk over hot coals to see you again. Now will you let me get you dressed?'

With a happy smile, Celine submitted to her maid's ministrations. Half an hour later she was seated before the dressing table, applying a last dusting of powder, when her father tapped on the door.

'Are you ready, my dear?' he asked. 'The first carriages are coming up the hill. We must be downstairs to greet our guests.'

Celine whisked the hare's-foot across her forehead and arose. Her brown eyes glowed and her cheeks and lips were softly rouged. Her taffeta gown was ivory-coloured, cut low over the bosom, and covered in tiny sprigs of green leaves and pink flowerbuds.

White satin shoes with emerald buckles peeped out from under her full petticoat of ruffled lace. Diamond drops trembled in her ears. Bess had brushed her hair into long curls that clustered about her shoulders, and a delicate diamond and emerald necklace lay on her white breast.

'Most becoming,' said Sir James, nodding his pleasure. 'Come. There's someone I want you to meet.'

Bess turned back into the bedroom and closed the door smartly. She tidied away the tangle of ribbons and laces that littered the floor and wiped up the spilt powder on the dressing table. Now there was only the bath to be

18

emptied and put away. Bess fetched a jug and then paused, thoughtfully.

Her best dress was laid out in the little closet where she slept. It would be a pity to put it on now, when she was all of a muck sweat.

Bess knew none of the other servants could challenge her for beauty. She was fair as a milkmaid and plump as a partridge, with blonde curls and sparkling blue eyes. And tonight all the coachmen who had driven guests in from the outlying plantations would be below-stairs. There would be grooms in smart livery, too, and the stalwart chairmen who had brought sedans up from the town. A pretty girl could pick and choose.

She picked up the soap and sniffed at it. The heady perfume decided her, and she stripped off her clothes. She was just about to step into the tub when a noise at the farthest window startled her into stillness.

The blue curtains bulged and swayed. Someone was hiding behind them. Bess snatched up a towel and huddled it around her.

'Who's there!' she cried, fearfully.

'It's me,' said a familiar voice, 'Martin.'

'I thought I told you to stay away,' snapped Bess. 'I can't be doing with you and your fly-be-night ways any more.'

The man stepped out of concealment and smiled at her ingratiatingly. Martin Piggott was a foxy, gypsy-like creature, roughly handsome. He was one of the indentured labourers – the scourings of Newgate – who'd been transported from England on the *Challenger*'s lowest deck.

'Thought you might change your mind,' he said, slinking closer. 'I've got a groom's place now. I came along ahead of the carriage, hoping to see you.'

'You should have waited,' she retorted. 'I'm not ready.'

'You look ready enough for what I've got in mind.'

Bess was very conscious of her nudity under the towel and, judging by the way he ogled her, Martin was too.

19

He looked quite different to the rough creature she had dallied with on the voyage. He was clean, for one thing, and he wore a suit of sober brown, with snowy linen at his neck and wrists. Only the tilted eyes, with their hungry expression, showed that the man inside was still untamed.

'Any road, I've been patient too long,' he added. 'She took her time bathing, that lady of yours. I was hard put to stay hidden.'

Bess could not prevent herself from looking down. The bulge in his breeches showed his eagerness all too clearly. She felt the first tingle of lust awaken. After all, it had been more than a week.

Martin reached out and took hold of the hand that held the towel bunched at her breast. Bess pouted, but allowed him to open her fingers one by one.

'She's a tasty bit, for those as like the lean ones,' he said, reflectively, 'I prefer something to get hold of, myself.'

Suiting the action to the word, he cupped Bess's breasts, one in each hand, teasing their tips with his thumbs. Sensitive tissue sprang erect under his touch. Desire overcame her resolution to have done with him and she felt the place between her legs grow wet and juicy as a split plum.

Bess slipped her hand down to feel the swelling at his groin. He was fully engorged, and hard as a broom handle. She traced the outline of his erection through the rough fabric of his breeches, squeezing its head gently until Martin groaned and buried his tongue in her mouth.

She loved the feeling of power it gave her to have him desperate for her but, as always, Martin was too eager. His hands were already probing her sex.

Well, if that's the way he wants it, thought Bess, and grasped his penis so tightly that he grunted and pulled away.

'Now you give over, Martin Piggott,' she said. 'I don't like being mauled about like that, and well you know it.'

Martin stared at her for a moment, breathing heavily. Then he bent his head and fastened his mouth on her left nipple, sucking and tugging at it. With a moan of desire, she put her arms around him, and pushed against his groin.

'That's better,' she whispered. 'Nice and slow.'

'You've missed me, haven't you?' he said, moving to the other breast.

'A bit,' she admitted.

Martin pulled her against his driving loins. Then, his mouth still greedy at her nipples, he lifted her bodily and carried her to Celine's bed.

His hands explored her moist crack, finding the pleasure-bud between the swollen lips of her sex and massaging it until Bess could wait no more. Eagerly, she reached between his legs, feeling the throbbing hardness there.

She unbuttoned his breeches and sprang his cock free, looking at it in desire and anticipation. It was thick and meaty, its head shiny, a drop of moisture hanging at its eye. Bess circled its shaft with her fingers, stroking the velvet skin until Martin could hold back no longer and, lifting her legs to rest on his hips, plunged his manhood into her to the root in one long stroke.

He pushed slowly, again and again, withdrawing almost the full length of his shaft each time, forcing her to clench the muscles of her vagina around the sensitive head of his cock in fear of losing it.

Looking up at him, she saw his face was twisted with the effort of holding back. Usually Martin was a selfish lover, ignoring her needs while he gratified his own, but this time he was really trying to please her.

As he thrust into her wet folds, Bess writhed and pulled his hands down to toy with her breasts. She was close, so close! This was different from their hurried couplings in holds and against bulkheads, and so much better.

Waves of tingling sensation spread through her entire being. They built rapidly, and swiftly reached the point of no return. Bess tossed her head from side to side on the blue damask coverlet as the spasms of climax overcame her.

Freed of constraint by her orgasm, Martin moved faster. His hands tightened on Bess's white breasts as he thundered on to his own release. Finding it quickly, he fell like a oak to lie still upon her.

He lay inert and panting, pinning her down with his full weight, until Bess pushed gently at his chest. Then he propped himself on his elbows and she was able to look up into his face. To her disappointment, he did not look particularly pleased to have satisfied her. He was even frowning a little.

'Penny for them?' Bess enquired.

'What?' he said. 'Oh. Yes. Who's this O'Brien fellow you've been meeting?'

'It's private,' said Bess, sounding rather guilty.

'I see,' replied Martin grimly. He pulled away from her and began to fasten his breeches.

Her heart melted. She had always thought she was just a convenience for him, but maybe he did care. He had certainly been very different tonight.

'Martin Piggott, I do believe you're jealous.'

'And what if I am?' he muttered, preparing to leave.

'Wait!' she cried. She could not let him go like this, angry and disappointed, after the pleasure he had given her.

He paused, and came slowly back across the room. Bess took his hand and pulled him down to sit by her side.

'You must keep what I tell you as quiet as the grave,' she whispered. 'It's not my secret, you see, it's milady's. No-one must know.'

'Trust me,' Martin said, drawing her head down onto his shoulder.

Held in his warm embrace, Bess told him in a low voice all about Liam and Celine; of their love, hopes, and fears. Piggott listened very carefully, a small calculating smile playing about his lips.

* * *

22

Celine stood beside her father in the entrance hall. The great doors were open to the velvet night. A myriad candles burned in the sconces, attracting glittering tropical insects and huge moths with powdery wings that circled and danced around the flames.

It was past midnight and the flood of guests was at last thinning to a trickle. She chafed to be free. Liam was in the ballroom, waiting for her. A few of the company lingered in the hallway, flirting and retailing Island news. A late carriage rolled up to the steps, its wheels crunching on the gravel.

Celine was chatting with a buxom widow in an astonishing blonde wig when she became aware of a sudden change in atmosphere. Men clustered in little groups, looking over their shoulders towards the door. Painted ladies whispered behind their fans.

Celine followed their eyes, and caught her breath.

A new arrival stood in the entrance, lit by the blowing flambeaux. He wore dull crimson, richly laced with gold. Mechlin lace foamed at his breast and fell in cascades over his hands. He carried a tall beribboned cane and his hair was foppishly curled. But the impression of inexorable power was still there: the angular face was the same, and the weary cynical glance. It was the man from the slave-market, the Viscount.

For a moment he waited, enjoying the *frisson* his coming had caused. Then he moved slowly up the hall to greet Celine and her father.

After that first shock of recognition, she kept her eyes lowered. She heard the man's heels clacking on the parquet. They stopped close in front of her. Celine stared resolutely at the floor.

'I vow, my Lord, you've kept us waiting,' said Sir James heartily. 'My dear, this is the gentleman I wished you to meet. Allow me to present you. My daughter, Lady Celine – Odo, Viscount Wraxall.'

'Enraptured,' drawled Lord Odo Wraxall, bowing extravagantly.

Celine unwillingly extended her hand. The Viscount

23

took it in cool, strong fingers. She felt his breath as his lips brushed across her skin.

'Good evening, my Lord,' she whispered.

Her father looked on indulgently for a moment. Then a stir at the entrance caught his attention, and he straightened his coat.

'You'll pardon me, Wraxall? There's someone I must welcome.'

When Celine tried to follow him, Lord Odo's fingers tightened on her hand.

'Your father would not relish your company just now,' he said softly, watching as Sir James descended to the carriage-sweep to greet the new guest.

It was a woman, cloaked and masked against the dust of the road, riding a grey mare. A huge African in white linen, mounted on a stallion as black and muscular as he, rode behind her. She swung down laughing from the saddle into Sir James's arms.

'I must go,' protested Celine, struggling to free herself.

'Without one glance?' the Viscount murmured. 'You were not so modest when I saw you last.'

Dismayed, she looked up and met his eyes. For a moment they widened. She read desire in them, and a frightening knowledge. Celine felt that they recognised secrets that she herself had hardly put a name to. His fingertips trailed over her palm, tickling softly.

She snatched back her hand, repressing an instinct to wipe it clean against her skirt. Hurriedly, she crossed to her father's side. She knew that she was running away, and that Lord Wraxall had allowed her to go; and that he watched her futile flight, as the cat watches the mouse.

Sir James came towards her, the masked woman swaying on his arm. He had slipped the riding cloak from her shoulders and she stood revealed, a lush-bodied mature siren all in cloth of gold. Flaming red hair tumbled around her shoulders, and green eyes inspected Celine through the eyeholes of the full-face black velvet vizard.

'What, tired of Wraxall so soon?' said Sir James when he saw Celine. 'That won't do! I want you to be better acquainted.'

'And may God have mercy on your soul,' said the woman.

Sir James laughed. 'Have done, Sal. You're prejudiced against the man.'

'Maybe,' said the woman. 'And maybe I know him better than you. Hell's teeth, I'm stifling in this thing. James, see if you can unfasten it. The strings are in the devil's own tangle.'

Celine stared. She had never dreamt that her father, whom she had found to be a stern, unbending character, would accept orders so meekly.

'At last!' the woman said, casting the mask aside. She had a tanned, open face, with jet-black brows and eyelashes. 'Damme, James, you've pulled every hair from my head with your ham-fisted fumbling. I'll have to devise a fitting revenge.'

Sir James shot a furtive look at Celine. He pressed the woman's hand.

'Later,' he said in a low voice. 'In the library.'

'When I say, and where I say,' replied the woman with a meaning glance. Then she turned and held out her hand to Celine in a forthright manner.

'Sarah Colney,' she said. 'Friends call me Sally. I'm the only woman planter on the island. My place, Laissez-Faire, is out by Morgan's Bay.'

'How interesting,' said Celine, with an uncertain smile.

Sally raised one eyebrow. When Celine remained tongue-tied, she shrugged dismissively and turned away. Linking arms with Sir James, she moved towards the ballroom. Unwilling to abandon the safety of numbers, Celine followed them. She did not mean to look back, but she could not prevent herself.

The Viscount had gathered a little court of sycophants around him, and seemed to be involved in languid discourse. But when she turned, his eyes were on her, intrusive as a stranger's touch.

Conversation flagged after Celine had left the room. Lord Wraxall responded with a cold smile to flatteries and witticisms alike. The juiciest scandal drew no more from him than a bored sigh. One by one the remaining guests fell silent, made their bows, and withdrew to the inner rooms where strings and harpsichord played a tinkling gavotte. Footmen closed the portals against the clouds of night insects and went about their business.

A great moth, its wings singed by candle-flame, flapped in a crippled circle on the floor at the Viscount's feet. He looked down at it lazily, but his thoughts were of Celine. Her beauty alone would have aroused his appetites, but her fear gave added piquancy to the dish, fitting it for the most jaded palate. Thin lips twisted in a smile, he lost himself in pleasurable speculation.

The click of a latch roused him at last. Martin Piggott hovered by a door in the panelled wall. Lord Wraxall beckoned, and the man slunk across to him.

'It's as I told you, milord. Lady Celine and O'Brien were making eyes for the whole voyage. Bess confirmed every word – once I softened her up a bit.'

Odo's grip tightened on the head of his cane.

'So, I have a rival. And has he beaten me to the prize?'

'Oh, no, milord, I'm sure not. They plan to marry. Bess said Mr O'Brien was a most honourable young man and wouldn't – '

'Then he's a fool.' He tossed a guinea down for Martin to grovel after. 'Take that, and get out of my sight.'

Odo Wraxall remained alone in the entrance hall for a minute or so after his servant had gone. He looked again at the crippled moth, fluttering on the parquet. Then he stepped forward and ground it slowly to pulp under his heel, before strolling away to the glitter and music of the ballroom.

* * *

26

It was past two o'clock before Celine had an opportunity to be alone with Liam. Finding a door opening on to the terrace, they slipped through it, hand in hand.

It was deliciously cool outside. They were not the only lovers who had sought privacy on the terrace. Here and there couples leant close in the shelter of pillars. As she passed, Celine heard murmurs, laughing protests and, once, a groan so full of agonised desire that it made her heart turn over.

The moon was high, and the air was heavy with the perfume of night-blooming flowers. Filled with tremulous anticipation she allowed Liam to lead her along the terrace and into a shadowed corner overlooking the gardens.

'At last!' he breathed, snatching her into his arms. 'Oh, Celine, I've dreamed of this every hour, every minute. I can't bear to part from you again. Come away with me. The *Challenger*'s captain can marry us.'

'Elope? But, Liam, why? I tell you, my father will consent!'

He shook his head, and his embrace tightened around her.

'My heart tells me no. But if you want it so, my love, I must obey.'

They clung together, kissing deeply, their tongues darting. A soft, wild frenzy grew in her as his hands moved on the tight bodice of her gown.

She felt them travel slowly up from her tiny, tight-drawn waist to caress the swell of her breasts. His fingers slipped along her neckline, dipping inside to feel the soft rounded flesh and brush against the sensitive buds prisoned within the silk.

Celine responded eagerly to his demanding touch. Liam thrust his loins forward, rubbing against her through the layers of gown and lacy underskirts.

His hand freed one breast from the silken confines of her bodice, and Celine cried out with pleasure as he bent to caress it with his lips. Never had she felt anything to equal this. She ran her fingers through the shining

27

darkness of his hair, and murmured his name over and over again.

While his tongue lapped at her nipple, Celine felt again the sense that there was a direct connection between the aching coral bud and the place between her legs. A creamy moisture seemed to be forming there.

When Liam parted her knees, pressing his thigh into her skirts, she could not help but move against him. And now there was no denying that she was getting wet. A warm, seeping fluid was oozing onto her thighs.

Her flesh cried out to take command, hurrying her onward to unknown pleasures. Clothes were too hot, too cumbrous, too constricting. She moved restlessly, wishing that she could be free of them, with nothing to separate her from the urgent male body of her lover.

How marvellous it would be to feel his lips and hands all over her. To be naked for him, as she had been in her bath; naked as the woman in the slave market. But with that thought came the memory of Lord Wraxall's dark and knowledgeable stare, and suddenly everything seemed to be going too fast.

'Please!' cried Celine, nervously. 'Liam, my darling, please wait!'

He groaned, and stilled his movements against her with an effort. He was panting, and she could feel his heart hammering against her breast.

'Don't be scared, *acushla*,' he said hoarsely. 'It's only this week without seeing you . . .'

She turned her face up to him. Liam's pupils were wide and dark, and she could feel that he was shaking a little. He took her hand and placed it on his loins. A long bulge lay diagonally across his belly.

'Oh, Celine, I need you so badly,' he whispered. 'Help me. Touch me.'

The thought frightened her a little, for she had never touched, or even seen, a man's sexual organ. But she could not refuse him. Liam unfastened the front flap of his breeches, and guided her hand within. The touch of his warm flesh was pleasant, and not too alarming.

28

He kissed her softly and encouraged her to investigate further. Trembling slightly, her fingers explored beneath his shirt until they found a stiff, pulsing staff of flesh. She would have withdrawn, then, but Liam gently forced her hand closed around it, and showed her how to pleasure him.

She was too shy to look but, after the first shock of handling it, Celine found the feel of Liam's erect penis exciting. The skin was so soft over the rigidity beneath. It was so thick and hard and hot, pulsing vitally in her palm. Obedient to his whispered instructions, she began to stroke her hand up and down the throbbing length.

'That's so good,' he sighed. 'Faster, love. That's right. What is it?'

'I thought I heard footsteps.'

Liam kissed her, thrusting his tongue into her mouth. His manhood drove eagerly through the circle of her fingers.

'There's no-one,' he murmured. 'Don't stop.'

A cough sounded behind them, shockingly close in the gloom.

Celine gasped, and looked around wildly. Liam jerked his cock from her hand and pulled his shirt down in a vain attempt to conceal it. But there was no time to do more before the intruder was upon them. A woman's gown rustled, and starlight glistened on cloth-of-gold as she glided out of the darkness.

Liam struggled with his breeches as he tried to imprison the unruly length of his erection. Celine's bodice was disarranged, and one pink nipple peeped alluringly above the low neckline.

'Mistress Colney!' she cried. 'How long, I mean . . .'

'Your father's looking for you,' said Sally, without preamble. 'And in no very good mood, either. Best come back to the ballroom with me now, my lady.'

'It's not what you think,' said Liam, a flush of colour burning on his cheekbones. 'We are betrothed, or nearly so. I plan to seek out Sir James tonight, and ask for Lady Celine's hand in marriage.'

'Good God, man! Nothing could be more fatal to your chances!' said Sally, sounding exasperated. 'He's in a tearing fury. Go back to your ship. Speak to him in the morning. If questions are asked, I'll swear I found her alone.'

Liam looked doubtfully back and forth between them.

'Oh, stop your dithering, and do as you're told, both of you,' snapped Sally. She grasped Celine's hand in hard fingers. 'Come along, my lady.'

Dragged along behind the determined Mistress Colney, Celine looked back over her shoulder until Liam was out of sight. She sighed deeply.

'Love him, do you?' asked Sally. 'Well, if you want him, you may have to fight. I think James has other plans for your future. A rich wife would be more than welcome to Lord Wraxall just now. His tastes are expensive: his plantation, Acheron, is mortgaged to the hilt.'

'Ah no!' exclaimed Celine, in horror. 'My father can't mean me to marry that roué, that satyr!'

'If you don't consent, they can do nothing,' said Sally urgently. 'Stick by your guns, girl. Hold out for that pretty boy of yours. I know your father's character. He'll bluster and bawl, but he's like our hurricanoes, soon blown out. You'll get your own way in the end, but only if you stand firm. Can you?'

Celine clenched her fists. Her chin came up, and her brown eyes glowed. For a moment, she had the stubborn look of Sir James in a rage.

'I can, and I will,' she said, between gritted teeth. 'Do what he may, I will never consent to be Lord Odo Wraxall's bride!'

'I'm glad to see you've some steel in you,' said Sally approvingly. 'Maybe you're more than the insipid society miss that you look. And now we'd best be getting back to the ballroom, before your father turns the militia out to look for you.'

Chapter Three

The cardroom was full, and noisy with shouts and laughter. Liam swore softly to himself: he shouldn't have let Mistress Colney put his back up with her orders. Better by far to have done as she'd said and returned to the *Challenger*. There, at least, he could be alone in his bunk and relieve the crying needs of his body.

A portly man, his face red as the militia coat that he wore, came over and clapped Liam on the shoulder.

'You remember me. Cathcart – Captain Cathcart. I signed for your load of transportees. Can't stand there all alone, man. Come and have a drink. Boy! More punch here!'

He linked arms with Liam and, weaving slightly, drew him across to a table in the corner.

'Here we are,' said Captain Cathcart. He waved his hand, introducing the others at the table. 'Viscount Wraxall, Mr Moffat – Mr O'Brien'.

Lord Wraxall shot a penetrating glance at Liam. Mr Moffat giggled.

'Drink up, lad,' said Captain Cathcart.

Liam drained his glass. It wouldn't hurt to have a couple more, just to be polite. He took a second drink, and a third. Then he stopped counting.

'It's my contention,' said Mr Moffat, an hour later,

'that fortune favours a man either at cards or in love, but not both.'

'Ah, but I've the luck of the Irish,' said Liam, as he gathered up the guineas. He beamed at his new friends. They were the most charming fellows, the best losers, the noblest drinking companions that a man could have.

Viscount Wraxall twirled the stem of his glass between his fingers.

'Speaking of love, I hear there's a new exhibition at Mother Midnight's.'

'Is there, by God?' said Cathcart, staring, and Mr Moffat licked his lips.

Lord Wraxall pushed back his chair and rose. 'Well, gentlemen, why do we wait? Come along, Mr O'Brien. Let's see if your luck holds among the ladies.'

Arm in arm with Mr Moffat and the militia captain, Liam happily left the card-room at Wraxall's heels. Right now a woman, any woman, seemed like a damned fine idea.

Viscount Wraxall stood aside and let the others lurch past him into Mother Midnight's bordello. He watched until Liam had collapsed onto a low couch, then caught the madame's eye with a commanding look.

The main saloon was a sultan's palace, hung with silks. Rose trees grew in tubs around the walls. A small fountain played in a niche. Its tinkling blended with the music played on flute and drum by two veiled Berber women.

Dozens of men sprawled on the divans and stared, in the silence of lust, towards the stage where the exhibition was beginning, while naked slaves with gilded nipples served them with hookahs and scented brandy.

His discussion ended, Lord Wraxall left the madame, and sauntered back to sit beside Liam. The young man was already transfixed. Odo smiled, and settled back to watch the performance with the critical eye of a connoisseur.

In the wall opposite the fountain, hangings framed a

deep, pillared alcove. Within it a woman lolled face down on a couch.

She was full-fleshed and olive-skinned. Black hair spread like a fan across her back and a wisp of gauze draped her loins. Behind her stood a muscular young man, his flesh the deep red-brown of polished mahogany. A bulging pouch of leather covered his genitals, and he held a tall peacock-feather fan.

Then the drum began a steady beat, and a tiny shiver ran across the woman's back. The reed flute twined its eerie whistling around the drumbeats and, stepping to the rhythm, four young women swayed onto the stage. They carried long-necked vases, seemingly of gold. Harem trousers of transparent silk clung low on their hips, half-concealing the satiny skin beneath.

Odo stifled a yawn and shifted his position so that he could watch the responses of his neighbour as well as the show on the stage. Liam was breathing hard and his lips were parted. So far, very satisfactory.

The girls knelt and, with oil poured from the vases, began to massage the prone woman. Slim hands slid up and down her arms, circled on calves and thighs. The woman shifted on the couch as the perfumed oil was rubbed across her skin. A scent of musk and jessamine spread through the saloon.

Now she was moving sinuously as the attendants oiled her back and the twin mounds of her buttocks. The drumbeat matched its tempo to the swaying of her hips. She stretched, languorously, and rose to sit on the edge of the couch. The flimsy covering fell away, leaving her unclothed.

She raised her arms, piling her hair above her head as her attendants kissed and cupped her breasts, rousing her nipples, oiling their round weight until they gleamed in the lamplight. Her lower body rocked back and forth on the couch. The flute cried out like a thing in pain.

Her attendants stroked her legs from ankle to thigh, and parted them gradually until she sat fully exposed.

33

Her mount of Venus was shaved bare, and the red lips of her sex were displayed to the men below.

She moved one hand, letting it drift down over her breasts and belly until it found her clitoris She teased and caressed herself, fingertips flicking. Here and there in the audience men groaned or panted. Lord Wraxall smiled to see Liam's erection, and the sweat beading his forehead.

The woman moved faster and faster, hips pumping to the drumbeat, the shrilling flute pacing her as she brought herself to the peak of sexual frenzy. At the moment of her climax, the youth beside the couch leapt forward.

He had been still for so long that the watchers had almost forgotten he was there. Now he sprang onto the couch beside the woman, tearing away the leather pouch to display his swollen phallus. The girl attendants scattered to the corners of the stage, miming dismay.

He grappled with the woman, snatching at her breasts. For a moment it seemed he would secure her, but she slipped from his grasp. The girls returned, bringing velvet ropes. They circled the youth, enmeshing him.

Lord Wraxall snapped his fingers for drinks, took one and passed a second to his companion. Liam accepted it absently, downed the powerful liquor in a single gulp, and turned his attention back to the stage.

The youth was bound to one of the pillars now, and the girls were gone. The woman prowled about him, wielding a silken whip. She teased his standing prick with it, and struck him smartly across the buttocks.

He writhed and struggled under the stinging blows that fell in rhythm with the drum, and the ropes began to loosen. He wrenched one hand free to tear at his bonds while she struck and struck again.

The ropes fell, and the youth was free.

The flute wailed, and the drum beat faster.

He sprang forward and seized the woman by her shoulders, bearing her down to kneel before him as she pleaded in dumbshow for mercy. He thrust his groin towards her, forcing the head of his erection between her lips.

Liam leant forward, his hands clenching and unclenching convulsively.

She stroked the youth's thighs, his hard-muscled arse. She licked and sucked his phallus. She took his whole length into her red mouth and deep into her throat, swallowing as he made each long thrust.

The drumbeats pattered like rain on a rooftop. The youth's loins pumped in time with them. His hands tangled in the woman's hair, pulling her to him. She stroked and suckled him, teasing his balls with the tips of her fingers.

The drumbeats reached a crescendo. The youth, with one mad lunge, spent his milk of pleasure in the woman's greedy mouth.

The drum stopped.

The flute wailed into silence.

The curtains fell.

'Jazus!' said Liam.

Mother Midnight allowed a moment of awed stillness before she struck the gong at her elbow.

At her signal, the curtains parted once more. A rainbow of girls – black, white, brown, tawny – stepped down from the stage. As the echoes of the gong-stroke died away, they moved forward, gauzes clinging to their tempting flesh.

Liam caught at the first who passed him. He pulled her down on to his lap and fondled her bare breasts hungrily. Lord Wraxall rose and strolled across to Mother Midnight. Together they watched Liam eagerly accompany his girl to the private rooms at the back of the house.

'That young man's brains are in his breeches,' she remarked.

'Madam,' said Lord Wraxall, with a bow. 'I have taken great trouble and expense this night to put them there.'

'Tell me,' she said, changing the subject, 'did you find the exhibition – '

'I found it predictable,' he said, crushingly. 'And banal. Visit my plantation theatre some time. Learn to be original.'

'This is a cash business,' retorted Mother Midnight, with a scowl. 'If we put on the *outré* diversions you fancy, Viscount, we'd be bankrupt in a week. Besides, I can see my poor show didn't leave you entirely unmoved.'

'What would you?' murmured Odo. 'I am, after all, only human.'

'That's not what I've heard,' said Mother Midnight. 'Now, milord, the business with O'Brien will take some time yet. Can't we offer you some entertainment? Perhaps an exhibitor? Melissa's mouth is a honeypot even you would not despise.'

'Very well,' said Lord Odo Wraxall wearily. 'But not Melissa. I'll take the boy. Just for a change, you understand.'

Bess looked up from the petticoat she was mending and made a tutting sound.

'You won't make the morning pass any faster by rampaging about, milady.'

Celine flung herself down on the sofa in the yellow parlour and snapped open her fan. Her hair was dressed in loose curls, dark tendrils waving about her neck and ears. Her lemon-coloured morning gown cast a creamy light upwards on to her bosom and face. She counted the ivory sticks of her fan with her finger, then flipped it shut again.

'What time is it?'

'Five to eleven,' said Bess. 'Two minutes later than when you last asked.'

Celine sighed, plaintively. 'Why doesn't he come?'

'Busy, probably,' said Bess, biting off a length of cotton. 'Some of us have work to do.'

They sat in silence while the streak of sunlight from the open window moved perhaps half an inch across the floor.

'What time is it now?'

Bess threw down her mending and started to her feet, arms akimbo.

'Now you listen to me, my lady – ' she began.

But Celine had no attention to spare for her maid. Downstairs. a caller had arrived. Bess ran out to peer down over the bannisters into the hallway. She came back shaking her head.

'Too late,' she said. 'But it was a gentleman, and he's gone into the library. He's with your father now.'

Celine pulled Bess down beside her, and clutched her hand. They sat together on the gold brocade sofa, waiting and hoping, while the clock on the mantlepiece struck the hour – quarter past – half past.

It was full morning, painfully bright and dazzling, when Liam awoke. He was sprawled on a heap of straw, dirty straw. Liam blinked and tried to sit up, but a wave of nausea forced him to fall back, retching.

'You're alive, then,' said a deep voice. 'I was beginning to think they'd given me a corpse for company. Here.'

An arm slipped around Liam's shoulders, and a cup of water was put to his lips. He drank it dry and lay back, feeling the sickness recede a little.

When he could open his eyes again Liam discovered that he was lying on the floor of a small stone room. A square of sunlight fell on to his face from the high barred window.

'Feeling better?' enquired the voice.

Liam turned his head gingerly to look at his companion. A muscular ogre squatted against the opposite wall and grinned at him through a great bird's-nest of beard. Every inch of his body that could be seen was matted with hair, dark and dense as a bear's pelt. One eye was missing and the other, small and mobile, looked down at Liam with a speculative glint.

'I'm Reuben Osset,' said the ogre. He waited for a reaction. 'You've heard of me, maybe? Black Reuben, the pirate? One of Tremaine's men?'

37

Liam pushed himself into a sitting position. He felt as if he'd been poisoned. He was filthy. His coat was stained and torn, one sleeve hanging off.

'What's this place?' he asked thickly; but he already knew. Drunk, like the fool he was: he'd probably been raising Cain and smashing lanterns down in the town. Damme that rum punch.

'The lock-up. Trial's next Friday.'

'Trial?' said Liam, aghast. 'I can't stand trial – it'll ruin my reputation as an officer. Besides, I've got to be at Government House this morning. Call the gaoler. I'll pay a fine.'

'Oh, will you, Mr High-and-Mighty,' said Reuben, with a snort. 'I'll tell you what you'll do, matey, you'll be tried with the rest of us commoners. And you'll swing alongside us on the gallows too, for all your officer's braid.'

'Swing?' croaked Liam. 'Dear God, what did I do last night that could possibly be a hanging matter?'

'Murder,' said the pirate cheerfully. 'They say you was in a brothel, fighting drunk: got in a brawl over one of the girls.'

'It isn't true!' cried Liam.

'That's as may be. But there's witnesses enough to hang you ten times over. A lord, no less, Mr Justice Moffat, and the Captain of the Militia.'

'It's a lie! I was at the Government House ball with Celine, and then – ah, my head's foggy. I can't remember.'

'Best try,' said Reuben with grim sympathy. 'Or you'll hang for sure.'

Liam thought back. He had been with Celine on the terrace, and then in the gaming room. He remembered drinking, and laughing, and winning at cards: winning great handfuls of golden guineas.

'Mother Midnight's!' he said suddenly. 'I was at Mother Midnight's!'

He clenched his fists and forced his clouded mind to rebuild the events of the night before. Even in his present

38

weakened state he felt a stir of excitement as he recalled the performance at the brothel – and the girl, afterwards, writhing on his lap as he stroked and kissed her breasts.

She was a mulatto girl, small and lithe, with great brown melancholy eyes like a deer's. She had slipped her hand into his breeches as they hurried towards her room, circling his erection with her fingers. He remembered how she'd gasped as she felt the size of his tool.

He'd seized her in his arms the moment the door closed behind them, tearing away her silken shift in his impatience to quench his lust in her supple body. She had seemed to be as eager for pleasure as he, thrusting her hand down to squeeze and rub the rampant length of his cock, as she deftly unfastened his breeches-flap.

Liam had fallen back onto the bed, his engorged penis thrusting proudly up from the nest of black curls at his groin.

The girl stepped out of the remaining rags of her garment and bent forward across him, rubbing her breasts over his face, teasing his lips with her hard brown nipples. Like all Mother Midnight's girls, her pudenda was shaved and he feasted his eyes and fingers on her naked sex.

She could see that Liam was in no mood for long preliminaries. She crawled on top of him, straddling him. He grunted with pleasure as she took his cock in her hand and guided it to the moist opening between her legs.

She lowered herself slowly on to him, inch by inch. The warm, soft embrace of her vagina enclosed his manhood, and her practised muscles clenched on it. He had never had a girl who was shaved before; he had never been so close, so deep inside a woman.

Sitting up, he grasped her buttocks. The girl arched her back, thrusting her breasts forward for him to suck and bite. She rose and fell on him like the tides, her tight wet love-passage sliding sensuously up and down his straining phallus.

Liam wanted the moment to last forever, his prick

39

buried to the hilt in her sweet brown body, but he was close to exploding with lust. The long abstinence of the sea-voyage, his delightful but frustrating episodes with Celine, and the arousal of the show, all combined against him.

His excitement built quickly to the crisis point. He clutched her avidly, his fingers digging into the cheeks of her arse as he thrust again and again.

He could hold back no longer. Crying out through clenched teeth, he climaxed, his seed spurting out of him. The girl gripped him firmly with her inner muscles, sweetly accentuating the pulses of his penis as he came.

He held her close, groaning with satisfaction. But after a short time she pushed Liam gently away from her and dismounted. Liam flopped back on the bed, panting. He heard the girl pour water to wash herself. Then he heard the door handle turn. He sat up, flinging the hair out of his eyes.

'Where are you going?'

The girl shrugged. 'You finished.'

'Not by a long chalk,' he said, grinning. 'You'll get no rest with me tonight, little darling.'

The girl looked at him appraisingly. 'You got money? All night costs more, lots more.'

Liam laughed, dug his hand into his breeches pocket, and tossed a handful of gold coins on to the rumpled bed. The girl rolled her eyes.

'Oh, you sailor-men!' she said, shaking her head. 'Wait one minute – I tell the madame.'

She slipped into the corridor, naked as she was. Liam shrugged out of his coat and glanced at the coins scattered across the coverlet. There was enough there – seven, eight guineas – to pay for any extras he might care to name. He thought about the woman on the stage and imagined the mulatto girl sucking him dry like that. His prick stirred and began to wake again.

By the time she returned, carrying a bottle and a glass, he was more than ready for her.

'Rum?' said the girl.

40

Liam knocked the proffered drink back in a single swallow.

'Odd taste,' he said. 'What's in it?'

The girl sat beside him and began to trail her fingers over his cock.

'Oh, lots of things. Herbs. Island spices.' She smiled mischievously and bit his earlobe 'Make you strong like a bull.'

She bent and took the head of his penis into her mouth, teasing its eye with the tip of her tongue. Liam pushed her away, frowning.

'You all right?' she said, looking at him slantwise.

Liam stood up. He swayed a little.

'I don't know about strong as a bull,' he said, in a slurred voice, 'but that stuff's made me feel damned diz –'

The crash of his fall had made the room shake.

Liam remembered lying on his side on the floor, feeling puzzled. He couldn't seem to move, not even a finger. He'd heard the creak of the door, and footsteps. A pair of black shoes, fine gentleman's shoes, with garnet buckles and high red heels, stood close in front of him.

'Goodbye, Mr O'Brien,' drawled Lord Odo Wraxall.

Liam's memory faded. He raised his head from his hands and looked across the cell at Reuben.

'That's all,' he said.

The pirate rose, and came across to squat on his hunkers beside Liam. He peered up into Liam's face with his single blue eye.

'You've been nobbled, mate,' said Black Reuben.

The parlour clock chimed the three-quarters. Celine heard the library door open. Her father came into the hall, talking in a loud voice about smuggling.

'I'd hang my own brother if I caught him at it,' he was saying as he mounted the stairs. 'It's a plague. It's got to be stamped out.'

His companion murmured something in a low voice.

Celine shooed Bess away and arranged herself in a

41

becoming attitude on the sofa. She blushed. Her brown eyes shone with happiness.

'I think we'll find her in the yellow room,' said Sir James. 'Yes, here she is. My dear, I've brought you a visitor. Come in, my lord. Come in.'

Every vestige of colour drained away from Celine's cheeks. The ivory fan dropped from her nerveless fingers and clattered on the floor.

Odo, Viscount Wraxall, stood tall in the doorway.

He wore a riding coat of dove-grey, and white kidskin breeches. Viciously rowelled spurs clinked at the heels of his high black boots as he paced across the floor to bend low over Celine's hand. His lips were cool and dry, and a strand of his silver-streaked hair brushed across her wrist as he bowed.

'You will permit me to join you, madam?' asked Lord Wraxall.

Celine squeezed herself as far into a corner as the bulging sofa cushions permitted and sat silent, staring at the toes of her shoes. She could smell his body. It was scented with some sharp, aromatic herb.

Sir James coughed and looked about him. He caught sight of Bess, standing quietly by the harpsichord in the window.

'Damme,' he said, irritably, 'Don't just stand there gaping at your betters, wench. Bring us some wine. You'll take a glass of claret, Wraxall?'

'Not at this hour.'

'A dish of coffee then. That's the dandy.'

Bess dropped a curtsey and scurried out. Sir James walked about the room, humming to himself. He fetched up in front of Celine and scowled at her.

'You're very dull, miss! Cat got your tongue?'

'I have a headache,' she said, putting up her chin.

'Rubbish!' said Sir James.

Lord Odo examined the fingernails on his left hand. The ticking of the clock sounded very loud. Sir James took another turn around the room.

'Where's that coffee?' he complained.

'I'll go and see.' said Celine. starting to her feet.

'You'll stay where you are!' said her father, with a frown. 'I'll go.'

'But – ' she began. He stared at her, and she sat down again.

'That's better,' said Sir James, walking to the door. 'Now be a good child and entertain Lord Wraxall. He has something to say to you.'

The door snapped to, and Sir James's footsteps retreated down the stairs. Lord Wraxall picked up Celine's forgotten fan. He looked it over critically.

'Too florid,' he said, tossing it into her lap. 'All that vulgar gilding.'

'It's the latest Paris fashion,' said Celine, coldly.

'I'll buy you a better,' said Lord Wraxall. He paused. 'As a bridal gift.'

'Never!' flashed Celine.

'Am I to take that as a refusal? Or as a repudiation of my taste?'

Celine turned to him. Two bright spots of colour burned on her cheekbones, and her eyes were hot.

'I will not be your wife, Lord Wraxall,' she said fiercely. 'No, not if you were the last man living. Not though my father orders it. Not even if King George himself commanded it! Never, do you understand me?'

'How disappointing.' He rose to stand above her, looking down with a saturnine smile. 'And yet, do you know, before I leave this room I believe you will have accepted my hand in marriage?'

'I'd sooner burn at the stake,' said Celine, contemptuously.

'You wouldn't, you know,' said Lord Wraxall. He moved, swift as a snake, and took her wrist, holding it in a grip so cruel that she cried out. He pulled her to her feet.

'I could light one of those candles on the harpischord there,' he said with a nod, 'and hold one of your fingers in the flame. Just the least little finger. Do not doubt I have the strength to do it, madam, no matter what your

43

struggles. Do you think you could bear the pain? Do you?' His eyes flashed wide, and he stared down at her. 'No. I thought not. So no more of these theatrical posturings, Lady Celine. Will you be my wife?'

'I won't!' she cried. 'And you cannot force me! I'll stick to my guns. I'll stand firm! Hold out!'

'You've been speaking to Sal Colney,' he said, and sighed. 'How meddlesome that woman is, to be sure. Will you marry me?'

Celine raised her fan and struck him angrily across the face. One of the slim ivory sticks broke with a crack.

'Spare your fan, madam,' he drawled. 'You grow heated, and will need it.'

Walking to the fireplace he examined himself in the mirror that hung above it. A drop of blood, like a cabochon ruby, lay on his swarthy skin. He paused for a moment.

'Your father is presiding at the Assizes next week, shall you be there?'

'No,' replied Celine shortly.

'A pity. You would find one case of interest. I stand witness in a trial for murder. A fatal stabbing; two sailors quarrelling over a whore. The defendant is a Mr O'Brien – do you know him?

Lord Wraxall watched her pale face reflected in the mirror. Her eyes, wide with horror, met his.

'How gratifying to have your interest at last,' he murmured. 'Now, let us put an end to this charming comedy.'

He turned and strode towards her, seizing her shoulders between iron hands and forcing her inexorably back to lie among the sofa cushions.

'You have a choice, my lady. Refuse me, and O'Brien hangs. Accept, and my memory, and that of the other witnesses, will be conveniently inconclusive.'

'You could not be so cruel!' protested Celine.

Lord Odo smiled. 'You don't yet know me. Well, is it a bargain?'

Celine's mind raced frantically, seeking a way out of

the trap he had caught her in. She found none. She shuddered at Lord Wraxall's touch, recoiled at the thought of him possessing her. Yet how might she refuse him? She could not let Liam die on the gallows when a word from her would buy his safety.

'Do you accept?'

'Yes,' she whispered.

His thin lips twisted in a smile of victory. Holding her down with one hand, he flung her petticoats up with the other. He looked down broodingly at the milky nakedness between her gartered stockings and her waist.

Celine lay still, with gritted teeth and clenched fists. Lord Wraxall's hand quested among the curls at her groin, twining the short hairs around his fingers. She pressed her thighs tightly together but Odo, not to be gainsaid, thrust his knee between her legs, parting them, and with the confidence of a practised libertine, found her clitoris.

His knowledgeable fingers teased and sensitised her. It was impossible to prevent their light caresses from waking a shiver of arousal. With shame and despair, she felt herself responding to his expert titillation. Her thighs relaxed, and opened to him like a flower. Odo laughed quietly and took his hand away. He looked down into her tear-stained countenance.

'I think you hate me, don't you?' he said in a low voice.

'Yes!' sobbed Celine.

Lord Wraxall closed his eyes.

'Exquisite,' he breathed.

And then, without another word, he was gone. The door clapped to behind him, leaving Lady Celine exposed and weeping among the lacy pillows.

Liam crouched by the outer wall, scraping away with a shoe-buckle at the mortar between the stones, while Reuben kept watch. It was Sunday. Liam had been working since Friday morning and had dug away maybe a quarter of an inch of mortar round one of the blocks.

'Someone coming,' whispered Reuben.

The tramp of a four-man guard approached the cell. Keys clattered, and the door swung open. Four long muskets targetted the prisoners as the gaoler thrust a woman into the cell.

'Good morning, sir,' said Bess, bobbing a curtsey.

She had brought a covered basket with a roast chicken, a loaf, and a bottle of Sir James's best port. The men tore the food apart and crammed it into their mouths. After days of prison slops they were half-starved.

'I've been stabbed in the back, Bess,' said Liam. 'I swear I'm innocent of this charge. Lady Celine doesn't believe it, does she?'

Bess took a letter from her bosom and held it out to him. She kept her eyes lowered, and twisted a corner of her apron between her fingers.

Liam felt a deep fury growing within him as he read Celine's words. How could she do this? If she loved him, she should know that he'd die a hundred times rather than see her Lord Wraxall's wife.

'I understand,' said Liam, when he had finished. 'She's abandoned me.'

'Oh, sir, don't say that!' cried Bess. She laid a hand on his arm. 'She loves you. She did it to save you.'

Liam cursed. 'She did for her own pleasure. That debauchee's a better catch than I am, that's all. Do you think I can't read between the lines, that I don't know she prefers him? How glad she must be of the excuse.'

'That's not true, and you know it!' said Bess hotly. 'She said Lord Wraxall may have her promise and her body, but you will forever have her heart. Those were her very words. And she told me to give you this, too, because she can't no more.'

Bess stood on tiptoe and took Liam's face between her work-roughened hands. She kissed him long and fiercely on the mouth. At first, he was too angry to respond. But at last his arms came up and around her, and he crushed her to him with the strength of despair.

Reuben turned his back and tactfully devoted his

46

attention to sucking the last rags of meat off the chicken bones.

Bess lay back on the straw, pulling Liam down with her. She unfastened the kerchief over her breasts and guided his hand to them. He lay on top of her, his face buried in her neck. Her flesh was soft and yielding. Her legs parted for him, offering him comfort.

She kissed him softly on the cheek and forehead, stroking his hair. She raised her knees to allow him in more deeply, rocking her hips gently as he thrust within her. She paced him, matching his movements until his climax gave him a moment of release.

Afterwards, he lay still, one forearm flung across his eyes, until the gaoler came and led Bess away. When she was gone he crawled over to the wall once more and began to dig grimly at the stubborn mortar.

Chapter Four

'Don't leave me,' said Celine. She caught a handful of Bess's gown and tugged. 'Not tonight – I couldn't bear to be alone.'

She sat huddled mournfully on the edge of the bed in her white nightgown. All around the bedchamber half-packed trunks and boxes stood open, candlelight gleaming on the rich fabrics and laces of her trousseau. Her wedding dress, of creamy figured satin, was laid out ready for the morning.

'It's past midnight,' said Bess. 'Can't you try to sleep a little?'

Celine shook her head.

'You lie down and make yourself cosy,' said Bess, drawing aside the covers. 'I'll stay with you. Are you scared of – you know – the wedding night?'

Celine got into bed and turned on her side, holding Bess's hand. One breast peeped from the disordered ruffles of her nightdress.

'It's Lord Wraxall,' she said, and paused, biting her lip. 'I can't bear that he should be the first: there's no love there, no tenderness. He'll just use me, for his pleasure. I wish I'd done it with Liam, that night on the terrace. Maybe then he wouldn't be so angry with me. We would have had time.'

'It ain't something you should hurry,' said Bess. 'A woman needs it slow, my dear, especially at first.'

Celine moved her head restlessly on the pillow.

'What's it like?' she asked, curiously.

'It's not something that I can describe.'

'Can't you try?'

'I could show you if you wanted,' said Bess slowly.

'But surely it's not possible! Not with another woman?'

'Close your eyes,' whispered Bess, bending over the bed. 'Imagine Mr O'Brien's here. No, keep them shut. He's in the room. Do you want him?'

Celine smiled. 'Liam . . .'

Candlelight shone red through her eyelids. She felt the mattress dip under the weight of a second occupant, and the covers being stripped away. An arm slipped round her, and a hand stroked her body, whispering on the silk.

Celine squeezed her eyes tighter. It was Liam's hand! Lips touched her forehead. A face nuzzled against her neck. She could feel the warmth of languorous breathing, close to her ear.

He is with me, now, Celine thought. She drew a shuddering breath. It is Liam's body pressing close against me. She sighed and opened her lips under the mouth that sought hers. Tongues met, toying together lasciviously.

Fingers found the open neck of her nightdress and slyly crept within, drifting across her flesh. Celine surrendered to the caressing hand as it stroked her breasts one after the other. Her lover found their flushed tips, rolling and teasing them until they stiffened and grew hard.

She moved her legs restlessly, feeling the heat and dampness of arousal beginning between them. When Bess pulled at her nightgown, raising it, it was Liam's loving hands that helped her, sliding the silk slowly upwards.

The mouth was travelling now, stealthily, finding its way down across her neck and shoulder until it joined the hand working at her breasts. Celine pushed against it, urging the busy lips to suck at her nipples.

She reacted instinctively to their touch, raising her knees and pushing urgently with her lower body as the wandering fingers quested amid the crisp hair of her mound, seeking the hidden dampness at its heart. They slid back and forth there in the slippery juices of her excitement, probing and squeezing, while Celine's eager movements and whimpering cries encouraged them to further intimacies.

Parting her legs wide, she pushed against the stimulation of the exploring hands. The mouth – she willed it to be Liam's mouth – circled her flat belly with a trail of kisses, before it resumed the downward journey.

A thumb lightly rubbed against her clitoris, teasing the nub of tissue into prominence. Celine panted and squirmed under the unceasing stimulation. It was Liam's face that burrowed between her thighs, his mouth that sucked and nibbled her so voluptuously.

Two fingers slid further down between her legs, seeking the narrow opening to her vagina and circling there, as if they were sipping the wine of her readiness. They pressed and squeezed the swollen lips of her sex, while her hips thrust and quivered with impatience.

They slipped inside her, pushing and withdrawing in a gradually increasing rhythm until Celine was all one intoxicating need: she moved faster and faster, pressing herself against the greedy mouth and probing fingers.

She cried out wordlessly as she felt her climax begin. It was a force she had never before experienced, a tidal wave that carried her irresistibly before it and burst with a shock and a delectable tumult, then slowly ebbed, leaving her shaken, stranded on the shore of a new land of delight.

And she knew that, no matter what the future held for her as the dissolute Viscount's bride, she and Bess – and somehow Liam too – had beaten him. His cold sensualities would not be all she ever knew of passion.

* * *

Church bells rang merrily for Celine's wedding. Liam tried to shut out the sound as he continued to gouge at the mortar. It was the fourth day since Bess's visit and his progress was negligible.

The great bell pealed its last stroke. The pastor would be speaking now. She was leaving him, for Lord Wraxall. She was gone.

Celine was gone.

It was as if the spring that had activated him had snapped. He slumped down on the straw and buried his face in his arms.

'Giving up?' asked Reuben Ossett.

Liam raised his head: he was deathly pale, but his eyes were blue steel.

'Never! If it takes my last breath, I'm going to escape from this place.'

'I don't know why you're so set on it,' said the pirate. 'You've got friends at court, ain't you? You've been promised.'

'Wraxall's promise!' snarled Liam. 'Wraxall's friendship! He's taken everything from me – Celine, my good name, my hopes for the future. Do you think I'll submit to having my life tossed to me, like a coin to a lackey? And by him, of all men!'

'You've spirit, at least,' said Reuben. 'That's a useful thing, in these parts of the world – for a seafaring man. Tell me, now. If you did break out, what was you thinking to do? How was you planning to get off the island, with a reward posted and the militia up and hunting for you?'

Liam shook his head, hopelessly. He had not thought further than the walls of the gaol. He did not want to think, or to feel; only to act. Digging had occupied his mind. It left him no time to examine his feelings of anger and pain. And why did he feel guilty?

It's not my fault, but Celine's, thought Liam furiously. If she'd truly loved me, she must have known I'd rather hang than live to know she shared Wraxall's bed. I was

51

just an expedient to her: something to pass the long boredom of the voyage. It was all lies!

'Well?' asked Reuben.

'I don't know,' groaned Liam. 'You're right; an island's just a bigger prison. There's no escape without a ship.'

'I knows of a vessel,' said Reuben, slowly. 'One that'll be anchored offshore, in a quiet bay, after moonset. A ship in need of a quartermaster, too. An educated man, what can write, and cipher up the profits.' Reuben raised his hand, stemming the eager spate of questions. 'Hear me out. You've heard me speak of Tremaine, maybe? It's Tremaine's pirate fleet that rules the Caribbean seas, for all the King's navy claim the crown. Tremaine's men don't swing, lad. Sign on the account, and I'll see you free as a gull by midnight.'

'Go on the account?' said Liam blankly. 'You mean, become a pirate?'

'Got no stomach for it?' asked Reuben, drawing closer and laying a hand on Liam's shoulder. 'It's a grand life in the Coast Brotherhood. There's no shilling a day for us: when we take a prize it's fair shares for all, and rolling in dollars 'til we make sail again. Who'd be governed by lords and magistrates? A pirate's a free prince, my bucko, not a snivelling puppy sneaking after the arses of those villains!'

'Enough,' said Liam. He bared his teeth. 'I'll join. What am I forfeiting? Love's lost, reputation's lost – this at least offers hope.'

'Give us your hand on the bargain, then,' said Reuben. 'And no regrets. There's other reputations to be gained on the account – think of Morgan, think of Blackbeard! And as for love, who'd refuse a handsome lad like you, his pockets jingling with Spanish gold?'

Liam threw back his head and laughed angrily.

'Women! They take your money and your soul, if you offer it, and betray you in the end. I'm done with women!'

'Are ye now?' murmured Reuben, with interest, and slid his hand down to the root of Liam's thigh.

Liam threw off the other man's clutch and started to his feet.

'Touch me again, Ossett, and I'll break your neck!'

'No need for that,' said Reuben, shrugging. 'Just being friendly, like.'

'Keep your hands to yourself and we'll get along fine,' said Liam. 'Now, how do we get out of here?'

Sir James had spared no expense over the wedding breakfast. Celine sat at the centre of the top table, stiffly ignoring the congratulations and bawdy jokes.

Viscount Wraxall was placed at her right. His fingers glittered with rings. He wore cloth of silver embroidered with jet, and the lace at his wrists and throat was black. Long hair, dark as his lace, curled about his shoulders.

They shared a gold goblet and plate. She hardly touched the rich dishes that were offered, and when Odo handed the tall cup of wine to her she turned it, surreptitiously, so that her lips would not rest where his had been.

On her other side, her father was deep in conversation with Mistress Colney. One of his hands was hidden beneath the table, and Celine suspected that it was busy among Sally's petticoats.

The red-headed woman had been out of town for some days, returning just in time to attend the wedding. It was clear from her scornful look that she thought Celine's courage had failed her, or that the lure of a noble name had tempted her; for Sir James was full of claret and self-importance, and was boasting about the alliance in a loud, drunken voice.

'A fine ol' family,' bawled Sir James, leaning close to Sally. 'Not a lot of money, but ver' ol'. Goes back to the Conquerer! Min' you,' he added, lowering his voice to what he thought was a whisper, 'He's a hard bargainer. You'd not believe what the marriage settlements cost me, first an' last.'

Lord Wraxall stirred beside her. He leant forward and

53

raised her chin with one jewelled finger, forcing her to meet his look.

'Do you recall where I saw you first?' he asked, quietly.

It was impossible to misunderstand him. Purchased for her dowry, sold for a great name: she did not need to be so cruelly reminded that she was now as much his property as any slave bought at the barracoon.

Her father lumbered to his feet and began a rambling speech. Odo released her abruptly, and stifled a yawn behind his hand.

Sir James broke off and glared at him.

'Am I boring you?' he asked belligerently.

'Not at all, sir,' said Odo. 'How could it be possible? But – forgive me – to a bridegroom all delay is tiresome.'

Sir James recovered his aplomb and roared with amusement.

'I'll swear it is!' he chuckled. 'Why, where the marriage-bed's concerned, you're as much of a virgin as my daughter. Damme, it must be the only thing you've never tried!'

Lord Odo bowed coldly. His expression of distaste silenced the sniggering of the guests almost before it began. He held out his hand.

'Lady Wraxall,' he said, 'The carriage awaits.'

She started. Lady Wraxall, she thought, with horror. Why, that's me.

Celine allowed herself to be led through a barrage of laughter and jests, and handed up into the chaise outside. Lord Odo gave his orders to the coachman, and sprang up beside her.

Celine was very aware of her new husband lounging beside her, his body swaying easily as they jolted over the cobbles. He neither spoke, nor touched her. She could not help but be grateful for the unexpected respite.

Twining her hands together in her lap, she looked determinedly out of the window. Liam was safe. She had made her bargain, and would stick to it.

The road took them west, and out of town. It plunged

into ancient forest, where trees overlaced the way and orchids grew among their dark foliage. Heat lay on Celine's skin, and her clothes stuck to her wherever they touched.

The carriage reached the top of one last hill and started to descend, swaying wildly over the rutted track. Little clearings opened beside the road, each with its tumbledown hut and meagre crops of yam and cassava.

Then the wheels slammed into a pot-hole, and the chaise lurched wildly. Celine cried out as she was flung from her seat. Moving with that disturbing swiftness that he sometimes showed, Lord Wraxall caught her back to safety.

Startled into speech, she whispered her thanks.

'It'll be easier once we get on to my lands,' he said.

His arm remained around her waist in a gesture of ownership. Celine could feel the warmth of his body through the heavy satin of her gown. She stole a dubious glance at him. His eyes were hooded, but he was watching her: waiting.

'I – I thought this was your land,' she faltered. 'Aren't those your slaves in the fields?'

'Those are small farmers,' said Lord Wraxall disdainfully, 'Free men. I'd be a fool to treat my slaves so poorly: starved animals cannot work. Why this sudden interest in things agricultural?'

Celine looked away. The road was sweeping down towards the sea, and a little way ahead two tall brick pillars marked the entrance to an estate.

'I mean to try to be a good wife, sir. I should know about such matters.'

'Hades! I did not marry you to get a gracious chatelaine!' he said, with a laugh. 'Let us be clear about this, madam. I wanted your person and your fortune. And when I have exhausted the pleasures of both – well, that's for the future. For the present we are at the gates of my plantation. Welcome to Acheron, Lady Wraxall.' His hands slid across the pearly satin of her gown. 'And to your new duties.'

With a final rattle and jerk, they swung to the left and through the pillared entrance, on to a smooth paved way. The chaise settled down, swaying slowly through acres of sugar-cane that stretched to the horizon. His touch grew bolder, more demanding, caressing her through the layers of cloth.

'Show me your breasts,' he said, softly.

He cannot mean it, thought Celine. Not here – not now! The carriage blinds were open. Any one of the labourers among the cane could look in and see her.

'Why this hesitation? Must I remind you that I have a husband's right?'

'Wait!' she pleaded. 'My lord, you've been so patient. If you will only give me time, just a little longer . . .'

'What, did you think I was showing gentlemanly forbearance?' he scoffed. 'How little you know me! If I have spared you until now it is only because I prefer my pleasures undisturbed by the jolting of an ill-made road.'

'I can't,' said Celine. She looked up at him imploringly. 'You must understand. I beg you, don't ask this of me.'

Lord Wraxall met her gaze calmly.

'I have no interest in rape as a pastime, though, now we are married, the concept has no legal foundation. The fact remains that I could force you – ' he said, hooking strong fingers into the low neckline of her bodice ' – if I had to,' he said.

His voice was quiet – he even smiled – but Celine had no doubt that he was serious. When she gave no answer he slowly closed his grip. Her lip trembled, but she met his eyes resolutely.

'Very well,' she said in a bitter voice. 'It's true I made my vows to you, and I'll keep my word – so far as I'm able. But honour, my lord, and love, I'm afraid will be beyond me. You must make do with obedience.'

She thrust his hand away with shaking fingers and jerked at the ribbons fastening the front of her gown. The bodice fell open, exposing the swell of Celine's firm young breasts above her tight-laced stays.

Compelling herself to breathe slowly, she stared at him and tried to make herself as still and cold as a marble stone. But the rocking carriage cheated her. As it swayed, her rosy nipples moved provocatively, now hidden, now displayed to Lord Wraxall's measuring gaze.

'Pretty enough,' he said.

Celine set her teeth as he bore her back against the cushions. She would do her duty, but no more. He leant over her, pushing the wedding dress back from her shoulders and freeing her breasts from the last vestige of covering. He ran his hands over every inch of her pale, exposed flesh.

Celine was a statue.

He caressed her expertly, his touch light but demanding, and dipped his tongue into the hollow at the base of her throat.

She lay rigid, looking up at the quilted lining of the chaise. It was pale fawn leather, held in place by gilded studs bearing the Wraxall crest. Celine counted them: left to right, and then diagonally.

'What, stubborn?' Odo murmured. 'Not for long, I think.'

He bent, and covered her breasts and throat with kisses. His hair trailed ticklingly across her skin. His thin, bejewelled hands moved on her with the skill of a practised seducer. Celine shivered and lost count for a moment.

His tongue flicked out, teasing her nipples. His cheeks hollowed as he sucked at them, nibbling gently.

Celine thought of dull sermons, of Aunt Prudence at her everlasting needlework, of anything but Odo's knowledgeable fondling. She did not want him. She hated him! But his hands held a power over her. It no longer seemed to matter if she cared, what she thought. Despite all her resolution she could feel a sullen excitement growing in her, like a black lily.

He knew her. He was aware of secrets, longings, urgencies that she herself could hardly put a name to.

He sensed the flower of eroticism that had its roots in her innermost being. And he fed it, tended it, ruthlessly playing on her awakening body until it turned traitor, fighting against her will.

Hopelessly, Celine felt her nipples respond to his unceasing stimulation, their soft tissue hardening and swelling until they were fully erect. She stifled a groan of despair as she felt an answering tingle between her legs.

Each moment it was harder to remain still and passive: soon, she knew, it would be beyond her power. Celine turned her head away, trying to call up Liam's image, trying to pretend – as she had last night – that the hands caressing her were his. But Lord Wraxall was too quick for her; he forced her back to face him, willing her to meet his eyes.

'Don't think you can escape that way,' he whispered. 'I tolerate no rivals, not even in imagination.'

Lifting her smoothly, until she lay half across his body, he crushed her close. The rough texture of the lace at his breast brushed against her already sensitised nipples, teasing them until they burned and throbbed.

Slowly, he raised her skirts and pushed up the froth of her petticoats. His hand slid along the taut silk of her stockings to the naked skin above.

Her heart fluttered. She dreaded the moment when his lazily questing fingers would reach their goal and learn from the seeping wetness there how much he had aroused her. But even the act of trying to shut him out excited her further. The pressure of her thighs and the swaying of the slow-moving carriage squeezed and massaged her swollen cleft.

He insinuated one hand between her legs, pushing them apart. She felt his fingers moving slowly upwards, sliding easily on her wet skin. He found her pleasure-bud and stroked it repeatedly, delicate as a feather. Celine quivered, unable to prevent herself opening to him.

Lord Wraxall gave a low laugh.

58

'Did you really think to resist me? Little fool: I knew your mother. I know how the tropic heat calls out to the inheritance in your blood.'

As he spoke, he tantalised the engorged flesh until she writhed and gasped under his expert titillation. She forgot hatred and thrust shame aside. Celine clung to him, past caring for anything but the excitement of his touch.

Gentle no longer, he parted the soft lips of her sex and plunged his fingers deeply within her, again and again. Celine whimpered with enjoyment, thrusting herself against his hand as he bent to kiss her.

She answered his lips with eager desire, feeling the foretaste of ecstasy as he found and teased the pleasure-spot on the wall of her vagina. She abandoned herself, intoxicated with need, pushing herself against him, wantonly encouraging his probing fingers

And then he took his hand away.

'I am master here,' he said, with a mocking smile. 'I could take my pleasure and deny you yours, if I chose. It's no more than many a bride endures. I could tease you and bring you to the brink, and leave you unsatisfied: each time, every time.'

Celine trembled. He could not mean it.

'If you want more,' he said, 'there is a price. Will you pay it?'

Celine sobbed her agreement. She would do anything – anything – if only he'd have mercy on her, satisfy the lust he had so cruelly aroused.

'Not anything: everything. What I demand, you will do. What I order, you will perform. You can hate me, if you want – you would be wise to fear me – but you will obey. Is it agreed?'

His eyes widened. She read unnamable depravities in them. But he already knew that she could deny him nothing. Her desire overwhelmed her fear.

'Is it agreed? Say it!'

'Yes!' cried Celine.

'Then take your reward,' said Lord Wraxall, huskily.

Celine moaned with relief as he kissed her breasts, suckling and tugging greedily at her nipples. His wrist pressed down hard against her clitoris. She could feel the embroidery on his cuff. The black lace of his ruffles, sodden with the juice of her arousal, rubbed fiercely against the sensitive bud.

'You can't imagine what delights your body can yield to you,' breathed Odo against her skin. 'You dream of simple pleasures, candid as the day. But I shall teach you other things. With me you'll take dark paths and hidden ways.'

His thumb thrust deeply into her vagina, pushing and circling. His index finger moved further back, finding and widening the tight ring of her anus, squeezing within. Celine gasped and twisted as he penetrated her, hardly knowing if it was pain or pleasure that she felt.

Her climax was near, she could feel it peaking. Nothing mattered but this growing ecstasy, the nearing moment of release. She surrendered entirely to Lord Wraxall as with cruel, unceasing stimulation he brought her to the edge.

He kept her teetering there a moment, as if to show his power. Then he took mercy, and pushed her over, sending her plunging into an orgasm so exquisite and long-lasting that it felt like a little death.

Chapter Five

Celine lay against Lord Wraxall, shaking to the thunder of her heartbeats. Now that her lust was satisfied she felt shame, and horror, and a deep remorse. How could she have surrendered to him so totally, so abjectly?

He pushed her away and busied himself with a handkerchief, drying his hands. The carriage was stationary. She had no idea how long it had been still. Keeping her eyes lowered, she fumbled for the fastenings of her gown.

'What are you doing?' he asked. He flicked her cheek with his fingertips: a light, stinging blow. 'Answer me.'

'I must make myself decent,' she whispered.

Leaning forward, he wrenched the satin bodice out of her hands, dragging it down and off her shoulders, leaving her naked breasts fully displayed.

'I think not,' he said. 'There was a price for your pleasure, my lady, remember? One that you agreed to pay. And now you begin.'

Celine swallowed convulsively and, for the first time, raised her eyes. Lord Wraxall was framed against the carriage window. Behind him, a great plantation house reared its pillars towards the burning sky. On the broad veranda the household staff were gathered, staring and craning.

A footman flung open the carriage door. Odo descended. He held out an imperative hand to her.

She did not stir. No matter what promises he had extorted from her in the heat of passion, she shrank from flaunting herself half-naked before that waiting crowd. But he would certainly have her dragged from the carriage if she continued to resist his will.

'You try my patience, madam,' said Lord Wraxall. 'Come: Acheron waits to greet its new mistress.'

Gathering all her courage, Celine let him help her down from the chaise. Every inch of her exposed flesh was suffused with blushes. She wanted nothing better than to run and hide within the house, but she made herself match his slow pace, sweeping up the shallow steps like a queen.

Formed up in a double line, the domestics flanked the entrance. They did not even pretend to spare her. Whispering together, they looked her over openly, and their eyes were hungry. Celine's nipples tightened involuntarily under their lascivious stares.

Lord Wraxall led her between their ranks, murmuring names: this was Mr Jeffries the steward, and this the cook François; Charles and Rupert the footmen, the upper-housemaid, the lower-housemaids, the between-stairs maid, the laundress, the gardeners, and half a hundred others.

A foxy fellow in the neat livery of a groom ogled her breasts with insolent desire. His undisguised lust woke dark tremors in her. Looking away hastily, she examined her new home with an interest only partly feigned.

Acheron rose above her, square and white-painted, each of its three storeys surrounded by deep, vine-draped verandas that protected the inner rooms from the direct rays of the sun.

To the west lay a low, circular building, its red-tiled roof supported by massive pillars. It stood apart from the main body of the house, connected to it by a colonnade: a library perhaps, or a music room.

Lord Wraxall caught the direction of her gaze.

'The Rotunda. The design is taken from a temple I visited in Antioch, many years ago. You will see it tonight. Let us go in.'

It was cool and dim inside the plantation house. Green light filtered in through the creepers. Celine freed herself from Lord Wraxall with a jerk and huddled her bodice around her.

'You don't deceive me with these prudish airs, madam wife,' Lord Wraxall said. 'You could feel their desire. You were stimulated by it.'

'No!' cried Celine.

'You're lying,' he said. He brushed her still-taut nipples with one fingertip. 'Do you think I am blind?'

Celine began a fierce rebuttal. Lord Wraxall smiled sardonically, and she found herself faltering into silence. In spite of her shame she could not deny that some part of her had warmed to the response she had drawn from his household. As he had known that it would.

'Do you begin to feel your body's power?' he whispered, leaning closer. 'They want you. They lust for you. And – for the present – you are mine.'

He took her hand, leading her towards the stairs. Celine could not help feeling that to obey so meekly was contemptible. She should resist, rebel somehow against his cool assumption of dominance. And yet it excited her in a way she could not understand.

Celine felt a dart of fear, not unmixed with anticipation. The moment of their union could not be far off now, and she caught herself looking covertly at him, wondering how it would be.

Lord Wraxall led her past the company rooms on the first storey, and up again to the bedroom floor. The house was very quiet. She could hear the susurrus of her gown dragging on the carpet. A trapped fly buzzed against the long window that lit the stairs.

Despite her trepidation Celine could not help staring about her. It was another world: richer, stranger, more corrupt. There were no familiar English appointments: no portraits, or pictures of pink shepherdesses among

63

their laundered flocks. Lord Wraxall had plundered the globe to furnish Acheron.

He seemed gratified by her awe, and broke his silence to draw her attention to Greek statuary and Chinese vases. The carpets were loot from Tangier and Smyrna. That suit of armour was from the hidden land of Japan. Persian miniatures glowed on the walls between scimitars and savage masks.

He did nothing so vulgar as boast, but it was clear that he was proud of his collection. Celine understood with a shock that she, too, was just one more item in his treasure-house. He had not made her expose herself before his servants merely to humiliate her.

Oh, he had enjoyed her shame: it was his nature. But he had displayed her with an owner's pride, like a man who shows off a precious diamond, increasing its value to himself by the envy of others.

Celine's chamber lay at the back of the house, its door guarded by the gigantic figure of a many-armed goddess, poised in a dance step.

'From Rajputana,' said Odo. 'Kali.'

He stroked the smooth metal. Where his hand lay on the statue's thigh the bronze was bright, polished by repeated caresses.

'*Beloved and lovely*,' he recited, softly. '*Deathless, pariah, drinker of blood. Valour in the form of a woman.* She cost nine men's lives to get away.'

The warmth of his tone piqued Celine. It seemed she was not even the most prized among his possessions. Though it brought the inevitable consummation closer, she was glad when Lord Wraxall left the statue and opened the door, standing aside to let her pass.

A pulse fluttering wildly in her throat, Celine crossed the threshold. Lord Wraxall followed close behind her. He closed the door and leant against the panels. With a little smile on his face he watched her look around the bridal chamber.

'I trust you approve my taste,' he said.

The room was high and shadowed, hung with mirrors

in ebony frames. It reflected itself endlessly, enclosing her like the heart of a sombre flower.

The furniture was black lacquer, writhing with dragons. A great bed, curtained and canopied with funereal silk, dominated the room's centre. With a lurch of the heart Celine noticed ring-bolts were set into each of its four towering posts. Was he going to tie her down?

The click of the lock startled her. Lord Wraxall twirled the key between long fingers. When he saw her looking, he pocketed it.

'I gave my word,' said Celine in an unsteady voice. 'Is that necessary?'

'I think so,' he replied coolly. 'You have a damnable streak of obstinacy in you, Lady Wraxall. You persist in making me work for every advantage. The day is too sultry for such labours. It's fatiguing, madam.'

He pushed himself away from the door and strolled towards her. In spite of herself, Celine took a step backwards. In the mirrors an infinity of doubles mimicked her actions.

'You see?' said Lord Wraxall.

Celine froze, and clasped her hands together.

'Then what must I do?' she asked helplessly.

Odo circled her slowly.

'You may take off my coat,' he said at last.

With shaking fingers she slipped it from his shoulders. She could smell the musk of his body, running like a base-note under the herbal scent. On his command, she unbuttoned and removed the long-skirted waistcoat, loosened and laid aside the lace at his throat.

His black lawn shirt, damp with heat, clung to the fine musculature of his chest. The tight breeches displayed, almost as much as they hid, his male member, fully erect and lying diagonally across his flat belly. It seemed impossibly huge to her: after one appalled glance, Celine averted her eyes.

Lord Wraxall shook back his hair and stretched luxuriously, crossing to a tall cabinet between the windows. He stood before it, stripping off his rings.

'Remove your gown,' he said, over his shoulder.

'But . . .' she began.

Lord Wraxall sighed.

When the heavy satin lay shimmering about her feet, he signed for her to continue. The tapes of her stiffened outer petticoat were knotted and she had to worry at them with her fingernails. It fell in a flurry of lace.

Lord Wraxall opened the cabinet, and searched through its multiplicity of drawers and pigeonholes.

Celine slipped out of shoes and stockings. She untied the ribbons at her waist and with trembling fingers let the silken underskirt flutter away.

Lord Wraxall turned to face her, weighing a book and a casket in his hands. His hooded eyes ran measuringly up and down her body. The corset pulled her waist in to a tiny compass, emphasising her hips and breasts.

The triangle of curls at her groin was startlingly black against her fair skin. She hid it from him with her hand and a myriad reflected Celines copied the shy gesture.

Seating himself on the edge of the bed, Odo up-ended the casket, spilling its contents on to the covers. Glass chinked against metal, metal against stone: an ivory ball the size of a turtle's egg rolled and fell soundlessly on the thick carpet.

'We will begin your education,' he said, and beckoned.

When she approached, Odo pulled her down beside him, and opened the book for her to see.

'*Aretino's Postures*,' he explained. 'Printed privately, in Geneva. It is your primer. I expect you to study it.'

He turned the pages slowly, so that her eye was forced to linger on the detailed engravings. In infinite variety they catalogued the positions of love. Bending, standing, supported on cushions, the little, stylised figures of men and women left nothing to the imagination.

Celine shifted nervously, the silk coverlet sliding under her naked thighs. What could it feel like to perform such acts? This one, where the woman's legs clasped her lover's hips like a girdle; or this, where she crouched above the man, kneeling over him and taking

66

his upstanding rod of flesh into her mouth? Despite her misgivings Celine could not help but feel a tremor of arousal.

When Lord Wraxall laid the book aside she knew he had sensed it. The moment was surely now. He would throw her back on the black bed and take her. She forced herself to relax, lying slack in his arms, waiting.

Lord Wraxall frowned: it was clear she had misjudged him.

'Virgins bore me,' he said coldly. 'Of late years I have avoided them: they do not know how to please a man of refinement. I am no peasant, requiring only passive flesh to copulate like a hog. Sit up.'

He jerked her upright and with firm hands ordered her position. Celine bit her lip as he made her perch on the very edge of the bed, parting her legs wide, wider still.

'Look in the glass,' he commanded. 'Watch me as I take my pleasure.'

Celine raised her head. The greatest of all the mirrors fronted the fourposter. Tropic heat and dampness had flaked away the silvering, here and there, but its depths were clear.

Her blatant, spread-legged pose showed every secret of her body. Under the fine black curls the outline of her sex stood out strongly, pursed and swollen, a line of dusky rose cleaving its centre.

She stiffened as Lord Wraxall reached down to open her, his darting fingers squeezing and fondling her gently. He parted the inner lips and she glimpsed the entrance to her vagina, pink and glistening, like the throat of a fleshy orchid. His eyes met hers in the mirror and her heart skipped a beat: who could tell what perversities he might demand of her? There were centuries of corruption in that lean, lined face.

It was degrading, vile, to watch herself being caressed so intimately. Ah, but it felt so good. Celine could not prevent herself responding. She flexed her spine, and with a tiny movement pushed against his fingers.

She saw Odo's lips twist in an arrogant smile. He had known she would succumb, she thought bitterly. He was a virtuoso. Over many years he had taken the art of love and made it a science: technical, perfect and cold.

His hand moved between her legs, teasing the bud of her clitoris free of its little hood of flesh. It was timid, shrinking away at first, then growing bolder, swelling, tingling, holding the sensation. He caressed her, leading her by subtle degrees from endurance, to urgency, to overwhelming desire.

Reaching behind him, Odo felt among the items spilt across the bed.

'This,' he said, showing her what he held, 'is an heirloom.'

A slim wand of jade lay in his palm. About six inches long, it was tipped with a rounded knob and inlaid with lilies.

'The Wraxall Fascinum,' Odo murmured. 'The brides of ancient Rome were deflowered with just such an instrument. Of course, my family has a long history, but it cannot be so old. A forgery, I suspect: possibly Arabic in origin, and brought back from the Second Crusade by an ancestor of mine. Still, one does not like to break a tradition.'

He pushed her, so that she fell back across the bed, and knelt beside her rubbing the jade up and down between the lips of her sex, turning it this way and that until the head was coated with wetness. Celine gasped as she felt the tip enter her vagina. It did not hurt, as she had feared, but it was alien: heavy, chill and unyielding.

'Such things had a dual purpose,' continued Lord Wraxall evenly. 'Firstly, they did away with the need to struggle with a reluctant maidenhead, since the hymen had already been broken and the bride prepared – thus.'

He plunged the tool to its full length inside her as he spoke. Celine yelped with shock, but he stifled her cries with a kiss and a velvet thrust of his tongue. He drove the jade wand repeatedly into her, taking her virginity with dispassionate calm.

'So: now we will have less trouble later. And now we come to the second purpose of the fascinum. It is to train you to please a man. Use the strength of your sex on it. Clench down hard on the withdrawal. I shall expect you to clasp me so, when I enter you as a husband. Concentrate, madam. Try it again.'

Celine moaned distractedly. She could not do as he commanded: it was too difficult. Her inner muscles refused to answer to her will. But Lord Wraxall was pitiless. He would accept no imperfection, allow her no rest, until she had proved to him the lesson was well learned.

The skill he demanded was slow to come. His lips and fingers distracted her as they moved caressingly across her body. Gradually she gained control; as she did so Celine began to take a pleasure in it. The feel of the jade shaft probing between the tightened walls of her sex was no longer repellent. It stimulated. It teased. She gripped it, alternately pulsing and relaxing.

'Yes. Again,' whispered Odo. 'Make me sweat with pleasure as I draw back for the stroke.'

There was no room in her any longer for shame or loathing. She wanted him. She was wet for him. She could smell the salty juices of her readiness, feel them trickling from her sex to wet his fingers. She drew up her knees and rocked her hips, flexing her vaginal muscles on the moving tool. She could feel her pleasure building, knew that if he gave her only a little more time she would reach her climax.

Odo gave a curt nod of satisfaction and sat back on his heels, withdrawing the fascinum. He looked down at Celine who lay open and waiting for him, sobbing for breath, the sodden bedcover bunched beneath her.

'What, surfeited already?' he asked mockingly. 'You disappoint me, madam. My wife should have as great an appetite as myself – and for the same exotic dishes. Shall I leave you to recover?'

Celine reached up to him, clung to him. He had to

stay. He had to satisfy the hunger he had roused in her flesh.

'Don't torment me so,' she groaned.

'I confess I am surprised,' said Lord Wraxall, with lazy affability. 'I seem to recall that – compared with another – my person was repugnant to you.'

Celine flinched as if he had struck her. She knew his casual reminder of Liam was meant to hurt – and it did. But it altered nothing. There would be a lifetime for regrets. Now there was only the present – and the needs of her awakened body. The Viscount's practised sensualities were beyond her power to resist. He repelled her – he fascinated her: she had not dreamt that such arousal was possible.

'I have altered my opinion,' she sighed: and in that moment it was true.

Lord Odo took her right hand and carried it to his loins.

'Prove it.'

Trembling at her own daring, Celine let her fingers rove up and down the length of his manhood. She could feel its heat even through the silver cloth. It was hard and straining, ready to press its way out through the flimsy covering, tearing its way through the silks and stitches.

When he released her, to loosen the fastenings of his breeches, Celine did not take her hand away. The thought of penetration no longer terrified her. The fascinum had done its work. She hungered for the feel of a greater tool, warm and resilient, moving vitally within her.

Freed from its tight containment, Lord Wraxall's erection jutted proudly forward, tenting the black lawn shirt. Even now the size of it daunted her a little, but her arousal – and her curiosity – was too strong to let her draw back. She had never really seen a man's genitals before, hardly daring to look at Liam's, and the idea excited her almost beyond bearing.

She clenched the muscles of her sex experimentally. A

honey-sweet dart of pleasure pierced her. Celine slipped her fingers into his breeches, pulling his shirt up, seeking for naked flesh. Lord Wraxall drew a hissing breath as she touched him, and she felt his penis throb impatiently.

'Are you so eager to see the sceptre you'll be ruled with?' he asked in a grating voice.

Celine felt herself flush. She nodded.

Lord Wraxall laughed harshly. He pushed her hand away and tugged his shirt off over his head with a single movement.

'Look, then,' he said.

His scarred torso tapered like a wedge from his shoulders to narrow hips. Exposed to the root, his phallus sprang from the bush of curls at his groin, thrusting potently towards her. Blue-veined, and curved like a sabre, its foreskin was fully retracted to expose the swollen, ruddy glans. Celine choked back an exclamation. Her fingers had prepared her for its prodigious size, but not for this.

Odo was pierced.

His cock was pierced. A ring, set with a bead of black opal, ran in through the eye at its tip and out again where the shaft joined the head. Like a second jewel, a drop of clear fluid hung on the gold. The sight was shocking, yet unbearably erotic. A pang of lust, so profound it made her catch her breath, shot through her, and she closed her eyes.

Odo knelt above Celine, watching her reaction with well-concealed surprise. He had not expected her to be so obviously aroused by the sight of his body.

It amused him to find that he felt slightly aggrieved. He had anticipated fright, and squeamish protests. This was almost too easy. He would have to be harsher, testing her limits, pushing her to acts of wantonness that would have her sobbing with shame as much as with lust.

And yet she was damnably beautiful in her abandonment: the tousled hair, the mouth half-opened, her

71

nipples hard with desire for him. Despite his apparent coolness, his own needs were overpowering. He fought to remain calm, breathing deeply, and the scent of her eagerness caught in his throat.

She was more than ready. A lesser man might have been unable to resist. Odo knew even he would not be able to hold back much longer. It irritated him that he must waste his pleasure in Celine with one soon-completed spasm. Such simple gratifications cloyed his palate now: too mawkish, too unsophisticated. He preferred the taste of bitters.

'Use your hands on me,' he said, and was pleased to note his voice betrayed none of the excitement he felt.

When Celine hesitated, he caught her fingers and closed them round the shaft of his cock. He felt her start: they hardly circled it.

With slow enjoyment, Odo guided her hand up the length of his manhood until its head filled her fist, then thrust fiercely downwards so that the ring rotated against her palm. The feel of the gold, moving through and inside the sensitive glans, sent a searing jolt of ecstasy through him.

'Yes,' he whispered through set teeth. 'Like that. Do it like that.'

She did not have to be taught for long what pleased him. Celine was quick to learn, sliding her grip up and down the full length of his velvety shaft, twirling the ring slowly through the swollen cock-tip at each stroke.

Sweat ran on the muscles of Odo's chest as he pushed her other hand between his legs, to cup his testicles. She stroked his balls, teasing them gently, as she masturbated him with a gradually quickening rhythm. Instinctively she found the pad of flesh behind his scrotum, trailing her fingertips along it until Odo could no longer repress a groan of pleasure.

It was a mistake, and he recognised it instantly.

Celine smiled and looked up at him languorously. She moved sinuously on the bed, legs parted wide. He knew she expected him to mount her now, plunge himself to the root in her, give her what she hungered for.

Such childishness diverted him. She thought she had him in her power, that she had conquered him with her unskilled, tyro's caresses. He, who had broached the Grand Turk's own harem, and been served in Delhi by the priestesses of Kama, god of love! No matter: she would learn.

Catching a handful of her hair Odo pulled her head between his thighs. He thrust his prick towards her, nudging her lips with its jewelled tip.

She was stubborn at first, complaining fretfully that he would choke her, and trying to push him away with soft hands. The challenge thrilled him.

Though it cost him much, he shrugged uncaringly and made to withdraw. A momentary flash of dismay lit her dark eyes and he suppressed a chuckle.

Slipping his fingers down to the wet cleft between her legs, Odo teased the hard nub of her clitoris, calling up all his art until she moaned and thrust against his hand with uncontrollable need. It excited him deeply to be able to override her will, to drive her step by faltering step along the path he had chosen. When he approached her lips a second time she opened for him with a sob, taking the head of his phallus into the warm cave of her mouth.

The feel of her tongue moving on his flesh excited him beyond measure. He wanted nothing better than to thrust his whole length into her throat, but he knew that Celine was not ready for such extremes. She was not yet skilled denough to swallow his manhood without spoiling his diversions by unaesthetic coughs and splutterings.

She was only entering her apprenticeship. There would be time enough to educate her in fellatio, and in his every other caprice. A beginning had been made. Already she was growing bolder, reassured by his caution, stroking her hands up and down the shaft of his cock while she suckled on his glans.

He pumped his hips in tiny movements as she licked the head of his phallus, turning the cock-ring with her tongue. Odo set his jaw, but he could not still the urgency of his need. He knew his crisis was near. He could feel it building, his body hurrying him onward. He thrust two fingers into the slippery depths of Celine's vagina and felt, with exquisite lust, her newly trained muscles clenching greedily on them.

It was too much, even for him.

Odo gave a single, deep, barking cry, and snatched himself out of her mouth. He surrendered totally to his orgasm. His seed spurted out in thick, pulsing jets, spattering Celine's face and breasts.

The intensity of his climax took him unawares. He had not expected Celine's body to yield him such delight. It felt as if his soul was bleeding out of him, drop by drop, to the accompaniment of his racking breath.

Even as he came he heard her cry of despair and knew that her ardour was still unsatisfied. Panting with gratified desire, he looked down at her and smiled slowly; her eyes were dark with loss and pleading.

That he could keep her thus wanting, waiting, set the seal on his enjoyment. Callously, he trailed his hand across her breasts. Her nipples were tight with arousal, and she moaned as he touched her, writhing beneath him. He gathered a drop of semen on one finger tip, and wiped it across her lips.

Then he stood, abruptly, and began to fasten his breeches.

From the corner of his eye he saw Celine push herself into a sitting position.

'You cannot mean to leave me thus! You promised me fulfillment – in the carriage. You promised!'

'Did I?' he said. He shook out his shirt, and pulled it on. 'I don't recall. My memory is somewhat selective, these days. Ah me, the effects of age.'

'Must I beg you to stay?'

'Save your breath, madam. You must learn that your pleasure is in my gift, to be granted or withheld as I choose. Besides, I have made plans for our wedding night. It's my wish that you should spend the intervening hours in anticipation. Your abigail will fetch you to me when all is ready.'

'Is she here yet?' asked Celine.

He smiled at the hope in her voice. Was she looking to find the satisfaction he had denied her at her maid's hands?

'Who do you mean?' he said.

'Bess. Bess Brown, my maid.'

'Not any more,' he said, and flung back his head, laughing at her expression of dismay.

'Did you really think I was going to let you keep your little confidante?' he sneered. 'Your go-between? Oh, yes, I know you have been sending her with messages to your dolt of a lover. No, madam. I have provided a servant for you, of my own choosing.'

He shrugged into his coat and sauntered back across the room to stand above her. Celine's eyes filled with tears.

'I hardly know whether sorrow or indignation shows your beauty to best advantage,' he said meditatively. 'Or perhaps desire. Yes, I think abandonment suits you best, my wife. The half-closed eyes, the wanton movements, the mouth pleading for pleasure – you tempt me. But why spoil the coming banquet? Such feasts are best eaten with a lusty appetite.'

'Stay,' pleaded Celine brokenly. 'Have you no mercy? I – I want you. I starve for you.'

Lord Wraxall looked back at her, his hand on the latch.

'Why, madam, the remedy lies in your own hands,' he said. 'I leave you the fascinum. It should take the edge from your hunger – until tonight.'

Chapter Six

*T*he last of the wedding guests had gone. Bess made her way back along the corridor to collect another load of dirty glasses. Her eyes were red and every so often she sniffled. Opening the door of Sir James's private office, she slipped inside.

Somebody's garters lay with two empty bottles on top of the steel-bound strongbox. A churchwarden pipe spilt ash across the carpet. Call them gentry? Pigs, that's what they were, every last one of them.

She wished she'd stayed in Surrey: she'd only come because she couldn't bear to be parted from Lady Celine. And what would happen to them now? Bess buried her face in her hands and sobbed silently.

The sun had set and it was already dark when the sound of hinges creaking open roused her from her misery. Someone was moving about next door.

Flint scratched on steel: a rectangle of light flickered and steadied, outlining the communicating door to the library. Oh, mercy. If that was Sir James he'd be coming into the office in a moment. It was about the time when he received the nightly report from the militia.

'So you finally choose to join me,' said a woman's voice, low and cold. 'Only an hour late. You forget yourself.'

'Forgive me, Sal,' groaned a man, weakly. 'I couldn't help it.'

Bess cocked her head. Surely that was never the Governor? She slipped off her shoes and stole across to ease the library door open half an inch.

A branch of candles, standing on the table, cast its light over the occupants of the adjoining room. The woman in riding dress had to be Mistress Colney: she was masked for the road, but that flaming hair was unmistakeable. And, though Bess could hardly believe it, the man was indeed Sir James. Look at him cringing there. Not so full of himself now, was he?

Sally trailed the thong of her riding whip through gloved fingers.

'Forgiveness, James? If one of your slaves is disobedient, what do you do? Listen to his lame excuses? Smile, and let him go unpunished, to flout your orders another time? I don't think so.'

Sir James bowed his head humbly.

'Sweet cruelty,' he said, in a trembling voice. 'Spare me!'

'And encourage future misconduct? Never! Prepare to receive your –'

'Wait!' interrupted Sir James.

'Great Caesar's ghost!' exclaimed Sally. 'Now what?'

Booted feet sounded along the corridor.

'It's Cathcart. Come to hand over his keys. I have to see him, Sal.'

'Well, do it quickly,' said Sally impatiently. 'Or it'll be the worse for you – don't try my good nature too far, James.'

She moved away as she spoke, crossing to a window. She opened it and leaned out into the night, whistling 'Lilliburlero' softly.

Bess heard the rumble of bass voices as the militia captain gave his report. Now was the time to be gone, while everyone was occupied. If she stayed where she was, Sir James would catch her when he came into the office. The master keys to the gaol and the arsenal were

77

always locked in his strongbox overnight, for safe keeping.

But she already knew she would not leave. What, miss seeing one of her betters take a thrashing? It was worth the risk. She'd hide under the desk if she had to.

The door clicked to, and Captain Cathcart stamped away.

'And where do you think you're going?' Sally demanded.

Sir James mumbled something about his duty to the King.

'There's only one sovereign here, and it's not Elector George. On your knees, you skulking villain.'

With a pounding heart, Bess watched as Sir James knelt.

'Pardon me,' he pleaded. 'On my honour, Sal, I'll reform.'

'Not good enough,' said Mistress Colney. 'Strip.'

With trembling hands Sir James unbuttoned his fine blue broadcloth coat. His waistcoat was watered silk, embroidered with birds of paradise.

He unfastened his neck-cloth and stripped off his long, curled periwig. His natural hair was dark, and cropped short to the skull. Bess looked him over. You couldn't call him handsome, but without the wig his hawk-like profile had a certain grim nobility.

Sally bent and picked up his discarded cravat.

'Tonight, you shall be blindfold,' she said.

'Be a little less severe, mistress!' cried Sir James. 'Don't deny me the right to see you!'

'A slave has no rights. Only privileges which can be taken away.' She threw the long strip of linen in his face. 'Do it.'

At first, Bess thought Sir James would refuse. His face set in stubborn lines. Mistress Colney stood immobile, staring down at him through the enigmatic velvet mask. Bess could feel the silent battle of wills.

He fought long and hard, but the end was never in doubt. With a deep sob, he fumbled the blindfold into place, binding it twice across his eyes. Bess trembled almost as much as Sir James. This was power. This was true strength. This – she knew with sudden clarity – was what had always been missing from her life of servitude. And oh, how she wanted it.

'Tighter,' said Sally.

Bess eased the door open a little further. Mistress Colney reknotted the blindfold, making sure that Sir James could not cheat her by leaving some crevice through which he could see.

'That will do,' said Sally. 'You may continue, James. I want you naked.'

She watched for a moment, until she was satisfied that he had no thought but to obey her. Then she turned away, and began to unfasten the top buttons of her riding coat.

Bess felt a stab of regret at the thought that the woman might also be about to disrobe. That wasn't how she would do it. No, she'd keep on every stitch to add to her triumph, even the rakish tricorn hat that lay forgotten on the table beside Sir James's keys.

But Mistress Colney did not undress. She slipped her hand into the open bosom of her coat, searching for something concealed there. Candlelight glinted on metal as she withdrew her hand. Was it a knife – fetters, perhaps? Bess craned to see. No, it was neither.

It was another ring of keys.

Sally glanced once at Sir James, who was having some difficulty in removing his breeches while still on his knees, and silently exchanged her keys for those Captain Cathcart had handed over.

As far as Bess could see, the bunches were identical: a broad brass ring holding two great iron keys for the outer doors of the gaol and armoury, and a clutch of smaller ones. Mistress Colney rustled swiftly to the open window and leant out.

Holding her petticoats close, so that they made no noise, Bess scurried over to the office window. She glimpsed a small, lithe figure darting from shade to shade: one of the ragged urchins of the town.

These were deep waters, sure enough. Nothing was what it seemed: the time, the place, the blindfold – even 'Lilliburlero' had been a signal to whoever waited outside. Bess frowned. She knew it was her duty to raise the alarm. But that would mean betraying her presence; and how could she ever explain what she'd seen – what she might still see?

The thought set her pulses racing. The library door, standing ajar, drew her like a magnet: she could not resist its pull. Thrusting her doubts aside, she took up her station in the shadows once more.

Sir James cowered in the pool of candlelight. He wore only his shirt.

'Stand up,' ordered Sally. 'Get rid of that rag.'

She snapped the whip. Its thong flickered like dark lightning across Sir James's shoulders. He started to his feet, turning his bandaged head this way and that as he listened fearfully for her approach.

'Must I flog it from your back? I said strip.'

Pleading for mercy in anguished tones, Sir James dragged off his last covering and stood naked before her, hunched forward a little, his hands cupping his genitals. The whiplash streaked out once more, and he snatched his fingers away with a cry.

He was in surprisingly good trim for his age, kept in shape by regular horsemanship. There was not an extra ounce of flesh on him anywhere – not even, Bess noted wryly, where it mattered most. His prick seemed almost shrunk into his body, only its head showing above the curls at his groin.

Bess sniffed disdainfully. Well, what a tiddler!

'Make yourself ready,' said Sally.

Sir James groped blindly forward, his hands held out before him, until he found the library table. Sally moved round him, ordering him laconically to bend over and straddle his legs. At last she was satisfied. He waited tensely for his punishment, bent forward at a right angle from the waist and supported only by his hands on the table. His knuckles whitened as he gripped its edge.

Bright colour burned on Bess's cheeks. She could hear Sir James panting, and knew that her breathing, though silent, was almost as heavy.

Mistress Colney slowly shook free the thong of her riding whip. It trailed on the carpet behind her. She paused. And then she struck.

Sir James flinched as the lash wrote its scarlet signature across his buttocks, but he made no sound.

'That for your disobedience, dog,' said Sally.

She snatched back the thong with a flick of her wrist, and struck again.

'And that for keeping me waiting. And this, and this, and this for marrying your daughter to that devil, Wraxall.'

Sir James groaned. 'Very fine old family,' he said faintly.

Bess shuddered as she watched the fall of the lash and the angry weals rising on his well-muscled arse. Her fierce response to the sight astounded her. She would have given anything to be in Mistress Colney's place, to have Sir James her slave and not her master. The thought of him, offering himself in fear and longing to her corrections, excited Bess beyond bearing.

She pressed her thighs together repeatedly. Her nipples, hard as acorns, rubbed against her kerchief. She could not resist touching them, stimulating herself still further as she watched his abasement.

Sir James was past dumb endurance now. He could no longer remain still. He heaved and squirmed under Sally's brutal caresses, gasping with pain and shuddering with pleasure. His prick, which Bess had dismissed as a mere lady's-finger, grew and swelled with each blow that his flesh received.

Shy no more, it thrust eagerly forward under his belly. It was still not the longest she had seen, perhaps, but so enormously broad and stout that it made her blink.

Mistress Colney laid the whip aside momentarily, and

ran one gloved hand over the abused skin of his behind, tracing the regular marks of the lash.

Sir James moaned and thrust himself back against her hand.

'Don't stop, Sal – mistress. Damme, I deserve it. Every stroke of it.'

Reaching beneath his belly, she took hold of his cock. The head of it alone filled her leather-clad grasp to capacity. She squeezed it tantalisingly, and began to move her hand up and down the swollen shaft.

Sir James moaned and wept in a frenzy of delight, thrusting through the circlet of Sally's fingers as, with her other hand, she rained a shower of blows on his smarting buttocks.

Watching this was more than flesh and blood could stand. Bess thrust her hand between her legs and grasped a handful of her petticoats. She rubbed the bunched fabric against her clitoris, timing herself to Sally's blows, sobbing gently as her sex-bud tingled and throbbed. It took less than a minute to bring herself to orgasm: a shattering burst of ecstasy that left her wobbly-kneed and gasping for breath.

She must have made more noise about it than she thought, though. Mistress Colney's head was raised alertly. Bess withdrew fearfully into the darkness. Had she been seen? For a moment she caught the glitter of eyes within the black velvet vizard: then Sally turned back to Sir James.

His mouth was twisted with passion. Bess could tell from his convulsive movements that he was on the edge of his climax.

'Not so fast, James,' said Sally, and released him, chuckling at his groan of frustrated lust. 'Let us observe precedence here. Mistress first, then man.'

She pushed him down to crouch before her and lifted her skirts to her waist. Flickering candles woke the glint of flame in the russet triangle at her groin. Parting her legs, she guided Sir James's head between them.

'Pleasure me, slave,' Sally whispered. 'Pleasure me – ah!'

She closed her eyes tightly; their lids showed white through the eyeholes of the mask. Her whole body tensed and quivered for a moment and then, drawing a deep breath, she relaxed.

Sir James thrust his face into her, drinking thirstily from the briny sweetness of her loins as he stroked his hands up and down the shaft of his prick. His shoulders shook as he pumped himself to climax.

Bess sighed deeply as Sally raised the whip a final time, bringing it down across his back, the lash curling between his legs. Sir James shrieked, and his come jetted in creamy spasms over the polished leather of her boots.

Mistress Colney laughed, and let fall the whip. She dropped her skirts and turned away from Sir James to stare directly across to the office door. Her eyes found the watcher in the shadows, and she winked.

Bess jumped violently. So she had been seen. But if the woman was thinking of betraying her to Sir James, she'd missed her chance. Bess had a tale of her own to tell now, about the keys. She returned Sally's look boldly.

After a moment, the red-haired woman shrugged and held out her hands, palms up, in a gesture of acceptance.

'The Blue Anchor – at midnight,' she said.

Sir James groaned and raised his blind head.

'Mistress?' he enquired.

Sally waited until Bess nodded her agreement. Then she glanced down, and spurned him with her foot.

'Nothing to do with you, dog. A private appointment I've just recalled. God's blood, look at the mess you've made of my boots. Lick 'em clean.'

Celine dreamt she was lost among black trees, and woke with a start. It was night. Shadows stood tall in the corners; the mirrors reflected a darkness only slightly less profound. The room smelt of sex and Wraxall's perfume.

She rose and padded across the floor, the silk bedcover draped around her. To her surprise, the French windows opened easily. Somehow she had expected them to be locked. Lord Wraxall was very sure of her. Celine pulled the coverlet tight around her shoulders and passed out on to the veranda.

The night was sultry. Carriage-lamps moved on the distant road, and from the Rotunda chinks of light showed between heavy curtains. Celine gazed out over the shadowed plantation, trying to make sense of her feelings.

Her body felt silky and relaxed, languid with eroticism. And yet it was Liam she loved, only Liam. Her feelings for Lord Wraxall were unchanged. No, she thought, say rather that something had been added: desire? Yes, and something darker. Dangerous yet alluring, it tempted her onwards.

She remembered he had known her mother. Where, and when? Had they been lovers? Was this fever in the blood, this need to submit, another legacy?

The door to her chamber opened, and light spilt across the floor.

'Madame?' said a woman, softly.

Celine cleared her throat. 'Here.'

'*Bon*,' said the newcomer. She pushed the bedroom door wide, murmuring orders to the servants accompanying her. Candles were lit: chambermaids brought in a clutter of cosmetics, silks, and ewers of perfumed water. The woman made a noise of disapproval.

'Come in at once, madame!' she snapped. 'Do you want to catch an ague?'

Celine could not help laughing a little as the woman closed the window and, scolding in island French, pulled the curtains to. Her abigail, sure enough. Being ordered around so brusquely was almost like having Bess back. She examined her new maid while the bath was brought in and filled. This was no English country rose, but an exotic – a hibiscus or an orchid.

The woman stared back with bold, bright eyes. She

was honey-gold and rounded: there was a haunting familiarity about her. Her tawny hair was crowned with a garland of wheat and poppies. Her thin robe, the colour of ripe corn, skimmed the ample contours of her body. She clapped her hands, and the lesser servants rustled away.

The abigail beckoned. 'Quickly, madame. There is little time. The company is gathering.'

'Company?' asked Celine. She knew she had seen this woman before. Not among the servants waiting on the steps, though: somewhere else.

'But of course. You think I dress like this to make beds? Milor' has ordered an entertainment for your wedding. Did he not tell you?'

'It was mentioned,' said Celine. She breathed a deep sigh of relief as her stays were unloosed. 'What's your name?'

'Does it matter?' said her new maid, with a shrug. 'I am a slave. I have no name. He calls me Ceres: my last master, something else.'

'But you must have a – ' began Celine. She broke off suddenly. A slave – the barracoon, the auctioneer chanting, the woman called the Nassau Hurricane writhing with pleasure under Odo's hands. And she knew, to a cold certainty, where she had seen Ceres before.

The woman lifted the hem of Celine's chemise. Her fingers trailed across bare flesh as she slowly raised the wisp of silk.

Celine shivered at her touch. She knew Lord Wraxall had taken this creature: perhaps in this very room, on the black bed, he had granted her the satisfaction he had refused his bride.

'You should not have slept in the corset, madame. It has left marks on the skin, you see? Milor' will be angry. We must see what the bath can do.'

Celine thrust her hands away. 'Don't touch me!'

'Oh la la, are you jealous?' asked Ceres, with a low chuckle. 'Does it pique you that he has had me – that he

85

will have me again? Then you must resent the whole house, madame, down to the boy who cleans the knives.'

She stepped closer. Her hands slipped down over Celine's hips.

'Come, *doudou*, let me wash you.'

Revolted, Celine pushed her off and stepped into the tub. Her nudity made her feel very vulnerable. She lowered herself into the warm water. It lapped around her, seeking out the tender folds of her body, supporting her breasts as she lay back so that they formed two swelling, snowy islands crowned with pink. She tried to ignore the maid, but remained very conscious of her gaze.

Celine soaped her arms, her torso. She rinsed the crawling suds from her stomach and long legs. She squeezed the sponge between her thighs, massaging the sensitive flesh. Ceres licked rouged lips.

'Let me help you, *chérie*,' she said huskily.

Celine glanced at her. The other woman's eyes were heavy with lust. Her nipples were huge and hard, peaking the fabric of her robe. Ceres knelt down and leant close, dabbling her fingertips in the tub. Celine could smell the musk of her arousal, even through the lily-perfume of the soap.

'Give the sponge here, to me,' purred Ceres, sliding her fingers up the inside of Celine's leg. 'I can show you things even milor' has not thought of.'

With an angry exclamation, Celine slashed her hand across the surface of the water, sending a great cascade of it into the kneeling maid's face. Ceres started to her feet with a scream of fury. The front of her gown was soaked to transparency, and foam dripped from the wilting corn-ears of her crown.

Celine stepped out of the bath and reached for a towel.

'You are a slave, Ceres: act like one,' she said, coldly. 'Address me as "milady" at all times. Take no further liberties. I have never flogged a servant yet, but by heaven, I will do it if you provoke me further!'

'You think you are so high above me,' sneered Ceres,

86

her eyes glowing with scorn. 'You are too good even for me to touch, yes? Well, let me tell you, he will tire of you. If I could not hold him for more than a week, what will you manage, *milady*? Two days? Three? Not much longer, I think. And then you will be ours to play with. After the footmen have finished with you, you will be begging me for a woman's gentleness.'

'That's five lashes, slut,' said Celine. She finished drying herself, and tossed the towel aside. 'You may dress me now.'

Ceres clenched her fists. 'I spit on you,' she hissed.

'Ten,' said Celine. 'Well? Am I to wait all night?'

Muttering under her breath, but not so loudly that Celine was forced to take notice and punish it, Ceres picked up a drift of white silk. She shook out its folds and held the garment up at arm's length, displaying it.

It was a *chlamys*, a long Grecian tunic. No more than two rectangles of spider-fine gauze, shot through with metallic threads, it was caught together at shoulder and hip with clasps of gold. The silk was so delicate that the flames of the candles could be seen through it, haloed as if by cloud.

'I won't wear that,' said Celine, flatly. 'It's indecent!'

'Milor's choice. Shall I tell him you do not care for it?'

Celine buried her face in her hands. It was outrageous, but, like every other of Lord Wraxall's demands, it had to be met.

'Very well,' she said. 'I swore obedience. How does it go on?'

It took nearly an hour before Ceres was satisfied. She gave a final twitch to the filmy draperies and stood back, frowning critically.

'Not my best effort, but it will do.'

Celine looked with awe at her reflection. A slender goddess, crowned with flowers, gazed back at her with soft, wild eyes. She had never dreamt that she could look so immodest – or so beautiful.

The *chlamys*, its glittering weave so fine as to be almost invisible, flowed in sculptured folds down to her naked feet, hiding nothing. Golden ribbons bound her waist and crossed between her high breasts. Her nipples were tinted to the same shade as her mouth, and Ceres had clipped short her pubic hair. The lips of her sex, delicately rouged by the same expert hand, glowed through the transparent fabric.

Celine swayed. The light of the candles shimmered on the spider-gauze. It was if she had dressed in water, or mist, gilded by the first sun of spring.

'It's wonderful,' said Celine, flushing. 'But I can't be seen like this. Haven't you heard the carriages? There must be dozens of guests assembled.'

'Milady will follow orders, as do we all,' snapped Ceres, and led her out.

The darkened house was silent. Celine's breath came fast as she followed her maid down stairs, through shadowed galleries, and out into the colonnade.

Looming overhead, the dark bulk of the Rotunda blotted out the stars. Ceres knocked twice. Tall double doors swung open at her signal, and sighed shut again behind them.

Inside was a small lobby, painted scarlet from ceiling to floor. The only light came from the eyes of a Balinese devil-mask set above a curtained doorway. From within came the sound of drums: loud, savage and insistent.

Ceres drew the hangings aside. The drums stopped short.

Her heart racing like a runner's, Celine stepped into the room beyond.

It was hung with sooty velvet and blazed with candles, black and myrrh-scented. The circular space was crowded with people, but she saw only one.

Her husband sprawled in an ebony throne opposite the entrance, all the light and darkness of the room concentrated in his eyes.

He was robed in brocade the colour of midnight, and crowned with black lilies. He smiled, and sipped red wine from a cup made of a skull.

'Welcome to the Underworld,' said Lord Odo Wraxall.

Chapter Seven

Celine stood at the head of a shallow stairway. On either hand, the interior of the Rotunda descended in tiers to a central space, and each broad circle was packed with watchers, sprawled among the cushions.

Every head was turned towards her. A hundred candles burned in the wall-sconces, as many more in the clawed, iron chandelier that hung from the centre of the gilded dome. Her thin tunic concealed nothing, merely accentuating her nudity. There was no place to hide from the stares.

Lord Wraxall set down the cup and rose, gathering his dark brocades around him. In silence, he stepped down from the dais and crossed the Rotunda to stoop above her.

His robe parted with a hiss of silks and he snatched her into its shadowy folds. He was naked beneath it. His body crushed against hers, breast to breast and thigh to thigh: she felt the quick response of his phallus, stirring into hardness against her groin.

Someone cheered hoarsely, and the watchers burst into applause. Celine cried out with shame and confusion, pushing against Lord Wraxall's chest.

Odo's grip tightened. 'Are you afraid?' he asked.

She buried her face in the hollow of his shoulder, and nodded.

'There is no need,' he whispered. 'Tonight, you are the Queen of Hades. Nothing shall be done without your consent. Come.'

He cloaked her in the parted wings of his mantle and guided her down the stairs. All eyes followed them as they went.

Celine clung to him, grateful for the concealment of his robe. She peeped curiously between her eyelashes at the room, as Odo led her across it.

Murals ringed the Rotunda's walls. Fallen angels, gold on red, copulated with beasts between the black-curtained windows. Behind the throne, a private room had been walled off. Three steps led up to its arched doorway. The hangings that screened it were caught back, and a low bed stood within.

From the inner chamber to the lobby, the Rotunda's topmost tier swept round in two half-moons, massed with servants. Women, shaved bare as babies, posed there among the ranks of drums: apart from their high-heeled shoes, they wore only scarlet stockings and half-masks.

The invited gentry, all male, lolled in full evening finery of silks and gems on the levels below. There were too many familiar faces among them: men Celine had danced with, friends of her father's, guests at his table.

Lowering her eyes, she drew closer to her husband. Together, they ascended the dais. He drew her down beside him on the black throne. There was room for two, if they sat close. His naked flank pressed against her.

Lord Wraxall raised his hand. The drums began a low muttering.

'Gentlemen, you know the rules. Let us commence.'

With a squeal of its chain, the central chandelier was lowered. Slaves doused its candles, and those burning round the walls, plunging the Rotunda each moment into deeper gloom.

Ceres danced in the growing darkness, her face an exaggerated mask of woe. She sang to the beat of the drums. The language was unknown to Celine, but every word spoke of tragedy, of a loss almost too great to be borne. Pain twisted inside her: she, too, had felt such a parting.

'What does she say?' she murmured. 'It sounds so sad.'

Lord Wraxall's hands drifted over Celine, just touching her.

'Forgive me, but I am disinclined for translation at this moment. It's Doric. A lament of Demeter.'

He moved the folds of his robe, so that he could see her body. Celine shrank away, embarrassed by his too-public caresses.

The Rotunda was in semi-darkness. A few flames still burned here and there among the guests, sparkling from buckles and jewelled sword-hilts.

Only the circular space in the middle of the room was fully lit, drawing the eye. Iron candle-holders, each as tall as a man, stood around its circumference, illuminating the heap of crimson cushions in its centre.

Odo's lips brushed her neck. Slowly he slipped the *chlamys* down from Celine's shoulder. His mouth left a track of kisses on her skin, following his hand over the swell of her breast to toy lightly with her rouged nipple. He found Celine's hand, lying loosely on her lap, and carried it to his loins.

His manhood was fully erect. For a moment Celine felt its virile heat pulsing within her palm. Then she recoiled, and snatched her hand away: she could not touch him so openly, before this crowd of lecherous onlookers.

On the lowest tier of the Rotunda, Ceres swayed and wailed. A man crouched at her feet, pawing her bare legs. It was Mr Moffat. He clutched at her and pulled her down beside him. Her song broke off with a most untragic squawk and giggle.

'I wonder why I invited that oaf,' Odo murmured pensively. 'No style. No finesse. The efforts of a Heliogabalus would be wasted on such dullards.'

He beckoned. A black slave, in stockings embroidered

with pearls, stepped into the centre of the room, and spread herself on the cushions heaped there.

She stretched out her limbs, making herself comfortable. More pearls were sewn into the tight cap of her hair and the triangle of her pubis. They trembled in the candle-light, gleaming against her sombre skin.

A bell chimed. The audience shifted in their places. After an introductory roll, the drums fell into a slow rhythm, like the beating of wings.

'First conundrum,' announced Lord Wraxall.

The curtains of the lobby parted with a sudden rush. As if blown there by a gale, a man stood poised on tiptoe at the head of the stairway. He was white, chalk-white, from head to foot: an albino. His hair was a snow-cloud, and his eyes were red. For an instant he waited there, arms outspread, and then with a slow, gliding pace, he began to descend the steps.

Lord Wraxall reached for the skull-cup, and passed it to Celine.

'You will drink,' he said. It was not a question.

Celine turned it in her hands, putting off the inevitable. The cup was wide and shallow, its polished bone bowl set on a stem of fluted gold.

The albino circled the supine slave-girl, his eyes fixed on her, his arms moving as if in flight. In the shadows, Mr Moffat reached orgasm with a grunt.

'Drink,' repeated Odo. 'Do you fear I mean to poison you?'

The wine was red: it burned in her mouth, heavy and sweet, with a faint aftertaste of bitterness. She closed her eyes and swallowed. Maybe it would be best if she was a little drunk. A last drop trickled from the corner of her mouth, and Odo bent to kiss it away.

'Now watch,' he said. 'See if you can guess my riddle.'

The black girl writhed on the cushions, caressing her breasts. She moaned softly and toyed with her sex, opening herself for all to see.

With a last flutter of his hands, the albino descended to settle between her legs. His pallid skin was a startling

92

contrast to the darkness of the woman moving beneath him. His arms stilled, and folded behind his back. He stretched out his neck over her. His white hair feathered across her breasts.

The wine coursed with a strange heat through Celine's veins. She could feel the skin of her nipples creasing as they tightened. Odo's hands, travelling across her body, seemed to imprint a pattern of fire that remained, and glowed, even after they had moved on.

On the stage below, the albino's phallus thrust at the gateway of pleasure. The woman held herself wide, guiding the blind guest within.

'Solomon and Sheba,' called a man. He stood up. His coat was red. Candle-light glinted on gold braid. Celine knew him.

'It's Solomon and Sheba, I say,' insisted Captain Cathcart. 'You know, "I am black but comely, oh ye daughters of Jerusalem."'

'Wrong,' said Lord Wraxall. He smiled. 'Pay your forfeit.'

Two of the masked women descended from among the servants. Captain Cathcart blustered insincerely as they began to unfasten his clothes. One of them slipped her hand into his breeches, and the officer's laughing protests changed to a groan of lust. The women twined their arms around him. They bore him back into the shadows.

Lord Wraxall held out his goblet to be refilled. 'Continue.'

The albino's manhood entered the woman's body by slow fractions. Their groins met and kissed, white hair tangling with black. He held himself there, pressed hard against her, while the drums beat ten times. Then, as gradually, he began to withdraw.

Fingers trailed across Celine's flesh.

'Shall I take you thus?' whispered Odo. 'Inch by inch until you whimper? Or would you like me to be rough, to handle you masterfully? Do you have a preference, madam? Answer me!'

93

He tweaked her nipple, and Celine cried out softly at the harsh caress. Excitement boiled inside her. Her sex throbbed, swollen and heavy. All the heat of the wine seemed to be concentrated there, radiating out from its centre to her every nerve-ending.

It could not just be wine that had brought her to such warmth and eagerness. She felt not far short of wanting any man. Celine moaned with despair and need. Something had been put in the cup.

She pressed against her husband, arching her back to bring her breasts forward to his mouth. In the lit circle at the centre of the Rotunda, the albino thrust again and again. He raised his head and called out once, wordlessly, then fell to lie upon the slave-girl, still as death.

'*Dieu*, I have it! Leda and the swan!'

'M. de Goudet wins,' said Odo. 'Will you choose your prize, sir?'

'Christ,' complained one of the watchers, bitterly. 'These aren't going to be *Greek* games, are they? Have a heart, Wraxall. We don't all know Homer.'

De Goudet, small and round, scrambled into the lit circle. He took the woman's arm and pulled her upright. He ran his hands across her dark skin.

'This one,' he said huskily, and retreated, taking his trophy with him.

The bell rang a second time.

'Next riddle,' proclaimed Lord Wraxall.

From opposite sides of the room, two naked men stepped down the tiers and into the light. Charles and Rupert, the footmen.

They were perfectly matched, of identical height and build. Their skins were the same shade of polished bronze: they might have been twins. Charles raised his right hand in an imploring gesture. Rupert mirrored it with his left. They moved closer. Palm met palm. Eyes reflected eyes.

Celine fidgeted on the throne. The aphrodisiac burned in her flesh: one thing alone could quench that fire. She slid her hand under Lord Wraxall's brocades, and ran

94

her fingers down the springing length of his cock, from the tip to the warm weight of his scrotum.

Odo shifted position, and his robe fell away, leaving him uncovered. His look was inscrutable, but his shuddering breath told its own tale. He, too, had drunk of the wine. He brushed away the transparent silk covering Celine loins, and sank his hand between her thighs. His fingers moved in the wetness between her labia: she thrust to meet them.

She was desperate for his body. Why didn't he take her into the inner room? He must know she wanted to feel him on her, wanted more than his fingers inside her. She moved the ring in his glans. His phallus jerked.

'By hell, you learn fast,' said Odo huskily. 'Leave me be, now.'

'I desire you,' she whispered. 'I need to have you. Why do we wait?'

'I said no more, woman! I'll not have those pretty fingers of yours make me spend before time. Watch the players.'

The footmen were very close now, face to face, their postures symmetrical. Charles took Rupert's cock in his right hand: his twin mirrored the gesture with his left. On the same beat of the drum they began to pump each other's engorged flesh. Celine made a little grimace and looked away.

'I know nothing of the classics,' she murmured.

'A pity. I like my wit to be appreciated. You should at least be familiar with the tale of Hades and Persephone. Shall I instruct you?'

'I had rather learn other things. Touch me.'

'Madam, you are importunate,' whispered Odo. 'Come, then, for once you shall be the teacher. Show me what you want.'

He allowed Celine to guide his hand once more between her thighs. The juices of her readiness slicked the skin. Lord Wraxall found the hood of her clitoris and drew it back, teasing her softly.

'In the ancient world,' he said, moving his thumb in

tiny circles, 'the goddess of crops and gardens was called Demeter – Ceres, if you prefer the Latin. She had a daughter, Persephone, fair as the spring. Are you listening?'

'Yes,' lied Celine.

The hot wetness of her sex throbbed around his fingers. She could feel the head of his erection against her leg. His lips were warm, and his long hair brushed over her breasts.

'One day, as the daughter of Demeter gathered flowers, the dark god Hades, Lord of the Underworld, passed by in his chariot.'

In the audience, someone cleared their throat.

'Hades saw Persephone, and wanted her in that instant. He – '

'Hm hmm!' came the sound again, louder.

'The devil!' Odo muttered, with uncharacteristic energy. 'How inopportune.'

A man stepped forward into the light. He was elderly, and stooped, and should have known better than to choose puce satin.

'Yes?' said Odo.

Celine panted with frustration. This interruption was agony to her. She pressed close to Lord Wraxall, tracing a line from his collar-bone to his nipple with her tongue. She bit the taut brown nubbin gently.

'Narcissus, who loved his own reflection in the pool?'

'Correct, sir. And your prize?'

The man considered, looking from Charles to Rupert, to Charles again. 'One hardly knows,' he said. 'They are both so . . .'

'Take the pair,' said Lord Wraxall, with a hint of impatience. As one, the footmen stood. They linked arms across the man's back. Walking in step, they ushered him into the darkness, eyes fixed on each other over his bent head.

'Now where were we, madam?' murmured Odo. 'Ah, yes, the legend.'

'No more delays,' said Celine passionately. 'You know

that I want you, that I need your body. Please, my lord . . .'

'You are sure?' he whispered. 'Shall I take you? Shall it be now?'

'Yes,' she answered, her voice shaking. He gathered her to him, picking her up in his arms. With a drive of his powerful thighs he rose smoothly to his feet. He looked down at her and smiled. His lean strength supported her weight without effort. Celine nuzzled against his chest, kissing the smooth tanned skin.

'Very well,' he said, and laughed. 'Remember, it was your choice.'

Holding her close, he looked out proudly across the silent room. The bell chimed. 'Gentlemen, the third riddle!' cried Lord Odo Wraxall.

At first she did not understand. It was only when he began to descend the stairs leading to the Rotunda's centre, that she realised what he had planned for their wedding night.

'My lord, not here!' she hissed, in horror. 'Not before them all!'

'Too late,' said Odo mockingly. 'Did you not, just now, consent?'

He sank to his knees, lowering her on to the heap of cushions. They were still warm from the previous occupants. Celine could smell sweat on the plush, sharp and masculine. From the audience, she heard a growing murmur.

Odo's hands trailed across her, teasing her back to arousal with his sensualist's skill. Celine was unable to still her body's response to his touch. He had tricked her: she would never have knowingly agreed to this. But her hunger for him was too deep. Even now, even here, she wanted him.

'Mother of God,' said someone, in heavily accented English. 'What then is the prize for this conundrum, Wraxall? You, or her?'

'I'll make you a gift of the answer, Don Alvaro,' he

said, 'Since I cannot give you my person, or that of my bride: the Rape of Persephone.'

He bent and kissed her. He parted her thighs.

'Look at me,' he breathed.

The robe had slipped from his shoulders: apart from the black flower-crown, he was naked. His body was that of an athlete, superbly conditioned: his face was the face of a jaded roué.

'You are mine: look only at me.'

He leant over her, his hands playing on her breasts. His hair fell down about her in dark curtains. He moved, and she felt the ring in his penis stir against the curls of her mound. Slowly, he unfastened the four clasps holding her last covering and let it fall. The watchers sighed.

'I am in hell!' cried Celine.

'Indeed you are. How quickly you have learnt to play the game.' His lips met hers, and his mouth held the taste of darkness. 'The Underworld, too, has its delights: I know them all. Let me show you, my Persephone.'

His fingers slipped briefly within her. His cock-tip rubbed against her clitoris. Torn between desire and anguish, she allowed him to bring her legs up, and around his waist. His phallus moved between her sex-lips.

He found the entrance to her vagina, and lingered there for a moment, supported on his outstretched arms. Candle-flames burned in the shadows of his eyes. Then, with a sigh, he thrust slowly forward, sheathing himself to the hilt in the scabbard of her loins.

His prick was warm, immense, filling her to capacity, almost to straining point. Celine moaned with shock and delight. She felt the ring in his glans nudge delicately at the neck of her womb. She felt it rolling as he drew back, felt it pressing against the pleasure-spot on her inner wall.

He thrust again, a little faster. Without conscious thought, she moved to meet the stroke, gripping the shaft of his cock, as he had taught her.

'Gently,' he said. 'Give me time to please you.'

Celine tightened her legs about his waist. She heard the rustle of silks as the watchers stirred on the tiers above. She tried to blot out her sense of them. Let them witness her passion. Only the moving hardness of her husband's phallus was of moment now: the feel of his pubic bone thrusting against her clitoris, and the heaviness of his balls brushing her inner thighs.

With leisurely skill, Lord Wraxall penetrated her again and again. She heaved beneath him, urging him on to push deeper, harder. Her hands slipped up and down his arms, across the muscles of his back and shoulders.

Her hips pumped. The muscles of her vagina fluttered, tensing and relaxing on his shaft in an increasing tempo. Celine had never known such ecstasy; the feel of him within her so sensual and erotic, that it was close to agony. She could not bear it. He could not continue; he must not stop.

Celine murmured little words of endearment, hardly coherent, as she felt the first sweet stirrings of her climax. Her need overmastered her. She clasped her hands behind Odo's neck and pulled herself up to him, sobbing against his mouth as her orgasm peaked, burst, and scattered, sending its piercing shards through every fibre of her body.

She sank away, gasping, but Lord Wraxall barely paused to let her get her breath. All slowness was abandoned now, all subtlety. He lay full-length upon her, crushing her beneath him. His kiss was savage. He grasped cruelly at her breast, and thrust in to her with a raw animal lust for satisfaction.

Lord Wraxall's rough dominance excited Celine even more than his earlier delay. Incredibly, she felt desire spark into life again. His ardour enflamed her. She raised her knees, clawing at his back and buttocks. Their loins drove together. She felt the heat run through her, and the tension building once more to the exploding point. Crying out wildly, she came.

And this time, Odo came with her, finding his release with a deep growl of fulfillment.

There was a minute's awed silence, then a tumult of applause.

Odo raised himself on one elbow. 'Well, Lady Wraxall,' he said, a little breathlessly. 'I was right about you, was I not? You have an inborn talent for the sport.'

Celine tightened her sex-muscles on his phallus: it was hardly less firm now than when he had first taken her. The feel of it thrilled her. Maybe it was the effect of the aphrodisiac, or – as he said – a natural hunger. Maybe it was his superlative skill at the act of love. It did not even matter that her heart was forever closed to him. She had tasted the pleasure of a man's body for the first time, and she wanted more.

There was no need for her to speak. Without once withdrawing, Lord Wraxall pulled her close, and got to his feet. Celine twined her limbs around him, and clasped her vagina around his hardening cock. He took her back to the throne and held her there, impaled on his manhood, while he kissed her, long and succulently.

Then he reached out for the skull-goblet, and placed it in her hand.

'Drink, Persephone,' he said. 'The night is long, and lies before us.'

Bess sat opposite Mistress Colney at a rough table in the Blue Anchor's taproom. They were alone, and the door was locked. She had been more than a little nervous about keeping the appointment; with who knows what dark deeds afoot, she could be an inconvenient witness. But the thought of Celine, terrified and struggling in the wicked Viscount's clutches, had decided her. Mistress Colney might be able to help.

'What the devil brought you to the library at such a time?' asked Sally. 'And why didn't you raise the alarm? I know you saw me take the gaol keys.'

Bess went very pink. Mumbling a little, she explained.

'You don't have to tell me why you stayed,' said Sally, when Bess faltered into embarrassed silence. 'That was clear enough. You made enough noise about taking your

100

pleasure. Does the idea of flogging a man really excite you so much? I always have to go masked when I serve James his punishment. He wants me to be severe, you see, and I find it hard to keep a straight face. Could you do it without laughing, do you think?'

Bess imagined wielding the whip; having Sir James, his fine airs forgotten, grovelling at her feet.

'Oh, yes,' she breathed. 'Milady's father, he's so uppity, ordering me about. It was wonderful to see him humbled. I went all of a tremble. I – '

'Wait on,' interrupted Sally. 'Someone's coming.'

Footsteps sounded on the cobbles outside: a man walking fast, but cautiously. Someone whistled, softly. Sally released the breath she had been holding and unbolted the door.

The newcomer was an African, broad and muscular, black as basalt. His shirt and breeches of white linen fitted him like a second skin. Gold rings hung in his ears, and he wore a wide straw hat. From the shadow of its brim, he examined Bess.

'This is Auguste Toussainte,' said Sally. She smiled, and rose on tip-toe to kiss him. 'He's my – well, what are you, Auguste?'

Auguste grinned back at her. His arm circled her waist.

'"General factotum" is a term one can use in company,' he said.

'Is it done?' she asked.

He nodded, and dropped a bunch of keys on the table.

'Reuben Ossett will be safe on board Tremaine's flagship within the hour.'

Sally picked up the keys and looked at Bess keenly.

'You've seen these before,' she said. 'And you could hang us both, if you gave the word. But I don't think you will. No: you'll go back home, and you'll leave the library window open, just by an inch. And then you'll forget all this ever happened. Won't you?'

'I'll do anything, if only you'll help poor Lady Celine,' said Bess, and burst into tears.

101

Sally patted her on the shoulder and made sympathetic noises as, between sobs, the sorry tale was unfolded: then she stiffened.

'He said what?' she asked, aghast.

Bess repeated Lord Wraxall's threat to have Liam hanged.

'Hell's bells and buckets of blood!' exclaimed Sally. 'Think of the worst thing you may, Odo Wraxall will top it, every time. Why was I away from town? Why, why, didn't that foolish child send to me?'

Bess looked up at her from swimming eyes.

'So you'll help her?' she hiccupped.

'Easier said than done, now they're married,' Sally replied, with a frown. 'Without she runs away from him, there's not much I can do. I'll keep my eye on things at Acheron: more I can't promise.'

'It's something, I suppose,' said Bess wanly. She blew her nose on her apron and arose. 'I'd best be getting back. I won't forget the library window.'

'Wait!' cried Sally. 'I pay my debts. What little I can do for Lady Celine, I will, and welcome. But you've still had no reward.'

'I don't want your money,' Bess said, bridling.

'You're not being offered it. How'd you like to be a lady yourself?'

'Me? Never. I'm not gentle-born.'

'That's no bar,' said Sally. 'I was born in the stews of Bermondsey: I've seen the inside of Newgate prison, and came to the New World on a transport ship. Now I'm a great landowner. Anything's possible out here.'

She looked Bess up and down, appreciatively noting her prettiness, the riot of blonde curls and the symmetry of her lush figure.

'A few lessons and some showy silks are all that's needed. You've everything else in plenty. And, I suspect, a certain special qualification as well. Meet me here tomorrow afternoon: we'll see what can be done.'

Auguste unfastened the bolts. Sally put an arm around Bess's waist and walked her to the door.

'Now get home with you,' she said, giving Bess a kiss. 'And don't speak to any strange men.'

Bess slipped away. The waning moon sank slowly towards the sea. One by one the taverns and bordellos of the town put out their lights and locked their shutters.

On the ramparts the sentries played dice for next month's pay. No officers came to disturb them: they were all at Acheron, with other things on their minds. In his ward-room, the sergeant snored under a red-spotted handkerchief, dreaming of sex in a hammock with three willing harlots, one of whom looked unaccountably like his mother. No-one saw the great ship, sliding across the moon's track, all sail set and drawing.

She rounded the island, running before the wind, and hove to in a quiet bay. A canoe put off from shore to meet her.

Two men bent to its paddles. One was squat and bearded; the second tall, with black hair and eyes that were blue, and bleak. They reached the waiting ship and swarmed aboard. Cordage creaked. Sails bellied. Heeling to the wind, the ship got under way, water chuckling at her forefoot.

The abandoned canoe bobbed briefly on her wake. Then the current took it, and it was washed round the headland and out of sight.

Chapter Eight

*I*t was dawn. Where early light penetrated the Rotunda's drapes the guttering candle-flames were wan and sick-looking. The drums were silent, overturned. The room was a chaos of torn garments and entangled bodies.

A bar of sun fell across Celine's eyes. She lay, with her head in Odo's lap, on the cushions of the lowest tier. Making a soft noise of protest, she turned away from the sudden brilliance.

Every muscle ached after the night's unceasing exercise in Lord Wraxall's arms. He had been a stranger to fatigue, taking her publicly and repeatedly in positions that made Celine flush with shame as she recalled them.

She had knelt for him, stood, crouched. She remembered straddling his hips while two of the masked women held her, supporting her weight as they raised and lowered her on the upright shaft of his penis.

The aphrodisiac's effects were fading, but still potent. Beneath her bitter remorse, Celine sensed a submerged excitement. Odo's hand lay on her neck, his fingers twining in her hair. She knew that he would only have to caress her breasts, her thighs, to bring that hunger boiling to the surface.

She sat up, and his hand slipped from her neck to her shoulder. He stroked it, fingers moving softly.

He lay, half-reclining, banked up by cushions. One knee was raised, supporting his outstretched right arm. He turned the goblet in his fingers. It still contained some dregs of wine.

Lord Wraxall's left hand moved from Celine's shoulder and down her arm, brushing the swell of her breast. A drowsy need awakened, and she sighed.

'What, still eager?' murmured Odo. 'Madam, you surprise me. I expected you to be exhausted by now.'

He pulled her close.

'Can't we go away from here?' she whispered, against his skin. 'Be alone?'

'Why this sudden need for seclusion? I thought you found my poor efforts at entertainment stimulating.'

Celine wanted to deny it, but the memory of some of the lewd games she had witnessed returned to refute her. The groom, who had ogled Celine's breasts so fiercely on the steps of Acheron, had urinated into his girl's mouth before satisfying his lust between her thighs. Captain Cathcart had guessed correctly for once: Danae and the Shower of Gold.

Odo's steward, in a false beard, played Zeus and Ganymede with one of the stable lads. The sight of the two men coupling had excited Celine dangerously. When Mr Jeffries had parted the young man's buttocks and thrust within, she had felt a desperate urge for Odo to spoil her of that second, secret virginity. But she had not voiced her thought, and now she was glad of it. She had been wanton enough: at least that shame had been spared her.

Lord Wraxall's hand cupped her breasts one after the other, squeezing the pale half-globes. Her nipples felt tender, and very sensitive from the greed with which he had suckled on them. It only needed a touch to send arousal darting swiftly down to the centre of her sex.

Only a very little more of this, and she would forget her reservations and be begging him to mount her again. It was too late for modesty. If anyone wanted to watch, they would see nothing which had not been done before them time and again.

She let her hand move down Lord Wraxall's body, and ringed his rapidly hardening cock with her fingers. Odo shifted an inch or two, making it easier for her to pleasure him.

'Will you drink?' he asked, offering her the goblet.

Celine shook her head.

'As you will, madam. It's true you don't appear to be in need of it.' He took a sip himself, and grimaced. 'Nor, for that matter, am I.'

The groom who had acted in 'Danae' snored noisily on the cushions a few feet away. With a flick of his wrist, Lord Wraxall sent the dregs of wine spattering into the man's face.

The groom started awake with an oath and dodged, adroitly, as Odo threw the cup at his head. It fell, and rolled clattering across the floor, leaving droplets that burned like rubies where they crossed the track of the sun.

'You, whatever your name is.'

The groom scowled into the shadows, slitting his tilted hazel eyes against the light. Then he realised who had spoken. He snapped to his feet.

'Martin Piggott, my lord. Undergroom, my lord.'

'Aptly named,' remarked Odo. 'You were grunting swinishly enough. Get me some coffee, Piggott, and quick about it.'

The man bowed himself obsequiously out. Lord Wraxall moved to the edge of the tier and sat there, raking through his hair with long fingers.

'Come round here in front of me,' he said.

Celine complied. Head a little to one side, he examined her naked body. His look was like his touch: intimate and exciting. She took a step closer. Odo slipped his hands up her flanks.

'Do you know, Lady Wraxall, you please me greatly,' he said, with idle courtesy. 'It's a pity I have to attend the assizes tomorrow. Even a half-day's absence from your charms will seem too long. I swear a man might use you for a month and not be wearied. A month? Say three!'

Celine had not forgotten her maid's warning that Odo would soon tire of her, nor the threat that she would then be made over to his servants. The idea was frightening, and she thrust it aside.

Better to think of the assize-court. Liam was to be tried tomorrow, and he would go free. She had purchased Lord Wraxall's testimony, and Liam's life, with this carnal marriage. That was worth any shame or remorse.

Odo's fingers closed on her waist; he pulled her towards him. He caressed the rounded flesh of her buttocks. His mouth, warm and wet, travelled across her stomach.

'Yes,' he whispered. 'I'd say at least three. We have a precedent, after all: that was the time Persephone stayed in the Underworld. But I never finished that tale, did I?'

He drew Celine down until she knelt before him, and bent to kiss her. She went to him easily, opening her lips under his. This new life need not be so bad: though she could not love Odo, he had taught her to desire him. And three months seemed to her endless – a lifetime

'Listen, now,' he continued softly, between kisses. 'Demeter went into mourning for the loss of her daughter, snatched away by Hades. The crops failed, the fields were sterile. It was the world's first winter.'

He guided her hands to the junction of his parted thighs. Celine stroked his balls, feeling their skin crawl and tighten.

'And then?' she murmured. 'Ah, God, I want you inside me.'

'Oh, the girl was found. But Hades refused to release her. She had eaten, while in his dark kingdom: only three pomegranate seeds, but it was enough. She was forced to be his, for as many months. As you will be mine. Though it is not pomegranate seed that you will swallow.'

Tangling his fingers in Celine's hair, he pulled her

107

down until her lips brushed the head of his fully erect manhood.

'Suck me, Persephone,' he said.

Obediently, she dipped her head, and ran her tongue down from the tip of his phallus to his scrotum. His prick throbbed with readiness for her, a drop of moisture exuding from its eye. His groin smelt musky with the juices of the night. She could taste herself on him.

Celine closed her hand around the thick shaft of his penis, masturbating him, while she kissed his testicles. She rubbed the hard length from head to root. very slowly. She could feel his need. He was sweating and trembling for her, eager as a rutting stallion.

'It's not your hands I want, madam. Suck my prick.'

He held his phallus at the base, and pressed it fiercely between her lips. As she had in the black bedchamber, Celine teased his glans with her tongue. But Odo's lust was keyed too high to be satisfied by half-measures. He made her take all of it, driving the full length of his shaft into her, deep within her throat. Celine fought for air. Her eyes watered.

Odo pulled back sharply. His penis still crammed her mouth, but at least she could breathe.

'This is a skill I expect you to acquire,' he said, hoarsely. 'And fast, madam. Hold your breath and swallow as I thrust: inhale on the withdrawal.'

He pushed in to her throat once more. Celine's hands tightened on him: her nails dug into his thighs.

'Yes!' he hissed. 'Once more.'

It was none too simple at first to follow the instructions he gasped out. Even when she had learned the knack of it, she sometimes lost the rhythm and had to come up for air, choking and sobbing.

'Don't stop, damn you!'

'But you go too fast!'

Cursing, Odo scrambled back on to the cushioned ledge, dragging her with him. He lay on his back and positioned her so that she crouched over him. With hard hands he pushed her down on his rigid phallus.

'Take me at your own pace then,' he panted. 'But do it. Do it, madam. Take my whole prick. Take all of me. I want to come in your mouth.'

His head was between her parted thighs. He kissed and sucked her sex, while he thrust his penis once more between her lips. It was better for her this way, easier, more exciting. Celine gave a muffled cry of pleasure as she felt his tongue on her clitoris. She palpated his testicles, and swallowed the great shaft of his cock, in slow, repeated mouthfuls.

Lord Wraxall heaved beneath her. His hands clenched on her arse. His lips and teeth aroused her wildly. He thrust his tongue inside her, lapping the juices trickling from her vagina.

She felt herself approaching climax and sucked him harder, faster. Odo's hands moved across her back and buttocks in soft, scattering motions. All his control was gone now, lost in lust. He moaned and nuzzled her clitoris: his hips rocked more rapidly. His prick pulsed with orgasm and he clutched her to him. His seed filled Celine's mouth in hot spurts.

The pungent semen burned on her tongue as her own pleasure reached its apogee. She came, with a sob of ecstasy, to the convulsive movements of his mouth, and sank down across his body. She lay there, shuddering, for a while.

Odo moved one of her legs so that he could lie pillowed against her thighs. Celine roused herself, and kissed his penis.

'The devil's in that mouth of yours, Lady Wraxall,' he said. 'A little more practice and you could seduce Satan himself, I believe.'

'I thought I already had,' murmured Celine.

Lord Wraxall laughed. 'I don't aspire so high. Though I have my moments.'

There was something in his tone that penetrated her trance of satisfaction. Celine rose on her elbow to look at him.

'Shall you come to town with me on Saturday?' he said.

'Why?' asked Celine, with some suspicion.

Odo shrugged. 'Any number of reasons. To visit your father; to show off your trousseau. To keep me company. Perhaps to say goodbye to that lover of yours: I won't deny you a last farewell, after the enjoyment I've had from you.'

Celine's heart leapt. 'Do you really mean it?' she exclaimed.

'Assuredly,' he said. His eyelids lifted: he gave her a hard stare. 'But in the market square, madam, before the whole town. You will not touch, nor will you say one word I do not hear. And you will never see him again.'

'I promise,' said Celine in a shaken voice. 'If you grant me this, my lord, I won't ever, ever forget it. I'll – '

'I dislike sentimentality,' he said. 'No more of this mawkishness, I beg.'

He shook her off, and padded across the room to retrieve his brocade robe. Celine propped her chin on her hands, and watched him go. Her dark eyes shone. It was unbelievable that he would be so generous.

The Rotunda's door banged in the wind, then slammed shut. The groom pushed through the curtains from the lobby and stood at the top of the steps.

'Have you not forgotten something, Piggott? I sent you for coffee.'

The man vacillated. His face was white in the shadows. Odo beckoned: Piggott came slowly down the stairs, and stopped just out of arm's reach. He was shaking: a nervous tic made the corner of his mouth twitch.

'My orders are not to be disobeyed: I thought all my people knew that.'

Piggott cringed, and began to babble.

'There's a messenger come from town, my lord. They've sent for Cathcart and the other officers. The gaol was broke last night: gaolers drugged, sentries sand-bagged, prisoners away!'

Lord Wraxall snatched a handful of Piggott's neck-cloth and twisted it.

'All the prisoners? All? O'Brien too?'

'Every one,' wheezed the groom. 'There'll be an empty gallows Saturday.'

At first Celine did not understand the implication of his words. Then the full horror of their meaning burst upon her. She started to her feet with a wail of anguish.

Lord Wraxall whirled to face her. 'You,' he said, 'will be silent!'

'I won't!' she cried, in a throbbing voice. 'That's what you meant, isn't it? "A last farewell in the market square, before all the town"! You were going to take me to see him hang, you whoreson bastard! You've never had any intention of letting Liam go. And you swore – and I believed you. God's death, I thought you were being kind! How could I have been so stupid!'

Lord Wraxall curled his lip.

'I told you, madam,' he said, coolly. 'I tolerate no rivals. And watch your language.'

She flung herself on him, nails raking at his eyes. Odo thrust the choking groom aside and caught Celine's wrists in an iron grip, twisting them until she shrieked. He forced her down, to lie sobbing on the floor at his feet. He smiled.

'I have remarked before how well tears suit you, madam. Don't dry them all before I return with O'Brien's head. Or would you prefer another part – for old times' sake?'

'I hate you!' screamed Celine.

'I know,' he said. 'I find it most enlivening.'

He turned his back on her, and shrugged into the robe. He glanced once at Piggott. The groom flinched and scrabbled away.

'As for your wagging tongue,' said Lord Wraxall, in tones of ice, 'I'll deal with that later. You've cost me a rare pleasure, my man. Her face, as she watched him die, would have been a picture. For now, get a saddle on

111

Brown Molly. And find my valet. I want riding clothes, my cloak, and my sword.'

'I can't go in there,' hissed Bess, eyeing the scarlet lantern hanging over Mother Midnight's door. 'It's a knocking shop!'

A panel in the door opened, and a scarred face appeared at the grille.

'It's me, Dennis,' said Sally. 'I've got an appointment.'

The panel snapped shut. Bess heard numerous locks and bars being unfastened. A burly man in a striped apron stood in the doorway. He held a shaving brush in one hand. Lather dripped on to his shoes.

Sally grabbed Bess, who was still protesting, and jerked her inside. A short corridor led them into an enclosed courtyard, where lemon trees grew. Bess looked around her, open-mouthed. She'd had vague ideas of red plush and gilding: nothing like this.

The courtyard was shaded by a silk awning, painted with birds in flight. Marble benches stood round its walls. There was a fountain, and a central pool. Two naked girls, one brown and one white, bathed in the cool waters. Giggling, they splashed each other.

Through pillared arches, Bess could see the interior rooms. Cleaners, with mops, washed tiles of blue, green and gold. More girls, still tousled from sleep, wandered yawning among the buckets and ladders.

'Lord!' said Bess. 'Isn't it fine?'

'It's a mess,' said the man lugubriously. 'Midnight decided it would be a good idea to spring-clean, what with all the tarts working up at Acheron last night. Lucky if we open on time, the way things are going.'

Still grumbling, Dennis stumped away across the courtyard. He picked up a cut-throat razor and began to strop it.

'Come on, Chloe, let's be having you,' he said, testing the razor's edge with his thumb. 'I ain't got all day.'

The white girl clambered out of the pool. She lay down on one of the benches, raised her legs, and spread them

112

wide with her hands. Dennis gave her sex a thorough lathering and bent to shave the fine blonde stubble of her mound. He whistled as he worked.

'Well, I never did,' said Bess, in awed tones. 'What must that feel like?'

'Damned prickly when it grows out,' said Sally. 'Come on.'

'Well I never,' repeated Bess, looking back over her shoulder as she followed Sally into the house.

'In here,' said Sally, opening a door.

The room they entered was dimly lit, and crowded with hampers and baskets. A short, padded bench had been pulled out in to the centre of the floor. There were straps, stout webbing straps with buckles, attached to each of its legs. Mother Midnight sat on it, making entries in a leather-bound volume, while a woman rooted through the boxes.

'Masks, red velvet, 22,' called the woman.

'22,' echoed the madame, scribbling.

'Stockings, red silk, um, 43.'

'Who lost one?' Mother Midnight demanded.

The woman raised her head: 'Matilda.'

'Dock it from her wages,' said Mother Midnight, standing. 'Now find me a whip, and get out. Mistress Colney's not paying us to take inventory.'

Bess took the weapon Mother Midnight gave her and weighed it in her hand. Could she really wield the lash, use it to beat her way out of servitude into a new future? Bess conjured up the image of Sir James Fortescue, pleading abjectly. Her nipples hardened with desire. Yes, she could: and she would.

She shook out the lash and flicked it. The thong flopped mutely on the floor.

'Not like that,' said Mother Midnight. 'Stand up: straight, now; and keep your grip light. The action's all in the wrist.'

Carefully following her instructions, Bess snapped the whip. The lash flickered out, faster than the eye could follow, and made a satisfactory crack.

113

Mother Midnight looked at Bess with some respect.

'A natural, sure enough. Let's get you looking a bit more the part, then we'll start work.' She bustled across the room and flung open a couple of hampers. 'Give me a hand here, ladies. I've just the things to suit, but it's anybody's guess where we'll find them. The house is at sixes and sevens today.'

A little reluctantly, Bess put down the whip and began to turn over the contents of a box. She found feather cloaks and gauzy trousers, handcuffs and masks, fur gloves fringed with seed-pearls, and peculiar-shaped bottles that gurgled when shaken, but nothing that matched Mother Midnight's description of the costume they were seeking.

Bess had no idea what outrageous purposes half of the items could serve. She picked up a harness of green leather, with bells, and tried to work out how it went on. Her imagination baulked at the task.

'This what we're looking for?' enquired Sally. She held out a bundle of net and purple velvet.

'That's it. You should find a hat to match – there it is – and a pair of thigh-boots.'

Sally stirred the pile. She shook her head.

'No boots. The rest is all lost property by the look of it. Gloves and handkerchiefs. Oh, and a periwig.'

'Wigs aren't the half of it,' remarked Mother Midnight, as she delved into another hamper. 'We had a wooden leg once. I often wonder how he got home without it.'

While the madame continued to search, Sally dressed Bess in the costume which had been selected. She tilted the hat at a becoming angle on Bess's blonde ringlets, and arranged the long skirts.

'Take a look in the glass,' said Sally. 'See what you think.'

Bess moved to the tall mirror which leant against one wall and admired her image. A tight corset of purple velvet supported her bare breasts. Her waist was laced as slim as a lady's and, from mid-hip, a wide skirt of stiffened black net flared out. Her lower body and thighs gleamed through it.

Best of all was the hat. It was black velvet with a wide, turned-up brim. A great flurry of ostrich plumes, dyed purple and clasped with a glittering buckle, swept round to frame her face and rest lightly on her right breast. The colour reflected in her eyes, turning them violet.

Bess smiled, and struck an attitude. Her skirts were split in the centre front. As she moved, they parted to reveal the plump mound of her pubis. The juicy pink of her labia showed clearly through the pale curls.

'You're right,' said Sally to Mother Midnight. 'It needs boots.'

'Teach your grandmother,' replied the madame shortly. 'The mischief is I can't find them. Unless they're with the stuff that went to Acheron last night.'

Finding the right box, she plunged her arms to the elbows into its contents. Instantly, she jumped back, with a startled shriek.

'There's something in there! Something alive! Something big!'

Sally produced a pistol from among the folds of her skirt. She signed to the others. Bess and Mother Midnight took hold of the box's handles.

'Now!' cried Sally.

They hauled the hamper over. 44 red shoes, a pair of black satin thigh-boots, and a man in groom's livery rolled across the floor.

'Lord have mercy!' exclaimed Bess. 'It's Martin!'

The man rose to his knees and peered through the gloom at her.

'Bess?' he said. 'Oh, Bess, darling, hide me, won't you? You know I've always loved you. Don't let Lord Wraxall know where I am – please!'

Piggott grabbed a handful of her skirt. Interspersed with pleas for her protection, he gasped out the tale of his flight from Acheron. He'd crept into the hamper, not daring to wait for his master's return, and the carrier's

115

cart had brought him to Fort George, along with its load of weary whores.

Bess took a long step away, displaying a white flash of thigh. Not for one moment did she believe his protestations of love. He hadn't been near her since the night of the Government House ball. The night, she remembered, when he'd wheedled the story of Celine and Liam out of her. And wasn't it strange how Lord Wraxall had known that story?

'Bess?' quavered Piggott.

She ignored him, and gathered the other two women close. They whispered for a while. Then Sally helped Bess into the long satin boots. Once they were fastened to the top, Bess strutted forward to confront Piggott.

'You can have my help on conditions,' she said, with a narrow smile. 'You may not like them. Take down your breeches.'

Piggott's jaw dropped, and she cracked the whip. He looked from her, to the implacable face of Mother Midnight, to Sally's steady eyes above the pistol barrel. Then, with a whimper, he began to fumble at his clothes.

Martin's obedience sent a charge of eroticism streaking through Bess. She loved the feeling of power his subjection gave her. Her pink nipples were so hard that they tingled, and she could feel seeping wetness in her sex.

Piggott stepped out of his breeches and, on Bess's further command, stripped off the rest of his clothes. He had the beginnings of an erection.

She moved forward, and handled his prick contemptuously. It stiffened in her fingers. He looked down at her breasts, and raised his hands as if to cup them. Bess squeezed his genitals, very hard.

'Lie face down on the bench,' she said. 'Sally – tie him down.'

When Piggott was fastened by wrists and ankles, Bess stooped over him.

'You told Lord Wraxall about my lady, didn't you, Martin?' she whispered.

'No, I swear it!' gasped Martin. 'On my life!'

Bess straightened up. The lash fell. Martin sobbed and shook his head. She struck again. He writhed on the bench, tugging frantically at his bonds. The sight of his sufferings sent a tremor of excitement straight to her clitoris. She cracked the whip a third time.

'Yes,' he wept. 'Yes, I told him. He put me in fear.'

But Bess no longer cared that she had his confession. She brought the lash down again and again. It felt so good: as if she could orgasm just by beating him. Martin screamed and fought against his bonds.

'Enough!' said Sally sternly, and caught Bess's wrist. 'The object is to make your victim delight in his punishment. This one's past enjoyment.'

Bess stared at her, white breasts heaving as she panted.

'I want to see him crawl.' she hissed. 'It pleasures me.'

'There's other ways of humiliating a man,' said Mother Midnight, with a meaning smile. 'Sally, in the box under the window you'll find a dimity gown, and all that goes with it. Bring the things here, will you? I think our friend will do whatever we ask.'

The idea thrilled Bess, and Piggott submitted tearfully to her orders. He was untied and made to stand. Sally dropped a short linen shift over his bent head, and Bess put her knee in his back, lacing a corset cruelly tight around his waist. Mother Midnight combed out his rusty hair and planted a frilled cap on his head.

Piggott stood before them, red with shame and arousal. As the pain in his buttocks dwindled to heat and soreness, his penis had hardened. It jutted out before him, fully erect. But Bess was not going to satisfy him, even though her sex ached with lust.

Again and again she teased his cock softly, bringing him close to orgasm, but never letting him come. When he tried to use his hands on himself she stung him with the whip, until he thought better of it.

On her cold command, Piggott stepped into the petticoats. He shivered as the lacy folds brushed against his hard cock and still-smarting buttocks.

Mother Midnight tossed the gown over his head, and

fastened the bodice. Wadded handkerchiefs from the lost property chest were stuffed into the front of his chemise, giving him a respectable bosom. Then the Madame left him, and opened the door.

'Dennis!' she called.

'The perfect lady,' said Bess, squeezing Martin's sore arse. 'Why, Lord Wraxall would never dream that Mistress Colney's new chambermaid was his runaway groom. Unless he investigated further.'

'No chance of that,' said Sally, with a grin. 'Wraxall's got taste, after all. The figure's not bad but, damme, if I've ever seen a plainer wench.'

Clumping footsteps approached along the corridor.

'Dennis,' said Mother Midnight, as the man entered the room. 'Take Patricia here down to The Blue Anchor, will you, and give her in to Auguste's charge? Oh, and find Daniel on your way out. Send him here. I think Miss Brown will appreciate his talents.'

Dennis slipped his arm around Piggott's waist, and gave him a squeeze.

'Lay off!' growled Piggott.

'My, that's a husky voice,' Dennis said, leading Piggott away. 'And you're shaking! Why don't we stop off for a glass of hot rum? Best thing for an ague.'

Bess hardly noticed them go. Her heart beat fast and she quivered all over with unfulfilled desire. Humbling Martin had excited her so much that she thought she'd burst if she didn't get some relief.

In answer to her prayers, a young man put his head round the door. His eyes widened when he saw Bess. They travelled to the whip, to the padded bench, and back to her face again.

'Come in, Daniel,' said Mother Midnight. 'Meet Mistress Brown.'

He licked his lips and, with a secret smile, entered the lion's den.

Bess looked him over. Very nice, she thought. Very nice indeed.

Sinking to his knees before her, the youth peered up

118

through devastatingly long eyelashes. He was about eighteen years old, still short of his full growth, and slender. His skin was a deep copper-colour and he wore nothing but a pair of knee-length white cotton drawers, fastened at the waist with a cord. She could see the outline of his erect member quite clearly through the thin cloth.

'Will I suit?' he enquired, softly.

Bess looked down at Daniel. She nodded, once.

The boy slowly unfastened the waist-cord of his trousers, and let the simple garment fall. He sighed happily as she tied him down, and rubbed his belly against the padding of the bench. She reached beneath him, feeling the satiny skin of his stiff phallus. Its tip was already wet.

'Don't spare me, mistress,' murmured Daniel, as she raised the whip.

Chapter Nine

Celine sat at the opposite end of the dining table to her husband: a waste of damask stretched between them. Four candelabra, spaced along its length, cast their flickering light over silver and crystal.

She pushed the food about on her plate. Though she had eaten nothing since the wedding breakfast, more than 24 hours before, the thought of dining in Lord Wraxall's company repelled her.

'No appetite, madam?' he enquired. 'Pining for your lover, perhaps?'

'I prefer not to air such subjects before the servants.'

He signed to the footmen. Rupert cleared the table and removed the cloth. Charles laid out dishes of nuts, salt biscuits and butter: a decanter of port was placed at Odo's left hand.

'And now let us discuss the situation,' said Lord Wraxall, when they were left to themselves. 'Nothing has really changed. Indeed, you are the gainer. Your Mr O'Brien is clear away: off the island, or so my spies inform me. Right has triumphed. Perhaps I should gnash my teeth.'

It was impossible for Celine to tell if he was speaking the truth, or deceiving her again. Liam had been enraged by her marriage: but surely he could not be so angry as to flee St Cecilia without trying first to contact her, to take her with him? Was it possible that he loved her no longer?

'I want a divorce,' she said flatly.

'Like your mother? It runs in the family, I perceive.'

'My mother was never divorced! She died: she died of a consumption.'

'I am desolated to have to contradict you,' said Lord Wraxall. 'But Lys de la Roche eloped with a half-pay captain six months after your birth. We met in Venice in 1702. She was notorious by then. I can't recall if it was the Grand Duke Alexei she took up with when I discarded her, or that Italian marquis, what was his name – Montecatini.'

'It's not true!' cried Celine, hotly.

'Ask your father, if you don't believe me,' said Odo, with a little smile. 'Or anyone else of an age to remember: the scandal was immense. But to return to our own case, I'm afraid you will find it is "'til death do us part". Comfort yourself with the thought that, by virtue of nature, I will predecease you.'

He held up his glass of port to the light and looked through it.

'Moreover,' he added, meditatively, 'I think we have proved, beyond refutation, that your dislike of me does not preclude your enjoyment of – let us say – certain wifely duties.'

'No longer!' said Celine, through her teeth.

Lord Wraxall tossed back his wine.

'I doubt that,' he said. 'Shall we put it to the test?'

He moved round the table towards her, unbuttoning as he came. Celine closed her eyes and dug her nails into her palms: she concentrated on the pain as a defence against pleasure. It was a forlorn hope, and she knew it.

Odo's hands fell on her bare shoulders.

'Consult your flesh: listen to its needs,' he whispered, close to her ear. 'We have only just begun our honeymoon. And honey is sweeter if some stings are taken in the gathering.'

His hands moved gently, seductively, on her breasts. Celine gasped as she felt her nipples harden to his teasing. She hated herself for responding to the caresses of this man: a betrayer, a murderer in will, if not in fact. But she could not help it – even now, she still lusted for him.

'Come, stand for me.'

Eyes still firmly shut, she rose to her feet. Odo pushed her forwards until the upper part of her body was pressed against the table. He flung up her petticoats behind and parted her thighs. Warm and thick, his stiff manhood insinuated itself between her legs.

His fingers moved on her clitoris, sensitising it. She spread herself wider and turned her head, resting her cheek on the polished mahogany. He teased her sex with his cock-tip until she grew wet with urgency.

'Stay as you are,' breathed Odo. 'Bear with me, madam, for a moment.'

His footsteps moved away, returned. Something clicked down on the table beside her. Celine opened her eyes. It was a dish of butter. He scooped a little up. She closed her eyes again, tightly, knowing what he was about to do. She wanted it: she had wanted it since the night before, though she had never dared to ask him.

Odo parted her buttocks and delicately worked the grease between them. She felt it, oily and rich on her skin. He lubricated the tight rose of her anus, loosening the ring of muscles.

Then, gently but inexorably, he penetrated her.

He moved slowly. Well greased, his penis slipped easily into the narrow passage. Celine felt him go further, deeper, into her until she had taken all of him. He withdrew and thrust again, harder. On the borderline between pain and pleasure, the sensation made her moan with excitement.

'Ah, you like that, don't you?' he whispered. 'Move for me.'

Celine bucked under him, arching her back and slamming herself into his belly. He increased the driving tempo of his loins, while his busy fingers rubbed and probed her wet sex. The feel of him roused Celine to a peak of wantonness so high that it could not long continue. She cried out hoarsely as she came for him.

'Keep moving!' hissed Odo. 'I have not finished with you yet.'

He plunged on deep into her anus, taking his own pleasure to the last limits. His control served him well, extending the time minute by minute until Celine shook with exhaustion. At last, very suddenly, he pulled out of her. She felt his hot semen spattering her thighs and buttocks. Odo drew a long breath of satisfaction and stood back.

'You may go, Lady Wraxall,' he said. 'I will take my port alone.'

Sir James Fortescue strode into the entrance hall and tossed his hat onto a marble-topped table. He'd wasted the morning at Acheron paying a courtesy call on his daughter and her husband, and taken the miles back at a gallop. He was impatient to be with Bess again.

Ever since that night, two weeks ago, when Sal Colney had brought her to him, he had been besotted. Absence from her was a greater torture than any she inflicted on his willing flesh.

Taking the stairs two at a time, he made for her room.

'Come in!' she called.

Bess lounged on a sofa under the window. She wore blue velvet, and she swung a diamond necklace on one finger, watching the sunlight glitter on the gems. Her mouth was set in an uncompromising straight line.

'You got my present, then,' he said, nervously. 'Don't you like it?'

She crooked a finger. 'Come here.'

Sir James took half a step forward. Bess gave him a long look, and his heart began to pound. She was going to be wonderfully hard on him.

Shaking, as much with fear as with excitement, Sir James stripped off wig and clothing. When he was

123

completely nude, he fell to his hands and knees and crawled across the carpet towards her. He was panting.

Bess extended one foot.

'If you make a present to a lady,' she explained, while he kissed her instep worshipfully, 'it ought to be something she wants. Get up now, put your hands behind your back. I'm vexed – very.'

Trembling a little, he obeyed her. Bess reached between his legs and began to play with his genitals. A plaited leather switch lay on the couch beside her. His prick swelled in anticipation of the sweet pain to come.

'Teach me better, mistress,' he said huskily.

'Not just yet,' replied Bess. 'There's something I want you to watch first. It's going to be your job from now on, James, so pay close attention!'

Bess lay back on the couch. She linked her hands behind her head, gazing at the fat cupids painted on the ceiling.

'You can come out now,' she called.

A man stepped from behind the screen which hid the washstand and commode. He was burly and scarred, and he wore a barber's apron.

'Meet Dennis,' said Bess.

The knowledge that another man was witness to his humiliation shook Sir James deeply, but he did not dare to complain. He merely looked at Bess with shamed and pleading eyes. Dennis handed him a shaving mug.

'Get a good lather up,' he said.

Bending over Bess, the barber rolled back her skirts and petticoats to her waist. He stroked the exuberant curls that covered her mount of Venus. Thrusting one meaty hand into her crotch, he felt about there.

Sir James worked the brush diligently, casting possessive glances at Bess. She was enjoying herself, trying to make him so jealous that he'd rebel. And then she'd devise some new torment in retribution. He shivered, remembering the time she had left him chained in the dog-kennel half the night.

Dennis snapped his fingers: 'Brush!'

Sulkily, Sir James handed it over. Dennis began to work the lather into Bess's pubic hair. He paid a lot of attention to her clitoris, soaping it luxuriantly until she sighed and squirmed.

'Razor!' demanded Dennis.

The barber whistled softly through his teeth as the sharp steel glided in long strokes over Bess's mound. Sir James could hear the crisp sound of the hair being cut away.

She had said this would be one of his duties from now on. The idea that she would permit him to soap and shave her regularly – perhaps even every day – made him sweat and lick his lips.

'Smooth as a baby's bum,' said Dennis. 'That'll be half a guinea.'

'Pay him, James,' murmured Bess, languorously.

She reached down and trailed her hands over the newly naked skin. Her clitoris protruded, bare of concealment: she played with it, purring with delight. Unable to look away, Sir James groped blindly for a coin in the pocket of his discarded coat.

The minute the barber was gone, Sir James sank to his knees and crawled back across the carpet to Bess. Beyond caring for the consequences, he plunged his face between her open legs, sucking and kissing her in a frenzy of jealous desire. She tasted of lavender soap.

Bess let him stay there, moaning and working his tongue inside her, while she moved restlessly under his caresses. Then she sat up abruptly and pushed him back until he fell full length on the floor. Holding her skirts high, she lowered herself slowly onto the thick shaft of his penis.

Sir James sobbed out his gratitude as he felt the warm clasp of her vagina around his cock. She clamped his shoulders to the floor and rode him hard and fast, careless of his pleasure, until she came with a yelp of enjoyment. Then she dismounted, and plumped herself down on the sofa again.

Sir James whimpered. He cupped his hands around

the root of his wet, erect phallus, holding it so that it pointed stiffly up at the pink bottom of a cherub on the ceiling. He looked at Bess longingly.

'Mistress, you aren't going to leave me like this, are you?' he asked, in a coaxing voice. 'Don't I deserve a little mercy? Please?'

'You might let a girl get her breath,' said Bess, with some severity.

Sir James wriggled with excitement at her tone. When she said nothing further, he dared to get to his knees. Bess picked up the riding-switch and teased the tip of his cock with it. Greatly encouraged, he shuffled closer.

'Not so fast,' she said. 'You haven't told me how Lady Celine is, yet. Did you give her my message?'

'I couldn't,' said Sir James. 'Oh, don't look at me that way! Wraxall was there the whole time. Very fond of her: hardly lets her out of his sight.'

'That I can believe,' replied Bess, with a frown. 'The question is, if she's fond of him? I've got my doubts. I'll have to think of some other way to get word from her. Drat! Can't you do anything right?'

Sir James bent to kiss the hem of her gown.

'It seems not,' he said humbly.

Bess sniffed. 'Bend over my lap,' she commanded.

Trembling, Sir James laid his body across her knees.

'Prepare yourself,' said Bess, and he tensed.

The first blow felt like fire, agonising and hot. He heard Bess sigh, and raised his backside eagerly to take the second stroke: this one cut like knives of ice. He drove his cock against her leg, loving the contrast between the sharp pains she inflicted on his arse, and the sweet excitement of her velvet-clad thigh, warm and rounded under his throbbing glans.

He writhed and groaned as the beating continued. Bess flogged him longer than she had ever done before, crying out with increasing passion at each blow of the switch. Sir James knew that she gained as much pleasure from inflicting his punishment, as he got from receiving it. They were perfectly matched.

126

He tried to stifle his cries of anguish, to endure as long as possible. He wanted Bess to join him in that melting moment where torture became ecstasy, and the getting and giving of pain brings supreme release.

'Bess, I love you!' he cried. 'I love you!'

And as he spoke, he came. The excruciating smart in his buttocks pulsed with each spurt of his semen. It was the best he had ever known.

'There, there,' she said, and stroked his sore arse.

When he was once more composed enough to pay attention to anything beyond the sensations of his flesh, Sir James turned his head to look at her. Bess was flushed and smiling. His heart leapt. He knew he had held back long enough for her to find satisfaction. He sank back to his knees and rubbed his cheek against her skirts.

'You've ruined my new frock, James,' she said.

'I'll buy you another,' he whispered. 'A hundred! Anything you want!'

She giggled. 'A set of razors might be nice.'

'I shall have them especially commissioned,' he said, extravagantly, 'with tortoiseshell handles, and your initials set in diamonds.'

'Ah, you're mad about diamonds,' she said. 'They don't suit me at all. Maybe you should wear them, since you like them so much.'

She made him stand, and knotted the fine chain firmly around his balls, until the bonds were tight, but not galling. The brilliants glinted among the grizzled bush of his pubic hair.

'Keep that on, to remind you that sapphires are my favorite stones,' said Bess. 'I'll have to get changed now. Come back to escort me to dinner.'

Sir James drew himself up. He managed to look remarkably dignified, despite his nudity and the jewels marking his subjection.

'No servant of the King ever accepted decoration by his sovereign with so great a feeling of honour,' he declared, emotionally. 'I am proud to wear your chains.'

He bowed, kissed her hand, and turned away to dress. When he was ready to leave, he paused and cleared his throat.

'I meant what I said, you know,' he told her, going red in the face. 'Damme, Bess, if I don't love you to distraction. I'll go and order the razors.'

Ceres finished buckling the last of the leather cuffs around Celine's wrists and ankles, and checked the snugness of their fit.

'*Fini*,' she said.

Celine marked her place in the book she was reading, and glanced at herself in one of the ebony-framed mirrors. She wore a robe of black silk strips, held together at the waist and neck with silver cord. Her breasts peeped out between the bands of silk: their nipples had been painted with vermilion. Her mouth was a scarlet slash and her hair hung loose down her back, as Odo preferred it.

'Is my lord back from town, do you know?' she asked.

'A few minutes since, madame,' said Ceres.

'Then why do you wait? I've no wish to watch you coquetting with him.'

The maid dropped a curtsey so exaggerated as to be verging on insult, and swished away. Celine went back to her book. A silver clip, hanging from the black leather cuff on her wrist, twinkled in the candlelight as she turned the page.

Nor shall our love-fits, Chloris, be forgot,
When each the well-looked linkboy strove t'enjoy,
And the best kiss was the deciding lot
Whether the boy fucked you, or I the boy.

It was just like Odo to make her a present of such lewd verses. She wondered if he wanted her to be shocked – horrified perhaps, and resistant to his demands. Maybe that was why he'd ordered the cuffs, and the chains on the bedposts, that waited to be snapped on to them.

Celine let her eye drift down the page, not taking in the rest of the poem, outrageous as it was. She had got through the last four weeks largely by not thinking at all about her situation. But sometimes, as now, she could not help herself. And then it hurt: dear God, it hurt.

If Lord Wraxall had been anything but a devil in human form Celine would, she knew, have been reconciled to her new life by now. He could even be tender: falling into softly breathing sleep, with her clasped in his arms, after a night of love as sweet and prolonged as any she had hoped to share with Liam. In the morning he would wake her with a kiss, and revive the hours of darkness one last time; looking down at her, and smiling to see her drowsy pleasure as he moved inside her.

But there were other times.

There were days when the glitter in his eyes warned her that she could expect no mercy. Days when he used her. Nights when he roused her to extremes of need and then refused to satisfy her, or made her wield the fascinum, while he watched, to bring herself to climax. Every room in the house had been witness to his lust, from the library to the servants' hall.

He had coupled with her on the floor, under the statue of dancing Kali; in the stable; on the stairs; on the spinet, reaching his orgasm with a great discordant clash as the keys stuck.

He had hunted her through the cane on horseback, flung her down and ripped her clothes to rags, before taking her as roughly as a beast. Then he abandoned her there, for the field-hands to find, while he rode on to Fort George; returning the next day heavy-lidded and languid from God knows what debaucheries.

A tear dropped on to the open book, then another. She was utterly alone. Liam had sent no word, as Odo daily – and hurtfully – reminded. She feared that he no longer cared, or even thought of her.

She dried her eyes, and smeared her hand angrily over

the open volume, wiping away the wetness there. She had to stop thinking. It did no good.

Turning another page she tried to concentrate, but all the time Celine felt her attention slipping away from the Earl of Rochester's bawdy verses into listening, listening, for Odo's footsteps in the corridor.

At last they came.

'I'm glad to find you so fond of reading,' said Lord Wraxall, lightly, as he entered. 'Perhaps I can find something else to suit your taste.'

He was in shirt-sleeves, and wore the kidskin breeches and high boots in which he'd ridden to town. His eyes were very still, the pupils so large that they almost eclipsed the iris.

She had never seen him look quite that way before. It woke a deep sense of alarm in her. Celine glanced nervously at the bed and its waiting chains. Tonight might not be the safest time to be bound and helpless.

Lord Wraxall bent to brush her forehead with his lips.

'Madam, I am heated with riding,' he said. 'Will it discompose you if I open the doors to the veranda?'

She watched him as he jerked the black curtains wide and stalked outside. He leant on the railing, looking in to the darkness. There was no moon, and the stars shone out all the more brightly in its absence.

A little wind rustled through the leaves of the vine. With the doors open Celine could hear the sound of drums, far off, pulsing heavily.

'Listen!' said Odo, 'The slaves are holding a fetish-dance in the forest. They are calling up the gods of Africa.'

'I wonder you don't forbid such heathen practices,' said Celine. There was something behind all this, she knew. A month's marriage had made her familiar with the way he went about things.

'Why should I? They are my faithful servants. Let them dance and drink and worship their bogeymen. The *umbanda* does no harm to them or me. Besides, they have my permission. Call it a reward.'

Celine bit her lip. Now it was coming.

'A reward for what?' she asked, with some trepidation.

Odo strolled back indoors and tossed a sheet of paper onto her lap.

'Why, madam, for bringing this to my hand, and not to yours,' he said.

It was a letter, addressed to her in an unfamiliar, flowing script.

'You've read it,' said Celine, looking at the broken seal.

'Indeed I have.'

With shaking fingers, she unfolded the paper.

My very dear Lady Celine, it began. *Let me have word quickly if you are well and happy. I am worried about you, as Lord W's reputation is what one does not like to think on. Being very close to your father now, I am sure that he can be brought around my finger if you want to return home. Put your answer in the hollow tree by the gates. The friend who writes this for me, will send it on by a safe hand. If you wish to leave him, and Lord W does not allow you ink and paper, ask your father, next time he calls, if he has had word from Miss Prudence about the figured satin she promised. I will know what to do. Your devoted servant. X. (Bess Brown, her mark).*

'It's Sal Colney's writing,' said Lord Wraxall, when she had finished. 'That woman is a constant irritation to me. You make no comment, madam.'

Celine tossed the letter aside. She knew she had to placate Odo immediately. The stillness of his eyes was uncanny. His voice, though quiet, was iron-cold: when he was cold, he was dangerous.

She put her arms round his neck, and kissed him.

'Why should I wish to leave you, my lord?' she whispered. 'Don't you know how impatiently I have been waiting for your return?'

Her nipples brushed the fabric of his shirt. Moving her hands down to his buttocks, she pulled him close. Within the the tight leather riding-breeches, she could feel his penis swelling into hardness.

131

Odo bore her back towards the bed and flung her down on to its sombre coverlet. He knelt above her, holding her between his thighs, and passed his hands slowly across her body.

'Your impudent friends have put me in a quandary, Lady Wraxall,' he said, caressing her absently. 'I fear a separation between us will not suit my purposes. Your father is a fool, with a lamentable taste for being humiliated by strapping viragos, but even he is not such a idiot as to let me keep your property while losing your person.'

She kissed him again, darting her tongue between his lips.

'Why need you part with either?' she murmured. 'No other man could satisfy me as you do.'

Odo cupped her breasts and began to tease her nipples with his thumbs.

'That is very likely so,' he said. 'Certainly it was true of your mother. I remember a time at the Carnival, just after I left her. She took every man she danced with, and the gondoliers as well; none of them could quench the fire I'd raised. You may well be the same. Shall we see?'

Celine grew suddenly very afraid.

'What do you mean to do?'

'I? Nothing. It is Charles and Rupert who will do all that needs to be done. You shall be chained, and used by them while I watch. Your hand, madam, if you please.'

'I won't do it!' cried Celine, struggling fiercely. She had accepted much from Odo, but not this. Never this. She would die rather than endure being prostituted to his footmen.

'Yes, you will,' he said, and leant across her to secure her right arm.

Half-crazy with fear, she snapped her teeth on his wrist. She kicked, shrieked and fought against him, finding from somewhere a strength she had never dreamt existed. There was blood on his shirt where her teeth had met.

She flailed her legs, and drove her fingers at his eyes.

Her nails dragged long streaks of red across his face. Laughing, he struck her hand aside. Then one of her thrashing legs connected sharply with his groin, and his laughter changed to a gasp of pain.

As his grip on her body loosened, she struck again. Her heel drove into the juncture of his parted thighs. This time, he screamed. She kicked him again, harder, and in the same place.

Lord Wraxall toppled from the bed and crashed to the floor. He rocked there, knees drawn up, his hands clutching his balls. His face was twisted with agony. He made a small, wet, mewing sound.

Celine raced for the open window and swung herself over the veranda rail, feeling for the vine's support with bare feet. Her silks caught on a projection and she ripped then away. In the black bedchamber, she could hear her husband groaning as he dragged himself upright.

Celine fought her way down through the vine, half climbing, half falling. She jumped the last five feet to the gravel drive.

Odo staggered out to the veranda above, shouting for his servants in a voice made harsh with pain. As Celine fled into the darkness, she heard him calling for the dogs to be unleashed.

She ran as she had never run before, fists balled and arms pumping, along the paths between the whispering cane, and in to the forest.

No starlight penetrated the thick canopy of leaves. Bushes snatched at her with thorny hands. The track was narrow, twisting: its stones cut her feet. Ahead of her, she glimpsed firelight, heard drumming. Behind, growing nearer, came the ferocious music of Lord Wraxall's hounds.

A tree put out its root to trip her, and Celine fell headlong.

Something moved in the thicket beside the trail, rustling, coming closer. She scrambled to her feet and ran on, weaving now, each breath painful. She fell again. The movement in the bushes was very close.

133

Celine turned at bay.

A black shadow rose from the undergrowth. Hard hands closed on her and she smelt the musky sweat of a man. She struggled with the last of her dwindling strength as he lifted her and slung her across one naked, brawny shoulder.

Birds, woken by her despairing scream, flew up with a great clatter of wings. They circled above the trees, calling to each other. As she fell into grateful unconsciousness, Celine heard them coming back to roost.

Chapter Ten

Celine ran through the forest of a dream. Black, swaying trees crowded a black landscape: they bent to touch her as she passed. Twigs that were fingers caressed her naked flesh.

Then she was running on water, across the sea to a ship. The ship was a house. Celine ran up and down its staircases, through corridors full of clocks, or black and white flowers, or familiar people with strangers' faces.

She ran into a room: a man was there. He was a shadow, but she knew he was Liam. He came to her, and touched her. His hands fitted themselves to her body, going around, above, below.

His manhood was stiff with desire. She stroked it until his ejaculation welled over on to her hands. It did not surprise her that his sperm was black, nor that he was not Liam at all, but Odo.

He sank down upon her. He filled her mouth, her vagina, her anus. He pleasured her slowly, with a master's skill. Her climax took her, but when she tried to cry out, she was dumb.

The man devoured her. He invaded her. If she could recognise him, name him, she could escape. But now he was not Odo either.

Between brow and chin his skin was featureless, he had no face. And, though there were no openings in the walls, the trees were looking in.

Celine's eyes snapped wide. Her heart thudded in her breast.

She was curled on her side, hands between her legs, on fine linen scented with rose-leaves. A silk nightgown was rucked up to her armpits. She stirred, looking around her in disorientation.

She had never seen this place before. The chamber she lay in was small, white, windowless: like a cell. Oblique afternoon light fell from a shaft in the ceiling and made a square on the wall. There was the narrow bed she lay on, a chair, a table. A door opened onto a spiral staircase. Someone out of sight was climbing it, their heels clacking on the treads.

Had she fled from Odo only to fall victim to a stranger? Or was it Lord Wraxall himself, coming to get her? Was this prison-like room the place he had chosen for her punishment, his revenge? Celine scrambled out of bed, and picked up the chair. She held it raised in defence.

'What the devil do you think you're doing?' said Sally, irritably, as she came round the last bend in the stairs and saw Celine, backed into a corner.

The chair clattered to the floor.

'Oh! Mistress Colney!' sobbed Celine, and flew into her arms.

Sally allowed her only a few moments to indulge in the relief of tears and grateful exclamations; then she drove Celine back to bed.

'I'm sorry I wasn't here when you woke,' she said. 'Auguste and I have been taking it turn and turn about to sit with you. He came to fetch me: said you were having a nightmare.'

Celine shivered, remembering.

'Well, I'm not surprised you had bad dreams,' said Sally. 'You're cursed lucky I had my watchers out. What in Hell's name made you attempt such an imprudent

136

escape? Of all the dam' fool, hare-brained things to do – didn't you get the letter?'

'Yes,' said Celine, bleakly. 'From Lord Wraxall's hand.'

Sally looked a little mollified.

'I understand,' she said. 'Hard on you, was he? Well, there was always a risk things might miscarry, and so I told Bess.'

'Is she here?' Celine asked. 'Can I see her? Is she all right?'

'Blooming,' said Sally. 'And, if she's the sense to match her God-given talents, well on her way to being your step-mama by now.'

She stemmed Celine's startled enquiries with a wave of her hand.

'It's not Bess Brown's future that must concern us now, girl, but yours,' she pointed out. 'Wraxall's already come here to Laissez Faire twice. He ain't advertising your flight – he's said nothing – but he knows I'm hiding you.'

Celine caught her hand in a painful grip.

'He mustn't take me!' she cried.

'Don't worry, this room's impregnable,' replied Sally, soothingly 'Old Sedley, who built this house, was a Jacobite. No-one ever found his chaplain during the religious wars, and Odo Wraxall won't find you. Have a heart, girl, you're breaking my fingers.'

'Sorry,' muttered Celine, releasing her. 'It's hard to believe I'm safe. And even if I am, what do I do now?'

'The question is, what do you want to do?' said Sally, somewhat tartly. She flexed her hand, and shook it, to restart the circulation.

Celine sat up and hugged her knees. Her flight from Lord Wraxall had been an act of the moment, born of fear. There had been moments of sweetness in her marriage; hours – even days – of passion, whose memory aroused her still. But there was a sour aftertaste to every recollection. Much she had learnt to enjoy, but he had pushed her too far. And the thought of the punishment he might exact for her rebellion terrified her.

137

'I can't return to Acheron,' she said slowly, working it out as she spoke. 'Will my father let me stay at Government House, protect me? Bess thought – '

'Bess is over-confident,' interrupted Sally. 'If Wraxall knows where you are, he'll take you back, as sure as gun's iron. And Sir James has invested too much in the alliance to protest about it. Here's an idea though: what about your Mr O'Brien? He's on the account now; quartermaster aboard one of Tremaine's ships. I've got friends who could take you to join him.'

'Oh, if only I could!' whispered Celine, her eyes filling with tears. 'But I don't know if Liam still loves me, you see. He was very bitter when I married.'

'Only natural he should be jealous,' said Sally. 'What of it? O'Brien would be a fool to turn a wench like you away. If he's doubtful, show him a few of the harlot's tricks I don't doubt you've been taught. After that, he'll be trailing you like a dog does a bitch.'

Celine floundered between hope and dread. She yearned to fly to Liam. But what if, despite Mistress Colney's assurances, he rejected her?

'I can't just throw myself at him like that,' she said, unhappily. 'I have to know he still wants me. Could your friends take him a message?'

Sally turned up her eyes in exasperation.

'Send him word if you must. But you're making a cursed mistake. If he's as angry as you say, a letter may not do the trick. Best take him by storm.'

'I'd rather write,' said Celine in a small, determined voice.

'Very well,' snapped Sally, turning to go. 'It's your decision. Now try to get some rest, or you'll not be fit to travel when the time comes.'

She left, closing the door behind her with an irritated bang.

Celine lay down again, and buried her nose in the pillow.

'If the time comes,' she said sadly to herself. 'Oh, Liam!'

* * *

138

'Faugh!' said Sally, under her breath. 'Milk and water!'

She clattered briskly down the spiral stair and let herself out of the priest's hole. Auguste was waiting for her in the gallery. He turned a boss on the panelling and the portrait of King James II, which masked the exit, swung back against the wall and locked into place.

'Of all the weak-minded, woolly-brained, idiotic nincompoops I've ever met, I declare,' said Sally roundly, 'that girl is the worst! Lord knows what Wraxall sees in her!'

'I could tell you,' said Auguste.

Sally looked at him sidelong. He had an erection.

'You didn't – ?'

'No, Sal, I didn't,' answered Auguste, with a rueful smile. 'But it wasn't for lack of wanting to. She was dreaming, touching herself: hot for it. I could have been in her before she woke.'

'Why weren't you?' asked Sally. She swayed her hips provocatively. 'Are you sure you're in good health, old friend?'

Auguste took her in his arms.

'Never better,' he said, as he nuzzled at her throat. 'But it would have been abuse to take her in her sleep. I'll leave rape to the plantation owners. I prefer my women to know what they want, and to ask me for it nicely.'

Sally laughed, low and husky.

'If you please, then, Monsieur Toussainte.'

'Here?'

'Here,' she said. 'Against the wall.'

He pressed her back to the panelling, and pulled up her skirts. His tongue thrust deep in to her mouth. Sally responded with a sigh of happiness. Her fingers found his belt and pulled it free of the buckle. Slowly, with long pauses while they caressed, she undid his buttons.

He was naked beneath the white linen breeches. His penis sprang forward, ready to her hand, and she stroked it with encircling fingers, delighting in its virile size and hardness, and its smooth, black skin.

Auguste freed her breasts from the bodice of her gown, squeezing and sucking them until Sally moaned with desire.

'Don't keep me waiting,' she said softly. 'No long preliminaries. I want to have you inside me.'

Auguste smiled at her, and parted her legs with his hand. Sally felt his fingers rubbing at her clitoris, then moving back to penetrate her. She was juicy and succulent, eager for the feel of his cock.

'Say please,' he whispered.

Sally nibbled his earlobe, and murmured her request again. She plunged her hand into his breeches, playing with his testicles, drawing them towards her until the whole of his manhood was bare. His prick stood up proudly, its foreskin retracted in readiness, its uncapped glans dark as a plum.

Auguste swung her up in his arms and entered her with an easy thrust of his hips. He covered her breasts with kisses. Sally twined her legs around his waist and clung to him, answering his movements. His cock was thick and warm, fitting her snugly. His strong hands clenched on her buttocks.

'Please!' Sally cried again.

Auguste drew back until he was almost outside her, and then gave her his cock again, every inch of it.

'You like me to do that?' he asked, rotating his hips. 'You like it? And this, and this?'

Sally groaned her agreement.

He fucked her greedily, using the strength of his legs to power his demanding prick. He moved in the tight, wet softness of her vagina, pulling out and pushing in until Sally lost all control. Her fingernails dug into his back. She felt herself coming, and sobbed his name repeatedly as the sweet satisfaction spent itself.

Auguste's prick pulsed with climax while the tingling aftershocks of her orgasm still lingered. For a few minutes she hung panting on his neck. Then, when she had caught her breath, he let her down.

'Thank you,' said Sally. 'I needed that.'

'The pleasure was all mine,' he said, buckling his belt.

Sally dimpled, and her green eyes narrowed with amusement. 'Not all of it.'

She leant against him comfortably as they walked down the gallery. Dead Stuarts looked down their noses as the pair passed between them.

'Better if we don't linger too near the priest's hole,' murmured Sally. 'We've been betrayed once, over the letter, and I don't want to risk it again.'

'Let's get our guest off the premises, then,' said Auguste.

'I'd like nothing more,' said Sally. 'The devil is the wench won't leave. Says she doubts that lover of hers still wants her. I was angry enough, at the time, but I can see the child's point.'

'If that's what she fears, she was right to refuse,' Auguste said, frowning. 'It'd be cruel to send her to New Providence on a venture. First, we don't know when O'Brien will fetch up there. Second, if he rejects the poor girl, where would she turn?'

'I thought of asking Kalinda to look out for her,' said Sally.

'You're crazy! I trust Kalinda – up to a point – but not the men she runs with. What would happen if Calico Jack Rackham got a sight of Lady Celine? Or that lecher Captain Everie? Or Blackbeard, God help us all?'

'I know, I know,' said Sally gloomily. 'She'd do better with Wraxall: he's no more perverse than they, and at least he washes. Blackbeard took his last bath at the midwife's hands. Well, it looks as if we'll have her quartered on us for a while, at least until we get the answer from O'Brien.'

'Let's hope he agrees to take her, then,' Auguste said, as he opened the gallery door. 'For if not, I can see we'll have the girl with us until doomsday. And next time she has a wet dream, I might not be able to resist waking her, and asking if there's any help I might give.'

* * *

141

More than four hundred leagues of sea lay northwest between the Windward Islands and the Bahamas, between St Cecilia and Nassau. An albatross might have made the journey in three days, never stopping, sleeping on the wing.

Celine's letter to Liam had to take a slower route.

A smuggling vessel carried the tear-blotted sheet to Guadeloupe. From there a native pirogue conveyed it on to Isla de Vecques. It passed through the hands of a cane-factor on Hispaniola, an emerald-dealer in Spanish Town, and a nun in Guantanama. It crossed Cuba and, nearly a month after Celine had written it, arrived at its destination: Cantina Kalinda in the pirate stronghold of New Providence.

The last in Sally's long line of messengers pushed his way into the cantina's main room. A fiddler perched on a barrel, sawing away at a jig. Gamblers outstared each other, pistols lying ready by their heaps of coin.

Dōna Kalinda Sagrado, the notorious Rose of Havana, took the letter held out to her and slowly spelt out the name on its cover. She'd never heard of Liam O'Brien, but she had no doubt he'd turn up. Everyone on the wrong side of the law did, sooner or later.

She raised her ruffled skirt high and slipped the letter into her garter for safe-keeping. She tossed one of the pieces of eight from the heap in front of her to the messenger. Picking up her cards once more, she arranged them in a fan and peeped over it at her opponent. He was very drunk and very youthful. If he didn't keep his mind more on the game, and less on her, he would also shortly be very poor.

She leant forward, making sure he caught a glimpse of her pointed, brown breasts down the neckline of her blouse.

'Your call,' she said.

The young buccaneer took another swig from his flagon of rum and gunpowder, and ogled her with helpless lust. Part Spanish, part Indio, and part black, Kalinda Sagrado combined the beauties of all three races in a mix of exotic perfection. From her high-piled hair to her tiny feet she was faultless, with skin like dusky satin and a waist two hands could span.

The buccaneer moaned softly as she moved her leg under his caressing hand. Then he stood up and pushed all his remaining money towards her.

'There's more'n three hundred there,' he slurred. 'All I've got. You can have it, Kalinda, every groat of it, if you'll jus' go upstairs with me.'

'A cardinal once paid more than that to touch my foot,' she said, proudly. 'I am the Rose of Havana. Any woman in New Providence would be cheaper, Davy.'

'I want you,' he growled.

Kalinda looked round the room, and caught the eye of one of her paid bullies. The thug nodded, and lounged across to stand beside the door.

'Let us make an agreement, then,' Kalinda said, once the man was in position. 'We shall draw just one card each. Aces high. If you win, I will forgo my price. If I win, you are mine.'

Davy stuck his thumbs in his belt and swaggered a little.

'Reckon I can handle that,' he said.

'I don't mean as my lover,' she told him. 'I mean I will own you. I can sell you. You're strong, young. The silver-mines at Potosi would pay well for your body. Will you play? Or are you scared?'

'I'll do it,' he said, through gritted teeth. 'But if I win, you've got to let me stay all night.'

Kalinda shuffled the deck and set it down before him with a snap.

'Cut,' she said.

With a hand that shook slightly, the young man made his play.

'Queen of Hearts!' he shouted, joyfully. 'Come on, you'll not beat that!'

The fiddler stopped in mid-chord. The dancers staggered to a standstill. Kalinda ran her fingers along the edge of the pack, feeling for the nick that marked the card she sought. She split the deck, turning it up.

'King of Clubs,' she said, and smiled. 'You lose.'

The young pirate looked around him wildly, and made a bolt for the open door. He did not get through it. The man waiting there struck him down with a cudgel. Davy dropped in a shapeless huddle to the floor.

Kalinda yawned daintily, and scooped the coins into the lap of her skirt.

'Foolish boy,' she said. 'Lock him away with the others.'

She picked her way among the revellers and went upstairs, where Captain Vane, her latest particular spark, was waiting.

The fiddler struck up again. Someone fired a brace of pistols into the ceiling, just to liven things up a bit. The party continued.

It was still in full swing at dawn, though there had been several more casualties by then. Blackbeard had accounted for two of them, explaining with engaging frankness that, if he didn't shoot someone, now and again, people would forget who he was.

The sound of a conch blowing woke Kalinda. Three blasts: a friendly ship had been sighted, coming into the roads. The sun was just rising. An offshore wind racketted among the palms. An hour, at least, for the vessel to beat in against it. Time enough. She smiled, and rolled on to her stomach.

Captain Vane lay sprawled across the bed. He was a large man; blonde, shaggy, and heavy set. His prick was as magnificently well-built as the rest of him, even in its flaccid state. Kalinda sucked it into her mouth.

'G'way,' he mumbled, turning on his side. 'Let a man get some rest.'

Kalinda looked at the pirate captain with unfriendly eyes. Vane by name, and by nature: but with little to be vain about. Last night he was unable to get it up more than twice, falling asleep while she still hungered for

144

more. And this morning he refused her! Nobody did that twice to the Rose.

She rose lithely to her feet, flung on some clothes and stormed out. Swaying down the trodden-earth street, Kalinda held her head high, as befitted one who was queen in her community.

When she reached the sheltered cove she used for bathing, Kalinda stripped, and ran into the surf. She swam hard and fast, heading far out to sea, hoping that exercise would still the aching need for a man.

The waters, still cool from the night, slipped between her thighs and found out the pouting cleft of her sex. Long Atlantic rollers, swinging in from half a world away, lifted her on their backs. She opened her legs to the sea, but it, like Vane, was insufficient for her.

Kalinda turned to shore again, and lay in the surf, her hair spread on the wet sand like a fan. One hand strayed over her breasts, squeezing and tweaking her hard, brown nipples; the other pressed hard between her legs. She drew her clitoris up towards her belly, rubbing herself eagerly, opening to the force of the waves. With half-closed eyes, and busy hands, Kalinda summoned up her favorite fantasy.

When she was rich, when she had doubled – no, tripled – her hidden store of jewels, she would go to Spain. She had a certain castle in her mind's eye, a glorious dream of thrusting pinnacles and creamy stone, perched on a rock above the Ebro river.

She raised her knees and thrust one finger inside herself, as far as she could reach. There would be a hundred bedrooms, and in each room a man, handsome and virile beyond belief. Tireless, ever erect, they would fight for her attention. She would make them wait, their hard pricks displayed, for her to choose among them.

Kalinda's hands moved faster. She moaned softly.

She would take them by turns, twenty in a night. She would have two, three of them together. She screwed her eyes tight against the strengthening sun. She imagined kneeling, sucking a potent youth, while another thrust in to her, doggy-fashion, from behind.

Her clitoris throbbed with excitement. She pressed her thumb down on it, frigging herself fiercely. A wave splashed her face, salty as sperm. Her finger moved and twisted in the wetness of her vagina. The tireless lovers of her dream drove into her in unison. Kalinda sobbed, and growled, and came.

She lay panting in the surf, then got slowly to her knees. The immediate need was over. The volcanic fires of her body sank to a glow. She waded into the sea, and bent to rinse the sand from her hair. Waves stroked her, still promising what they could not perform.

The conch sounded again from the earthworks which commanded the harbour. A tall ship, beating in against the wind, loosed a cannon-shot in answer. Kalinda stood thigh-deep in the sea and looked out, shading her eyes with her hand.

A black flag broke above the ship's foretopsail. It bore a grinning death's head above an hourglass and two crossed cutlasses: one of Tremaine's squadron. By the rake of her masts it was the *Sugaree*, and full of plunder from the way she wallowed.

Still wet, Kalinda scrambled into her clothes. She turned back to the town, walking fast. There might be a replacement for Vane aboard.

The ship slowed, headed into the wind, and hove to. By the time the crew rioted ashore, the cantina – and Kalinda – would be ready to supply any diversion the men might fancy after their long weeks afloat.

Singing and shouting, the crew of the *Sugaree* came thundering up the street. Kalinda took a last look around the room. Last night's drunks were gone to whatever dens they could find to sleep off their hangovers. The tables had been scrubbed. A fresh covey of whores was waiting. Kalinda riffled her deck of marked cards. Her eyes and lips were freshly painted, and she wore golden lilies behind her ears.

Shadows crowded the door. Men jostled each other to be first at the bar, or at the women. Kalinda ignored them, for behind the fo'csle hands stalked the officers, the navigators and gunners: the wild aristocracy of the sea.

She nodded to each, as he entered. Most were old friends. There was Mark Read, pale and slender, who was rumoured to be still a virgin; Ben Everie, Jehu McPherson, Black Reuben Ossett. Only one was a stranger.

Kalinda looked him over, and her red lips curved in a smile.

He was tall and slim: perhaps twenty-five, in the prime of his manhood. A cutlass and a long knife were thrust negligently through the scarlet sash that bound his narrow hips. His shirt was open to the waist, and a bandolier of pistols lay crosswise on his tanned, muscular chest. His hair was raven black as Kalinda's own, but his eyes were reckless blue fire.

Yes, she thought. That one. That one is mine.

Reuben Ossett shouldered his way through the crowd. Kalinda received his bear-hug and bristly kiss without once taking her eyes from the young stranger.

'Like him, do you?' Reuben asked, with a bitter smile. 'You're not alone. Reckon you've a better chance than I, though.' He swung an arm round the man's shoulders and pulled him forward. 'This is the Rose of Havana, lad, of whom you've heard tell. Kalinda, meet our new quartermaster, Liam O'Brien.'

Chapter Eleven

'I need to know how much space to clear in the store-room,' said Kalinda, with a flash of her dark eyes at Liam.

He emptied his glass of spirits and poured another. The randy little slut wanted him, sure enough, for all she talked nothing but business. She was preening, flaunting her tits, and her foot pressed his under the table.

Well, he'd give her what she asked for, but not until he was good and ready. And that wouldn't be yet awhile.

Liam soaked up the raw alcohol as if it was a duty, without tasting it. These days, one bottle of rum was use-less. It took two to make him even mildly tipsy: four to get him dead drunk. And if he wasn't fighting or fucking, he wanted to be dead drunk. In oblivion was peace.

Reuben laid a hand on his arm. There was concern in his single blue eye.

'Take it easy, lad,' he said. 'We've work to finish.'

Liam leant back and gave Kalinda a careless glance.

'The plunder's mainly hides and indigo,' he said. 'Some bar silver: a couple of chests of gee-gaws – altar furniture and such. When the men have had their spree, we'll get it packed up here. Tomorrow morning, at the earliest. Have you got sufficient coin? The crew will want their shares in cash.'

'But of course,' she said, rubbing her leg against him. 'At Cantina Kalinda, you will find everything a man could need. You have only to ask.'

'And pay,' said Liam. He slapped his hand on the table. 'More rum here!'

He would not think of Celine. Her love had been a lie from start to finish. She cared only for titles and riches – and one thing more.

Liam jerked out the cork from the second bottle, and filled his glass to the brim. He drained it, filled again.

The story of her wedding night had run through the islands like fire: there had been witnesses enough. Within a week of his joining the pirates Liam had heard a dozen versions. In one sense only had the salacious tales agreed: she had been more than willing – she loved the feel of Wraxall's cock inside her.

She loved it. And she'd sworn she loved only him.

Liam clenched his fist on the glass until it shattered. His blood mixed with the spirits, ran across the table and dripped to the floor.

Kalinda turned up his palm, and began to pick the splinters out of it with delicate, slender fingers.

'This needs seeing to,' she said. 'Come to my room.'

'All right,' said Liam, indifferently. 'I need a fuck. My prick's not been dipped since Jamaica.'

Turning his back on Reuben, who was watching with a sad, resigned expression, Liam followed Kalinda up the stairs.

He barged through the door ahead of her and cast his eye over the room: a rumpled bed, a chest littered with papers, clothing hanging from rough pegs driven into the whitewashed wall. There was a squat flask of Hollands, and two glasses, standing on a low table under the window.

He tossed down a couple of gold pieces, in payment for the gin and his pleasure, poured a glass and drank deeply. A welcome haziness was coming on and, with it, a fierce need for a woman. His prick was hard as iron, hot as hell. He looked round for the girl. She was busy at the chest.

149

'Come here,' he said.

'One moment.' She thrust a handful of papers inside, slammed the lid.

'Right now!' he said, harshly, and took her by the arm. His fingers dug into her. He knew they would leave bruises: what was that to him? He dragged Kalinda across the room, and threw her on the bed.

'Get that skirt up,' he said, through his teeth, as he tore at the fastenings of his breeches.

Trembling, the dusky beauty obeyed. She spread her legs wide, offering herself to him. She raised her knees, and swung her hips.

Liam needed no encouragement. The minute his cock was bared, he fell on her. He plunged his manhood violently into her, thrusting strong and heavy. It was a bitter joy to be in a woman again. He ripped away her blouse, baring her breasts, and crushed her taut nipples between finger and thumb.

'Yes,' hissed Kalinda. 'Yes. Harder.'

Liam rammed himself against her. His cock slid in her tightness. He felt his glans pressing at the entrance of her womb. He forced himself higher. He wanted to lose himself in her, to fuck himself unconscious.

Kalinda clung to him, grinding her hips and fluttering the muscles of her sex. Groaning and sweating, he plunged deep in to her, chasing his release. He hunted grimly after it. It eluded him, flew from him. He had not yet run it down, when Kalinda reached her climax. Her pleasure incensed him.

'Bitch.' gasped Liam, against her satin skin. 'Whore. Bitch. You want a man's prick, don't you? As long as he pays. Gold for you; a noble name for her. All the same: you're all the same.'

Kalinda whimpered, and tried to kiss him. Liam turned his face away. He could not stop now, not even if she begged for mercy. But it seemed she was was made of sterner stuff; she showed no signs of tiring.

Her vagina clenched on him, as wet and soft and mobile as a mouth. The feel of her, still pacing him, gave

Liam the last impetus to grasp the fleeting ecstasy. His balls tightened: his cock throbbed. With a volley of curses, he climaxed.

The relief of emission did not last. Depression clamped down on him, almost as soon as the thrill of orgasm passed. Liam pulled out of the girl, and reached across for the flask of gin. He knew he had been rough with her: she would have the marks of his lust on her for days. He was damned if he would apologise.

'Want a drink?' he asked, morosely.

Kalinda nodded. She rubbed at her ribs, where the hilt of his cutlass had dug into her. Liam sat down on the edge of the bed. They passed the bottle between them.

After a little while, Kalinda's hand slipped round Liam's waist and tugged at his shirt. She pulled it free of his sash.

'Take this off,' she whispered.

'Thought once would be enough for you,' he said. 'It usually is. I'm not very kind.'

'Kindness is for boys,' said Kalinda. She bit his nipples, one after the other. 'I like a real man. Take me again.'

Liam sucked the last dregs from the flask, and let it fall. He turned his head and looked into her glowing eyes.

'You want it, Kalinda,' he said. 'You do the work.'

The next day, the *Sugaree*'s loot was brought up to the cantina for division. As each man got his share Kalinda counted out its value, less a substantial handling fee, from the box of coins before her.

In exchange she received cathedral candlesticks of solid gold, enamelled crosses, madonnas and statues of the saints. Jewelled rosaries dripped through her fingers, scintillating in the morning light.

'All done,' said Liam. 'Any complaints?'

'It ain't likely anyone'd argue, lad,' said Reuben, pulling up a stool. 'They trust you. There's none among the Coast Brotherhood that's got a better reputation for fair dealing.'

Liam gave a twisted smile, and called for rum.

'I was a man of honour, once. Old habits die hard, it seems.'

Now the share-out was finally over, Kalinda allowed the cantina's door to be unlocked. The scavengers of New Providence fought to be first inside. Tawdry prostitutes of both sexes, fortune-tellers, gamblers and beggars, all jostled to help the *Sugaree's* crew spend the gold burning in their pockets.

Kalinda ran her hand lustfully up Liam's leg. He had proved to be all she hoped for, all she dreamt of: virile, handsome, brutal, and untiring.

Reuben opened his jack-knife and glowered at her.

'Let him alone for a minute, can't you?'

'Ah, you're just jealous,' Kalinda sneered. 'You want him yourself.'

Reuben kept his head down and concentrated on prising the stones from an altar cross. Liam picked up a ruby, and rolled it in his fingers.

'Sure, you're spoiling the thing,' he said. 'It seems a pity.'

'We sell gold by weight here, friend,' said Reuben. 'The gems – they're Tremaine's cut: portable, precious – untraceable, out of their settings.'

'Ah, the mysterious Tremaine,' said Liam pensively. 'Ever since I've been on the account, I've been hearing tell of Tremaine. And do you know, I've yet to meet a man who's seen him?'

'Is that so?' said Reuben, shortly. He threw down the despoiled cross and picked up a chalice, set with topaz flowers and leaves of pale beryl.

Kalinda filled Liam's glass again.

Reuben frowned as the level in the bottle fell. Kalinda kept her eye on the hairy pirate. He was like an old hen with one chick, she thought. His protectiveness made him ridiculous.

He could do nothing: she had no fear of competition from the likes of Reuben Ossett. Long weeks at sea frequently inclined the pirates to seek pleasure in each other's bodies. Even the unregretted Captain Vane had not been immune to the charms of a good-looking youth. But not Liam: no. She had never known so fiercely heterosexual a man.

A female rival might be a different matter.

A group of late arrivals swaggered into the cantina. Kalinda gave them hardly a glance. Her mind was on the letter, hidden in her chest upstairs.

There had been a distinctly feminine turn to the handwriting. And then there was the mysterious 'she' he had mentioned, who had sold herself for a noble name. Whoever she was, had she now regretted her decision, written to say she wanted Liam back? More than that: if Kalinda gave him the letter, would he go?

Not if the Rose of Havana had a word to say.

She slipped her hand into the front flap of Liam's breeches. His prick stirred under her hand: soon he would be ready.

A shadow fell across the table and Kalinda glanced up. Her teasing fingers stilled, and her heart beat fast. Ringed by light from the open door, Captain Vane towered like a giant above her. His teeth were bared. He gripped a naked cutlass in one brawny hand.

Reuben hastily scooped up the jewels, and thrust them into the bosom of his shirt. Glancing once at Vane, Liam filled his glass again.

'Keep going, Kalinda,' he said. 'I was just beginning to enjoy it.'

'Don't be a fool,' muttered Reuben. 'You're unarmed, man.'

Kalinda felt her heart begin to pound with excitement. Holding Vane's eyes, she resumed her intimate caressing of Liam's manhood.

With a roar of inarticulate fury, Vane brought the cutlass down, embedding it a good inch in the wooden table. Kalinda squeaked, and jumped away. Eyes wide with anticipation, she withdrew against the wall.

Liam rang his empty glass against Vane's blade.

'Now, that was a foolish thing to do. You've taken the edge off it.'

Vane wrenched his cutlass free and leapt forward, overturning the table. Gold and glasses clattered on the floor.

Kalinda pressed one hand to her fluttering heart. Liam drove himself backwards, chair and all, and sprang to his feet, catching the sword Reuben tossed to him. Steel rang: fire sparked from the meeting blades.

'You've a damned bad temper, my buck,' said Liam, and flung himself into the attack.

Rouged lips parted with excitement, Kalinda watched her lovers do battle for her. This was no matter of honour that could be resolved by a little blood-letting and an apology, but a hacking, mortal duel for her favours that would end in death.

In the safety of her corner, she panted harder than either of the fighting men. One would win the right to possess her. The thought of being taken by the victor aroused Kalinda wildly. At that moment, she hardly cared which it would be.

At first all the advantage seemed to be with the larger man. Vane had the longer reach, the heavier muscles, and could bring the slicing edge to bear. Liam was forced to fall back before him, parrying the swinging blade.

Kalinda squeezed her legs together, feeling the little pleasure-bud that lay between them throb and tingle. As the cutlasses clashed, creamy moisture oozed from her sex and on to her thighs, making them slippery.

It was impossible to touch herself before the crowd of onlookers, and the gamblers who shouted the odds, but she was hungry to do it. How often had she dreamt of this, teasing herself to satisfaction while she imagined two men fighting for her charms?

Liam was fast. Vane was tiring: he breathed hard, gasping for air, and the flashing arc of his cutlass moved a little slower. Eyes burning, Liam drove in under the blade, his point darting at face, heart, belly.

So stimulated that she was beyond caring who saw, Kalinda pressed her thighs together again and again, sending little jolts of pleasure through her sex. Her nipples thrust against the thin fabric of her blouse. Each time she moved, the linen brushed on their sensitive tissue. If the fight did not end soon, she would have no choice but to pleasure herself in front of the whole room.

Vane stamped forward, blade raised, and Liam caught his wrist as the blow descended. For an instant, the man was open, defenceless. With steely strength, Liam drove the point of his sword between Vane's ribs and through his heart. The pirate captain's eyes widened with the surprise of death. Then they glazed over. And he fell.

Before Vane hit the floor, Kalinda flung herself into Liam's arms. She rubbed her body against him, mad with the desire the fight had raised in her. Her sex throbbed. Her clitoris itched for his rough caresses.

Liam's eyes were pale, and distant. It was almost as if he had forgotten who she was. Then he seemed to come back from far away. With a catch of her breath, she saw the moment his battle-fury changed to lust. He squeezed her breasts harshly, tweaking their nipples.

'To the victor, the spoils, is it? Let's go to your room.'

She was on him, almost before the door was closed, pushing him back towards the bed. Panting with her need for his cock, Kalinda ripped open the fastenings to his breeches and dragged them down to his knees.

She licked at his manhood, teasing its eye with her tongue. She sucked his balls. His phallus swelled and grew, pumping erect, until it was more than ready for her, hard and warm, its head wet with her saliva.

'Ride me,' said Liam, hoarsely. 'Do it now.'

Needing no second word, she wriggled out of her clothes and crawled on top of him. Liam pushed open her sex with his fingers and jerked her down on his prick, impaling her on the stiff rod of flesh. Burying his face in her breast, he sucked greedily on the rigid nipple until she moaned.

The feel of his cock's magnificent hardness was almost too much for Kalinda to bear. Vane's death had stimulated her wickedly. Liam took her with the same ferocity he brought to the combat, stabbing her to the heart. She reached orgasm quickly, wailing her enjoyment.

Liam outlasted her pleasure, as he had the night before. His hard cock lunged and thrust within her, giving her no rest. He was the only man she knew whose hunger approached, nay, overtook, her own. Before he came, he had given her satisfaction a second time. When at last Liam climaxed, she was exhausted; drained.

He pushed her roughly away and rolled out from under her. While Kalinda still sobbed for breath, he tugged up his breeches, feeling in the pocket.

'Here, these are for you,' he said, and flung a rope of pearls, part of his share of the loot, over her head.

Kalinda looked down at the pale gems hanging between her breasts. They were beautiful, luminous against her dark skin. She gasped.

'I don't want thanks,' said Liam, before she could get out a word. 'They're payment, not a gift. I'll expect full value for them before I ship out again.'

The thought of losing him, so soon, brought Kalinda up short. Up to now, she had been glad to see the back of her lovers: none could keep up with her demands. But this one was different. She could not let him get away: or at least not yet.

'Why not stay here, in New Providence?' she said. 'I have plans for the future – you could be part of them. Have you ever visited Spain?'

'Now don't be telling me you love me,' said Liam, wearily. 'It's not the truth, and if it was, I'd be gone the sooner. I'm done with that. Let's keep things straight between us, Kalinda. You're a whore, and I'm your cully.'

'I prefer to be called a courtesan,' she said. 'Why are you always angry?'

'Me?' he said. 'Faith, I'm the happiest man on earth. More money than I can spend, plenty to drink, and a woman who can't get enough of my cock.'

'And that's all you want?'

'Just one thing more,' said Liam, between his teeth.

'There's a man I aim to kill. He's powerful, though; rich. I'll need my own command before I can go after him. I'll have my revenge, but not die for it.'

'I could get you a ship,' said Kalinda, slowly. 'I know Tremaine.'

As Liam stared, she rose to her knees, and put her arms around him. She brushed his hair aside, and kissed his throat. Her hands slipped down over his chest, smooth and bare within the open shirt.

'I'll be taking the jewels to – a certain place – soon,' she whispered. 'My pinnace, The *Paramour*, is ready to sail. You could come along. I have influence. You could be Captain O'Brien within a month.'

Liam pulled her round until he could look into her eyes. His grip was tight, painful on last night's bruises.

'You're not gulling me?' he said.

Kalinda gravely shook her head.

'I need a drink,' he said, starting to his feet. 'I need to consider. I'm not one to be beholden. But if it'll help me to that man . . .' His voice trailed off for a moment. 'I'll talk about it with Reuben, over a bottle or so. I'll come back tonight, if you're willing.'

Kalinda ran the pearls through her fingers. She thought the bait was taken, but she knew better than to try the line just yet.

'For you, Liam O'Brien,' she said, 'the Rose of Havana is always willing.'

Liam let himself out. When she was sure he was gone, Kalinda struck fire and lit a candle. She opened the chest and found the letter. Holding it by one corner, she dipped it into the flame. She caught a single phrase as the paper curled and blackened: *I have loved no man but you*. Then fire licked up the words, and they were gone. Kalinda crushed the ashes into powder, and threw them out into the wind.

'*Adios*,' she breathed.

Afterwards, she washed her hands three times to make sure no atom of the letter remained.

* * *

157

It was late, dark; a blustering gale from the south rattled tiles on Laissez Faire's roof. In the house below, doors banged and timbers creaked.

Celine lay on her bed in the secret room, her hand moving back and forth between her thighs. Sensation thrilled through the swollen bud she touched, and she gasped softly as she stroked and teased herself.

She fantasised about Lord Wraxall. He had chained her down on the black bed and roused her with lips and fingers. Rock-hard and enormous, his prick drove into her mouth while he sucked her clitoris. She was bound and helpless, unable to escape from his darting tongue, his probing hands. The bitter-sweet memory of his ringed phallus brought her to orgasm, as it did every time.

Gasping softly into her pillow, she felt the pulsing spasms shake her. She clenched her thighs repeatedly, pressing them together, and tried to make the feeling stronger.

It was useless. The climaxes she achieved for herself were nothing compared to the ecstasy she had experienced with her husband. They were paltry things, hardly fit to be called pleasure at all.

And yet she could not stop stimulating herself. In the six weeks during which she had been in hiding, she resorted to her fingers for satisfaction several times a day.

At night, it was a necessity: the only thing that made sleep possible. But sometimes, as now, even that expedient failed.

She rolled onto her back and lay staring up into blackness. Her body was slick with sweat, her pounding heart hammered against her ribs. Doubts and terrors, magnified by the dark, invaded her mind.

Why was it always Odo's phantom, not Liam's, that she called up when the hunger of her flesh gave her no peace? She tried to tell herself that it was only natural: she had never lain with Liam. But she feared it was something quite different.

Odo had said that her mother could never be satisfied by anyone but him. Was she the same? In these past weeks she had more than once felt the urge to approach Auguste. Her need was so urgent, and the African had a rare beauty, bearing himself like a savage king.

But – ghastly thought – suppose he gave her no more than she could find in self-caresses? Was she, like Lys, beginning an endless, fruitless search for past delight? Would Auguste be the first of a thousand faceless lovers?

Would even Liam have been capable of giving her what she longed for?

Celine turned over and prodded her pillow. It was hot, squashed into uncomfortable knots.

No answer had ever come to her letter. Sally tried to comfort her with tales of delays, missed tides, and suchlike children's stories, but Celine knew Liam no longer cared at all. He would have come to her by now if his love had still been alive. There had been ample time.

She turned over again. The sheet, clammy with sweat, wound itself around her legs. This was ridiculous. She could not lie here, letting the same thoughts of loss, fear and lust go around and around in her head. Reaching a sudden decision, Celine got out of bed and began to dress herself.

She would go and find Auguste. She would face her dread, once and for all. And afterwards, whatever happened, she would tell Sally that she wanted passage to America. Her mother's family lived in one of the French colonies. She would throw herself on the mercy of Tante Heléne in St Louis, and try to forget both Lord Wraxall and Liam.

'Go on, let me try the green silk,' said Piggott-Patricia, coaxingly. 'I'm sure it'll fit.'

'That's my best gown,' said Sally. 'I'm not having it split across the shoulders like the last two.'

Piggott sidled closer, his pink skirts rustling. He had become quite reconciled to wearing women's clothes in these last weeks. He liked the feel of lacy petticoats brushing against his naked cock and balls, and the tight constriction of his corset.

For a while he had wondered if he was going queer: but Mistress Colney had soon put that worry out of his mind. Just looking at her, sitting there on the edge of the bed, naked as the day she was born, gave him an erection.

No, he definitely wasn't turning into a nance. He just liked wearing dresses: they were sensual. They kept him in mind of his body all the time, made him feel sexy. The only problem was they had no pockets, nowhere for a man to keep his baccy.

'You know you'd like to see me in it,' said Piggott, sitting down next to Sally and running his hand up her bare thigh. 'Green's my colour. And silk's sweet to the touch. Wouldn't you like to put your hands up under some nice soft sliding material and find what I've got hidden away for you there?'

'I can do that now,' she murmured, lifting his skirts. 'And while it's true pink's not best suited to a redhead like you, or me for that matter, I'm not going to wait while you change. You always take hours.'

Baring his cock as she spoke, she began to run her fingers along its thickness until Piggott couldn't help jerking and whining with desire.

'Come on, Miss Patricia,' Sally said, when she had teased him to distraction. 'Show me how one woman can really pleasure another. If it's as good as last time, I'll buy you a green gown all of your own.'

She lay back on the coverlet, moving restlessly up and down. Piggott joined her eagerly, and knelt between her thighs.

Mistress Colney seemed to like his women's clothes as much as he did himself. Only two days after arriving at her plantation, she caught him making beds, and threw his petticoats up so she could play with his prick. Ever since then, he had shared her favours with Auguste. And Martin had ambitions to be more than just her lover. Much more.

Sally raised her legs, holding them open with her hands, so that he could get closer. He slotted his penis into her with a quick pump of his hips, and began to thrust.

She was all wet and lovely inside, just how he liked it. He began to pat and tease her breasts, pulling at her nipples until they swelled up as hard as the buttons on his best blue taffeta.

'My goodness,' said Sally, langourously. 'What a big clitoris you've got, Patricia. It goes all the way up – ah, God! that's wonderful.'

Piggott drove lustily into her, his mind occupied with happy thoughts. He was on a winning streak. It just went to show how a man who kept his wits about him, and his eyes open, could go far.

Mistress Colney was involved in the moonlight trade. He had collected quite a lot of evidence against her: times, dates, places, all were written down and hidden behind a loose board in the stables with his pipe and tobacco.

Smuggling was a hanging matter: everyone knew how tough the Governor was on it. Martin was sure that Sally would do anything he wanted, if he threatened to expose her. They could be married. He fancied being a planter.

They would look a picture, walking up the aisle in matching wedding gowns.

Martin gave Sally several long strokes of his cock until she whimpered and began to thrash about beneath him. He loved the feel of her, writhing out of control with pleasure. He thrust deeper, groaning with enjoyment.

Downstairs, a door slammed.

Rapid footsteps sounded below; someone was coming up the stairs and along the corridor in a hurry. Whoever it was, it sounded as if they were on their way to Sally's bedchamber.

Martin didn't care: only let them give him enough time to reach the climax already beginning to tingle in his flesh. He lunged again and again, his eyes half-closed. He was on the brink of orgasm when the bedroom door burst open and Auguste strode in.

Martin was incapable of stopping. He held Sally where she was and plunged his cock into her deeper and harder.

'You're needed downstairs, Sal,' said Auguste. 'It's urgent.'

'Can't it wait?' gasped Sally.

'Not for a minute,' Auguste said. 'Wraxall's come calling.'

'All right,' she said, pushing at Martin's padded chest. 'I'm coming.'

'So am I,' whimpered Martin, softly. 'Right now.'

There was no time to enjoy the aftermath. As soon as Piggott had reached his climax, Sally shooed him out.

Rather disgruntled – he had been looking forward to discussing the promised new gown – he stepped into the corridor. He paused before a glass, straightening his cap. A movement in the mirror's depths caught his eye: Auguste and a woman. A woman that Martin surely knew. Holding his petticoats close, he stole after them, up the stairs and as far as the portrait gallery. There, he paused in the shadows.

It was Lady Celine, large as life and twice as tasty. And cuddling, like a shameless hussy, with that big black stud Toussainte.

The wind that blustered around the house made it impossible to hear what they were saying, but from the way she blushed and clung to Auguste there was no need to guess what was being planned between them.

The question was, what the devil was she doing here? Most like, she had run away from Acheron, but Martin had heard not a whisper of her being missing. If she had run away, there were those who would pay highly to know where she was concealed: and others, no doubt, offering more to keep that knowledge close.

He watched narrowly as Celine disappeared behind one of the portraits. Auguste pressed a boss on the panelling. Piggott counted: third across from the window, second row down. The portrait shut with a click.

Piggott scuttled down the corridor, bolted into the first room he came to, and hid behind the curtains. Outside the window he glimpsed clouds scudding across the moon as a tall ship heeled to the gale, coming into the bay under shortened sail. Some more of Mistress Colney's smuggling friends, no doubt. Midnight visitors, secret doors: Laissez Faire had more mysteries than a dog had fleas.

As soon as he heard Auguste leave, Martin went straight to the gallery. He swayed across to the section of panelling he had made a note of.

Two down, three across.

After a few attempts he discovered that the boss had to be pressed at the same time as he gave it a half-turn to the left. The picture sprang open. Light filtered down a spiral stair. A woman was singing 'Greensleeves.'

He took off his high-heeled shoes and crept upwards. There was another door at the top. Piggott crouched and looked through the keyhole.

Lady Celine was undressing. She was touching herself: caressing her taut young breasts, her thighs and belly. She lay across the bed and dipped her fingers in between her legs, playing with her sex.

Wasn't she just the goer? thought Martin. Maybe she would like a little friendly visit – a bit of girl-talk. He lifted his skirts and grasped his penis, pumping it hopefully. It flopped in his hand, stubbornly refusing to rise. Martin looked at it glumly: dead as a doornail.

Then he brightened. Now he knew the secret of the hidden room, he could get in any time. He would bet his best blue gown that Lady Celine would let him have her any way he asked, if he threatened to betray her whereabouts to Viscount Wraxall.

Piggott straightened his skirts and stole back to the gallery, well pleased. All in all, things were looking up for him.

Chapter Twelve

*B*efore she went in to confront Lord Wraxall, Sally paused and glanced at herself in a mirror. She had not waited to dress, merely throwing on a loose powdering gown over her nudity.

She looked very well, she thought. The shot silk changed colour, green to bronze, as she moved; and the iridiscent fabric clung to her lush curves.

Auguste had interrupted her assignation with Piggott-Patricia at a damned inopportune time. She was roused, but not satisfied: in the mood for adventure.

Sally had known Odo Wraxall a long time, and there were things she could not forgive him. But the way she felt now, she might be tempted to overlook past events – for an hour or so. Swinging her hips, so that the silk whispered, she went to meet him.

The saloon at Laissez Faire was a large room, its panelling painted in dull ivory. Lord Wraxall stood with his hands linked behind him, examining a tapestried sea-battle which covered the whole of one wall. He wore black, and silver lace: a diamond-hilted rapier hung at his side.

'It's a Gobelin,' said Sally.

'I know,' he replied. 'A king's ransom to purchase: one wonders where the money came from. It was not so long ago that you were an indentured servant.'

'As you so gallantly remind me, my lord, I'm only a commoner,' said Sally. 'I don't have the expensive tastes of the nobility – or their debts. I hear you've had to put the *Nemesis* up for sale. A fine vessel: I'm sure I can find a few odd guineas to purchase her.'

She draped herself comfortably across a sofa, and picked up a palm leaf fan. Her loose gown fell open, baring one long, tanned leg.

'Did you come here to admire my furnishings?' she asked. 'Or is there another reason?'

His nostrils flared as he approached her. She knew he could smell that she had recently had sex, and that it stimulated him; challenged him.

'Why, madam, I came to kiss your hand,' he said, suiting the action to the words. 'May I sit down?'

'You're unusually complimentary, my lord,' said Sally. 'What do you want?'

'At this moment, a glass of wine would suffice,' Odo said. 'But I am sure that other items will occur to me later. If I put my mind to it.'

Sally reached out and struck the bell. While they waited for service, she watched Lord Wraxall from under her eyelashes. He had come to try and find out about Celine, of course. He could have no proof that the girl was concealed at Laissez Faire, but his suspicions must have the force of certainty.

Their long silence was broken by a tap on the door. Auguste entered, leading a little parade of servants who brought wine and sweetmeats. At his direction, they laid the refreshments out on the table, and were dismissed.

'Will there be anything else?' asked Auguste.

Sally shook her head. Auguste shot a glance at Lord Wraxall.

'You're sure?' he said. 'I could stay within hearing.'

'Not tonight,' said Sally, curtly. She could handle Wraxall, even at his worst. She had done it before.

Auguste bowed, and retreated. Sally listened to his footsteps on the stairs, waiting to hear him turn off to her room. Instead, he continued upwards: he was going to the gallery.

So he was going to pluck the pretty blossom in the secret room tonight. Perhaps Celine would prefer Auguste's loving. He would be gentle, considerate: for a young girl affection might be a better aphrodisiac than Odo's dark confusion of lust and power. Ye gods, but Wraxall would hate that.

When Sally rose, Wraxall followed her. She poured wine, and handed him his glass. Odo's hair was scented with rosemary. It hung, in silver-streaked curls, over his shoulders and down his back, almost to the waist. She remembered a time when it had been all black.

Auguste would be with Celine now: perhaps they were already touching.

'To absent friends,' said Sally.

Crystal chimed. Lord Wraxall rolled the wine on his palate.

'I taught you how to judge a claret, at least. That was where? Savannah?'

'Charleston.'

Odo looked down into his wine.

'I'm glad to see you remember my teachings. Tell me, the man you were with just now: was he better than I?'

She pretended to consider. There was, of course, no comparison.

'I hardly recall what you were like, my lord. I vow, it's been an age since the last time. Nine years? Ten?'

'So it seems longer to you. That's gratifying. I, however, am precise. Seven years, five months and eight days. Do you want the hour? I know it.'

Sally leant back against the table. The shining robe clung to her body.

'Memories are such melancholy things,' she said. 'I'm for the present.'

Odo set down his glass. 'Is that an offer?'

'There was a time when you would not have waited to ask,' she said. 'Has marriage softened you? Or is it age?'

He took a strand of her hair and drew it towards him, twining it around his fingers.

'Caution, I believe,' he said. 'This could be mere distraction. What, advances from you, of all women? Is my wife in the next room? Are you buying her safety, by thus throwing yourself at my head after years of enmity?'

'Good Lord, is she missing?' asked Sally, with assumed astonishment.

'It's not something I have cared to make public. Why, scandal would say she'd tired of my body. But with you, of course, I need have no reserve. I know you're hiding her. I can make you tell me, Sal.'

'How?' she demanded. 'Even if I could inform you where the child was concealed – which I can't – how would you possibly get the secret from me? Do you think to make me so desirous that I'll babble out any-thing, just to have the pleasure of your body? A prick's a prick, Odo, not a magic wand.'

Lord Wraxall dropped one hand to the rapier's hilt.

'I had a somewhat less enjoyable method in mind,' he said.

Sally swore, and put the table between them. In all probability, this was another of his games. The Viscount had some extraordinary tastes in foreplay, as she well remembered. But it didn't do to be certain of anything where he was concerned. She fumbled open a drawer and felt for the pistol hidden there.

Steel scraped as Lord Wraxall drew. The rapier gleamed in the candlelight. He raised his point.

'I could spoil your beauty for you, Sal,' he said. 'I've long resented the way you share it so widely.'

He made a pass at her cheek. She felt the wind of the blade as it whispered past, a calculated fraction from the skin. Sally cocked the pistol and took aim.

'I can cover a scar or two with paint. What would you do if I blew your balls off?'

'Termagant,' he said, baring his teeth, and feinted

again. A rent opened in the sleeve of her gown. Sally sidestepped, and his third cut went wide.

'You're cheating,' she said. 'I have but the one bullet.'

'I know,' said Odo, and lunged. Silk ripped from shoulder to thigh.

The light material bellied open as Sally swayed to avoid the sword, displaying one rounded breast and the long curve of her flank.

They circled each other slowly, eyes locked. Lord Wraxall's blade licked out, shredding the fabric, never touching the flesh beneath. Sally's aim was unfaltering. Let him draw a single drop of blood: she would shoot, and damn the consequences. But he knew that: he was only playing with her. Wraxall was too fine a fencer to miss so often, and so narrowly.

Testing him, Sally leant in to the next blow, instead of away. It threw him, as she thought it would. The blade sheered wildly through the powdering gown, and he was hard put to recover with even a semblance of grace.

Odo took another pass. Sally made no move to avoid it. A panel of silk fell away and fluttered to the floor. It left her entirely bare on one side.

She gave a choke of laughter. This was ridiculous. Why couldn't he just undress her, like any normal man?

Odo's mouth twitched at the corner: it was clear he, too, was beginning to find some humour in the proceedings. He slashed away a last swathe of fabric, and lowered his blade.

'Curse it, don't you take anything seriously?' he asked. 'I could have killed you, Sal. I still can.'

Sally's finger curled on the hair-trigger.

'Try it,' she said, proudly. 'Though you were a greater swordsman than Inigo Montoya himself, I could put a bullet through you before you came back on guard. Disarm, Wraxall, or I swear I'll fire.'

For a second, Sally thought she had gone too far, and that he would take her at her word. But then, with a flicker of a smile, Odo raised the rapier in capitulation and salute.

His grip relaxed. The blade fell from his open palm, clattering on the waxed floor. He kicked it aside, and stepped close. Holding her gaze, he took her right hand and guided the gun to his breast.

'Shoot then, virago,' he said. 'Here's my heart.'

'You have no heart,' scoffed Sally.

'Not now, perhaps. But seven years ago . . .'

She uncocked the pistol, and laid it aside.

'I told you,' she said, in a softer voice. 'I'm for the present.'

Lord Wraxall pulled her close, and kissed her. Sally opened her mouth under his; she sighed with pleasure as their tongues met in a softer duel. His hands found their way in, through slashes torn by his rapier, and moved on her naked body under the silk.

He stroked her back, down from the wings of her shoulder-blades, counting each one of her vertebrae if he told a rosary. He cupped her buttocks, their muscles firm under the soft skin, and drew her loins to his. He kissed each eyelid, closing them. His tongue teased her earlobe: his breathing, deep and languid, ruffled the strands of her hair.

Odo sipped briefly at her mouth again. He kissed the angle of her jaw, her cheek, her neck. His tongue trailed a line along one collar bone, dipped in to the hollow at her throat, setting out on a slow exploration downwards.

Sally let her hands rest easily on Lord Wraxall's shoulders. Head back, and eyes closed, she surrendered to his caresses. She appreciated the time he was taking to give her pleasure; there was a sweet nostalgia in his touch. But she had no illusions. He might be tender now: let her once lose the advantage, though, and he would crush her.

She moved against him, sighing. His hands, his mouth, kindled a devouring ardour in her. She felt the erect staff of his manhood, hard against her belly, through breeches and long-skirted waistcoat.

Her hand went down to touch his phallus. She needed

to feel its potent warmth, to stroke its velvet skin, to kiss and suck its head.

Lord Wraxall caught his breath.

'Wait, now,' he whispered. 'I will not disappoint you, Sal, but this is too rare a pleasure for me to enjoy with my boots on.'

'Don't delay too far, then,' she said, biting his neck gently. 'I might grow impatient, and seek an understudy to replace the leading man.'

'Not once you see what you're getting,' said Odo, as he unbuckled his sword-belt.

Sally retreated to the sofa and spread herself on its cushions. She moved luxuriously on them, and caressed herself sensuously as she watched him undress, dabbling her fingers in the moisture between her legs.

'I've seen this play before,' she said, lazily. 'Don't you think the overture's a little long?'

'For a single act, perhaps,' said Odo, pulling off his shirt. 'But if you remember your lines, we might keep the stage for three. Besides, there have been alterations to the scenery since we last trod the boards together.'

He pushed his breeches slowly down from his lean hips, and stepped out of them. He stood proudly before her, displaying his jutting manhood. Above the asymetric sac of his scrotum, his penis thrust out and upwards from the dark curls. Light glinted on the golden hoop that transfixed his glans.

'Christ!' said Sally, in a startled voice. 'Didn't that hurt?'

Odo stalked towards her and got to his knees beside the sofa.

'Do you like it, Sal?' he asked, huskily. 'Does it excite you?'

She reached out to touch him. His phallus lay in her palm, warm and hard as animate stone. A tracery of blue veins snaked on its shaft. The upturned head, deep rose, was fully uncapped. She stroked the tender skin of his glans with her fingertips, turning the metal through its eye.

'I had an earring like that once,' she said.

'What a coincidence,' said Odo, and bent to kiss her breasts.

His hands closed on the tanned skin, pressing the globes of flesh close, so that he could move more easily from one nipple to the next. Sally whimpered softly and writhed on the cushions. Her breasts had always been sensitive: a touch there was enough to arouse her. Odo's single-minded stimulation of them, using hands, lips, teeth and tongue, was unbearable ecstasy.

She grasped his phallus, working her fist along the silken skin of its shaft from base to head. Odo thrust his glans into her hand, pushing it against her palm; she felt the ring shift. She used her thumb to move it back and forth. The gold was wet.

Odo growled softly, and raised his head to look at her.

'The past is dead,' he said, hoarsely. 'The future's yet to come. Let us take this minute's pleasure in each other, Sal, and forget the rest.'

Joining her on the cushions, he drew her to him: his mouth met hers in a sweet exchange of tongues. He parted her legs still wider, and sliding between them. He raised her knees and pressed them outward, so that her sex opened to him. He looked down, into the shadowed secret places. She heard him sigh.

His touch was delicate, light. Sally bucked against his hand, crooning with desire. He used the wetness that seeped from her vagina to slick his fingers. He drew back the hood of her clitoris, and circled there. The little nub throbbed, sending tremors of lust through her entire being.

While he still teased her clitoris, Odo slipped two long fingers inside her. They pressed on the wall of her vagina, sought and found the sensitive spot within. Sally drew up her thighs, holding them wide so that he could get still deeper into her. She tightened on his fingers and rocked to their repeated thrusts. She felt her orgasm approaching.

And at the exact moment that she came, Odo took

away his fingers and gave her instead the full length of his phallus.

He stayed there, immobile, until her last spasms of satisfaction had passed. Sally gasped and shuddered with the delight that spent itself in her.

Still Odo waited, looking down at her. Only when her trembling had stopped did he lower himself upon her. He kissed her hungrily, and crushed her in his arms. With infinite slowness he began to move.

Sally tangled her fingers in the dark strands of his hair. Her hands moved down to stroke the taut muscles of his buttocks. Odo began to move faster. He used a subtle variation in his penetration of her: sometimes teasingly shallow, sometimes so deep that she felt the ring in his cock brush the neck of her womb. Sally's clitoris still tingled from her first orgasm; satisfaction melted into new lust, fresh eagerness.

She hooked her ankles over the backs of his thighs, and gave him thrust for thrust. Tensing the muscles of her vagina, she gripped him hard, rejoicing in the feel of his glans, his shaft, pressing into her. Their sweat mingled. Flesh slid on flesh. Their pubic hair, soaked with the juices of pleasure, rubbed and tangled together.

His climax was near: she could feel it in his convulsive movements, his gasping breath. His arms tightened around her. He drove into her steadily, as Sally pulled him closer. Her nails dug into his back. It was enough to feel him in her. His need was infectious: it took her to the point of no return, and she came with a soft shriek of ecstasy.

Odo was too close to fulfillment to stop. He pulled her on to his moving phallus. He sank himself into her.

'I die,' he whispered. 'Oh, Sal, I die.'

His spasms lasted a long time. His cock pulsed and throbbed within her as he made a last few diminishing motions. He lay full length upon her, his face buried in her hair. His hold on her relaxed a little, but he did not let her go. They lay close linked together, their hearts thudding in unison.

172

Recovery was slow. Sally's entire body felt suffused with the afterglow of pleasure. She looked dreamily at the ceiling, and stroked his back. Wraxall was a haughty swine, and dangerous to boot. But if he was vain of his prowess, it was not without reason. She fluttered the muscles of her vagina on his prick.

'Again?' he said. 'Give me time, you witch.'

He slipped out of her and lay at her side. Propping himself on one elbow, he ran his other hand over her breasts and belly to clasp the pursed and swollen flesh between her legs. She responded with an automatic thrust.

'Ah, Sal, Sal, you never should have left me,' he murmured. 'What a pair we would have made.'

'I don't remember leaving.' said Sally. 'I seem to recall you sold my indentures to a whoremaster.'

Odo stroked the flattened curls of her pubic hair with his thumb.

'I would have bought you back. I waited only for one word, one look.'

'Of submission.'

'Yes,' he said.

Sally raised one knee to give his wandering fingers more freedom.

'Not then, not now,' she said, flatly. 'Never.'

Lord Wraxall looked down at the woman lying beside him. It was difficult to keep his impassivity in the face of Sally's rejection. She had just used him. Her willingness had been nothing to do with any feelings for him. She had been with an unsatisfactory lover, that was all.

At the time, it had aroused him wildly. The musky scent of her; the ready heat and wetness of her vagina; the knowledge that a lesser prick had prepared the way for his; all these had combined to raise a need he could not control. Even now, there was a bitter contentment in the thought that he had been able to give her release where another had failed.

There was anger, too, now that his lust for her was momentarily sated. Of all his uncounted women she, and she alone, had stood out against him. Sally had been his servant, his slave in all but name: but he had never owned more than her body.

'Death, but I hate you, Sarah Colney,' he said, in a shaken whisper. 'I've never hated any woman so long, or so much.'

'The feeling's mutual,' said Sally. 'Let me know when you're ready.'

She rolled onto her stomach, and reached out for her wine-glass. A faint criss-cross pattern marked her back. Odo traced the lines with his hand: they were the scars of a whip. Faded and silvery against Sally's brown skin, they were not recent. But, like the ring in his penis, they were new since the last time. Someone had laid on hard; hard enough to cut.

'Who was responsible for this?' asked Odo, quietly.

Sally glanced at him across her shoulder. 'You.'

Odo drew her head back so that he could look down into her face.

'Don't lie,' he said. 'I was crazy, the night we parted, but not so out of my senses that I can't remember. You cannot say that I ever hurt you so.'

Sally pulled away from him, and sipped at her wine.

'No, flogging isn't your style, is it?' she said, distantly. 'You choose different ways to impose your will on women. Humiliation, for instance. You knew what that brothel was like before you sold me into it. I got these stripes for my third escape attempt: they held an auction to see who would have the privilege of punishing me. Oh, the bidding ran high indeed. Forgive me if I have forgot the sum.'

'Whatever it was, I would have paid double to save you, Sal.'

She thumped down the empty glass, and turned on him.

'By God, Wraxall, if you had been in the very room, I wouldn't have lifted one finger to ask for your help. Leave the subject now, man, or I'll call my servants to turn you out, bare-arsed as you are. It makes me mad to remember.'

Odo caught back a retort. There was nothing to say, unless he wanted Sally to make good her threat. And he was not yet ready to leave: far from it.

Her closeness, even her scorn aroused him. He could feel himself getting hard again, his balls tightening, and the blood pumping into his phallus. Odo bent his head and began to kiss the whip-marks on her back. He followed the lines with his tongue as if he could lick them away. Too late for that, of course. Except in bed, his timing had always been a little off with Sally.

After he had sold her, he travelled for three months, coasting slowly up from Carolina to Rhode Island and Providence Plantations. Constantly, at the back of his mind, had been the thought of his triumphant return.

But when he reached Savannah again, she was gone.

Odo slipped his arm round Sally's waist, and gathered her to him. His prick brushed against her, eager for the soft welcome of her loins.

His desire for her had never waned. It was inexplicable to him. He had lovers of both sexes who were more beautiful, younger, more skilled in the erotic arts. Men and women had risked, and lost, everything for him: position, reputation, even life. They were less than the dust on Sally's shoes.

Her mouth opened under his kisses. His hand moved on her breasts and her nipples hardened at his touch. Odo brushed the firm buds with his tongue. Her pubis, still wet, moved warmly against his thigh.

It mortified him to remember how hard he had searched for her. All he had ever been able to discover was that a besotted tobacco-planter had bought her indentures, and taken her up-country, no-one knew where.

Then two years ago she had streaked into sight again, bright as a comet; she had bought the Sedley estate with ready cash, and settled there. She had cut him dead in

Fort George the day she arrived. It was a declaration of war: a war he did not intend to lose.

Sally reached down to hold his erect penis between cool, strong fingers.

'Stop brooding, and come here,' she said. 'I want to suck your prick.'

He moved up her body and settled beside her. She rolled her head into his groin and began to lick his phallus, washing him like a cat. A drop of clear liquid oozed from the slitted eye. She took it on her tongue and smoothed it on to his glans, out to the rim of his cock-helmet, and back in again to the centre.

Sally burrowed between his thighs. She parted her lips and drew his left testicle deep into her mouth, rolling it against her tongue, grazing it with her teeth. She sucked harder: her caresses were on the borderline of discomfort, driving him mad with an aching mixture of dread and desire.

'Stop that, Sal,' he whispered. 'Stop it. I can't bear it.'

But she knew exactly how much he could bear, to the minim's weight. She always had done. No matter what he said, she knew that ending the sweet agony she was giving him would be worse than continuing.

Odo's prick pressed against her cheek, thrust into her hair. He would be reduced to begging for her soon. That's what she wanted. Damn her. Might she be damned to the uttermost pits of hell.

'Please, Sal,' he cried, ashamed and needy. 'Please!'

And she had mercy.

Parting her lips, she let his testis slip free. She looked up at him, and smiled. Then, very slowly, Sally took his rigid cock deep into her mouth.

Odo thrust his manhood eagerly into her, felt her take the whole shaft, felt her throat ripple as she swallowed his glans. She drew back. Her tongue teased the ring. Then she gulped him down again.

Odo began to push gently into her. His hand, between her thighs, mirrored the movement of his loins. She had always loved to suck his prick, to swallow down his sperm like fine wine.

'Ah, sweet,' he whispered. 'Do it. Do it, Sal. Take me to the root in your mouth. Take all of me. Suck me 'til I come.'

He could feel her clitoris throbbing under his hand. The old ways of pleasing her, while she in turn brought him to the heights of sensuality, came easily to him. It was as if it was yesterday. He caught one of her nipples between his fingers, crushing it. He heard, he felt, her gasp of delight.

Her hand gripped the base of his cock. She cupped the heavy sac of his balls, still wet with her saliva. He groaned, and thrust in to her, his phallus sliding through the mobile circlet of her lips.

Sally pushed against his fingers, moving faster. She was fiery as a furnace, wet as the sea. Her clitoris was hot and hard. He pressed his thumb down on it, rubbing fiercely. Her vagina flexed around his fingers, hungry as her mouth. He felt her come.

Odo struggled to prevent himself from joining her. He had to regain the mastery, had to keep going. He wanted to stay inside her forever; poised on the brink of dissolution, but strong enough to refuse the final surrender. Faint hope. He knew himself incapable of control, unable to prevent himself from rushing towards his doom.

He felt the dizzying onset of his climax and cried out: needful, incoherent. His cock pumped. His semen jetted on to her tongue in tearing spurts. In the midst of his ecstasy, Odo knew himself defeated.

He bowed over her, drained and groaning, trying to remind himself that it was only a battle lost, not the war. Next time, next time, he would be the victor. His hands stroked her body, quiet and lax with fulfillment.

Sally raised her head. A trickle of his sperm ran from the corner of her mouth, white on the tanned skin. He watched her, waiting for the moment when she would finish savouring the salty taste, and drink it down.

Sally smiled, close-lipped, and groped for the empty glass.

Then she turned away, and spat out his seed.

The blatant contempt of it infuriated him. Sally spat several times. She ran her tongue over her teeth, so as not to miss a single drop. Odo watched, grimly, as the sluggish white liquid oozed down the crystal and pooled at the bottom, mingling with the dregs of her wine.

It surprised him to see how small a quantity there was. When he climaxed, it had felt like a tidal wave.

'Another time, I'll know to hold your nose,' he said, when he could trust his voice.

Sally got up and stretched. 'You're very confident,' she said, as she sounded the bell. 'Who said anything about another time? I need to sleep.'

'I thought we decided on a three-act play,' said Odo, lazily. 'Is it that you doubt your ability to pace me?'

Sally threw back her hair and examined the love-bites he had left on her breasts. A servant scratched at the door.

'Lord Wraxall's leaving: have his horse brought round,' she said, without turning. 'And bring me something to wear.'

When the man left, Odo prowled across and stood close behind Sally. He slipped his arms around her waist and pulled her back against him.

'The old fires burn yet, Sal. I can feel their heat in you. You need my body. Do you think you can hide it from me, of all men? Lie with me tonight, or promise me tomorrow. You know the pleasure I can give you.'

Sally shook her head and pushed his hands away.

'I remember the price, too. Best get dressed, Wraxall. It's finished.'

'What if I – ' Odo began, and broke off suddenly.

He dressed with slow precision, spending a long time on arranging the folds of his lace cravat just so. In a moment's weakness he had thought to offer Sally his wife's freedom. If she complied, it would be worth the sacrifice of Celine and her wealth. But she might refuse. Hell's gate, she would, the spitfire!

Servants came and went. The table was cleared. He heard his horse led clattering up to the entrance. He did not once look at Sally, though he was conscious of her, veiling her nudity in a golden robe.

Odo slammed his rapier back into its sheath, and turned, head held high. He would not be reduced to haggling with her. He would have them both: Celine and Sally in the same bed, or he would have nothing. He was Wraxall: he had his pride.

Sally extended her hand for him to kiss. He bowed over her fingertips. Let her wait. His time would come.

'I bid you goodnight,' said Lord Wraxall, coldly. 'Your servant, madam.'

Chapter Thirteen

*L*ord Wraxall hauled back on Brown Molly's reins, pulling her to a plunging stop just outside the plantation gates. The sinking moon cast long shadows of horse and rider on the road ahead. Leaves hissed in the gale. Palms tossed and bowed.

Turning in the saddle, he looked back the way he had come. The moonlit road stretched, straight as a sword-blade, to Laissez Faire's door. Sally and Celine, under the same roof, and he was riding away?

The mare stamped and snorted. Lord Wraxall slipped from the saddle, tethered her beside the road, and made his way back towards the house along a circuitous side-path.

Celine rubbed her head against Auguste's arm, and sighed. She lay face down, one hand enclosing his manhood. The past hour had been full of frustrations. She had been aching with desire by the time he'd joined her in the priest's hole. But satisfaction was not so readily got, it seemed.

'Disappointed?' asked Auguste.

'No,' lied Celine. 'It was wonderful. You were superb.'

'I'm not a child, or a fool,' Auguste said. 'I know you didn't come. What do you expect? Why wouldn't you tell me what you wanted, what you liked?'

He sounded irritated. It had not occurred to her that he might also have found their first encounter less than adequate.

'If it bothers you so much, why don't you go?' she said, peevishly.

When he pushed at her shoulder, Celine turned over, stiff as a plank of wood. She avoided looking at him.

'Do you really want me to leave? Tell me, now.'

Celine thought about it. She was hungry for the touch of a man, and she desired Auguste fiercely. She wanted to come with his phallus inside her: maybe, a second time, it would happen.

'No, stay,' she said, shyly. 'I want – I need – I'm still . . .'

Auguste teased her nipple with the tips of his fingers. The brief touch sent a shiver of excitement down to Celine's loins.

'Ah, you liked that, didn't you?' said Auguste.

Celine nodded. She had, indeed.

'Do you want me to do it some more?'

She nodded again.

Auguste looked at her, and smiled, but did nothing.

'You'll have to ask,' he said softly.

'Stroke my breasts, please,' she breathed, after a while.

His hand caressed the pale shallow curves.

'Not like that,' Celine whispered. 'What you did before.'

'Touch your nipples, you mean? But that's not what you asked for.'

'It's what I meant,' she answered.

'Then tell me,' he said softly. 'I'll do whatever you want, sweetheart. I'd like to please you; and I will, as long as you're clear.'

'I find it difficult to talk about these things,' she said, huskily.

'But you can do them,' said Auguste. 'You're eager enough for loving, so why not speak of it? Didn't you let your husband know what you enjoyed?'

'Lord Wraxall? Never!' she said. 'He didn't talk to me

181

very much at all. Just to tell me how he wanted to use me, you understand.'

'Well, that explains a lot,' he said. 'Wraxall might have shown you how to satisfy his lust, but he's been deuced lax in teaching you how to make love. It's a partnership, Celine. How do you expect to enjoy sex with a man if you don't know what you want? Or if you know, but don't say?'

'I'll try,' she murmured.

She took his hand, and placed it on her breast again. In a whisper, with pauses to fumble for the right words, she told him exactly how to excite her.

Auguste followed her soft instructions. His fingers circled on the taut crests of her nipples. When she asked, he sucked them, teasing them until they were hard as beads of coral.

'Touch me,' she sighed.

Auguste grinned at her affectionately. 'I am touching you, sugar.'

'No. Down there. Between my legs. Pet me there.'

'Your clitoris?'

'Yes,' she answered, and gave his neck a kitten-bite. 'Touch my clitoris. Rub it. I want to feel your hand on it.'

'How do you want it? Up and down?' he asked, demonstrating with one fingertip. 'From side to side? In circles?'

Celine kissed him, thrusting her tongue into his mouth. Auguste's hand remained still.

'Up and down,' she said, huskily.

'Hard?' he said, as his finger began to move. 'Or gentle?'

It felt so good. She could feel Auguste quivering with tension. He was holding back, for her. And he would continue to do so for as long as she needed. Not, like Lord Wraxall, because it gave him pleasure; but because he wanted to give her fulfillment, as a free gift, between equals.

'Yes, I like that,' she said. 'A little faster now. That's right.'

The whole of the sensitive flesh of her sex pulsated and burned. The nerve endings at the opening to her vagina tingled, urgent for his entry.

She whispered her desire. One of his fingers moved back, and thrust slowly into the wet opening. He widened its tightness, and slipped a second finger inside. She loved to feel it, and the firmness and heat of his cock moving against her thigh. Her sex was swollen and engorged, the little pleasure-bud so hard that it ached.

Auguste's thumb circled the hot nubbin of flesh. Celine gasped. She could feel herself close to climax. She raised her knees and pumped her hips.

'Don't stop,' she sighed. 'Go deeper. Rub me faster.'

Willingly, he did as she asked. But when her orgasm came, it was no more than a single tiny pulse, so disappointing, so feeble, that she groaned aloud. Auguste took it for a sound of pleasure.

'There, that was better for you, wasn't it?' he asked, softly.

Celine embraced him, hid her face in his shoulder so that he could not see her expression of dismay. Even her fingers had given her greater delight. Was it true, then, that only Odo could bring her to ecstasy? Or was it because Auguste had made her talk – made her ask? Please, please, let it be that!

With a happy sigh, he turned on his back, and placed her fingers around the base of his erect phallus.

'Rest now, little dove,' he said. 'And when you're ready, I'll show you what I like.'

A thorny creeper hooked itself into the ruffle at Lord Wraxall's wrist. He untangled the the fragile lace carefully, and continued his silent approach. Laissez Faire drew him, as the moon draws the tides. He imagined padding through Sally's hushed and darkened rooms like a figure in a dream.

Would Celine sense his presence, would it give her

nightmares? The idea amused him. He thought of standing at her bedside, erect and still, the guardian of her unquiet sleep. She would be naked, defenceless, clasped in Sally's brown arms. And the door would have a very stout lock.

Lord Wraxall paused in the gloom cast by a flamboyant tree, and looked over the moonlit gardens to the house.

A woman came out of a side door and slipped furtively across to the stables. She was tall, and her hair was russet under the moonlight: Sally, perhaps? He turned aside, and began to circle through the bushes.

The stable door was open. The scent of sleeping horses, heavy and warm, filled the air. Down at the end, past the stalls and loose-boxes, a lantern burned in the tackroom. If it was Sally, she was out here alone, far from the house, her servants too distant to hear her call.

Odo flexed his right hand. One blow would do it. He could have her shut up at Acheron before she regained consciousness. Perhaps she would be more amenable when it was a case of exchanging Celine's freedom for her own. It wasn't what he had planned, but there was an elegant symmetry about the idea.

He stalked closer. The woman stood sidelong to him, a gawky creature in pink calico. With practiced fingers, she filled and lit a stubby clay pipe. Burning tobacco cast a lurid light on her harsh features. Not Sally, but he knew that face. This was proving to be a night full of interest.

'Well, the devil damn me black, if it isn't my late absconding groom,' he said, kicking the door open.

Martin Piggott choked, dropped his pipe, and fell into a fit of coughing.

'My Lord Wraxall!' he wheezed.

'I should have known that woman would be hiding you too,' said Odo. He looked the quaking man over, from his beribboned cap to the frill of his petticoat. 'Take my advice, my man: avoid pink. It does nothing for you.'

Piggott backed away, until his shoulders were pressed against the wall.

'My name's Patricia,' he squeaked. 'Honest! I'm the chambermaid!'

'Is that so?' said Odo, drawing his sword. 'Well, if you're truly tired of masculinity, I'll help. It's only the removal of certain accessories.'

'I'd sooner die!' said Piggott, through gritted teeth.

'That, too, can be arranged. Afterwards.'

'Mercy!' cried Piggott.

'Justice. I've not forgotten your wagging tongue.'

Piggott fell to his knees, hands clutched protectively at his groin.

'Spare me, my lord! I'll give you Sal Colney – I've evidence against her, hanging evidence. And I know where Lady Celine's hiding. I know how to get in. I can tell you! Isn't that worth something?'

Odo withdrew the rapier's point by a fraction.

'It may buy you a clean death.' he said. 'Speak!'

The clock above the card room's fireplace played a tinkling tune and then struck the hour. It was three in the morning, but the game was far from over.

Sir James laid his hand out on the green baize. 'Dear me, lost again!' he said. 'What shall I take off next?'

Not much much choice remained, for he was down to his shirt, his periwig, and one buckled shoe. Bess looked at him sharply, through the eyeholes of her half-face mask.

'I think he's cheating,' she said. 'Don't you, Midnight?'

'Definitely,' said the madame, fanning herself.

Sir James fidgeted guiltily, as Bess got up and strolled towards him.

She was all in sky-blue leather, from mask to boots. A buckled corset left her swelling breasts bare, and her skin-tight breeches were split at the crotch. Her sex, shaved naked, pushed the seams apart.

Bess was more than pleased with the outfit. It was one of several made to her own design by Mother Midnight's

185

specialist tailors. The madame had brought the completed order up to Government House that very night.

The exotic costumes lay draped over a nearby table: the black lace, the silver satin, and the red, each with its matching whip. A set of gilded shackles and a monogrammed ivory dildo lay on a chair, along with Bess's evening dress. James had begged her to wear the blue, as soon as he saw it.

Bess leant across him, and lifted his left wrist. She shook it. A couple of low diamonds fell out of his sleeve.

'I thought so,' said Bess. 'No-one could hold such bad hands all night without a little help. You know what this means, don't you, James?'

Shamefaced, he hung his head. 'Yes, mistress mine.'

'Bend over the table,' Bess commanded. 'Midnight, hold his wrists.'

'I thought this was a social occasion,' said the madame.

'I'll let you take payment in kind,' said Bess.

Mother Midnight gave Sir James an interested look. 'Is he willing?'

'He'll do as he's told,' said Bess. 'Won't you?'

Sir James nodded, and got heavily to his feet. On Bess's instruction, he tucked up his shirt, leaving himself bare from his armpits to the single shoe. His squat phallus thrust out rigidly from between his legs.

Bess smiled, remembering the first time she had seen James taking his punishment. Sal Colney had flogged him a good half-dozen times before he got an erection. All she needed was a threat, and he was ready for anything.

Not that it would do to be too puffed up, Bess told herself. Her power was far from total. She had made little headway over Celine's marriage. James knew nothing of his daughter's flight. There was no point in telling him. His search parties would only disrupt certain illicit activities of Sally's and, in the end, he would only send Celine back to Acheron.

His stubborness annoyed Bess, but it piqued her too: kept her on her toes.

She toyed absently with his prick as she thought. When she squeezed the thick, shiny head above the cock-ridge, its slitted orifice gaped and closed like a tiny mouth, silently begging for satisfaction.

'Oh, Bess,' said Sir James, in a voice that shook.

She released him, and chose a supple switch.

'I told you to bend over,' she said.

Sir James lowered himself so that his broad chest was flat on the table-top. Mother Midnight caught his wrists between skinny fingers, and tugged.

He grunted as she pulled his arms painfully tight. The bones of his pelvis ground against the table's edge. His erection thrust out under his belly. A drop of clear liquid fell from its tip to the Turkish carpet.

Bess kicked lightly at Sir James's ankles, to make him straddle.

'No, wider. Wider than that,' she said. 'You'll need to be fully open to take what I'm going to give you tonight.'

She brought down the switch, smartly. Where it landed, an angry line streaked across his buttocks, and the skin rose, puffy and red.

'Be a little gentle, mistress,' whimpered Sir James. 'Please? I've got exchequer business all day tomorrow. If you knew how those damned chairs hurt, after you've been rough with me. I won't be able to concentrate, and I must. I'm the Governor, damn it. I have obligations – duties.'

Angered, she struck him again. The switch whistled through the air and his buttocks quivered to the force of the blow. When five more lines lay beside the first, she gave him a rest.

Sir James lay panting across the table among the scattered cards. He had managed not to cry out, but only by biting his tongue.

Spreading her palms across the abused skin of his behind, she felt its heat. Soon the pain would fade a little, change to a tingling and a need. She knew that Sir James expected her to command his services now, first for herself, then for Mother Midnight. The madame was

187

breathing fast, and small spots of colour burned on her white face. She wanted it as much as he did.

The thought of watching him burrow his head between Midnight's scrawny legs, licking her salt cleft, was so erotic that Bess almost succumbed. She would make him do it, right enough, and flog him on to better efforts. But not yet. He was going to get something else first.

Leaving Sir James to anticipation, she fetched the ivory dildo.

It was craftsman's work, a perfect duplicate of an erect male member, and polished to a dull sheen. Entwined initials, inlaid with gold, were cut into its head. Bess traced them with a fingertip, wishing she could read. She had asked for a B and a J, but it might have said 'Vote Whig' for all she knew.

Sir James spoke her name softly: the delay was telling on him. Bess moved round to Mother Midnight's side, and raised his head so that his chin rested on the table. His look of abject surrender made her dizzy with desire.

'Open,' said Bess, and slipped the dildo between his parted lips. She twisted and turned it in his mouth. 'Suck it. Make it good and wet: dripping. If you skimp on the spittle, the next part might hurt more than you like.'

Bess watched with delight as Sir James realised her intention. His eyes bulged, and he struggled fiercely. Mother Midnight clamped down on his wrists.

Bess pushed the dildo further into his mouth. She leant close. Her nipples brushed on the green baize, and hardened still further.

'You don't fool me,' she whispered in his ear. 'I know you could get loose if you wanted to. You say you're mine, James. Well, tonight I'm going to make you prove exactly how much.'

Not even trying to answer, he licked and sucked helplessly at the ivory cock in his mouth. When she was sure of his obedience, Bess slowly withdrew the dildo, and checked its wetness.

'Don't make me do it, Bess,' he pleaded. 'I've never –

no-one's ever – that thing's too big for me. I won't be able to take it.'

'Don't listen to him,' said Mother Midnight, hoarsely. 'He can bear twice that thickness. It's only the moment of penetration that's difficult. If he fights it, though, I might not be able to hold him.'

'He won't,' said Bess, confidently.

She walked round behind Sir James and thrust his buttocks apart. His anus was a little puckered ring, darker than the surrounding skin. She spat on it, and smoothed her saliva around the opening. He shuddered, wide-spread legs trembling so hard that, without the support of the table, he would have fallen.

Bess placed the dildo in the centre of the dull rose of flesh. She pushed, gently, but with increasing force His muscles tightened against her attempts at invasion.

'Relax,' said Bess, softly. 'Or you'll make it worse.'

She sensed the effort of will it took for him to obey her. Slowly, the resistance ebbed out of him. His fists, that had been clenched, opened.

Bess gave a low laugh.

'You want it, don't you?' she asked. 'You fear it, but you want it more.'

Sir James nodded, dumbly.

'Say it!' commanded Bess.

'Yes!' cried Sir James, in humiliation. 'Do anything you want to me.'

'Turn your head,' she murmured. 'I want to see your face as it goes in.'

Sir James laid his cheek on the table, among the scattered cards. Bess thrust with a steady pressure. Sir James's mouth twisted, and he began to cry.

Ignoring his tears and protests, Bess pushed harder. The tip of the dildo slipped into him. His tight orifice dilated to take it.

'No more,' he pleaded. 'I can't. It's too much, Bess.'

'Be a man, James,' she said, and eased the shaft further inside. 'You'll take as much as I choose to give you. Push on it. There. Do you like it?'

'No!' wept Sir James. 'Ah, God, yes.'

Bess thrust the dildo into him until only an inch remained outside. The sight of it, protruding from the straining ring of his anus, made love-juice trickle from her sex, darkening the blue leather at her thighs. Bess had never wanted him so much. She knew she could not last much longer.

'You'll keep that in place while you serve us,' Bess said. 'Stand up now, and ask Midnight how she wants to use you. And James, don't let it come out. For if you do, I'll make you wear it all day tomorrow, meetings or no.'

Sir James pushed himself slowly back into an upright position, flinching at the feel of the intrusive shaft penetrating his vitals. His prick, flushed and angry-looking, stuck out from his groin in counterpoint to the dildo's end, jutting obscenely from between the cheeks of his arse.

He gave Bess a long look, half dread, half worship, and bowed his head.

'I will submit,' he said. 'May my sufferings bring you joy, my love.'

Mother Midnight pulled a chair forward and settled herself on it. She beckoned. Sir James approached her. His single shoe made him hobble. He clenched his buttocks tightly, but his uneven gait was enough to cause a slippage of the rod.

To Bess's delight, without further commands from her, he thrust the ivory back in to position. Using his hands to hold it inside himself, he shuffled across to stand before Mother Midnight.

'My mistress . . .' he began hoarsely, and broke down.

His shoulders shook with sobs. Bess picked up the switch and went to stand beside him. His shame aroused her more than she thought possible. She squeezed her wet thighs together, putting pressure on her clitoris, and the resulting flash of sensation made her gasp. She tapped the shiny glans of his penis sharply with her switch.

Sir James winced, and tried again.

'My mistress has put me at your command,' he whispered. 'What is your pleasure with me?'

Without a word, Mother Midnight pointed to the floor. Arms linked behind his back, hands on the dildo's end, he dropped to a kneeling position before her. Bess watched avidly as the madam began to draw up her skirts.

'Give me a good licking,' said Midnight, crudely. 'Don't stop until I say.'

Covering her sex with his mouth, he sucked at it. His tongue dipped into the cleft between the madame's labia, and parted the wet folds. When he licked her clitoris, Mother Midnight grasped his head and crushed it in to her sex. She jerked up and down, mashing him against her groin.

Bess encouraged him with a flurry of light blows to the back of his thighs. Putting one hand on his, she made him thrust the dildo in and out of his own arse. Sir James moaned loud enough to wake the dead.

She wanted to stroke his cock, but she knew that he would spend at a touch. And James was going to have to last. She wouldn't let him come until she had her turn: maybe not then. She might make him wait until morning.

His face was wet with tears and Mother Midnight's juices. He rubbed his mouth and chin against her roughly, lashing her with his tongue until the madame flopped back in her chair, eyes closed, and lay there panting.

Obedient to his orders, for she had not told him to stop, Sir James continued to lick desperately at her sex.

'Forgive me,' said a quiet voice from the door, 'but how much longer is this going to go on?'

Bess turned, feeling as if she was moving through molasses.

Odo, Viscount Wraxall, stood at the entrance to the card room.

'I'm desolated to disturb your pleasures, Fortescue,'

he said. 'But the matter is urgent. I've received information that there's a smuggling vessel about to unload
in Morgan's Bay. It will be gone by dawn.'

Sir James rose, unsteadily, and pulled down his shirt
to cover himself. Bess drew herself up, quivering all over
with rage and disappointed lust.

'Get out!' she stormed. 'Go on, sling your hook, you
toad!'

'One of your troupe, Midnight?' asked Lord Wraxall,
with contempt. 'Send her to Acheron, the day after
tomorrow. She needs a lesson in manners.'

Raising the whip, Bess took a step forward. Sir James
caught her arm.

'Smuggling's against the King's law,' he said, sternly.
'I won't let it pass, Bess, not even for you. I must make
out a warrant, alert the militia.'

'Very well,' said Bess, coldly furious. 'But that dildo
stays up your arse, understand? Just to remind you of
what will be waiting when you return. Now get dressed,
and go. And keep your mind on King George if you can.'

She turned away, and stalked to the window. She did
not look round again until the door was closed behind
him.

'Looks like Sal Colney's in for a surprise,' remarked
Mother Midnight.

Bess stiffened. Morgan's Bay: that's where Laissez
Faire was – and Lady Celine. If the militia searched, and
they would, she might be found. But Sir James would be
back shortly, eager to submit, and her need to punish
him was like a fire in her blood. What to do?

'You alright?' enquired Mother Midnight.

Bess nodded, absently. Odo Wraxall would not take
Celine, if she had to die to prevent it. The men would be
in the office by now. She had to hear what was said. She
had to know what was happening, and fast.

'I'm going to the library,' she said. 'Wait for me.'

Mother Midnight began to lay out a game of clock
patience.

'Take your time,' she said.

Chapter Fourteen

*I*t was past moonset, dark as pitch. But as Sally made her way to the stables, a single bird chirruped, sensing the approach of dawn.

She must have spent longer brooding about Wraxall than she thought. It had been stupid to renew their liaison. All she had done was remind herself of days best forgotten. She had loved him once.

Better to think of business, she told herself, crossly. Morning would be here all too soon and, in truth, there was enough to be done. Dozens of barrels of gunpowder and shot were hidden in the barn, waiting to be exchanged for the *Queen Royal*'s cargo of contraband. A long job, and one best started.

She broke into a run, glad not to be encumbered by skirts. Male attire was better suited for her after-dark activities.

The severity of shirt and breeches suited Sally, emphasising the lush femininity of her figure. A ribbon knotted back her auburn mane, and there were two pistols slipped under the green silk sash that wrapped her waist.

Against all orders, the stable door was open. The horses were restless, stamping in their stalls. There was a lantern burning in the tack-room.

She pushed open the door, and walked across to lift her saddle from its place by the wall. A clay pipe crunched underfoot.

Those damned grooms, Sally thought. They knew it was forbidden to smoke in the stable; the place was a fire-trap. All it needed was for one wind-blown spark to reach the barn and the whole place would be blown to Bermuda.

She bent to pick up the pipe, hoping to identify its owner. There was a foot sticking out under the workbench. A foot too large for the high-heeled lady's shoe it wore.

Piggott sat propped against the wall. For a moment, Sally thought she saw his expression change, but it was only a vagary of the light. Martin would not move again. Blood bloomed like a flower on the breast of his gown.

Her fingers shook slightly as she parted his lace kerchief. Piggott had been killed with a single blow from a rapier's point. There were no signs of a struggle, no defence cuts on his hands. An efficient murder, and a quick one: Wraxall's work, without a doubt.

A sound startled her. Cocked pistols ready in her hands, Sally listened alertly. She heard a distant pounding on the hard-packed road: galloping hoofbeats, growing nearer.

Sally raced outside. The first grey light of morning was seeping into the sky. A horse turned through the gates, and thundered towards her. Its hooves struck sparks from the stony road. A small figure crouched, jockey-style, on its back, yelling like the Wild Hurt.

'Mistress Colney! Mistress Colney!'

It was Bess Brown.

Celine knelt above Auguste, straddling him, and ran her hands over the sculptured muscles of his torso.

During their night together, she had reached the heights of arousal. She craved Auguste's body, loved the feel of his hardness thrusting inside her.

But her orgasms continued to be disappointing, almost

194

non-existent: tiny spurts of satisfaction which only sharpened her appetite and made her greedy for more.

At that moment, shaming though the reflection was, she almost wished she had stayed at Acheron, and allowed the footmen to use her body. At least then she would still be subject to Lord Wraxall's perverse, inventive lust, and the ecstasy it woke in her.

She bent and teased the tip of Auguste's phallus with her tongue. It tasted of salt and musk. The scent of it made her wild with desire and frustration.

He moved sharply in her arms.

'Stop!' he said. 'Someone's coming.'

Footsteps raced up the secret stair. The door crashed open and Sally hurtled through it. Behind her, a masked woman, with a voluminous coat buttoned up to her chin, panted into the room.

'Good morning, milady,' said the stranger, and bobbed a curtsey.

'Bess?' gasped Celine.

Bewildered, she looked from one to the other. Bess was covered in the dust of travel: Sally's face was wild and strained.

'Wraxall's on his way with a militia escort,' said Sally, grimly. 'He's got a warrant to arrest me for smuggling, and enough proof to hang me five times over, though God knows how he got it. I won't wait to be taken. I'm for the *Queen Royal*, and freedom.'

Auguste pulled on his breeches and shrugged into his shirt.

'I'm with you,' he said.

'What about you, Bess?' asked Sally. 'Take the chance on a new life?'

'I've already got a new life, thank you very much,' said Bess, tartly.

Celine knew her turn was coming.

It was too late to go back now. Yes, she missed Lord Wraxall. Perhaps she always would. But just thinking about the revenge he would take on her for the injuries to his body, and his pride, made her sweat with terror.

'Well?' said Sally. 'The secret of this room is still safe.'

'I'll sail with you, of course,' she said.

'Take my coat, miss,' said Bess, slipping out of it. 'You can't go naked.'

Bess had not stopped to change before setting out on her desperate ride, and the blue leather outfit she wore made Celine's eyes widen with shock.

While she was being buttoned into the coat, Celine stole covert looks at her maid's bare breasts above the tightly buckled corset, and the pouting cleft of her sex. She was shaved, too!

Celine knew Bess was now her father's mistress, but she had no idea his tastes were so extreme. She had never seen such a wanton costume, not even among the exotica of Acheron.

'Are you ready?' asked Sally, breaking off a low-voiced argument with Auguste. 'Good, then let's go. Time's short.'

'I still don't like it,' said Auguste, as they piled out of the priest's hole. 'I'm no more disposed to make Wraxall a present of the powder and shot than you, Sal. But – '

'I know what I'm doing,' interrupted Sally. 'Your job is to get Lady Celine aboard the *Queen* and set the sails. Let me handle blowing up the barn.'

The warm light of sunrise striped the gallery floor. Leaving the portrait of James II swinging, the four raced down the stairs and outside.

Bess's horse cropped quietly at the grass. Auguste swung into the saddle, and pulled Celine up to sit before him. She clung on firmly, glad of the warmth and security of the African's muscular body.

He gathered the reins, and looked down into Sally's drawn face.

'It won't serve!' he said. 'Fortescue's probably on his way by sea in a Revenue cutter. If we wait for you, he'll trap us in the bay.'

'No, he won't,' said Bess, unexpectedly. She cast an apologetic glance at Celine. 'I'm ever so sorry, miss, but I left him tied to the bedpost.'

'What!' said Celine, in horror, as Auguste urged the horse into a trot.

'It's all right, my lady,' Bess called after her. 'He likes it!'

Lord Wraxall threw up one hand, Captain Cathcart shouted the command to halt, and the mounted militia came to a jingling, stamping stop behind them. The white walls of Laissez Faire shone in the rising sun. A faint wisp of smoke from the outbuildings was the only thing that moved.

'Column of fours, men,' said Cathcart. 'Lieutenant Bellamy with Company A takes the house, Jones and Company B the bay. At the trot, now: advance.'

Odo kicked his horse into a canter, outstripping his escort. He wanted this moment to be all his, as Sally – and Celine – would shortly be his. He smiled. Perhaps he would give a victory entertainment in the Rotunda.

He could see now that the barn was burning. Flames, almost invisible in the light of the rising sun, licked from between its planking. Above them, the air rippled with heat. The stable doors opened and a scatter of horses galloped free.

Mounted on the last came Sally.

She rode astride, guiding the beast with her knees. A pair of long pistols were in her hands: they pointed at his heart. Odo rose in his stirrups.

End it now, if you dare, he thought, with fierce exaltation.

Her gaze did not falter, but the pistols moved the tiniest fraction. She fired and Cathcart crashed from the saddle just behind him. His riderless horse went blundering through the column, sending it into disarray.

Sally fled. Odo spurred after her. And the gunpowder in the barn blew up.

The explosion was shattering, deafening. The very earth shook. The windows of Laissez Faire came apart in shards of crystal. The air was filled with flying splinters of wood and glass.

Brown Molly reared and squealed. Odo clung to the mare's neck, his ears ringing. Lieutenant Bellamy careered across to him, calling for orders.

'Get down to the bay!' commanded Odo. 'I want that woman caught. Ten guineas to the man who does it.'

Bellamy drew his sabre. Odo grasped his arm.

'Alive!' If you can't take her alive, then let her go. You hear me?'

He waited for the lieutenant's nod before he released his hold. Then he turned to the house. Sally, for the moment, was beyond his reach. His wife remained, in the secret room. Might she have pleasure in their meeting.

Celine leant on *Queen Royal*'s taffrail, scanning the shore-line. Overhead, the great sails were being shaken free. Sweating gun-crews unlashed the cannon from their places and ran them out.

'Load canister!' commanded Auguste. 'Check your elevation!'

'There!' cried Celine. 'There, look!'

Sally shot out from the cover of the trees. Her auburn hair had come loose; it trailed behind her like a flag in the wind. Bent low, to present the smallest possible target, she drove her horse onward into the surf.

A company of militia ran down to the beach, and drew up in two ranks. Carrying clearly over the water, Celine heard their officer give the command to fire. A volley crashed out, and she ducked instinctively and need-lessly. They were not aiming at the *Queen Royal*.

Having ridden as deep as her horse could take her, Sally flung herself from its back and began to swim for the ship with a racing stroke. The first rank of the militia knelt and reloaded, and the second rank let fly. Musket balls pattered and splashed around her.

Auguste strode to the head of the ladder and raised his hand.

'Port side gunners! On my mark.'

Celine put her fingers in her ears. Auguste brought his hand down.

Six slow-matches met the touch-holes.

Six cannon lurched backwards on their wheeled carriages.

In a man-made storm of fire and brimstone smoke, six thunderbolts of canister sped towards the shore. They struck and shattered, their lethal fragments bursting full in the faces of the militia waiting there.

When the smoke cleared, the sand was red with more than the coats of the fallen men.

Sally came up the anchor cable like a cat. She vaulted the taffrail and was scooped up into Auguste's arms.

'No time for dalliance,' said Sally, wriggling free. 'Let's slip our cable and get out of this. It's too hot for my liking.'

'What course?' cried the man at the wheel.

'To the Bahamas, where else? New Providence, and the freedom of the seas!'

Bess sat on the edge of the bed in the priest's hole, biting her nails. She could hear the noise of battle all too well.

I want to go home, she thought, fiercely. I want to go back to James.

She pictured him waiting, bound and helpless, patiently trusting in her return. The image sent a little shiver of excitement up her spine. Bess told herself off severely. How could she think about sex at a time like this?

She squeezed her thighs together. The pressure on her clitoris sent a thrill of guilty pleasure through her.

It was awful but, after all, it couldn't hurt. Better than just sitting and waiting. In fact, there wasn't even any reason why she had to sit. She could make herself comfortable.

Feeling very wicked, Bess lay back on the bed, and put one hand between her legs. She teased herself gently. Just until the cannon-fire stops, she thought. And then I'll find out what's happening before I ride home again.

Bess closed her eyes. Her fingers sought the moistness of her sex and began to move there. She thought about riding down the shore – riding home.

It was stormy weather, and she was mounted on Sir James's back. He was bridled with silk and bitted with silver. He went on all fours down the beach, very slowly. Her open sex rubbed against his spine, wetting it.

When the cannon – no, Bess corrected herself – when the thunder roared, James shied and startled. She had to tug back on the reins, holding him in, and school him to obedience with flicks of her whip on his rump.

A cool wind blew away the clouds. It brushed across her breasts and hardened their nipples. Her clitoris pressed against Sir James's flesh. There was no sound but the hush, hush of waves on the sand, or sometimes a click as two stones struck together in the retreating foam.

Bess's eyes popped open.

A click? Like the sound of a latch opening?

The guns were silent and, in the quiet, someone was coming up the staircase, very slow and stealthy.

As quietly as she could, Bess crawled beneath the bed, and curled up close to the wall. The door opened. A pair of riding boots came in.

'Well, madam wife,' said Lord Wraxall, suavely. 'We meet again. How fortuitous that it should be alone!'

The baleful promise in his words made Bess shiver.

'Come out from under there, if you please,' he said.

I won't, she thought.

'You will do as you are told,' said Lord Wraxall.

Try and make me, thought Bess. Put one hand under this bed and I'll bite your fingers off.

'Do you expect me to grovel about on the floor?' he asked. 'For the last time, madam, will you obey me?'

Not a chance, thought Bess.

'Very well,' said Lord Wraxall, and overturned the bed.

Bess blinked up at him, in the sudden light.

Drat, she thought. Now that, I didn't expect.

Lord Wraxall, too, had been taken unawares. It was too much to say that he looked surprised. But for a moment, before the heavy lids hooded them again, Bess caught a flash of some dark emotion in his eyes.

'I see,' he said. 'Fortescue's little playmate. I suppose it would be redundant to enquire what you are doing here. My wife, I then take it, is with Sal Colney on board the ship that has just left the bay. Did you race me from Fort George with your warning?'

Bess sighed with relief. Sally had won the battle. And what would Wraxall do now? Get a ship and follow, of course. Immediately.

She uncoiled herself, and got to her feet. Not if she could help it.

'And if I did?' she demanded.

Lord Wraxall gave her a look of chilling malice.

'It's unwise to meddle in my affairs,' he said. 'I promised you a lesson before, did I not? If I had more time – as it is, your punishment will have to be deferred. Rest assured, doxy, the delay will not make it lighter.'

Bess took a gliding step closer. She drew a deep breath that made her full breasts quiver. She noticed, with secret glee, that her startling costume was not without its effect. He was unable to resist a glance down at her shaved sex, pouting from the split seam of her blue leather breeches.

'Why wait?' she asked, provocatively. 'Or can't you get it up?'

Her hand darted down to his groin. Bess was hard put not to let her wonder show at the size of his manhood. It stiffened in response to her touch. He was as thick as Sir James, and longer – much longer. She felt slowly along his phallus, seeking its end.

'Are you satisfied?' asked Lord Wraxall, coolly.

'Far from it,' breathed Bess.

'I can't spare the time for this,' he said, but he did not move away.

She came still closer. Her erect nipples brushed against

his coat. She found the fastenings of his breeches and began to unloose them.

'No?' said Bess. 'Are you going to turn me down, then?'

His breeches flap fell open, and she slipped her hand inside. The shaft of his penis was warm and immense in her palm. She stroked it rhythmically, looking up into his set, inscrutable face.

Bess could feel a growing wetness in the cleft between her legs. Her arousal surprised her. This had started as play-acting, but it was swiftly becoming something more. He could not refuse her: he must not.

Her hand reached the head of his prick. She felt his piercing, and could not prevent a gasp of surprise. Lord Wraxall drew a hissing breath as her fingers toyed inquisitively about the ring.

Got him! thought Bess. Oh, yes, he likes that. She moved the metal back and forth through his glans.

'What's this?' she whispered. 'What's it for? Let me see.'

'It's for my pleasure,' said Lord Wraxall, coldly. 'On your knees.'

'We'd do better on the bed,' murmured Bess, as she teased his cock. 'It won't take a moment to put it to rights. We could get comfy.'

'I said, kneel,' he snarled.

He seized her shoulder with hard fingers, and spun her around, driving her to the floor. Bess struggled instinctively against his roughness. He caught her before she had crawled a yard. His hand closed on the nape of her neck like a band of iron, holding her still.

'Not so eager, now?' asked Lord Wraxall, mockingly. 'Having regrets?'

He hooked his fingers into the entrance of her vagina and pulled her back against his loins. He nudged her thighs apart. She felt the swollen head of his cock probing between them.

'Don't hurt me!' she whimpered.

'You started this,' he said. 'I'll do as I please.'

His arms tightened around her waist and he tilted her hips up towards him. With a thrust of his groin, he lodged his prick's head in her vagina. His rigid phallus stretched her to capacity. Even though she was wet and receptive, it was hard to take him.

Lord Wraxall drove into her strongly, cramming his shaft in her to its root. Bess parted her legs wide, to accept him more comfortably.

She braced herself as he began to move in her. Each time he withdrew almost his whole length. With each deep penetration, his belly rammed hard against her leather-clad behind. She could feel the ring in his glans quite distinctly, pressing against the rear wall of her sex.

A wave of intoxicating lust flooded over her, and Bess surrendered totally to Lord Wraxall's prick. She loosened to him. Slippery juices seeped from her vagina, smearing his phallus and making each thrust easier, better. God, but it was good. She had not thought she would enjoy it so much.

'Yes,' she murmured, pressing herself back against him. 'Yes. Oh, I want it. Come on; show me what you can do.'

His balls brushed against the inside of her thighs as he pushed in and drew back, fast and steady. With every withdrawal she could feel her clitoral hood tighten, sending tingles through the little pleasure-bud.

She ached for him to use his fingers on her, and she squirmed against him, begging in incoherent whispers for a touch on the burning flesh. She needed it, wanted it so fiercely that she almost wept.

Lord Wraxall ignored her pleas. He pushed her back and forth on the shaft of his cock, using her for his pleasure, oblivious to hers. Bess writhed and twisted, impaled on his stiffness, sobbing with arousal and need.

'Faster,' said Lord Wraxall, through his teeth. 'You hear me, wench?'

She panted and struggled, trying to reach the fulfillment he denied her. She heaved beneath him, responding with growing desperation to the movements of his rigid member. She could tell from his broken breathing and the increasing fury of his thrusts that his crisis was near.

'Wait for me,' she wailed. 'I'm not ready – please . . .'

It was no use. Bess heard his grunt as the spasms took him. In the instant that she felt the first pulsations of his prick, he snatched it from her. He released her abruptly, and she slumped gasping to the floor. His seed spattered the backs of her legs.

Lord Wraxall fastened his breeches, and tossed a shilling down to her.

'More than you're worth,' he commented.

Without another look in her direction, he strode towards the door.

Bess pushed herself up on her elbows. Tears of frustration and rage trickled down her cheeks, and out from under the mask.

'Go on, leave,' she spat. 'Much good may it do you, now.'

He stopped, one hand on the doorlatch.

'And that means?' he asked.

Bess rose to her feet.

'It means I've bought Lady Celine's freedom. By the time you get back to Fort George and set sail, she'll be long gone. Don't you think that was worth the loss of a little pleasure?'

'Indubitably,' said Lord Wraxall, with a thin smile. 'If it was true. My plans, however, are not so easily overset. I gave orders for the *Nemesis* to leave harbour before I set out. With this wind, she should be close on Morgan's Bay by now. I will only have to go aboard.'

Stunned into silence, Bess watched him leave. He had to be lying. Please, God, let him be lying. She tried hard to convince herself, all the time knowing that it had been for nothing. She felt soiled, degraded; and knew that he had intended that very thing.

Stiffly, for his use of her body had been strenuous, Bess bent and picked up the piece of silver. She turned

204

the coin in her fingers. Her eyes darkened with anger, to the deepest indigo.

She searched in a chest for some less revealing clothes in which to make her escape, but her mind was not on the garments that she turned over. She thought of cellars, and shackles bolted shut, and branding irons.

'I swear, that if I ever get that man in my power,' said Bess, in a low, throbbing voice. 'He will rue this day. He'll rue it sorely.'

Chapter Fifteen

Celine opened her eyes to rippled wave-reflections moving across the ceiling of the *Queen Royal*'s great cabin. She lay cuddled between Sally and Auguste, and accepted the tired kisses they gave her. All three were naked.

Celine flushed, remembering the long afternoon's pleasure. It had been wonderful to have the two of them ministering to her; but her lust, roused beyond bearing by their doubled caresses, still wanted more. Her doubts were justified. Without Odo, she feared she would not taste true satisfaction again.

A part of me longs to be his, yet I loathe him, she thought. He terrifies me. And Liam no longer cares: that is over, I have sealed the hurt away. It's time for a new beginning.

She stirred in Auguste's arms, and he groaned.

'Not again: I'm outnumbered, ladies, have a heart.'

'Maybe we should leave you out next time,' said Sally, yawning.

'At the moment, that sounds like a damned good idea,' he said, climbing out of the bed.

Celine rolled on to her stomach and watched him dress. Once Auguste had gone on deck, Sally unearthed a shirt and a pair of damson plush breeches for Celine from a cupboard built into the bulkheads.

It felt very peculiar to have fabric enclosing her legs. The breeches bagged at the waist. Celine hitched at them: a seam brushed her most intimate places, as if someone touched her covertly.

'You need a belt,' commented Sally. 'Or better, a sash.'

'I saw some,' said Celine. 'No, not there, up on the shelf.'

Standing on tiptoe, she tugged at a confusion of silks, black and scarlet. The bundle opened as it fell. They were not sashes, but flags.

And the topmost bore a grinning skull.

'That's the pirate flag,' said Celine, shocked. 'The Jolly Roger.'

'No, it ain't,' Sally corrected her. 'But the red one is. We fly the death's head first, to give a ship the opportunity to surrender. The *Joli Rouge* only goes up if they refuse. It means no quarter will be given. It doesn't get used often. Few have the courage to oppose Tremaine.'

'You mean the captain?' gasped Celine. 'He's Tremaine? And I hardly even noticed him!'

'The captain's Bartholmew Pollock,' said Sally. 'Tremaine is aboard, though. Haven't you guessed yet?'

'Oh my God. Not you?'

Sally burst out laughing. 'If you could see your face!'

'But are you?' asked Celine. She could not believe it.

'Well, partly,' said Sally. 'Tremaine don't exist. It's what you might call a company name. A very profitable company. There are three of us altogether. Me, Auguste, and Kalinda Sagrado: she runs the shore operation.'

Unable to find a word to say, Celine let Sally bind a sash about her waist and lead her outside, on to the poop deck.

She found it hard to assimilate the fact that she was sailing with the most feared sea-thief in the Caribbean. Tremaine, the bogeyman that Island mothers used to scare their children into obedience. Tremaine, whom her father had sworn to hang. And Sally had danced with Sir James, flirted with him, on the night of the Government House Ball!

Auguste stood at the rail, scanning the distance through a long telescope. Captain Pollock, who looked more like a starved preacher than a pirate, gave the women a brief nod of acknowledgement as they came up.

Gulls wheeled above their wake. St Cecilia was a blue smudge on the horizon. Far behind, a vessel paralleled their course, its sails like white sparks in the sun.

Auguste passed the spy-glass to Sally.

'No doubt about it,' grunted Captain Pollock. 'She's after us. What do you reckon: Navy, or Coastguard?'

Sally stared through the telescope, her mouth set.

'Neither,' she said. 'I'd recognise those gilded top-masts anywhere. That's Wraxall's *Nemesis*.'

'We can't outgun her,' said Auguste. 'We've hardly enough powder for a single broadside. Can we outrun her?'

'She was up for sale,' replied Sally, with a shake of her head. 'Wraxall had her careened and new fitted to get a better price. There's not a barnacle or a weed anywhere on the hull, to slow her down.'

Celine's hands tightened on the rail. She tried to tell herself that the beating of her heart was only fear. He was coming after her. She could not, would not, willingly go back. But he might take her.

'We'll change course, make for the mainland.' said Sally. 'Kalinda's *Paramour* should be moored off Catzu-mel by now. With her help, and a wind to hold him on a lee-shore, we'll turn the tables on Odo Wraxall. So much for sentiment. I should have killed him when I had the chance.'

'And if the *Paramour*'s not there?' asked Auguste, doubtfully.

Sally shot a glance at Pollock.

'We could always go ashore,' she said, in a low voice. 'You know where.'

'Without Kalinda to guide us? It's a desperate venture!'

'So's falling into Wraxall's hands,' said Sally, and turned away. 'Best get those guns loaded.'

The rainforest at Catzumel swept down from mountains so great that Liam had to crane his neck to see their peaks. Beyond the treetops was a space of purple distance and above it – up, up, impossibly high – the snowfields shone and the condors circled.

They left the *Paramour* tugging at her anchor in a brown river, and walked inland through the forest for a day and a night, and half another day. The air was heavy as sweat. It smelt of fever.

Liam and Reuben carried the chest of jewels between them, slung from an oar for portage. Kalinda led them, moving easily despite the great bundle balanced on her head.

At noon, on the second day, they reached the clearing.

Liam swung the oar off his shoulder and rubbed his aching muscles. The sunlit space crowned a steep rise. He could see the sky again. He could see the *Paramour*, small and perfect as a toy. The forest, stretching out on every side, looked no more than a field of tussocky grass. In two strides he could be down there, picking the ship up in the palm of his hand.

'Now what?' he asked.

'We wait,' said Kalinda. 'We have to get permission to enter the city.'

Liam looked around him again.

'A city? In this wilderness? And permission from whom?'

'Friends,' said Kalinda.

Reuben snorted. He was busy about the bundle she had carried.

'Savages,' he said. 'Poison blow-pipes: nasty habits.'

'They are my grandmother's people,' said Kalinda. 'And they were great once, before the Spaniards came. We – they still remember, a little. And they are trustworthy. Can you think of a better guard for treasure?'

'Only because they don't know what it's worth,' said Reuben. 'Quartz is the same as diamonds to them.'

He jerked open the bundle and shook out its contents: mirrors with bright tin backs, machetes and strings of scarlet beads.

'Lend a hand here, lad, will you? This Brummagem rubbish has to be hung up on the branches.'

Kalinda drew close, and touched Liam briefly between the legs.

'He doesn't really need your help,' she said, huskily. 'I do.'

Reuben hunched his shoulders, and turned his back. Liam knew he was hurting. Curse the man, what did he expect?

'I know a place nearby,' said Kalinda.

Leaves rustled as she disappeared into the undergrowth. Liam turned his face to the sun and felt his skin tighten under its rays. His hair stirred in the little wind that hung about the hill-top. He did not want to go back between the dripping aisles of trees. He found them oppressive. But at his groin he felt other tightenings, other stirrings.

Kalinda was waiting for him in a tiny enclosure hardly large enough for them to lie down together. Bushes with shiny, dark-green leaves and white blossoms made a wall around it. The scent of the flowers was acrid, faintly medicinal. It mingled with the smell of her arousal. She was already naked, wearing nothing but the pearls he had given her.

She kissed him. Her tongue slipped demandingly between his lips. She pressed against him, tugging at his clothes. Her hands eased his shirt free and over his head. The urgent trembling of her body transmitted itself to his. Liam crushed his mouth hard against hers, and pulled her to him.

Kalinda clawed her fingers down his back, and bit sharply on his lower lip. Closing her mouth on his nipple, she teased it with sensual skill until he groaned, feeling it harden under the flicking of her tongue.

210

This was what he wanted, this oblivion of the senses, where nothing could reach him but pleasure. No memories, no doubts, nothing but a sweating urgency and the knowledge that he could relieve it in Kalinda's body.

She sucked harder, almost painfully. One hand moved to his other nipple and began to torment it. His hands dug into the skin of her back.

'Ah, God, Kalinda,' he gasped. 'I can't bear it. Let me take you now.'

Kalinda's free hand caressed the hard muscles of his belly. Her fingers slipped into the waist of his breeches. They brushed his swollen cock-tip. He was ready, more than ready. His balls felt full to bursting; they ached to be discharged.

'Come on,' groaned Liam. 'Come on, don't keep me waiting.'

Sliding down his body, scratching and biting as she went, Kalinda reached his groin. His breeches were painfully tight over the rigid line of his cock. She kissed his erection's length through the fabric. She dipped her head, rubbing her face against the bulge of his testicles.

Her lips moved about the horn buttons of his breeches. Without using her hands, she tongued the first one free. The glossy head of his penis escaped.

Liam pumped his hips, pushing against her face. Dizzy with need, he wanted to feel her soft mouth enclosing the tip of his manhood. Her mobile lips opened the second button, the third.

He knew she was going to drive him to such an extreme of lust that he would fall on her like a rutting beast. Kalinda liked it hard and heavy, and the rougher the better. And Liam had sources of anger in him that never failed to fuel the brutal sex that Kalinda craved. But it wasn't all he wanted.

Sometimes, even when he was deep within her body, he despaired. He would have liked a kiss that was gentle, arms that encircled him softly. Not love – never love any more, only some tenderness. But it was not

Kalinda's way. He had more chance of affection from Reuben: and that was impossible.

Kalinda took his breeches down and slipped them from his feet, leaving him naked. His cock was hot and red, jutting out towards her. While her fingers moved on his tight buttocks, she kissed and sucked his balls, knowing that the feel of her tongue there took him to the point of frenzy.

He thrust her roughly back, so that she fell to the earth under his weight. Raising her knees, he pushed violently between them. As she accepted the drive of his loins that put his phallus into her, she hissed and spat.

Liam's hands gripped her waist, pulling her up on to him. If she wanted him to be an animal, well, that's what he would be. In the past weeks she had shown little interest in him as a human being. They hardly spoke except when coupling, and then only to urge each other on to fiercer passion.

'Is that all you want?' he snarled. 'Is it? My prick up you? Take it, then, the whole of it. I'll give it you.'

They wrestled together, copulating on the dirt like beasts. Their kisses were savage. She fought with claws and teeth, trying to get above him, for she climaxed more easily when she bestrode him.

Liam held her down by her shoulders, using all his strength. That was better: he could get in deeper that way. But it was still not sufficient.

'Get your legs up,' he said, hoarsely.

He felt the sucking warmth of her vagina enclosing him. She milked him with a greedy willingness that contradicted her struggles. She could not move him, could not escape. Kalinda bit and growled, but she obeyed. Her thighs clasped his hips. Her hard heels dug into his arse.

Liam gave a grunt of satisfaction, and threw back his hair. Leaves of the overhanging bushes brushed his face. The breeze riffled them and they turned to show their silvery undersides. The shadows changed. For a

212

moment, it seemed as if the undergrowth was alive, inhabited.

He stilled his thrusts. It was only sunlight ringstraking the branches.

Kalinda writhed impatiently beneath him. Liam rose on outstretched arms, preparing to use the whole force of his body to power his thrusts into her.

Suddenly he stopped. Stopped dead. Kalinda hissed with frustration, and clawed at his chest.

There were people in the bushes.

It was like waking in the night and seeing a figure sitting at the end of the bed who, when you looked, was a chance arrangement of curtains and bedclothes. Only this was the other way round. What he had thought was a branch became the curve of a hip; leaf-shine was the gleam on a naked arm.

He lay on Kalinda in the centre of a ring of women.

Kalinda locked her ankles together around his waist. She clenched her arms around his back, pulling him down, holding him on her, not allowing him the freedom to bring his arms into play. Her nails dug into his back.

The watchers stirred and moved closer, encircling them. Now they were more than half-seen shapes. Lithe women, naked and tawny as woodsprites, with conical breasts. Women with hair cut in lines as straight as their eyebrows.

'Don't stop, Liam. I need it. Don't stop.'

'Let me go,' he said, hoarsely. 'We're not alone.'

'They mean us no harm,' Kalinda murmured. 'They are only interested.'

She thrust up under him, flexing her sex-muscles around his prick and pleading for his thrusts. Liam shuddered and made an involuntary movement into her welcoming folds.

'Yes,' whispered Kalinda. 'Again.'

Something – a leaf, a fern? – trailed across his leg. Liam turned his head sharply, catching a movement from the corner of his eye. There was no leaf. There was no frond that could have moved across his back and touched his testicles so lightly, so teasingly.

There was only the women. All of them watching. Not salaciously, but with an open curiosity. They spoke together: a language of liquid, throaty syllables.

Kalinda's sex was wet and welcoming around his hardness. She heaved under him with an urgency impossible to resist. Liam thrust up into her. He tried to close his eyes, his ears, to the movement all around them.

But he could not shut out their touch.

A woman stroked his shoulder. Another ran her palm over his legs. She reached between them, weighing his balls in slender fingers, and made some comment in a low voice. Liam could not help but respond to her caresses. She laughed, softly. And then they were all around him.

Their hands were like petals falling, like the wind.

'They like you,' whispered Kalinda. 'They like your eyes – so blue. They like your – ah! Yes, do that again.'

His buttocks tensed and relaxed as he drove into her. The feel of her enveloping sex thrilled him. Warm and spicy, the scent of her excitement was so strong that he could almost taste it.

The light hands of the women were all over him. They caressed him unceasingly, inescapably. Each time he withdrew for a new stroke, slim fingers touched the shaft of his cock. They moved on his thighs, his balls, his neck. They slipped in to his mouth, they investigated the soles of his feet.

As he came, Liam cried out wordlessly. Soft hands squeezed his tightening balls. Then his orgasm took him and he could feel nothing but the ecstatic pulsing as his seed jetted from him.

He lay against Kalinda's flesh, gasping. Among the bushes, he heard a murmur, a breath, a rustle. And when he could raise his head again, the women were gone.

Chapter Sixteen

Celine stood beside Sally at the *Queen Royal*'s prow. The forested shore of the Spanish Main had been in sight since dawn, but they would never reach it. Over the past three days, the other ship had eaten up their lead.

'She'll be in range soon,' said Sally.

'Let me help,' blurted Celine.

'I'd feel better if I had no need to worry about you in the mêlée,' said Sally. 'Stay in the cabin: you've got a pistol for defence. I'll have enough to do in killing Wraxall.'

'Must he die?' asked Celine, feeling a sudden chill run down her spine.

'You miss him, don't you?' said Sally. 'You wake up in the night and think, and dream: being his woman could be so sweet if he was just a little different, just a little kinder, eh?'

'I can't deny that I still want Lord Wraxall bodily,' Celine said, softly. 'I thought I hid it well. How did you know?'

'Woman's intuition,' said Sally. 'Best get below.'

Celine made for the cabin and shut herself in. Her pistol lay on the bed. Gingerly, she picked it up. She was not a warrior. Sally had been in the right when she told her to stay hidden: but it still felt like shirking.

The *Nemesis* was running alongside now. She could see Lord Wraxall on the poop deck, erect and elegant in silver brocade.

With a six-fold crash that shook her to the keel, the *Queen Royal*'s guns let fly. The *Nemesis* wallowed at the impact. Then Lord Wraxall answered with all his metal. His broadside swept their decks. Louder even than the guns, Celine heard the long groaning fall of a mast. The mizzen, and its load of canvas, crashed to the deck.

The *Queen Royal* was crippled. Celine could feel it in the way she yawed to the wind. Timbers crunched as the *Nemesis* came alongside.

She fidgeted with the pistol. It was hand to hand out there, now. Sally and Auguste were fighting for their lives, while she stood by, inactive.

I can't just wait here, Celine thought. It's only one bullet, but there must be somewhere it would be of use. Stifling the inner voice that told her she was being every kind of fool, she eased open the cabin door.

The *Queen Royal*'s deck was a chaos of corpses, stench and steel. Celine hugged the shadow of the fallen mast. As she sidled along the bulkhead, her feet slipped in blood, and worse. Auguste lay trapped below a spar. She could not tell if he was dead, or merely stunned.

The battle on the gun-deck swirled and parted. Taking the moment's chance, Celine bolted up to the poop. The steersman was gone. Captain Pollock's body lay huddled beneath the loosely twirling wheel.

And by the taffrail, Sally and Odo confronted each other, blade to blade.

Balanced lightly on the balls of their feet, they were utterly intent on each other, eyes locked. There was a kind of formal grace about their duel. It contrasted strangely with the butchery below, where Sally's out-numbered men were being driven to the side.

Odo circled, and Sally matched him, pace for pace. They were like dancers, like lovers. They inhabited a private world, their bodies answering each other, at one in the swift attack and parry, in the long, repeated

216

lunges. Sally even smiled. It was the smile of the dancing Kali.

Beloved and lovely, he had said. *Valour in the form of a woman*. Celine's hand shook on the pistol grip. What past had those two shared, when she was sewing samplers, and learning her hornbook?

The rapier flashed. Sally riposted, and Lord Wraxall moved smoothly away. He fell back, pace by pace. She pressed him hard. Their blades rang as they met. Then his wrist turned in a subtle pass, and caught her blade as it drove forward. With an upward movement that was almost a salute, he struck the sword up and out of Sally's grip.

Her cutlass spun away, wheeling in the air. Celine did not wait to see it fall into the sea. On tip-toe, she crept forward.

Lord Wraxall drew back his blade. Its point was at Sally's throat. A line of blood leaked from the tiny wound and trickled down to stain her shirt.

'Yield, Sal,' he said, softly. 'I want to hear you say it.'

Celine rammed the barrel of her gun into Odo's side, and her finger curled on the trigger.

'One move,' she said, 'and I'm a widow.'

Lord Wraxall never blinked.

'Nonsense, madam. You've forgotten to cock it.'

It was no more than a glance she took, an instant's slackening of the pressure. But it was enough. She had forgotten how swiftly he could move.

Odo's hand closed on hers like a vice and drove it down. Celine cried out, her fingers numbed by the force of his grip. He eased the pistol free, and stepped back, so that he could cover both women.

'*Veni vidi vici*,' said Lord Wraxall.

Hugging her knees, Celine sat on the bed in the darkened great cabin, and tried not to think too much about the coming reunion. It would be soon.

Beyond locking her away to await his evening's leisure, Lord Wraxall had not been near. There was work to be done. The decks had been cleared, the dead tossed overboard. Auguste had woken from unconsciousness to find himself in chains. Celine had seen him and Sally dragged below. The *Nemesis* was holed and listing badly. Not caring to get his feet wet, Odo had transferred his command to the *Queen Royal*.

She heard the key rattle in the lock, and raised her head. Lord Wraxall entered, two crewmen at his heels.

Lanterns were lit. Celine hid her eyes from the glare. And from more than that. Odo had given her a single look before he turned away; it set her blood pounding with apprehension.

She pushed herself into the farthest corner of the bed. Odo was deep in discussion with his companions. Why had he brought these men with him? Were they a maritime Charles and Rupert?

'I doubt the *Nemesis* will stay afloat much longer,' said one. 'The pumps can only just keep up as it is. If the wind rises, we'll lose her.'

'Can she be repaired?' asked Odo.

'Given the timber, yes,' said the other, evidently the ship's carpenter. 'But she'll not last until we reach a shipyard.'

'Very well,' said Odo. 'There's a river off Cape Catzumel, if my memory serves. Good deep moorings, and a virgin rainforest, waiting for the axe. Set a course for it. And now, men . . .'

His pause was short. But it left ample time for Celine's imagination to present her with a dozen different pictures, all abominable.

'. . . I will bid you goodnight,' he completed.

Celine gave a low sob of relief. Lord Wraxall was watching her, and smiling. Of course he had done it deliberately.

Once the others had slouched away, Odo strolled across to her.

'Were you frightened?' he enquired, pleasantly.

Celine nodded. There was no point in pretending. She

still shook with the sudden release of tension. Her pulses were loud enough for him to hear.

'I intended that you should be. You are aware that, if I chose to turn you over to the crew, there is not a damned thing you could do about it? No open window this time, Madam Runaway. No convenient vine.'

'I won't ...' began Celine. She cleared her throat, and tried again. 'I won't fight you. I'll do whatever you say. Even – that – if you insist.'

'I shall, madam, never doubt me. But not tonight. This voyage has been wearisome in the extreme and, enforcedly, celibate. I am not disposed to let anyone precede me in the use of your body. Stand up, Lady Wraxall.'

Celine obeyed him. This was too easy. He could not forgive her so lightly for her escape. He had to have some ghastly surprise in store.

Odo unfastened his coat. He laid aside the rapier in its sheath.

'Think of this as a second honeymoon,' he said, taking off his waistcoat. 'At sea, in the tropic night, with only the stars to witness our marital bliss. Does not the idea charm you? Turn around, madam. and face the bed.'

'What are you going to do?' she cried, unable to bear the suspense.

'Why, madam, teach you who wears the breeches in our marriage. I have never beaten a woman before, but those kicks of yours came close to unmanning me. I pissed blood for a week after. You need to learn what pain is.'

His hand closed on the nape of her neck. It was a caress of velvet, but when she struggled she could feel the iron beneath.

'I do not intend to wrestle,' said Odo. 'This is my right as your husband, under law. Will you submit to discipline, or do I chain you on the orlop deck, down below sea-level, with your friends?'

Paradoxically, his threat calmed her. She had forgotten Sally and Auguste. If she submitted, Lord Wraxall might leave her free, and perhaps she could find some way of helping them.

'There's no need for that,' she whispered. 'I will accept my punishment.'

Odo relaxed his grip and gave a brief nod of satisfaction.

'Then bend, madam, and place your hands on the bed,' he said. 'Believe me, I will take no more pleasure in this than you. But it is necessary.'

Celine did as he told her. Odo slipped his hands around her waist from behind to unfasten her breeches and pull them down around her ankles. She felt him lift her shirt and toss it up. He picked up the rapier.

'No, my lord!' cried Celine, in terror. 'I beg you, not the blade!'

'What a monster you think me,' said Odo, in an amused voice. 'I have been without a woman for three days; without your services, my wife, for longer than I care to contemplate. Do you think I would render you unusable? Be calm, madam. The sheath stays on.'

Celine bit her lip, waiting for the blow. She knew it would hurt, but when the supple Toledo steel, leather-coated, lashed across her buttocks, it was worse that anything she had believed possible.

'That's the first,' said Odo.

Celine whimpered with anguish and sagged at the knees. Impatiently, Odo raised her, and made her spread her legs wider. The intial three or four lashes were so excruciating that shock insulated her from the next few. In the part of her mind not overwhelmed by pain, Celine knew he must be enjoying the sight of her pouting sex. It was fully exposed to his eye as she squirmed and writhed under the repeated strokes.

The last four blows were agony. Good intentions went by the board: she could not help but struggle to get free. Odo held her down firmly, and pushed away the hands with which she tried to protect her tender flesh.

Tears ran from her eyes, but she made no sound. It

was not bravery. The torment was so great it was impossible to get her breath.

'Twelfth,' said Odo. 'And last.'

Her correction was over. Celine hardly had room for relief. The scalding pain in her bottom was all she could think about. It felt red-hot, and sent twinges like burning wires through every part of her.

He stood back, and tossed the rapier onto the bed.

'I trust you now know your master?'

Celine fought to regain the ability to speak, to move.

'Yes,' she managed at last, in a humiliated whisper.

'I will expect proof,' he said. 'No, don't get up yet.'

Celine winced as he brushed his fingertips over the rose-glowing, painful globes of her behind. She felt him tracing the lines he had written there.

'I find that sight surprisingly erotic,' he said, softly.

He bent close; he stroked and kissed her smarting buttocks. He licked the weals he had made, his tongue trailing along them. His mouth was cool. Its soft wetness eased Celine's discomfort a little.

As he continued to caress her, the initial hurt of the beating began to subside. It died away slowly from a blaze, to a prickling heat, to a glow.

To her astonishment, as her pain moderated, the soreness of her bottom excited her. The smart of the lashes was converted to an itching arousal. Fiery messengers of pleasure travelled from the abused and sensitive skin of her behind to her sex. Creamy juices seeped from her vagina.

She sighed, and shifted restlessly under his hand. Her clitoris burned and thrilled as if it, too, had felt the rod.

'I see you are Fortescue's daughter indeed,' said Odo. 'Just as well. For I find there is one more thing which must be attended to immediately.'

He loosed the flap of his breeches, and pressed up close behind her. Celine could not prevent herself from crying out in renewed pain, as she felt him bearing down on the stinging weals that criss-crossed her buttocks.

He thrust inside her, his arms wrapped around her

221

waist. Making no concession to her soreness, his belly slapped hard against her upturned bottom each time he went in to her.

It hurt, but how pleasing that pain was. Every touch on her burning skin recharged the tingling of her sex. She sobbed and wept, and pleaded for a respite, but she could not help responding. She had never felt such violent pleasure. She was half mad with it.

Celine lost all track of herself, only aware that, with each impact of Odo's groin against her smarting rump, he was bringing her closer to a release she craved as a drowning man craves air.

His hands tightened, and she heard him groaning softly. His thighs battered against hers as he used his powerful legs to give increased strength to his thrusts. He drove his prick into her eagerly, plunging in and out.

When he came, and pulled away from her, she was on the brink of climax.

He stepped back, and covered himself. Celine raised her buttocks to him, offering herself to his hand.

'Don't stop,' she whimpered. 'Please – touch my clitoris. Rub it. You can make me spend with your fingers.'

'Indeed I can,' said Lord Wraxall. 'But I do not intend to. I told you once that your pleasure was in my gift. I may grant you release later. But you must earn it, madam. All depends on your compliance.'

Celine burned, she ached: but she would have to contain her lust, somehow. Now that Odo had relieved the most urgent of his desires, he could play with her for the whole night.

How could she ever have pined for this servitude? And yet she knew that, even if she were given the freedom to leave, she would not take it.

'Get up,' he said. 'I have tasks for you to perform yet, madam wife.'

She lifted her tear-streaked face. Cruel and uncaring he was, hateful to her he might be; but he knew how to enslave her with passion.

'As you wish, my lord,' she whispered. 'What must I do?'

He left her standing, while he strode to the door and called for wine. Then he flung himself into a chair and looked Celine up and down, while he waited for his command to be fulfilled.

'Take off the breeches,' he ordered.

The wine arrived while he was re-examining the damage done to her buttocks. Her shirt was bunched around her waist and Odo made her stay that way, continuing to handle her intimately while his glass was filled.

'Your cheeks are as red as your arse, my lady,' commented Odo, after the crewman had left. 'You can pull the shirt down. I have seen enough.'

He caught her around the waist and pulled her on to his lap. The silk of his breeches was cool against the weals on Celine's buttocks. She could not prevent herself moving softly against his groin.

Lord Wraxall smiled faintly, and sipped at his glass. 'It seems I am not the only one with a thirst.'

'Can I help it if you make me want you?' she said, bitterly. 'Must I admit how I have missed you? How I want the ecstasy you taught me to need? How much I crave your mouth sucking on my nipples, your prick inside me?'

'Flattering,' he said. 'But a pretty reluctance is more to my taste, Lady Wraxall, as you should remember. Do you know, I find you changed.'

'Changed?' she said, nervously. 'How?'

Odo did not answer until he had finished two more glasses of wine. In the silence she could hear the ship talking in creaks, whines and liquid gurgles, and the staccato tapping of blocks against the masts.

'Well, to take but one example: when you left me, you did not know what your clitoris was, save that when I teased it you trembled with lust. And yet tonight you named it, pleaded with me to touch it. I fear, madam, that you have not been faithful. My glass is empty.'

Celine refilled it. Her hand shook a little.

'No denials?' asked Odo. 'No protestations of innocence?'

'No,' said Celine. 'You wouldn't believe them.'

'How wise you have become,' he said. 'You need not fear to confess it. I find the idea of you coupling with others arousing, as you know. But I expect your gallants to be my choice, and your infidelities to be conducted under my eye. Lean back against me, madam, and open your legs wider.'

He pushed back her clitoral hood with the pad of his thumb, and began to toy with the little pleasure bud.

'And now, you will relate to me all your little adventures with Auguste Toussainte,' he continued. 'In detail, madam, and using every indelicacy of language. Don't look so startled. The whole world knew that he slept in this cabin with you and Sal Colney. It took very little persuasion before her men told me that.'

'W-what do you intend to do to him?' asked Celine.

'I've not decided yet,' Odo said. 'Either the noose or slavery. It depends on what you tell me. I'd like to turn a profit from this cruise, and any number of rich degenerates of my acquaintance might bid for him. If, that is, his performance at stud is sufficiently vigorous. Enlighten me.'

Her body's hunger made it desperately hard to think. The right answer might ensure survival – of a sort – for Auguste. But what was the right answer? Odo had promised her a man's life before, and she knew how he had planned to honour that vow.

'I will have your obedience in this, madam. When was the first time?'

'The night we took ship,' she whispered.

'I find that unbelievable,' he said, flatly. 'I trained you too well. You could not have gone three days without offering yourself to the first standing prick.'

'It's true,' insisted Celine. 'I used to do it to myself: with my fingers.'

Odo removed his hand, and reached for the wineglass.

'Kneel down between my legs, and excite yourself,' he said. 'Show me how you manage when you don't have a man.'

He pushed his chair back from the table. Celine positioned herself at his feet, spreading her thighs wide open. She needed relief, and the thought of showing herself off to him sent a thrill of shamed arousal through her.

Very slowly, Celine began to stroke the damply curled hairs that clothed her mount of Venus. At his order, she trussed up her shirt above her breasts so that he could see better. She slipped one hand between the outer lips of her sex. As she pressed open the plump petals of flesh, love-juices coated her fingers.

She massaged the tingling bud of her desire: it was hard and hot. How often had she felt for that wet, pulsing nubbin and caressed it into orgasm? How often had she tossed and moaned, wide-legged on the bed, dreaming of him thrusting into her?

Holding his eyes, she began to circle on her clitoris, just as she had done time and again, in the hidden room. In a low voice she told him how it felt, and how she fantasised of him while she frigged herself to exhaustion.

Sweat glistened on Celine's belly. Her hand swept back and forth between her thighs. Her breasts quivered and jiggled as she moved faster and faster. She was close to climax.

'You have not earned your pleasure yet,' said Odo, and poured more wine. 'Take your hand away.'

It was unthinkable. He could not make her wait again. In reckless defiance of his orders, she continued to stimulate herself. Only a minute more was needed, less than a minute, a fraction of a second.

She was poised on the very brink. But she was not permitted to take the final plunge into release. Odo leaned forward abruptly and seized her wrists. She was unable to prevent him pulling her hands away, and outwards, holding them extended to the sides.

Celine's hips pushed and jerked in a desperate need

for satisfaction. Hopelessly, she fought against his strength. He would not even allow her to press her thighs together, and ease her throbbing clitoris that way, but kept them wide-spread by thrusting a foot between her knees.

'I beg you,' she wept. 'I implore you! I will take you in any way you demand, be as lewd as even you could wish: but first have mercy!'

'Conditions, madam?' he said. 'I fear you are in no position to make them, or ever will be.'

He brought her wrists together, holding them both easily with a single hand, and stripped off his cravat. Taking her arms behind her, he tied her hands firmly with the strip of lace.

Celine's enforced powerlessness only excited her further. Odo poured the last of the wine, and tossed it back. Taking a cynical delight in teasing her, he tweaked and rolled the aching buds of her nipples.

He lifted one foot and let her rub herself on the smooth leather that clothed his ankle. But as soon as he saw she was close to orgasm, he ceased, and left her whimpering.

'Now tell me about Toussainte,' he said. 'Did you lick his cock? Did you take his penis between those soft red lips of yours? Did you let him spend in your mouth?'

'Yes! No – I sucked him a little. Just to make him eager. Just to make him want it. And then I got on top of him, and I fucked him. And lt wasn't as good as it was with you. Is that what you wanted to hear?'

'It was,' said Odo. He opened his breeches, and dragged her closer. 'You will now do the same for me. Kiss my prick, madam. Suck it a little.'

He pushed her head down between his parted thighs and stuffed his phallus into her mouth. To her surprise, it was only half-hard.

She licked his cock. She suckled on it. She worked the ring that pierced its glans back and forth. No matter how fiercely she laboured with lips and tongue, it obstinately refused to stiffen further.

Celine let him slide from her mouth.

'It isn't any good. You're angry. You don't want me.'

'On the contrary,' he said. 'I plan to use your fair flesh often tonight. It's simple enough. I have drunk overmuch. You will have no trouble in rousing me, once my bladder's empty.'

She snapped her head back and looked up at him, wide-eyed.

'Yes: the final act of surrender. Take me in your mouth. Come, the choice is yours. You can refuse. I will not force you. But I will be only be hard again once you have done it.'

Celine closed her eyes tight. Could she, dare she, give him this last proof of her abasement? It horrified her: but she needed him so badly.

'Indulge me in this,' he said, coolly. 'I will give you full satisfaction, I swear – afterwards.

'You aren't lying? I could not bear it.'

'On my manhood,' he said.

Her shoulders shook; but her silence was the silence of consent.

She felt the tip of his penis nudge her mouth, and opened to it. A drop of his water, hot and pungent, fell on her tongue. And then it was gushing from him in a heavy stream, spattering her lips and running down her chin.

He groaned and pulled her close as his urine spurted over her. The tucked-up wisp of her shirt was soaked with the salty effusion. His phallus swelled to a fierce hardness.

'Come here,' he said, hoarsely. 'Mount me. Move on me.'

He snatched her on to his penis. The chair protested, creaking under the weight and movement of their conjoined bodies. Odo buried his face between her breasts, rubbing it on the wet skin and mouthing at her nipples hungrily.

Celine could feel how unbearable his arousal was. His prick, warm and thick, was in her to its root. He cupped her buttocks, drawing her up and down the shaft. His

227

hips worked below her, and he pressed close, rubbing his lower belly against her clitoris. She struggled with the bonds that still tied her wrists, wanting to hold him.

'It's so good – you promised – don't stop,' she gasped.

He shook and moaned with the effort of control, but he kept his word. He thrust up hard underneath her, the cock-ring rolling on the wall of her vagina until she nearly fainted with the pleasure of it.

Celine felt her orgasm peaking, building to the point of delirum that only he could bring her to. Wailing and writhing against his loins she spasmed again and again around his driving manhood.

Released by her climax, Odo took himself to the point of no return with five hard strokes that jolted Celine's spine.

She lay against him, gasping for breath, and feeling the wild pulsings of pleasure fade to trembling satisfaction.

Odo raised his head and looked into her face.

'Well, madam, was it worth waiting for?' he enquired.

Chapter Seventeen

*L*iam rolled on to his back, putting one arm across his eyes to shield them from the morning sun. Kalinda pushed his blanket aside.

'You want to go in to the bushes?' she said, touching him.

'At least let me get the sleep out of my eyes, Kalinda,' he complained. 'And while we're about it, tell your friends to keep away, as well.'

'I thought you liked being caressed all over by a dozen women.'

Liam sat up and gave her a perfunctory smile.

'Don't get me wrong,' he said. 'It ain't unpleasant. It's just odd: not what I'm used to. And something else is damned odd, too. Where are the men?

Reuben poked the fire, and snorted. 'There are no men. Just my luck, eh?'

'But that's not possible!'

Kalinda made a face at the hairy pirate, and turned back to Liam.

'Of course it isn't,' she said. 'The men are hunters, their place is the forest. Those who are married have their wives and children with them. The city is – well, I suppose you'd call it holy. Only the unwed girls live there, and one man: Chochipil, the Flower Prince. Shall we go into the bushes now?'

'In a minute,' said Liam.

He wandered away from her and went a little way down the hill. To his relief, Kalinda did not follow him. It was always such heavy weather with her. Sometimes a man wanted light airs and easy sailing.

Hands in pockets, and shoulders hunched, Liam mooched along a faint track through the undergrowth. Sunlight seeped through the forest canopy, and spilt on the spongy leaf-litter underfoot.

Soon Tremaine would arrive, and he would have his own command. And after that? Liam wondered. Once he had his ship, and his revenge, what then?

An interminable life of fighting and loveless fornication stretched before him, Kalinda clinging as close as a barnacle. By Christ, he was tired of her demands and her temper.

Suddenly, more than anything in the world, he found himself wanting to turn the clock back. What if he had refused to listen to Celine on the night of the Government House ball? What if he had carried her off?

Liam sat down on a boulder and put his head in his hands.

'God forgive me!' he groaned.

All his anger, his hatred, his wild jealousy, had just been a way of avoiding what he knew in his heart to be true.

It was his fault.

Celine would have gone with him. Not after the ball, perhaps. But if her father had insisted on the Wraxall match, she would willingly have eloped.

If only he had gone back on board the *Challenger* that night and not got drunk and gone a-whoring, they would have been settled in Virginia by now. And he had been drunk and whoring ever since, trying to hide from that knowledge.

'Celine!' he cried softly. 'Oh, my love, what have I done?'

And what could he do now? She was forever lost.

Liam sprang to his feet and paced back and forth between the trees, a prey to guilt and misery.

It was with relief that, some minutes later, he heard Reuben shouting his name. Liam went to meet him. The matter sounded urgent, and he craved something to silence the clamour of his thoughts. Action, sex, alcohol: anything would do.

'There's a ship coming into the river,' Reuben told him, as they walked back to the clearing. 'One of Tremaine's squadron, but Kalinda don't like it. She's got a feeling, if you please.'

Kalinda was perched on a rock, and peering out across the tree-tops. Not one, but two ships had joined the *Paramour*. They had evidently seen hard fighting. The larger vessel had lost her mizzen-mast: the smaller rode low in the water, listing badly.

'Didn't I tell you?' said Reuben. 'It's the *Queen Royal*. Plain as a pikestaff what's happened. Some fool thought he could match her metal, and got taken as a prize for his pains. They've put in to make repairs.'

'I still say there's something wrong,' insisted Kalinda. 'She's not flying Tremaine's colours.'

Leaving them to continue their squabble, Liam slumped down by the fire. It was just his luck that Kalinda was occupied. Despite his growing distaste for her, he could do with a woman right now.

Like Reuben, he paid little mind to her doubts. No, Tremaine had arrived, and a bleak future was beginning. He pulled over the provision-sack and hunted in it for rum: the last bottle was three-quarters empty. He was uncorking it when the sound of distant cannon-fire brought him to his feet.

As he watched, the *Queen Royal*'s guns fired again. Smoke and flame blossomed from her side: a long time later, the sound reached him. The little *Paramour* tugged backwards on her cable. She went down by the stern, slowly, like a wounded animal sinking on its haunches.

'Ah, Jazus, she's going,' he murmured. 'Isn't that fit to break your heart?'

'Don't be so soft. It's only wood and canvas,' Kalinda retorted, acidly. 'Well, one of us will have to go back. Find out what's happening.'

'I'll do it,' said Liam. 'Anything's better than sitting around.'

'Forget it, lad,' said Reuben. 'You can't go. It has to be someone familiar with Tremaine. I'll – '

'Yes, and how will you get there?' snapped Kalinda. 'You'd be dead in an hour. There's a thousand things you need to know before the tribes will let you through. Signs and passwords. Charms that you repeat, herbs that have to be carried for protection. It must be me.'

'While we sit here twiddling our thumbs, I suppose?' said Liam.

Reuben nudged him. 'I don't think so, mate,' he said. 'Take a look over your shoulder.'

Without a breath, without a whisper, the clearing behind had filled with tawny, dark-haired women. All were naked, but for one.

Her inky hair was crowned with an elaborate arrange-ment of feathers, blue and scarlet. A band of beadwork was slung around her hips. Where the strings of beads met, a narrow plate of polished bone held the top of her sex-cleft open. He could see her clitoris, enlarged and poking forward. It wasn't meant to be an erotic display, or at least he did not think so, but he hardened anyway.

'Who's that?' he asked, pointing her out. Kalinda struck down his hand.

'Be respectful!' she hissed. 'That is Chochiquetzal, Flower Feather. She is the mother and the wife and the virgin daughter of Chochipil. You wouldn't understand .'

She left him, hurriedly, and made a complex gesture of obeisance before the crowned woman. Heads together, they held conclave.

Liam tried not to stare. Kalinda was right, he didn't understand. But one thing was sure: if Flower Feather was a virgin, he was William of Orange.

'It has been decided,' said Kalinda, rejoining them at last. 'You two are permitted to take the jewels on to the city. I am to discover what is happening below. Some of the men, warriors, are to be sent with me.'

Liam looked at Flower Feather. She stirred her hips slightly.

Kalinda grasped him by the hands and he glanced down at her.

'I have to go now,' she said. 'But one word of warning. There is a festival soon. From sunset to sunset of a single day, men are permitted to enter the city. If I'm not back before it starts, refuse what you are offered. You are my man, Liam, remember that. If you do not – '

Flower Feather gave an order. A band of women moved between them and Kalinda's grip on his hands was broken.

'Remember!' she cried, as she was swept away.

'Sure,' said Liam, his eyes on the savage queen. 'Whatever you say.'

The scent of coffee woke Sally. She opened her eyes by the tiniest fraction, but did not stir. She lay sprawled on the great cabin's bed, a chain about her wrist padlocked firmly to one of its posts. Across the room, Lord Wraxall breakfasted with Celine.

Sally's guts growled softly with hunger. She had been on bread and water since the capture and, until last night, had been imprisoned below the waterline with Auguste. She shivered, remembering.

On Odo's orders, they had been dragged to the orlop, the lowest of the *Queen Royal*'s decks. Down there it stank of tar, and tallow, and the nearby bilges. Long chains had been fastened to their wrists, and run through a great ringbolt in one of the ship's main timbers.

Strong though it was, that ringbolt was the weakest point in their bonds. From the first, Sally and Auguste had attacked it, tugging and twisting, and by the time the *Queen Royal* had moored at Catzumel their efforts had been rewarded. At first imperceptibly, then more easily, it began to move, loosening in the heavy oak.

'Rest now,' said Auguste. 'It'll take another twelve

hours steady work before we're free. There's no point in exhausting ourselves.'

It was agony to feel the minutes of inactivity pass. Wraxall had had a day to slake his lust for Celine, and Sally knew she would be next. She doubted whether twelve hours remained to her, and she was right.

They had only just resumed work when footsteps sounded overhead, and a growing light illuminated the hatchway above. When Lord Wraxall descended the ladder, they were sitting side by side, stony-faced.

He stepped towards them, holding a lantern high.

'How do you find the accomodation, Mistress Colney?' he enquired, sweetly.

'I've bedded down in worse places,' returned Sally, with a shrug. 'It takes more than a few rats to disturb my rest.'

'I'm surprised your companion permitted sleep,' he said. 'From what my wife has told me, I understood him to be inexhaustible. I confess my curiosity is aroused. Hence this visit. I'd like to see for myself. Excite him.'

Sally glanced at Auguste. Would he submit? She knew his pride: but if he fought, Wraxall would likely hang him, and she could not bear the thought.

'You, Toussainte! On your back!' commanded Odo.

Auguste stared at the other man for a long minute, his eyes burning with more than the reflected lantern-light. Then he lowered his head.

'Yes, sir,' he said, through his teeth.

When he lay spreadeagled on the deck, Lord Wraxall set down the lantern.

'You may commence,' he said.

With a great effort, Sally choked back the impulse to curse Odo to hell and all points south. If Auguste could endure this, then so could she. Whispering an apology, she unfastened the waistband of his tight linen breeches. Raising his shirt, she laid all bare.

'My wife found it excited him to be sucked,' said Lord Wraxall. There was the tiniest tremor in his voice. 'Why don't you try it?'

234

Sally descended to Auguste's loins, and took the whole of his gradually swelling manhood into her mouth. Anger made him slow to respond. It took long minutes of licking and caresses before his cock grew to its full majesty.

Lord Wraxall's cool fingers pulled her breeches away.

'Mount him: slowly. I want to see his prick going inside you.'

Sally obediently moved up Auguste's body and placed the tip of his penis in position. By degrees she allowed Auguste's thickness to push the walls of her vagina apart, until his full shaft was inside. Lord Wraxall sighed deeply. His hands caressed her back, under the shirt. They were shaking.

'Rise up,' he said into her ear. 'And do that again. But not so fast.'

Auguste panted softly. He heaved beneath her, aroused beyond bearing by the slowness of Sally's movements. The lamplight flickered, and steadied again. Lord Wraxall's shadow moved across them.

He knelt behind her. His naked belly pressed on her, and he bore a fierce erection between his thighs. His hands, coated with the warm oil he had spilled from the lantern, moved on her bottom.

'Be still, Sal,' he murmured. 'Let me take my part in this.'

He parted her buttocks and began to rub the oil between them. Gently, but without hesitation, he eased his shaft into her anus, driving her forward on to Auguste's cock. Odo waited a long moment for her to feel the full sensuality of the dual intrusion. Then he began to thrust.

Sally whimpered as Auguste caught the rhythm. His hips pumped beneath her. Sometimes in unison, sometimes in subtle counterpoint, both men pleasured her until she was sobbing with frantic lust.

Such ecstasy could not continue long. Sally thrashed to and fro as both men drove their pricks into her flesh.

She climaxed in a series of spasms, accompanied by cries that were almost screams, so intense was her arousal.

Auguste came almost immediately he felt the increased heat and tightness that enclosed him. Odo outlasted them both, reaching his orgasm at last with a hoarse yell of triumph.

Then he withdrew from her, and fastened his clothes. Unlocking one end of the chain confining Sally's wrists, he pulled her towards the hatchway, leaving Auguste chained to the ringbolt.

'Come with me,' he said. 'I have promised myself the luxury of you and my wife in the same bed, and I am not disposed to wait.'

Sally glanced across at Odo who now sat calmly sipping his morning coffee. Well, he had had that indulgence; and taken his pleasure with them – variously – during the watches of the night. Sally was only grateful he had not seen fit to demand their services this morning.

She cast a sympathetic look at Celine, drooping at the breakfast table. The girl had had far the worst time of it. Odo had refused to satisfy her; he'd taken a vicious delight in humiliating his wife. Even now, he still taunted and threatened her cruelly.

'What could you possibly do that is worse than I have already experienced at your hands?' Celine said, in a low voice.

Odo laughed, and pushed back his chair.

'I will tell you, madam,' he said, smiling down at her. 'As you know, the repairs do not progress as fast as I would like. So I intend to offer your body to my men as an incentive; a daily prize, awarded to he who works hardest. What do you think? Does the scheme appeal?'

Sally winced inwardly as Celine began to plead for mercy. That was no way to handle Wraxall: the more she begged, the more he enjoyed it. The girl was sorely in need of some sage advice. If it went on much longer, Sally thought, she would have to intervene; try and draw Wraxall's fire herself.

But it proved unnecessary. A knock on the cabin door

interrupted Odo's lascivious description of the fate in store for his wife.

'What the devil do you mean, Toussainte's gone?' demanded Lord Wraxall, when the crewman had stammered out his news.

'Clean vanished, my lord. Not a trace of him, on board or ashore.'

Celine started, and Sally's heart beat with a fierce hope. Auguste was free; the unmanned sloop whose masthead still showed above the river meant that Kalinda was somewhere near. There was a chance yet.

Lord Wraxall closed the door on the man's departing back and strolled across to stand above Sally.

'I know you're awake, Sal,' he said. 'Does the news please you? It shouldn't. I had intended to hang the man: a kinder end than being marooned, and starving to death, in this wilderness, don't you think?'

Sally rolled over, with a clink of chain.

'Kiss my arse, Odo,' she said, pleasantly.

'Willingly,' he murmured. 'But later. I have the ships to attend to.'

All morning Kalinda had crept from shadow to shortening shadow on the outskirts of the wound Lord Wraxall's men were hacking in the rainforest. All morning she had spied on Odo's strutting figure as he directed the prisoners at their labour. At last, when the sun was at its height, he left them and walked down to the river.

Screened by the undergrowth, she stalked him.

Auguste had been brought in by her scouts last night. Their plans were made. If they could split Lord Wraxall's forces, Auguste and the remainder of the *Queen Royal*'s crew could take care of the men left at the ships. Axes could be used for more than felling trees. Her warriors would handle the rest.

But all hinged on separating Wraxall's band. And that was her task.

Up-river from the moorings, a stream came down from the high ground.

Where it passed, the trees opened out into a hidden glade. Transparent brown water poured smoothly over rocks and tree-roots, making pools and bubbling cascades and waterfalls, before it fell into the sulky river and was stilled.

When Kalinda reached the glade, all that could be seen of Lord Wraxall were his clothes, neatly piled on the bank. Soap and a towel lay ready beside them. Brushing aside a final barrier of leaves, she stepped in to the open.

She was all bare brown flesh but for a single ornament: a spread-winged condor, made of hammered gold. It was the sole piece of precious metal her grandmother's tribe had saved from the *conquistadores*, and belonged to the hunting chief. He had made some trouble about letting her wear it.

But hopefully, it would do her business for her.

Kalinda stole uphill a small way and leant across a boulder overlooking the linked pools. Lord Wraxall floated in the largest, further down. His eyes were closed. His arms, outspread, lay on the water. His hair drifted like weed in the moving current. Between his legs, a little parted to give him buoyancy, his penis played laxly to every eddy of the stream.

Even in its flaccid state, it was sizeable enough to give her pause, and she noted his piercing with deep appreciation. Kalinda had a little plan of her own, a secret she had not bothered to share with Auguste.

Everything she had heard about Lord Wraxall – and she had heard much – attracted her mightily. If the tales were true, it would be a crying shame to have such a stallion killed. She let the stream carry her down a level, and threw a flower at the floating man. He opened his eyes. Star-shaped, and deep mauve, the flower hung in his pubic hair.

Kalinda sent a handful of blossoms over the cascade towards him. They span on the pool. He traced their course upwards until he found her. She leant on her elbows, and gave him an encouraging smile.

238

Lord Wraxall rose. The water reached his hips.

'Come here to me,' he said.

'I don't understand,' said Kalinda, in the language of the tribe.

But she did, and better than he thought. His eyes had never left her breasts. It was not their firm curves alone that woke the fire in his gaze, but the gold that lay on them. There were lusts other than those of the flesh.

He tried again, this time in Spanish.

Kalinda slithered down the rocks and into the pool. The cool stream, falling from above, pounded her shoulders and gushed over her upper body. Her brown nipples stood. Drops fell on them from the golden condor.

'And what might you be?' he asked. 'A naiad?'

'I am Xingari,' answered Kalinda, pretending to stumble over the Spanish words. 'I do not know the tribe you speak of. I came to fish, but your boats have scared them all away. Now I wash, and go home.'

'I too,' said Lord Wraxall. 'Wash, that is. By all means share my bath.'

Holding his eyes, she sank down briefly and then rose, letting the water spill down over her hard, pointed breasts. Lord Wraxall picked up the soap, and waded closer.

'Allow me, water-sprite,' he said.

He turned her, and began to soap her back. His palms circled on her shoulder-blades, and slid beneath her arms. They moved on her breasts. He weighed the golden condor in his hands for a moment.

'Does your tribe have many baubles such as these?'

'Oh yes,' said Kalinda. 'We trade for them, with the city of Chochipil.'

'Indeed?' said Lord Wraxall, with deep interest. 'A lost city? One hears legends of such things, of course.'

'Stupid! How can the city be lost, when I know where to find it?'

Lord Wraxall laughed softly. His fingertips moved down her spine to the double dimple that marked the top of her anal cleft. He stroked the soap down the soft valley, and began to raise a lather there.

'Where is this city?' he asked, huskily.

Kalinda felt the tip of his penis brush her thigh. He was fully erect. Was it the gold he wanted, or her? She took the soap from him and began to wash his cock, her fingers sliding on the thick, foamed shaft.

'In the forest,' she whispered. 'You want to go there?'

'Later,' said Lord Wraxall, and grabbed her.

He seized her around the waist and pulled her hard against him. His phallus, still slick with soap, slid into her body on the first lunge.

Kalinda lost her footing, shrieked, and went under with a mighty splash. He followed her down, still coupled to her. Their breath rose up in bright bubbles to burst on the surface of the pool. He took three strokes within her before they had to come up for air.

Gasping, they broke water. Lord Wraxall's mouth came down on hers, and his thrusting tongue went deep into her mouth. Kalinda fought a little, for the pleasure of being overpowered. He did not disappoint her, but held her tightly while he thrust his ringed cock into her again and again.

She wrapped his lean hips with her legs. Her nails raked down his back, raising long lines of scarlet. He met her desire with eager strength, grappling her wet body to him, and pushing her back against the smooth rock wall.

The falling water broke and spattered on their shoulders, coursing between their bodies. The last of the soap frothed at their loins, forming rainbows in the curling hair.

With the stone behind her, Kalinda felt every drive of Odo's prick with redoubled force. She accepted his thrusts with greedy pleasure, panting hard as the wave built within her. Her orgasm broke and spilled all through her to reach as far as her fingertips, tingle, and withdraw.

Lord Wraxall pulled out of her. She watched his

phallus jerk and pump as his sperm entered the water. It curdled, like white of egg, and sank slowly.

As slowly, he let her down. With a scissoring thrust of his legs, he took himself to the lip of the pool, and climbed out.

Kalinda lay in the water, letting her body trail out along the current. Its coolness eddied between her thighs and soothed the heat that pulsed there.

Odo's prowess had impressed her greatly. She had not taken such pleasure in a man since the first time with Liam. Once was not enough. She wanted to feel him inside her again . . . And again. She imagined taking him and O'Brien at one and the same time, and quivered with renewed lust at the thought.

Reaching a decision, she scrambled up the bank. Picking a handful of foliage, she laid out a *patteran* for her warriors to read.

Five twigs arranged in a fan-shape stood for the city, and a scarlet flower was Odo. She encircled the flower with tiny leaves, added a dead caterpillar and a wavy line of pebbles.

And there it was, a clear command for those who knew the language of signs: *The leader of these strangers is not to be killed. Bind him, and bring him secretly to the city of Chochipil, there to await my pleasure.*

Kalinda signed her message with one of the mauve, star-shaped blossoms, and sauntered back to the pool.

'Now we go to the city?' she asked, all wide-eyed innocence.

Lord Wraxall looked up from drying his hair.

'Now we go back to the ships to fit out an expedition. And you shall meet some lady friends of mine. I wonder, naiad, do you perform as well on land?'

241

Chapter Eighteen

Not a ray of moonlight, nor the gleam of a star, penetrated the blackness of the forest from above. Odo strolled around the expedition's encampment, making a last inspection before he retired to his tent for the night's pleasures.

Men snored, rolled in their blankets, or sat talking in low voices of the gold. They were eager to get their hands on a share of the riches of Eldorado. Such fools, thought Odo. It would be a waste to let them fritter a fortune away on harbour drabs and gambling. Great wealth demanded great skill in the handling: a gentleman's touch.

Perhaps he would purchase one of the smaller European princedoms. Andorra, or maybe Lichtenstein. Grand Duke Odo, he thought. *Odo Superbus, Rex.*

Smiling, he stepped into his tent, and let the flap fall behind him. The shelter was primitive enough, for a future monarch. One of the *Queen Royal*'s topsails was slung over a ridgepole, and supported by two pairs of oars. But he had ordered certain conveniences, necessary for a man of taste and appetite, to be brought along from the ships.

The three women were curled together on the heap of silks and cut fern that was his bed: Sally, Celine and his new acquistion, the dusky Indian maiden whose name he had not bothered to ask.

He looked them over slowly, pretending to deliberate. Then he beckoned to Celine. She was very pale. She knew he had not forgotten his threat of the morning, nor the competition in which she was to be the prize. Her gallant was already chosen, and waited only to be called into the tent.

Odo felt a stirring of perverse pleasure. Would she struggle, he wondered, or endure? Would she weep?

'Come closer, Lady Wraxall,' he said, softly. 'It is time you were made ready for the dance. Your new partner grows impatient.'

It puzzled him that she did not protest: he knew she was frightened. He ran his hands over her body, feeling her tremble with tension.

'Aren't you afraid I might prefer this stranger?' she asked.

Her words were bold, challenging, but she could not keep her voice from shaking. Odo shot a glance at Sally, who was lying back, calmly chewing a stalk of fern. So that was the answer: Sal had been meddling again.

He pushed Celine's velvet breeches down, and ripped her shirt open. He began to arouse her, with brief, light touches to her clitoris and nipples.

'I have no fear of that,' he said, with sensual pride. 'Like mother, like daughter, remember? He will take you from behind, madam. Get down on all fours, sideways to me. I will want to see him enter you. Sal, take your clothes off. I'll have you while I watch.'

'Christ, Odo, don't you ever get tired?' said Sally, wearily. 'Why don't you just satisfy the poor child, and yourself, and then let us all have some sleep. We got little enough last night, in all faith.'

Odo laughed. 'You once had more stamina, Sal,' he said.

He positioned Celine to his liking and reached beneath her to flick gently at her hard nipples. His fingers slipped in and out of her vagina, exciting her until he felt the salty juices of need begin to gather.

But before he could call in her chosen partner, six muskets went off together and the forest silence was broken by a cacophony of savage howls.

'I think the camp's being attacked,' said Sally, helpfully.

Swearing with pardonable irritation, Lord Wraxall seized his sword.

'You will stay as you are, madam,' he commanded, as he strode out. 'Don't make another move until I return, understand?'

Rapier in hand, Odo ducked from the tent. His men were huddled in the centre of the ring of fires which guarded the encampment, their musket barrels waving to every point of the compass.

Arrows flew out of the darkness, thick as slanting rain. At Odo's left hand, a crewman dropped to the ground and lay writhing as the poisoned dart took its effect. Two other men flung down their weapons in panic and fled in to the forest. One staggered back instantly, slashed from breastbone to groin by razor-edged obsidian: the other shrieked once, and was silent.

Furiously, Odo shouted and struck out at the wavering ranks of his crew.

'Form a square, damn you! Front rank, on your knees, and take aim. They're nothing but a parcel of savages, in Hell's name. Where's your backbone?'

'Take aim at what?' growled the bo'sun, fumbling with his powder horn. 'I can't shoot what I can't see!'

Odo cursed him, but the man could no longer hear. Musket and horn fell from his hands: a long spear transfixed his throat.

Yowling like jungle cats, naked warriors leapt from the shadows, struck, and were gone again. Arrows pattered around Odo's beleaguered crew, a scratch from their envenomed points enough to bring agonised death.

Inch by inch, Lord Wraxall's company was forced back across the encampment, away from the tent, and into the forest. Odo seized a pistol from a corpse's hand. It was empty: useless. He threw it down.

The man at his side was snatched into darkness and was gone, as if he had never been. Lord Wraxall lashed out with the rapier, and felt his steel connect with flesh. The little victory heartened him, and he set his back against a tree. Invisible enemies surrounded him, closing in.

'Sa-ha!' he hissed, lashing out. 'Have at you!'

A spear shot past him, and into the tree-trunk with a thud. Odo ducked, and lunged. From the tail of his eye, he could see the clearing, a lit space that only made the darkness where he stood deeper. The tent was burning. Against its light he glimpsed the women – one, two, three – slip across the open ground and into the forest.

A club crashed into his ribs, driving his breath away. Hard hands grasped his body. The rapier was twisted from his grip. Lust and power at last forgotten, Odo struck out with his fists in a desperate fight for life.

Liam sat half-way up a staircase that ended in air, looking over the ruined city. Its buildings were tumbled down, roofless. The great pyramid that dominated the city's centre was shaggy with trees and creepers that had grown up between its stones. What he had thought were roads had proved, on exploration, to be a cross-hatching of canals, silted up and overgrown, in which toads gulped, and stared at him from gold-flecked eyes.

He had been there four days. More than enough time for memory, for regrets. He wanted a drink, but the rum had run out. He wanted a woman, but Kalinda was away, and Flower Feather kept her distance. It maddened him to see the pointed breasts and shiny buttocks of the Indian maidens as they went about the business of preparing for tonight's festival.

He didn't even have Reuben to talk to, for the pirate had disappeared in to the maze of ruins, taking the chest of jewels with him. Liam sighed deeply and descended to stretch his legs.

It was late afternoon, and long shadows fell across the cracked and stained pavement of the plaza. Pots were boiling. Bark was being scraped and pulped. In one place, the ground was a rainbow of colour where elaborate headdresses of feathers were being refurbished.

When Flower Feather touched his arm, he jumped.

She stood in a semicircle of twenty or so girls. Dozens of small wooden strips were hung about her in festoons, each on a thong of plaited grass. They clacked as she moved.

At her signal, the women seized him. They held his wrists. They encircled his waist. They took away his weapons. Small, soft hands pushed at his shoulders and the small of his back.

His captors laughed and chattered as they tugged him up to the summit of the pyramid, and thrust him through the temple door. Liam felt a momentary qualm as he entered. But if the temple had ever been used for sacrifice, it had been centuries before. Now, not even the statue of a god remained. It was somebody's living-place. A clutter of pots and feathers and straw cushions lay on the floor. Two hammocks hung from the roof-beams.

To his surprise, in one of them was a man, the first he had seen. Of course, Kalinda had said that there was just one in the city. He had forgotten the name, but it meant Flower Prince. And he was Flower Feather's husband.

The prince was no more than eighteen. Dark hair was cut straight across his brows and shadowed his eyes. He was naked, but for ornaments of bead and shell. A red dog had been drawn on his chest, and his limbs were gaudy with patterns in black and yellow. His penis, fully erect, was painted scarlet.

He was also uproariously drunk. He took one look at Liam and fell into hoots of laughter, pointing, and kicking up his heels until the hammock shook.

Flower Feather gave an order, and the two men were given bowls of a thick, yeasty liquor.

Liam sniffed, and took a sip. The liquid tasted rich

246

and soupy. Its pungent fumes filled his nose and made him sneeze. The Flower Prince drank, and giggled: whatever it was, it had certainly done him no harm.

'Mud in your eye,' said Liam, and gratefully drained the bowl.

The liquor went quickly to his head, surprising him with its strength. Flower Feather had him served with more. Two women started to undress him. Ignoring Liam's not very sincere protests, they stripped his breeches down and pulled off his shirt.

When he was completely nude, they began to paint him.

It tickled.

Liam emptied his fourth, or was it his fifth, bowl and swayed a little. His feet seemed a very long way off. Two women knelt there, small as ants, putting the finishing touches to his decorations.

He had been painted deep blue, a blue that was almost black. Lines of sparkling mica striped his face, and zigzagged down his limbs. He wore necklaces, belts and armbands, and a tall crown of feathers swayed on his head, but he had on nothing that could be called clothes: it was all adornment.

The Flower Prince – Chochipil, that was the name, how could he have forgotten it? – swung in his hammock. One of the girls had climbed up beside him, and they were exploring each other's bodies with eager interest.

Liam could not help but watch. He grew hard as the two played together. The girl put her legs around Chochipil's hips and lowered herself on to his phallus. The hammock rocked to and fro as they pleasured each other.

'Wish I was in your shoes,' said Liam, enviously.

Then he chuckled. What a damned silly thing to say. Chochipil had no shoes. Neither had he, any more. It suddenly seemed very funny.

'Wish I was in your paint,' he corrected himself.

As if in answer to his words, Flower Feather knelt and

began to rub a greasy, scarlet dye into the skin of his penis and testicles.

'I didn't mean that,' said Liam. 'I meant – oh, hell, carry on.'

He couldn't have drawn back if he'd wanted to. The feel of her hands on him was driving him wild with desire. The paint felt warm on his manhood: it glowed, growing hotter every minute. It wasn't uncomfortable. Far from it. But, hell, it made him hungry for sex.

Flower Feather's fingers ringed his cock-head and she began to stimulate him. She ran her hand up and down his shaft with a light, arousing grip. Liam stroked down across her buttocks, and pulled her towards him.

Without once letting go of his manhood, or stopping her soft pumping, she sank down on the floor among the bowls of paint. Dizzy with the drink and his desire, Liam let her take him down with her.

He did not care that the room was full of people, or that Flower Feather's husband was there. He only wanted to be inside her.

He took her quickly, simply, with a gentle eagerness. Her vagina was wet and heated. She gripped his shoulders and worked her body under his with lithe, wriggling movements, grinding her hips.

He felt no embarrassment or modesty. There was a primal innocence in her love-making. It was like the first time ever; the first time in the world.

Liam's cock throbbed and pulsed. Her soft body enclosed him, lapping around him. All his consciousness was centred on his phallus, piercing the woman, and the pleasure that made his whole body sweat and tremble.

He thrust into her, trying to give back to her the delight he felt. Climax came all too soon, and he hung above her, crying out his satisfaction. He felt her shuddering as she came, and was so glad he almost wept.

'Thank you, sweetheart,' he said. 'It must have been like that in Eden.'

He was still hard when he withdrew, totally hard: his painted prick looked as if it had been carved from polished coral. Liam could not believe it. He was as potent as the next man, but this had never happened to him in his life before. It had to be either the drink or the paint; either way, he was happy enough.

He felt like dancing. He felt like singing. He tried a few bars of 'The Beckoning Fair One'. A tame macaw walked up and down the roof-beam, twisting its neck and looking at Liam in beady astonishment. Someone handed him another drink and he supped it down.

Flower Feather turned his palm upwards, and placed on it one of the wooden sticks. It was a tally: with one notch. Outside, the sun had set. Drums were beginning to mutter.

Liam whirled in a circle with six other men, clapping his hands to the music of conch and drum. A full moon was poised above the pyramid. Dozens of fires burned around the grand plaza. Couples took each other by their light.

Flutes shrilled. Liam moved his feet to the licking of a wooden instrument like a two-keyed xylophone. His erect phallus leapt between his thighs and there were five notches on the tally-stick that bounced among the necklaces on his chest. The last time he had orgasmed without ejaculating; something he had never done before, nor even dreamt possible.

There had been no real beginning to the festival. Men had appeared in pairs and scattered groups. They materialised from the shadows. One moment the space between two fires would be empty, and in the next a warrior stood there, bright as a pheasant in paint and feathers.

The shining brown of the women was drab by comparison. The men glittered with coloured dust, shone with oil and paint. Their faces were haloed with plumes, the lovely green of the quetzal, and the polychrome of parrots. Their penises, scarlet with unguent, were proudly displayed as they strutted and danced to attract their mates.

Liam had seen a tall, supple man whose tally had notches down both sides; and one, spotted with black and yellow like a jaguar, whose conquests had required a second stick.

He was not drunk, though he had lost count of the bowls passed to him. He was too happy even to laugh. He was trying to teach the jaguar-man how to dance the hornpipe when he saw Celine.

She stood in the midst of a group, just come in from the forest. The others were nothing: shadows. Liam saw only her.

She was naked, her pale body as white as the moon. Her wondering eyes passed over him with no more interest than she gave to any of the other men.

She did not know him.

All Liam's joy burnt out and fell to cold ash in that instant.

And in the next, Kalinda flung herself into his arms.

She kissed him fiercely, her tongue hunting his with sensual greed. Eyes closed, groaning with lust, she pressed against Liam's body. Her nipples were as hard as the pearls that were her only garment.

He hardly moved his lips under hers, and his hands lay loosely on her waist. Kalinda pulled back sharply. She flipped the tally on his chest.

'Five already?' she said. 'Have you worn yourself out, then? I told you not to take what was offered.'

'Ah, what does it matter?' he growled. 'I never promised to be faithful.'

'I never asked you to,' she said. 'I don't mind you having other women – as long as there's plenty left for me. But tomorrow the red dog comes for Chochipil, and the most popular of the men replaces him as Flower Prince. You wouldn't want the honour, believe me.'

'What?' said Liam, absently. He looked past her, searching the crowd.

Kalinda kissed him again. Her fingers clawed his buttocks; she ground her loins against his rigid, painted phallus.

250

'Come on,' she said, hoarsely. 'You're ready. Let's do it.'

'I'm not interested, Kalinda.'

She grappled with him, thrusting her bare brown thigh between his legs.

'I am the Rose of Havana, man. And I want it. Here! Now!'

Liam tore himself free of her, and thrust her violently away. Kalinda stumbled. Her necklace caught, and snapped. Unstrung pearls pattered around their feet.

'Say goodbye to your command, Mr Liam O'Brien,' she hissed, her face twisted with rage. 'And forget your revenge. At my side you could have been a prince of the seas; but now you are nothing, understand me? Nothing!'

'I don't care for any of those things,' he said, in a low voice. 'I just want my girl, that's all.'

'You've lost her, too,' sneered Kalinda. 'I have already found another lover – a real man. You've missed your chance. No one refuses me a second time.'

He met her eyes.

'What made you think I meant you?' he asked, and left her.

Celine scrambled up the last of the broken steps to the platform on top of the pyramid. Warm light spilt from the temple's doorway; inside someone was playing on a breathy flute.

She hesitated, deliberating whether to enter. She was frightened, but not of the Indians. She had not needed Kalinda's explanations to tell her that they would not approach a woman unless she first made her desire clear.

No one would force her to have sex. But if she did, she might find out, once and for all, that what she dreaded was true. That Odo, and he alone, could quench the fires that burned in her body.

And if it was the truth, what then? Was she doomed to become another Lys, so desperate to recapture a lost delight that she would lie with anybody?

251

The flute-player broke off. From within the temple a man's voice, soft and rather plaintive, asked a question in an unknown language.

Celine gripped her hands together to still their trembling.

There was only one way to find out.

It was dim inside, lit by a flickering fire-pot. A young Indian man sat cross-legged on a cloak of feathers. His limbs were striped with black and yellow, and a dog was painted on his chest. At the juncture of his parted thighs his phallus stood, deep red and upright.

Even with her misgivings, Celine found the sight arousing. And he was young, and handsome, and looked gentle. She could do worse.

He looked up at her with dark eyes whose sombreness contradicted his smile of welcome. Laying aside his flute, he held out one hand to her.

She knelt and touched his face. Shaking fingers slipped down his neck and over his shoulders. His skin was smooth, with a faint surface roughness from the paint. She took his hand, and laid it on her left breast. Her nipple hardened as he fondled the sensitive bud. He made an enquiry.

'Yes,' she whispered. 'It's nice. Won't you do it some more?'

She reached down and stroked his penis from balls to tip. The feel of it, warm and springing beneath her hand, made her breath come fast.

The young man opened his arms and took her into them. They lay down, facing each other on the warm feathers. He rubbed his cheek against hers, and brushed his palm down her back, rhythmically, repeatedly.

His touch was soft at first, just skimming her flesh. She arched her back and thrust her buttocks against his hand, showing him that she liked it, and soon he grew bolder. She nuzzled his throat, making a soft crooning noise.

'I want you,' she sighed, knowing he could not understand her.

252

But desire needed no interpreter. He laid her on her back, and parted her thighs. She opened for him, and took him inside her with a murmur of delight.

Celine moved beneath his weight with increasing vigour, dreamily looking up into his eyes. His manhood thrust and returned in her wet vagina with gentle persistence. She used all the skills of lust which Lord Wraxall had taught her. But now she brought them in to play in her own service, flexing the mobile warmth of her inner passage on the young man's shaft. She felt the onset of her orgasm and thrust her lower body hard against him.

He grunted softly, responding to her movements, and his hands tightened around her. She came with a tiny shiver, and lay back under his body, waiting for him to finish.

So now she knew.

When she moved to go, the young man's arms tensed for a moment, as if to keep her.

'Not again,' she said, putting him aside. 'No, never again.'

As she stepped out of the temple and into the night, he began to play the flute once more: a small sad tune.

The sky above the pyramid was black velvet; the moon looked only inches from Celine's fingertips. If she stood on her toes, she thought, she could reach it, draw it down from the sky. She tried, and failed. It was all of a piece.

She had her answer. Only with Lord Wraxall could she know ecstasy: but his price was her soul, her self-respect.

A part of her still hoped, still yearned. Surely, somewhere, somehow, there would be a man who could give her the pleasure, without the darkness.

She crushed the longing mercilessly. That was how Lys must have felt. That was what made her take those endless, faceless lovers. What had Odo said? Every man at a ball, and the servants beside? How well she could understand her mother's promiscuities!

She could even duplicate them.

'I won't!' said Celine, stubbornly. 'I'll use my fingers for the rest of my life, rather!'

Slowly, she began to descend the pyramid. She would find somewhere quiet, and sleep, and try to forget. Sleep would be best.

She did not see the waiting Indian until she was almost upon him. As she passed, he rose and followed her. When she reached the ground, he was only three steps behind.

'Go away,' she said, dully. 'Find someone else.'

He came forward into the light and pulled off his crown of feathers.

'Celine, don't you know me?' he asked.

She recognised Liam in two heartbeats. The first hesitated, and the second caught up with it, so that they both came down together, with a thud like a falling stone.

Celine looked away from him, dry-eyed. She had hurt for Liam: she had wept. After the silence that had been his only reply to her letter, she had thought the wound skinned over. But it broke out now, and bled afresh.

If she had never been Lord Wraxall's bride, she supposed they could have been happy enough. But all that was long ago. Now he would just be another in the long line of men who were not Odo.

He took a half-step towards her.

'Is it too late?' he asked. 'Is there nothing left for me at all?'

'I'll have sex with you, if that's what you mean,' she said, evenly. 'This place will serve as well as any other. How do you want me, Liam?'

With a cry of pain, he fell to his knees before her, and clasped her round the waist. He pressed his face against the skin of her belly. She knew he suffered, and a small vengeful part of her was glad.

'Don't,' he whispered. 'Please don't.'

Celine sighed, and stroked his hair.

'All right then,' she said. 'Where?'

Chapter Nineteen

Celine opened her eyes on greenery. Dim, pre-dawn light was filtering through the leaves. Birds were calling. Liam's body was cuddled against her back, and his strong arms surrounded her. She could feel his face pressed against her neck, and his breath moved the loose tendrils of her hair.

She had followed him to this secret place among the city ruins last night. They had been together there for hours. And not once had he attempted to make love to her.

A little bird, grey with a blue tail, perched on a branch above Celine's resting-place. It flirted its wings, and chirruped once or twice. Then it began to sing. She could see its throat pulsing, even the tongue in its open beak.

Liam had led her away from the plaza, into the moonlit quiet of the ruins. They had walked along the bank of an overgrown canal, and turned aside into what had once been a house. A leaning wall, sheltered from time's hand, still showed formal patterns in faded red on white. He made a nest of fern and rushes for her, under its shadow.

She had waited, then, for him to take her. Instead he went to the canal, and spent a long time washing. She heard him splashing, watched him scrubbing himself with bunches of grass. When he came back to her, clean of paint, his tanned body was wet. He smelt of earth and water.

After a while, he took her hand, and held it very tight.

And then, at last, they talked.

It was about trivialities, to begin with. And then, with 'Do you remember?', 'Do you recall?', they tremblingly touched on shared memories: little incidents that had happened on board the *Challenger*; or the night of the Government House ball, and the harpsichord playing far away, as they held each other on the dark veranda.

Liam had never got her letter. His voice ached when he admitted it might have made no difference.

'I tried to hate you,' he had said. 'I should have hated myself.'

And another time he said: 'I could not forgive you for saving my life. For choosing him.'

And again: 'I'm so sorry, Celine.'

When he embraced her, a long time later, she could feel him tremble. There was comfort without passion in their kisses. They huddled together like children seeking reassurance and, as the moon set, they slumbered.

Liam jerked in his sleep and his arms tightened around her. He muttered something she could not catch. Celine closed her eyes. She tried to convince herself that this had come too late; but all the same hope, like the bird, sang in her heart.

I should leave now, she thought. Get up and leave. At least that way I would have this moment to remember: unspoiled and perfect.

But when she stirred, he woke.

He did not move, but she felt the difference instantly. And she heard his breath catch.

'Don't go,' said Liam.

Tears leaked from behind her closed eyelids.

'I must,' she said. 'I told you: Lord Wraxall – I fear no other man will be able to – don't you understand that I could not bear the pain? The hunger? Not with you, Liam. Least of all with you.'

'We could live together platonically,' he said, sounding agonised. 'If only you stayed with me, loved me, I could stand it. I think.'

'I couldn't,' said Celine, in flat despair.

He moved, turning her in his arms so that they clung breast to breast.

'Then try me,' he whispered 'Allow me to pleasure you. I'm begging, Celine: just the once.'

He bent his head and kissed her on the lips. Celine opened her eyes, and looked into his. They were so blue: she had forgotten how beautiful they were, the dark lashes as long as a woman's.

His hand moved on her neck, fingers tangling in the waves of her hair. His thumb brushed the tip of her ear, and his lips followed it. She felt a shock run through her as his tongue touched the lobe. Liam's breathing was uneven, heavy.

'Lie back, my love.' he said. 'Give me this chance.'

Against doubt and judgement, Celine allowed him to stretch her out on the scented grasses of their bed. She gazed up, through the overhanging leaves, in to a sky that was gilded by sunrise. The little bird had gone out of sight, but she could hear it somewhere nearby: still singing, still singing.

Liam knelt above her, close but not touching. She could sense his tension, and knew that he was as nervous as her. Suddenly he began to speak of his feelings, the shaken words tumbling from his lips. She had not known that his jealousy of Lord Wraxall went so deep, or hurt so much. Haltingly, she tried to explain to Liam the hatred, shame and lust that had been her marriage.

'The tale of your wedding night nearly killed me,' he confessed. 'You loved him, they said, could not get enough of him. How could I know what lay behind?'

She watched his face as he spoke; he swallowed repeatedly, fighting against breakdown. He was very pale under the tan, almost ashen. How shaken he looked, how sad. A muscle jumped at the corner of his jaw.

When she reached out to him, Liam took her hand in

both of his, and caught it to his heart. She could feel it beating. The scent of his maleness mingled with the smells of grass and earth.

His restraint confused her a little. Though nothing had been spoken, Liam knew he had her tacit agreement. What was he waiting for? By now, Lord Wraxall would have had his fingers deep inside her – unless, that is, he had chosen some darker method of taking his gratification.

It was unexpected, but Celine felt no disappointment. It was better this way. They had been so long apart; there had to be a kind of shyness.

I want him; and in a way that I had forgotten feeling, she thought. Maybe love will make the difference, some-how make the insufficient enough.

Gradually, but every moment more intensely, his delay aroused her. She could feel herself softening, opening. Liam kissed the palm of her hand, each finger-tip, each joint, the pad at the base of her thumb.

She drew a long breath, and let it out with a shiver.

His head was bent, and the shining fall of his sable hair brushed against her arm. All she could see of his face was the strong line of his cheekbone and the dark, finely shaped brows.

Within the pursed groove of her sex she could feel her labia thickening and swelling. There was a sense of moisture growing there. If she stirred her thighs, no matter how slightly, the movement sent pleasure pulsing through the little bud that burned between them. Her hand trembled in his. She did not want to speak her desire; she did not want to ask. But if he continued to keep his distance, she would have to.

In answer to her thought, Liam stooped above her. She let her fingers stray across his shoulder, feeling the muscles slide beneath the smoothness of his skin. His pupils were wide with passion. He embraced her, pull-ing her close.

'We could stop,' she said, against his neck. 'We need not court sorrow.'

258

His mouth tenderly brushed her forehead. 'Do we not? I think we have to: win or lose all, Celine.'

He pressed her down on the sap-scented cushion of foliage, and sought her lips with his own. Celine's tongue met his in a kiss of shared longing. His body, firm and masculine, lay over hers; she felt his erect penis push against her thigh. Her hand slid down to stroke the glossy skin of its head, and its long hard shaft.

Liam moaned softly at her touch.

'Can't you feel how much I need you? I have done this over and again in my dreams, Celine: and woken with the cooling seed wet on my belly. I thought you were lost to me, gone forever. Dear God, I love you so much. I want to give you pleasure such as you've never had. We can reach the heights together, I swear it. Won't you surrender yourself to me? Won't you let me satisfy you?'

His arms were painfully tight around her: she was caught in their bonds.

'Oh, Liam, yes,' she cried. 'I want you – I love you.'

She gave a sharp cry of pleasure as his hands sought her breasts. He was demanding, a little harsh. He squeezed her nipples between finger and thumb until they burned, then soothed the hardened nubs of flesh with his tongue.

Thrusting herself up to meet his touch, Celine felt excitement churning inside her. She had not thought that he would be so forceful a lover. Her fingers combed and stroked his hair as he pulled her close, biting and suckling on the coral buds that crowned her breasts.

When at last Liam gave her a respite, she was shaking with desire. He pushed himself up on one elbow and gazed at her, while his hand travelled over her milky skin. She responded to his touch with little sighs and gasps of pleasure.

'I could look at you forever,' he whispered. 'Your eyes, your face, your sweet body: I could come, just by looking at you. One day I'll prove that: but not now. This time is yours. I am here to please you.'

Celine smiled at him, and clasped her hands behind

her head, so that her breasts were raised and the skin tautened on the curve of her belly. She arched her back, and moved her hips a little from side to side, displaying herself. She could read from his expression how beautiful she was to him.

With hands and lips, with gentle bites that made her start and whimper, he moved slowly down her body.

'I'm going to taste you, Celine,' he said, in a voice made heavy with desire. 'I'm going to lick your juices, bury my tongue inside you. I'm going to kiss and tease your secret places until you squirm with pleasure and beg for mercy. And then I'll hold you down and do it some more. Open for me now, open.'

Celine trembled as his hands pressed her legs wide apart.

She felt his mouth questing among the dark, curling tendrils that clothed her mound. Exploring fingers moved between her thighs, and his tongue darted out to touch the aching pleasure-bud that hid there. His words had excited her wildly, even more the tone in which they were spoken; she hoped he would not spare her a single one of the delights he promised.

Liam pushed apart the swollen outer lips of her sex with his thumbs, exposing the pinkness within. She could feel the moisture gathering there, knew that he could see how ready she was.

Her vagina, like the throat of a fleshy flower, was open to him. His tongue dipped in to it, and circled on the sensitive nerve-endings that rimmed the shadowed entrance.

'You taste like the Indies,' he murmured. 'Like the coast of Coromandel; hot salt and spices.'

As his mouth greedily claimed her sex, the pleasure of it made Celine cry out softly. Liam's tongue lashed between her thighs. With gentle ferocity he stimulated her until the tingling became an itch, a glow, a fire, that had her moaning and thrusting in uncontrollable passion.

Wrapping his arms around her, he pulled her hard

against him and held her still. He sucked and nibbled softly on the burning pleasure-bud, pushing its fleshy hood away with his tongue. The sensation was almost unbearable in its intensity.

She tried to escape from it, pleading with him to stop, and pushing at his dark head, but Liam's grip never slackened. His face burrowed in to her. With lips and teeth, and wet mobile tongue, he drove her to climax.

The pleasure grew like an egg of cool fire. It filled her up. She was all sensation. The shell broke: her orgasm, a bird of flame, shivered its pinions and took flight.

Liam did not stop pleasuring her until the last wing-beat had faded. Then he turned his head and rested it on her belly.

'Was it enough, Celine? Please, love, tell me it was. Tell me there's a future for us – isn't there?'

The doubt in his voice, so humble, so hopeful, made her heart turn over. She stroked his hair, and murmured his name. When he raised his eyes and looked into hers, she knew that he could read her answer there.

'Yes!' he cried, and snatched her into his arms.

They kissed with passionate delight, and murmured little love-names and endearments against each other's lips. Liam held her close, rocking her in his arms. Celine nuzzled into his shoulder. The afterglow of satisfaction, warm as the now-risen sun, pulsed within her.

'You don't have any regrets, do you?' asked Liam. 'I mean, you don't still miss him? It is as good with me? Truly?'

It charmed her that he should need reassurance. Celine smiled, and tenderly kissed his neck.

'As good at the time, and better afterwards,' she whispered. 'Oh, so much better, Liam. I did not know, I could not imagine how sweet love could be.'

'It can be sweeter,' said Liam, huskily, and moved the hard tip of his phallus against her.

She drew away from him a little, and he turned on to his back to let her eyes rove across his body. From broad shoulders, his torso tapered to narrow hips. His chest was slabbed and his abdomen ribbed with muscle, firm but not over-developed. Between long, strong legs his penis reared up above the ample weight of his balls. The skin of his scrotum was darker than the rest of his flesh, plushy-looking, and tempting to the touch.

Hot desire burned in his eyes, and the moisture of readiness seeped from his prick. Celine knew he was yearning to enter her.

I'm going to drive him wild with arousal, as he did me, she thought. To take him beyond control. I want him to lose himself in his lust for me.

Pushing away his eagerly reaching hands, she began to caress him. Liam groaned and bit his lip as she smoothed his shoulders, and brushed down across his chest. His nipples hardened under her touch. They rubbed ticklingly against her palms.

Slowly, teasingly, she moved her fingers over his belly and along the outside of his thighs. Liam made a pleading noise, deep in his throat. His hips rocked forward. She knew how much he ached for her to touch his cock.

She looked down, with love and desire, at his thrusting manhood. It stood up at an angle from the sprout of dark hair at his groin. He was strainingly hard, his foreskin fully retracted from the heart-shaped tip. As she watched, a drop of fluid oozed from the slitted eye.

Bending her head, she lapped up the little pearl of liquid and then, without once using her hands on him, she started to kiss his prick all over. It jerked upwards under her mouth. She ran her tongue down Liam's shaft and planted kisses on every inch of its velvety skin. The feel of his potency moving against her lips made her thrill with excitement.

'Celine, darling, stop! Please stop!' Liam sobbed, as she took his glans between her lips and suckled on it.

Tugging himself free of her mouth, Liam drew her up to lie upon him. He clasped her fiercely, kissing her, and driving the saliva-wet length of his cock against her belly.

'Give yourself to me,' he gasped, hoarsely. 'Now, Celine. I can wait no longer. I must have you. I must be inside you.'

Celine did not have time to voice her need, desperate though it was. Liam was already pushing into the opening of her vagina, his hot cock-head distending her as he spoke.

He thrust up greedily into her, gorging her with the thick hardness of his phallus. She felt her soft folds being parted, invaded, by his rigid member. Moaning with her desire for him, she pushed against his surges.

'Yes, Liam. Oh, yes. That's so good. Take me; pleasure me.'

But he needed no encouragement beyond the soft enfolding wetness of her body. He took her with such passion that Celine felt utterly powerless before it. Liam was fierce, but gentle; wholly focussed in sensation. His dominance excited her as much as the driving force of his cock inside her.

His hands grasped her buttocks, fingers digging into her soft skin. Kisses rained on her face and neck. His pubis ground against hers, setting the pleasure-bud palpitating wildly.

One of his fingers, still wet, thrust down in to the tender cleft between her buttocks. She felt it pressing against the tight rose of her anus, pushing for admission, and she whimpered as it gained entry.

Liam's head jerked up. 'Do I hurt you?' he gasped. 'Don't you like it?'

'I want it. Don't stop. I love it.'

Glorying in her lust, Celine clenched and relaxed the trained muscles of her sex on his manhood. Liam snugged his finger to the knuckle in her anus, and moved it in and out as his cock penetrated her vagina with deep lunges.

The feeling was so exquisite that it brought her quickly to a second peak of pleasure. Her orgasm swept through every part of her body: a series of shattering spasms that left her breathless. She clutched Liam to her, sobbing out half-words of ecstasy against his neck.

He thrust in to her with the shallow, speedy rhythm of near-climax.

'Don't make me stop, love,' he whispered. 'I can't stop, Celine, I need you too much. I – ah, God, Celine! Yes! Yes!'

She felt his cock pulsing and he pulled her to him, burying his face in her hair and groaning with fulfillment.

'I love you so much,' he said, when he could speak.

They lay nestled together in drowsy satisfaction, listening to the beating of their hearts. Celine rubbed the top of her head against the angle of Liam's jaw, and sighed, happily.

'I suppose we ought to go back,' she said, after a long while.

Liam shook his head.

'Not yet. This is our bridal, Celine. I want to know every part of your body. We have only just begun, love. And I don't intend to stint you. Anything you desire; anything.'

The promise in his voice made her shiver with pleasure. Celine looked at him with shy speculation. Brushing aside his hair, she whispered into his ear.

'If you want to,' said Liam, smiling. 'I'd like to try that.'

'You're not shocked?' asked Celine, and blushed.

He pulled her down into the grass and kissed her, long and deeply.

'Love can't be shocked,' he said. 'Only pleasantly surprised.'

The sun had long passed its zenith, and was declinIng in to the west, by the time Celine and Liam left their nest by the painted wall. Slender clouds, rose and gold and crimson, flew like pennants in the air.

Celine glowed with love. Their day had been one of voyages, discoveries. Fingers, like pilgrims, had wan-

264

dered from sea cave to stiff-stretched peninsula. Tongues had travelled among shadowed grasslands and swelling hills.

Naked, hand in hand, they made their slow way back to the plaza, stopping now and then to kiss, or just to look deep into each other's eyes.

With the approach of sunset, the festival was coming to its end. Broken feathers and overturned bowls lay on the paving among the exhausted celebrants. Sally, Kalinda and Reuben were sitting on the steps of the pyramid, locked in discussion.

Kalinda turned her shoulder when she saw them. Sally grinned.

'At last. Best get dressed, both of you,' she said. 'News has come in: Auguste's taken the *Queen Royal*. I'm anxious to get back to him and under way.'

Celine went to find her clothes. She scrambled into them hastily but, even so, the sun was setting and the swift tropical night coming on, by the time she rejoined Liam.

He was fully dressed and deep in conversation with Sally. He swept Celine in to his arms and kissed her as deeply and passionately as if they had been separated for a week, not merely a few minutes.

'Well, what about it, O'Brien?' Sally asked. 'We – Tremaine could do with a man like you. Ossett says you're one in a thousand.'

'You can give us passage to Virginia,' said Liam, smiling down at Celine. 'That's all we need. I'm sorry, Reuben.'

The pirate looked at his shoes. 'As long as you're happy, lad. It's all I ever wanted for you.'

'Oh, aye?' said Sally. 'All the same to me. Let's be going, then. This city always did give me the fantods. Too quiet.'

Giving her the lie, a conch sounded. At its signal, the tribespeople, men and women, formed a huddle around Flower Feather. They chanted quietly, rhythmically, and among them, Celine glimpsed movement. What with the

265

gathering dusk, she could not tell if what she saw was animal or human; but it was red and went on all fours. There was something about the way it moved she did not like.

'Keep your eyes down as you pass,' said Kalinda, in a low voice. 'The red dog has come: a new Flower Prince is being chosen. It is something strangers should not see. Wait at the end of the causeway. The men will take you when they leave. It won't be long now.'

'But what about you?' asked Sally.

'I am staying,' murmured Kalinda. 'And with good reason.'

The crowd parted before them as she led the way across the plaza. Flower Feather stooped above something on the ground.

'Don't look,' hissed Kalinda.

But Celine could not help herself.

Lord Wraxall lay there on the paving.

His hair was braided with feathers. His erect phallus was red-painted. Torchlight gleamed on the gold ring that transfixed his glans. Three wooden tallies lay on his breast; they rose and fell to his gentle breathing. His lips were curved in a small, vainglorious smile.

With a shivering whisper of steel, Liam's cutlass swept from its sheath. Celine put her hand on his arm.

'Leave him,' she said. 'Let him live.'

Liam stared at her, blue eyes darkening with pain.

'Oh, love, don't tell me you still feel something for him!' he said.

Celine touched his lips with one finger. 'Put up your sword. It's not for me that I'm asking.' She turned to the red-haired woman. 'He's yours, Sal. He always was, wasn't he?'

Sally went bright pink and traced a pattern on the paving with her shoe.

'Hells bells, I don't want him!' she muttered. 'At least, that is . . .'

'It would do no good if you did,' said Kalinda. 'He is ours, now. Look!'

Six of the Indian women raised Odo to their shoulders. His head hung back; his long curls brushed the ground. Flower Feather laid a cloak of feathers over his sleeping form.

With solemn step, they took him across the plaza. Celine watched as Flower Feather led them up the long staircase to the pyramid temple. It was dark. The moon was rising.

'He has found favour. He will be Flower Prince: all the women he wants, all the pleasure, all the power. He will be able to command everything his fancy dictates until the red dog comes again next year. You must leave now. The rest is not for your eyes.'

As they passed onwards to the causeway, Celine took a last glance over her shoulder. A light shone from the door of the pyramid-temple. It flickered, like the blink of an eye, as someone passed across it. Lord Wraxall would be a king, a god, for the next twelve months. But though he lived and breathed, he was a dead man. There could be no escape – could there?

She caught her breath, and ran to rejoin Liam. He kissed her, and murmured her name. Celine clung to him, safe in his encircling arms. A warm wind blew a veil of cloud across the moon above them. And the scent of tropical flowers filled the air they breathed.

Envoi

To: Mistress Celine O'Brien
Battlesboro
Virginnia

Mid Yeare's Day, 1719

Dear Mistress O'Brien or should I say my dear Friend Celine. I hope all is well with You and Your Husband as it is with me. Sir James has taught me to write as you see but I am not so good yet. Mayhap I am too old for this and should have gone to Schoole along of you. Write to me soon and let me have all the News from Virginia. That Lord Wraxall has never come back and the Servants have taken over Acheron and made it a Bawdy House. Not much Change there! Must stop now as the Packet leaves soon with the Mails for the Americas. My blessings on You and Yours. I hope ever to remain your loving Mamma-In-Law.

Lady Elizabeth Fortescue (Bess)

Post Scriptum: Your Father would send his Love too but he is in disgrace locked in the Broome-Cupboard.

x x x B

BLUE HOTEL – Cherri Pickford
ISBN 0 352 32858 4

CASSANDRA'S CONFLICT – Fredrica Alleyn
ISBN 0 352 32859 2

THE CAPTIVE FLESH – Cleo Cordell
ISBN 0 352 32872 X

PLEASURE HUNT – Sophie Danson
ISBN 0 352 32880 0

OUTLANDIA – Georgia Angelis
ISBN 0 352 32883 5

BLACK ORCHID – Roxanne Carr
ISBN 0 352 32888 6

ODALISQUE – Fleur Reynolds
ISBN 0 352 32887 8

THE SENSES BEJEWELLED – Cleo Cordell
ISBN 0 352 32904 1

VIRTUOSO – Katrina Vincenzi
ISBN 0 352 32907 6

FIONA'S FATE – Fredrica Alleyn
ISBN 0 352 32913 0

HANDMAIDEN OF PALMYRA – Fleur Reynolds
ISBN 0 352 32919 X

THE SILKEN CAGE – Sophie Danson
ISBN 0 352 32928 9

THE GIFT OF SHAME – Sarah Hope-Walker
ISBN 0 352 32935 1

SUMMER OF ENLIGHTENMENT – Cheryl Mildenhall
ISBN 0 352 32937 8

A BOUQUET OF BLACK ORCHIDS – Roxanne Carr
ISBN 0 352 32939 4

JULIET RISING – Cleo Cordell
ISBN 0 352 32938 6

DEBORAH'S DISCOVERY – Fredrica Alleyn
ISBN 0 352 32945 9

THE TUTOR – Portia Da Costa
ISBN 0 352 32946 7

THE HOUSE IN NEW ORLEANS – Fleur Reynolds
ISBN 0 352 32951 3

ELENA'S CONQUEST – Lisette Allen
ISBN 0 352 32950 5

CASSANDRA'S CHATEAU – Fredrica Alleyn
ISBN 0 352 32955 6

WICKED WORK – Pamela Kyle
ISBN 0 352 32958 0

DREAM LOVER – Katrina Vincenzi
ISBN 0 352 32956 4

PATH OF THE TIGER – Cleo Cordell
ISBN 0 352 32959 9

BELLA'S BLADE – Georgia Angelis
ISBN 0 352 32965 3

THE DEVIL AND THE DEEP BLUE SEA – Cheryl
Mildenhall
ISBN 0 352 32966 1

WESTERN STAR – Roxanne Carr
ISBN 0 352 32969 6

A PRIVATE COLLECTION – Sarah Fisher
ISBN 0 352 32970 X

NICOLE'S REVENGE – Lisette Allen
ISBN 0 352 32984 X

UNFINISHED BUSINESS – Sarah Hope-Walker
ISBN 0 352 32983 1

CRIMSON BUCCANEER – Cleo Cordell
ISBN 0 352 32987 4

LA BASQUAISE – Angel Strand
ISBN 0 352 329888 2

THE LURE OF SATYRIA – Cheryl Mildenhall
ISBN 0 352 32994 7

THE DEVIL INSIDE – Portia Da Costa
ISBN 0 352 32993 9

HEALING PASSION – Sylvie Ouellette
ISBN 0 352 32998 X

THE SEDUCTRESS   Vivienne LaFay
ISBN 0 352 32997 1

THE STALLION – Georgina Brown
ISBN 0 352 33005 8

CRASH COURSE – Juliet Hastings
ISBN 0 352 33018 X

THE INTIMATE EYE – Georgia Angelis
ISBN 0 352 33004 X

THE AMULET – Lisette Allen
ISBN 0 352 33019 8

CONQUERED – Fleur Reynolds
ISBN 0 352 33025 2

DARK OBSESSION – Fredrica Alleyn
ISBN 0 352 33026 0

LED ON BY COMPULSION – Leila James
ISBN 0 352 33032 5

OPAL DARKNESS – Cleo Cordell
ISBN 0 352 33033 3

JEWEL OF XANADU – Roxanne Carr
ISBN 0 352 33037 6

RUDE AWAKENING – Pamela Kyle
ISBN 0 352 33036 8

GOLD FEVER – Louisa Francis
ISBN 0 352 33043 0

EYE OF THE STORM – Georgina Brown
ISBN 0 352 330044 9

WHITE ROSE ENSNARED – Juliet Hastings
ISBN 0 352 33052 X

A SENSE OF ENTITLEMENT – Cheryl Mildenhall
ISBN 0 352 33053 8

ARIA APPASSIONATA – Juliet Hastings
ISBN 0 352 33056 2

THE MISTRESS – Vivienne LaFay
ISBN 0 352 33057 0

ACE OF HEARTS – Lisette Allen
ISBN 0 352 33059 7

DREAMERS IN TIME – Sarah Copeland
ISBN 0 352 33064 3

GOTHIC BLUE – Portia Da Costa
ISBN 0 352 33075 9

THE HOUSE OF GABRIEL – Rafaella
ISBN 0 352 33063 5

PANDORA'S BOX – ed. Kerri Sharp
ISBN 0 352 33074 0

THE NINETY DAYS OF GENEVIEVE – Lucinda
Carrington
ISBN 0 352 33070 8

Published in June

THE BIG CLASS
Angel Strand

1930s Europe. As Hitler and Mussolini are building their war machine, Cia – a young Anglo-Italian woman – is on her way back to England, leaving behind a complex web of sexual adventures. Her enemies are plotting revenge and deception and her Italian lover has disappeared – as has her collection of designer clothes. In England her friends are sailing their yachts and partying, but this facade hides tensions, rivalries and forbidden pleasures in which Cia becomes embroiled. It's only a matter of time before her two worlds collide – and everyone has to face up to their responsibilities.

ISBN 0 352 33076 7

THE BLACK ORCHID HOTEL
Roxanne Carr

Many contented female clients have passed through the Black Orchid Hotel, and, as joint owner of this luxurious pleasure palace, Maggie can have her every need satisfied at any time. But she has begun to tire of her sophisticated lovers, and is soon encouraging the attentions of the more rugged men in the area – including the local fire officer and a notorious biker. But she had better beware. There is one new friendship which may prove to be too hot to handle.

ISBN 0 352 33060 0

Published in July

LORD WRAXALL'S FANCY
Anna Lieff Saxby

1720, the Caribbean. Lady Celine Fortescue has fallen in love with Liam, a young ship's officer, unaware that her father has another man in mind for her – the handsome but cruel Lord Odo Wraxall. When Liam's life is threatened, Wraxall takes advantage of the situation to dupe Celine into marrying him. He does not, however, take into account her determination to see justice done, nor Liam's unlikely new alliance with some of the lustiest pirates – male and female – to sail the Spanish Main.

ISBN 0 352 33080 5

FORBIDDEN CRUSADE
Juliet Hastings

1186, the Holy Land. Forbidden to marry beneath her rank, Melisende, a beautiful young noblewoman, uses her cunning – and natural sensuality – to seduce Robert, the chivalrous, honourable but poor young castellan she loves. Capture, exposure, shame and betrayal follow, however, and, in her brother's castle and the harem of the Emir, she has to exert her resourcefulness and appetite for pleasure to secure the prize of her forbidden crusade.

ISBN 0 352 33079 1

To be published in August

THE HOUSESHARE
Pat O'Brien

When Rupe reveals his most intimate desires over the Internet, he does not know that his electronic confidante is Tine, his landlady. With anonymity guaranteed, steamy encounters in cyberspace are limited only by the bounds of the imagination, but what will happen when Tine attemps to make the virtual real?

ISBN 0 352 33094 5

THE KING'S GIRL
Sylvie Ouellette

The early 1600s. Under the care of the decadent Monsieur and Madame Lampron, Laure, a spirited and sensual young Frenchwoman, is taught much about the darker pleasures of the flesh. Sent to the newly established colony in North America, she tries in vain to behave as a young Catholic girl should, and is soon embarking on a mission of seduction and adventure.

ISBN 0 352 33095 3

If you would like a complete list of plot summaries of Black Lace titles, please fill out the questionnaire overleaf or send a stamped addressed envelope to:-

Black Lace
332 Ladbroke Grove
London W10 5AH

WE NEED YOUR HELP . . .
to plan the future of women's erotic fiction –

– and no stamp required!

Yours are the only opinions that matter.

Black Lace is the first series of books devoted to erotic fiction by women for women.

We intend to keep providing the best-written, sexiest books you can buy. And we'd appreciate your help and valued opinion of the books so far. Tell us what you want to read.

THE BLACK LACE QUESTIONNAIRE

SECTION ONE: ABOUT YOU

1.1 Sex (*we presume you are female, but so as not to discriminate*)
Are you?

Male ☐
Female ☐

1.2 Age

under 21 ☐   21–30 ☐
31–40 ☐   41–50 ☐
51–60 ☐   over 60 ☐

1.3 At what age did you leave full-time education?

still in education ☐   16 or younger ☐
17–19 ☐   20 or older ☐

1.4 Occupation _____

1.5 Annual household income

    under £10,000   ☐   £10–£20,000   ☐

    £20–£30,000   ☐   £30–£40,000   ☐

    over £40,000   ☐

1.6 We are perfectly happy for you to remain anonymous;
but if you would like to receive information on other
publications available, please insert your name and
address

    _____

    _____

    _____

    _____

SECTION TWO: ABOUT BUYING BLACK LACE BOOKS

2.1 How did you acquire this copy of *Lord Wraxall's Fancy*?

    I bought it myself   ☐   My partner bought it   ☐

    I borrowed/found it   ☐

2.2 How did you find out about Black Lace books?

    I saw them in a shop   ☐

    I saw them advertised in a magazine   ☐

    I saw the London Underground posters   ☐

    I read about them in _____

    Other _____

2.3 Please tick the following statements you agree with:

    I would be less embarrassed about buying Black
Lace books if the cover pictures were less explicit   ☐

    I think that in general the pictures on Black
Lace books are about right   ☐

    I think Black Lace cover pictures should be as
explicit as possible   ☐

2.4 Would you read a Black Lace book in a public place – on
a train for instance?

    Yes   ☐   No   ☐

SECTION THREE: ABOUT THIS BLACK LACE BOOK

3.1 Do you think the sex content in this book is:
   Too much ☐ About right ☐
   Not enough ☐

3.2 Do you think the writing style in this book is:
   Too unreal/escapist ☐ About right ☐
   Too down to earth ☐

3.3 Do you think the story in this book is:
   Too complicated ☐ About right ☐
   Too boring/simple ☐

3.4 Do you think the cover of this book is:
   Too explicit ☐ About right ☐
   Not explicit enough ☐

Here's a space for any other comments:

SECTION FOUR: ABOUT OTHER BLACK LACE BOOKS

4.1 How many Black Lace books have you read? ☐

4.2 If more than one, which one did you prefer?

4.3 Why?

SECTION FIVE: ABOUT YOUR IDEAL EROTIC NOVEL

We want to publish the books you want to read – so this is your chance to tell us exactly what your ideal erotic novel would be like.

5.1   Using a scale of 1 to 5 (1 = no interest at all, 5 = your ideal), please rate the following possible settings for an erotic novel:

Medieval/barbarian/sword 'n' sorcery ☐
Renaissance/Elizabethan/Restoration ☐
Victorian/Edwardian ☐
1920s & 1930s – the Jazz Age ☐
Present day ☐
Future/Science Fiction ☐

5.2   Using the same scale of 1 to 5, please rate the following themes you may find in an erotic novel:

Submissive male/dominant female ☐
Submissive female/dominant male ☐
Lesbianism ☐
Bondage/fetishism ☐
Romantic love ☐
Experimental sex e.g. anal/watersports/sex toys ☐
Gay male sex ☐
Group sex ☐

Using the same scale of 1 to 5, please rate the following styles in which an erotic novel could be written:

Realistic, down to earth, set in real life ☐
Escapist fantasy, but just about believable ☐
Completely unreal, impressionistic, dreamlike ☐

5.3   Would you prefer your ideal erotic novel to be written from the viewpoint of the main male characters or the main female characters?

Male ☐   Female ☐
Both ☐

5.4 What would your ideal Black Lace heroine be like? Tick as many as you like:

Dominant	☐	Glamorous	☐
Extroverted	☐	Contemporary	☐
Independent	☐	Bisexual	☐
Adventurous	☐	Naive	☐
Intellectual	☐	Introverted	☐
Professional	☐	Kinky	☐
Submissive	☐	Anything else?	☐
Ordinary	☐	_____	

5.5 What would your ideal male lead character be like? Again, tick as many as you like:

Rugged	☐		
Athletic	☐	Caring	☐
Sophisticated	☐	Cruel	☐
Retiring	☐	Debonair	☐
Outdoor-type	☐	Naive	☐
Executive-type	☐	Intellectual	☐
Ordinary	☐	Professional	☐
Kinky	☐	Romantic	☐
Hunky	☐		
Sexually dominant	☐	Anything else?	☐
Sexually submissive	☐	_____	

5.6 Is there one particular setting or subject matter that your ideal erotic novel would contain?

_____

SECTION SIX: LAST WORDS

6.1 What do you like best about Black Lace books?

_____

6.2 What do you most dislike about Black Lace books?

_____

6.3 In what way, if any, would you like to change Black Lace covers?

_____

6.4   Here's a space for any other comments:

_____

_____

_____

_____

_____

Thank you for completing this questionnaire. Now tear it out of the book – carefully! – put it in an envelope and send it to:

Black Lace
FREEPOST
London
W10 5BR

No stamp is required if you are resident in the U.K.